MISTLETOE AND HOLLY
"Alone at last," he murmured.

All the lights in the room had been turned off except for the winking Christmas tree lights and the flickering glow from the fireplace.

Leslie lay on the warm carpet beside him with her head pillowed on his arm. He turned on his side, facing her, and kissed her lips, then drew back.

"It's always possible Holly might decide she wants a drink of water," Leslie murmured, to tease him.

"If she does, I'll drown her." Tagg growled the mock threat.

"No, you won't." She laughed softly.

"Don't be too sure," he warned. "I've wanted to be alone with you for a long time."

SWEET S
"How long hav
Sandy

"Long enough to wonder if y
by one leg out of a magnolia

"I'm a woman," Sandy said.

"Define your terms," Tyler countered.

"I'm twenty-one, old enough to drink and vote. That makes me a woman."

Tyler's blue eyes swept her body. "If you think that's what makes you a woman, Sandy," he drawled, "then you're more of an innocent than I thought."

Suddenly Sandy realized that working with Tyler was not going to be easy. Unless the faint sparks that were kindling between them were stamped out, her well-laid plans would be in jeopardy. Tyler Hamilton was a man she could lose her heart to, and with it, her new job.

Dear Reader,

At this special season, we bring you our Editors' Choice of two full-length memorable holiday novels written by two of your favorite authors.

We hope you have a season of joy, and we wish you the very best for the New Year. As Leslie and Sandy, the two heroines featured here, discover, Christmas is a time for love and sharing.

Best wishes for a Happy New Year.

Candy Lee
Reader Service

Harlequin Books

TORONTO • NEW YORK • LONDON
AMSTERDAM • PARIS • SYDNEY • HAMBURG
STOCKHOLM • ATHENS • TOKYO • MILAN

JANET DAILEY

Mistletoe and Holly

Chapter One

The sunlight glistened on the snow's icy crust, creating a diamond shimmer that dazzled Leslie's eyes. A frown of irritation crossed her usually smooth features as she made a one-handed search of her purse on the car seat beside her, looking for her sunglasses without taking her attention from the road. The snowplows had cleared the road two or three days before, judging by the melting piles of mud-spattered snow along the shoulders, but there were still slick patches where the plow blade hadn't scraped all the way to the road's surface.

Skidding on one of those icy patches was definitely not on her list of thrills she wanted to experience. Leslie Stiles had already had her fill of accidents for one winter. Her hand's blind search came up with the sunglasses, which she immediately slipped onto the bridge of her nose, her hazel eyes instantly feeling the relief from the sun's glare on the sparkling white mantle of snow that covered the Vermont country-side.

A stop sign stood at the crossroads and Leslie slowed the car to a halt as she approached it. Melting snow dripped onto the car roof from an overhanging tree branch. The drops made a tinny sound as they landed. A dirty pickup truck that might have been green had the right of way. Her fingers tapped the steering wheel impatiently as she waited for its putting speed to carry it across the intersection.

The strain of the drive from Manhattan was beginning to show on her—the strain and her own physical pain. Leslie attempted to shift into a more comfortable position, but the thick plaster cast on her left leg severely limited movement and position. It was a lucky thing the car had a lot of leg room—and an automatic transmission. There was a steady throb of pain that tensed all her nerves and planted her teeth together. In her purse, Leslie had a bottle of pain pills, prescribed by the doctor, but they made her sleepy so she hadn't taken any, certain she could grit her way through the trip to her aunt's home. It was turning into more of an ordeal than she had thought it would be.

The pickup passed and Leslie made her turn onto the intersecting highway. She clung to the knowledge that she only had a few more miles to go. Already she could see the white spire of the church steeple poking above the tops of the trees.

There was a distinct New England character to the village nestled in the mountain fastness. There was something changeless and nostalgic about its steepled church and village green, and its old houses all in neat repair. Too many artists had captured towns like it on canvas, which gave even strangers the sense of coming home.

Leslie wasn't a stranger, but neither did she view it as home. When she approached her aunt's two story Victorian-style house on the outskirts of the rural community, she saw it merely as a refuge, a place to recuperate from this damnable broken leg, and avoid all of December's holiday hoopla.

No attempt had been made to clear the driveway of snow, although there was a set of parallel tracks going in and out. Leslie slowed her car to make the turn, barely noticing the man pulling a red-suited child on a sled in the next yard. The car tires crunched in the crusty snow as she wheeled the vehicle into the drive, stopping short of the side door.

Relief sighed through her strained nerves as she removed the sunglasses and smoothed a side of her sand-colored hair where it was pulled sleekly back and secured at the nape of her neck to trail between her shoulder blades. As December went, it was a mild day with the temperature hovering above the freezing mark, so Leslie didn't bother to put on the rusty-brown, fake fur jacket that lay on the passenger seat. It would only hamper her movements, and maneuvering her cast-rigid leg out of the car wasn't going to be an easy task.

Her crutches were propped against the passenger door. She pulled them over, so they'd be within reach once she was outside, then opened her door. Scooting sideways, she managed to gain enough room to swing her left leg around and aim it out the door.

The sound of footsteps and sled runners cutting through the snow's crust signaled the approach of the next-door neighbor as she edged forward to test the footing before she made a one-legged attempt to stand up. It was something she hadn't mastered too well as yet, so she regarded his appearance at that moment as ill-timed. Broken legs and graceful movements simply did not go together.

Her smile was a bit tight when he hove into view with the sled in tow. Leslie tried to keep the flash of annoyance out of her eyes as she glanced toward him. He was tall, easily six foot if not more, which forced her to tip her head back in order to focus her gaze higher. A network of smile lines fanned out from the corners of his icy blue eyes, framed by dark, male lashes. The winter sun had added the finishing touches to the tan the summer sun had started, giving a certain ruggedness to his leanly handsome features. Hatless, his dark hair had a black sheen to it, thick and attractively rumpled by a playful breeze.

If it hadn't been for the strain of the drive and the nagging pain in her leg, Leslie probably would have found him physically disturbing. But her least concern at the moment was how good-looking he was. She just wanted to get into her aunt's house, take a pain pill, and lie down.

His gaze glittered down on her with friendly interest, yet managed to take her apart at the same time. He observed the annoyance behind the polite smile she gave him, the high cheekbones that kept her features from being average, and the rounded right knee where her long skirt had ridden up higher than her fur-lined winter boot. A stretched-out woolen sock protected the bare toes that peeked out of the left leg cast.

"Let me give you a hand," he offered and reached out to give her the steadying support of his grip while she held on to the door with her other hand.

"Thank you," Leslie murmured when she was upright and precariously balanced on one foot.

"You must be Leslie," he guessed and kept a light hold on her arm until she was more sure of her footing. "Your aunt said you'd be arriving today. I'm Tagg Williams and this is my daughter, Holly. We live in the house next door."

"How do you do." It was a polite phrase with little meaning behind it. Leslie wasn't intentionally trying to be rude or unfriendly. She was just tired and plagued by the dull pain of her injury.

The little girl had climbed off the sled and waded through the hard snow for a closer look at the white cast on Leslie's leg. She was all of six years old. Her beguilingly innocent face was framed by the red hood of her parka trimmed in white fur. She was wearing a pair of matching red snow pants and white boots, and a pair of white, furry mittens. Her eyes were a darker blue than her father's and blessed with long, naturally curling dark lashes.

"Holly, get the crutches for her, will you?" Tagg Williams took it upon himself to make the request of his daughter, so Leslie wouldn't have to make the hopping turn to reach them.

"Sure." The young girl half-climbed into the seat to drag the metal crutches out by their padded tops and gave them to Leslie.

"Thank you." She managed to keep her balance long enough to maneuver the crutches, one under each arm, and let them take her weight.

"Did you have an accident skiing?" the little girl asked.

Her mouth slanted wryly. "Nothing so glamorous, I'm afraid," Leslie replied. "There was a patch of ice on the sidewalk in front of my apartment building. I slipped and fell and broke my leg."

"I bet it hurt." She gave Leslie a wide-eyed look of sympathy.

"It did. It hurt a lot." Leslie didn't believe in downplaying the harsh facts of reality, especially with children. In the long run, honesty would do them more good than pretence or white lies.

Hinges creaked when the storm door to the house was pushed open. A fairly tall, gray-haired woman stood in the opening, dressed in a pair of loose-fitting brown slacks, a heavily knitted tan pullover with an orange and brown blouse underneath.

"She's here, Mrs. Evans!" The little girl named Holly hurried toward the side door to announce the arrival to Leslie's aunt. "I saw her car drive in!"

"And you guessed right away that she was my niece. That's very clever of you, Holly." As a former schoolteacher, it was an ingrained habit for Patsy Evans to comment on a child's observation, which she did warmly, but not effusively. Then she greeted her niece. "Did you have a good trip up, Leslie?"

"Yes. Thankfully there was very little traffic." The rutted tracks in the snow made by previous vehicles made it difficult to negotiate with the crutches when Leslie tried to keep her balance and open the rear car door where her bags were.

"I'll bring your luggage in." Tagg Williams moved effortlessly to intercept her and eliminate the need for the attempt.

"Thank you." This time her smile was much more genuine in its show of gratitude. His alert gaze seemed to notice that, too, and lingered on the curving movement of her lips. But Leslie was already busy making the turn toward the house, so she wasn't aware of his heightened interest.

"Most of the traffic comes during the weekend when the skiers descend on the area," her aunt replied to Leslie's initial remark and watched with sharp concern while Leslie awkwardly approached the house.

The concrete steps leading to the back door were clear of any snow or ice, although they were wet. Icicles dripped water from the eaves overhead, plopping and splattering when the large droplets hit the ground. Leslie paused in front of the bottom step.

"Can you manage all right?" her aunt asked, ready to go to her aid if she couldn't.

"Three steps I can manage," Leslie replied with a short, dry laugh. "It's the three flights of stairs to my apartment that were impossible." Then she remembered. "Damn. I left my purse in the car."

"Holly will get it for you." Autocratically Patsy Evans motioned to the young girl to fetch Leslie's purse.

"It's in the front seat." She called the information to the blue-eyed girl in the red snowsuit who was already dashing toward the car.

With her aunt holding the door open, Leslie mounted the steps one at a time and swung across the threshold to enter the house. It had been five years since she had last visited her aunt, yet time hadn't seemed to change anything.

The large kitchen with its birch cabinets looked just the same. The pussycat clock on the wall was still swinging its pendulum tail, marking off the seconds. Even the plaid curtains at the windows were the same pattern if not the same curtains that had hung there before. It was funny that she remembered these little details after all this time. It wasn't as if she'd grown up in the house, or even been a frequent visitor to her aunt's home.

Actually, it had only been during her college years that Leslie had become really acquainted with her aunt. It was a case of liking the person, rather than a relative. Patsy Evans had a keen sense of humor and a ready smile, but Leslie was drawn more by her aunt's no-nonsense attitude. Patsy was her father's sister, and it was difficult to imagine two people with more divergent personalities.

As her scanning gaze finished its sweep of the kitchen and stopped on her aunt, Leslie smiled. There was contentment in her otherwise tired expression.

"I always did like this house," she declared. "It's so strong and solid."

"Yes." There was a musing quality about her aunt's agreement. "It's what you look for in a home, isn't it? Yet those same traits are regarded as unflattering in a person."

The rattle of the doorknob interrupted any reply Leslie might have made. Then a small hand succeeded in turning it and little Holly Williams came into the house, followed by her father with Leslie's suitcases under his arms. Both stopped on the large rug so they wouldn't track on the floor.

"Here's your purse." Holly stretched to hand it to her, careful not to overbalance and step off the rug with the snow-wet boots.

"Thank you, Holly." Leslie rested her weight on the crutches and leaned to take it from the girl. "And thank you, Mr. Williams, for bringing my luggage in." It seemed she had been thanking the pair ever since she had arrived.

"You had your hands full. It was the least I could do." The corners of his mouth deepened in a smile as he glanced pointedly at her crutches. Then his attention was swinging to her aunt. "Where would you like me to set them, Mrs. Evans?"

"There by the counter, is fine." She nodded and turned to Leslie. "I don't believe you've met my new neighbors, have you Leslie?"

"We more or less introduced ourselves outside," Tagg Williams inserted, flashing another smile at her.

"Good," her aunt stated in her typically decisive voice. "I was just going to put some water on to heat for tea. Would you like to stay and have a cup with us, Taggart?''

"Another time, perhaps," he refused as his astute blue eyes skimmed Leslie with another thorough glance. "Your niece looks tired after her journey." With one hand, he was reaching behind him to open the door and steering his daughter in that direction with the other. "Enjoy your stay." The last was directed to Leslie.

Something in his final look touched her feminine core that had been too tired to care about anything before, and attracted her interest. She managed to assimilate a few impressions like the width of his shoulders under the heavy winter jacket and the lean-jawed strength of his profile, then the inner door was closing behind him, followed by the storm door.

The corners of her mouth were pulled down by a dry smile as she glanced sideways at her aunt, busy at the sink filling the teakettle with water. "Why is it the good-looking ones are always married?''

Patsy Evans laughed, a low sound that came from her throat. "I'm not so sure he is."

"Oh?" Leslie opened her purse and took out the prescription bottle, then hobbled on her crutches to the sink for a glass of water.

"Unless he has locked his wife in the attic, I haven't seen a sign of anyone except Taggart and the little girl since they moved in the first of November." She set the teakettle on the stove's gas burner and lighted the flame with a match. "I really can't tell you whether he's divorced or widowed. Since he has never volunteered the information, I have respected his privacy and not asked."

"His daughter certainly seemed happy and well-behaved for the offspring of a single parent." Leslie made the observation almost absently as she took the prescribed dosage of medicine and washed the pills down with water. Being the only child of divorced parents herself, Leslie had firsthand knowledge of what that was like. "How old is she?"

"Holly is six years old now but she'll be seven the day after Christmas. She was obviously named for the season." Patsy Evans didn't pause from her task to answer the question as she took a set of cups and saucers from the cupboard and placed them on the counter.

"What does he do?" Leslie wondered, again aloud.

"You mean for a living?" Her aunt stopped to think. "I don't believe he's said. He doesn't talk about himself very much. For all his outward friendliness and charm, he seems to be a private person." She slid a glance at Leslie, curiosity gleaming in her shrewd, brown eyes. "Are you in the market for a husband with a ready-made family, Leslie?" she chided, and let the affection in her voice take any sting from her words.

"Hardly." Leslie pushed away from the sink and gripped her crutches. "I've seen enough bad marriages to keep me single for the rest of my life." Not just her parents, but those of her friends as well.

"You'll change your mind someday," her aunt declared with certainty.

Leslie glanced at her, then laughed. "You're probably right. What is it they say about 'famous last words'?" It was a rhetorical question that trailed off tiredly at the end.

Patsy Evans took a closer look at her niece and suggested, "Why don't you go into the living room and get that leg propped up? I'll bring the tea when it's ready."

The prospect was too inviting for Leslie to refuse. "I think I'll do that and give this pain pill a chance to work." As she pivoted on her good leg and swung the crutches around to start for the living room, one of the crutches banged into a kitchen chair. "I'm like a bull in a china shop with these things," she grumbled in irritation. "I'd like to know why it's more difficult to maneuver on four legs than it is on two."

"Coordination will come with practice," her aunt assured.

"I'll be a pro with these things by the time this cast comes off in five weeks," Leslie agreed and clumped out of the kitchen.

Like the house itself, the furniture in it was strong and solidly built, some of the pieces bordering on antique. The thick cushions on the gold corduroy sofa were firm, indicating to Leslie that the upholstery was new, but the sofa wasn't. She sat at one end and lifted her casted leg onto the cushions, plumping handmade crewelwork pillows behind her back for additional support. Closing her eyes, she let the quiet of the old house spill over her. Peace was something she had always appreciated, and it was no less precious to her now at twenty-five.

A reflective expression stole over her features in repose. It was true that, despite all her antimarriage remarks, she secretly desired a lifelong partner to love, and to be loved by him. There had been moments in her life when she had thought she had found him, only to discover fundamental differences of opinion. Those relationships, like most others, had died an early death. Leslie knew she was wary; sometimes she wondered if she wasn't expecting too much, but she wasn't prepared to settle for less.

A sigh broke from her lips. An instant later, she heard her aunt's footsteps entering the living room. She opened her eyes, smelling the fragrance of freshly brewed tea. A cup was set on the table within easy reach for Leslie as her aunt took a seat in the matching armchair that faced the fireplace.

"How's your father? I haven't heard from him lately." Her aunt asked to be filled in on the family.

"He and Millie and the kids are spending the holidays at their condominium in Hawaii. They're all fine." Both of her parents had remarried after their divorce when Leslie was fourteen. Each had stepchildren.

Having wanted brothers and sisters all through childhood, she had been disillusioned when she had finally acquired both. The sibling rivalry and setting parent against stepparent were painful things for her; almost as painful as the way her parents had tore at her, trying to be the sole object of her love and depriving the other of her affection. Her parents' marriage and divorce had both been fought with Leslie as the battleground. Growing up had been unpleasant, dimming what few happy memories she possessed.

"Hawaii," her aunt repeated. "It must be wonderful to escape all this snow and cold."

"As soon as Daddy was notified about my fall, he had prepaid tickets waiting at the airport for me to fly over there and stay with them." Her grimace showed her opinion of that invitation. "You know what it's like at Christmas—everyone trying to outdo the other and complaining if their present isn't as expensive as the one they gave. The endless parties. Decorations all over the place." She shook her head to show her dislike for such things. "Needless to say, Daddy was upset when I told him I wasn't coming." There was no humor in her laugh. "He was convinced I was going to Mother's for the holidays. She drove into New York from Baltimore just to take me home with her. Then she got angry because she thought I was going to Hawaii."

"Why didn't you tell them you were coming here?" A dark gray eyebrow was lifted in puzzled amusement.

"I did, but they didn't believe me." Leslie shrugged. "They thought I was just saying that to avoid hurting their feelings."

"Your mother and father are too much alike. Both of them are too intense, too quick to anger, and too possessive," she pronounced with a degree of sadness. "A marriage of opposites is better than that. One has a stabilizing influence on the other."

"Do you really think so?" Leslie was skeptical.

"You need to have the basis of love and common interests, but with two different personalities involved," her aunt elaborated on her initial statement.

"I suppose that makes sense, as long as one didn't try to change the other," she conceded. "Either way, I'm glad I'm here. And I'm really grateful that you're letting me stay with you."

"It's a big, old house. There is always plenty of room for you to come anytime you want," her aunt insisted. "Besides, I had no plans for the Christmas holidays, except to spend it quietly here. I suppose we could get a tree if you want."

"No. I don't believe in that nonsense," Leslie stated firmly. "I've been called a female Scrooge, but I think Christmas has lost its meaning. It's all decorations and gifts and parties. It's an excuse to celebrate rather than a reason."

"That's a cynical attitude." The remark was almost an admonition.

"It's true," she insisted. "It used to be Christmas merchandise was never displayed in stores until after Thanksgiving. Now it's on the shelves before Halloween. Personally, I think they should ban Christmas."

"Unfortunately the economy would suffer if that was attempted," Patsy Evans murmured dryly and changed the subject. "How's your job? It was certainly understanding of your employer to grant you a leave of absence until after New Year's."

"Mr. Chamber had planned to be gone most of the month attending a sales conference anyway, and he always takes off a few days before Christmas, so there wouldn't have been much for me to do at the office except handle the mail and answer the phone. The receptionist can do that.'' She knew her boss too well to believe he had been motivated solely by compassion. He had given her a leave of absence because it was both practical and economical.

''Then both of you are benefiting from it since you don't have to worry about going back and forth to work in bad weather. You'll have a chance to rest while your leg heals,'' her aunt reasoned.

''Yes.'' It just seemed bad luck that she had broken her leg at this time of year, presuming there was a good time for an accident like that. She had an aversion to the holiday season, a holdover from her childhood probably. Usually she could escape it with work or physical activity. Both those were taken from her.

She sipped at her tea and tried not to think about it.

Chapter Two

Christmas seemed inescapable. Nearly every other song the disc jockey played on the radio was oriented toward the season. After trying for almost an hour to tune in other stations, Leslie gave up and switched the radio off. She had already read two books since she had arrived at her aunt's. She liked reading, but not all the time.

In desperation, she picked up a deck of cards and propped her leg on a kitchen chair to begin playing solitaire to pass the time until her aunt returned from her shopping trip. Leslie wished now she hadn't decided to stay at the house.

The knock at the side door startled her. No car had driven in; there hadn't been the sound of footsteps climbing the back steps to the door; and no movement in the kitchen window facing the driveway. Leslie pushed the cards into a pile at the end of the table and grabbed for her crutches. With growing deftness, she maneuvered them under her arms and swung toward the door in long strides. Steam and frost covered the glass pane in the door, preventing Leslie from seeing who was outside.

In New York, she wouldn't have dreamed of opening the door without knowing who was out there, but this was Vermont. She opened the inner door and saw a short, red-coated child standing on the other side of the storm door. Leslie pushed it open too, her glance running past the little girl, but there was no sign of her father.

"Hello." The hood to her red snow jacket wasn't covering her head, revealing long, shining black hair. Its blackness made the girl's eyes seem all the more blue.

"Hello, Holly." Leslie was a bit confused as she glanced at the paper sack the girl clutched against the front of her unbuttoned jacket. A pair of blue barrettes secured the black hair swept away from her temples.

"May I come in?" she asked with a look that fairly beamed with friendly warmth.

"Of course." She shifted her crutches to back out of the opening and let the young girl step inside.

Holly paused on the rug and painstakingly wiped all traces of snow and moisture from her shoes. "I forgot to wear my boots." There was a hint of mischief in the rueful expression. "My dad's probably gonna be mad when he finds out." But she obviously wasn't concerned.

"Was there something you wanted?" Leslie still wasn't too sure about the reason for this visit. Her aunt hadn't indicated the little girl was in the practice of coming over.

"I saw Mrs. Evans drive away a while ago and I thought you might like some company," she declared and walked to the kitchen table to lay her paper sack on it.

"That's very thoughtful of you." Leslie had been wishing for someone to talk to, but she wryly wondered if her desperation for company stretched to conversing with a six-going-on-seven-year-old girl.

"I know," the girl agreed blandly and shrugged out of her jacket, draping it on a chair back. Underneath the jacket, she was wearing a pair of blue corduroy overalls and a white blouse with a ruffled collar. She managed to look both the little lady and the tomboy. "Is it all right if I call you Leslie? Dad said I should ask before I called you that," she explained to Leslie over her shoulder.

"I don't mind if you call me Leslie." A little bemused, she edged around the girl to resume her seat in the kitchen chair.

"Do you want me to put your crutches somewhere?" Holly volunteered.

"No, that's all right," Leslie refused gently. "I'll just stand them up against the wall where I can reach them."

"I always thought Leslie was a boy's name, but Daddy said it can be a girl's name, too." She emptied the contents of her paper sack onto the table. There were a dozen pieces of red and green construction paper, a bottle of glue, and a pair of blunt-ended, child's scissors.

"I guess it must be true since my name is Leslie and I'm a girl," she offered, containing an amused smile. "What's all this you have here?"

"I remembered when I was sick with the measles, it made me feel better if I had something to do. So I brought this over. I thought you might like to help me make a paper-chain to hang on our Christmas tree."

"I see." Actually what Leslie saw was the irony of the situation. She, who abhorred the commercialized Christmas and all its trappings, was being asked by a little girl to help make a Christmas decoration. She liked children, so how could she refuse without appearing heartless and cold.

"I can show you if you don't know how to make them. It's real easy," Holly assured her and picked up the scissors to cut a strip of green construction paper crosswise. "You start with a piece of paper like this— it can be red or green—then you glue the ends together like this." She squired a glob of white glue on one end and stuck them together with the excess glue oozing out the sides. "Then you take a different color." She picked up the red paper and crookedly cut off another strip. "And you put it through the first one before you glue it. That's how you make a chain."

"That's very good." Leslie managed to force an approving nod.

Holly wrinkled her nose in rueful disagreement. "But I don't cut straight."

"It just takes practice."

"Why don't you cut the paper and I'll paste it together? It will go faster," the girl suggested with bright-eyed eagerness.

Leslie opened her mouth twice, but couldn't find an adequate excuse to refuse. "All right."

She took the small scissors Holly held out to her. The handles were so small she could barely get her fingers in them, but she began cutting. The edges were so dull it was closer to sawing. Holly pulled a kitchen chair closer to Leslie and sat on her knees to begin the task of pasting the chain together.

"Do you have a boyfriend, Leslie?" she asked.

Leslie threw her a look, wondering what prompted that question. "No."

"I do. His name is Bobby Jenkins and he always sits beside me at Sunday School. He says he wants to marry me." She frowned and tipped her head to one side to look at Leslie. "Has anyone ever wanted to marry you?"

"Yes, a couple of boys have asked me," she admitted and tried not to appear too amused by the subject matter. Neither did she explain the last serious marriage proposal had been when she was a freshman in college.

"How come you didn't marry them?"

"Because I didn't love them." Leslie kept cutting the strips of colored construction paper, pausing now and then to flex her fingers.

Holly sighed heavily and began pasting again. "I'm too young to be in love."

"You are a bit young." Leslie had trouble keeping her tongue out of her cheek.

"Do you think my daddy is handsome?" Holly wanted to know. "A lot of women do."

"Yes, he's a good-looking man." She tried to sound disinterested, and failed, although she doubted that his daughter knew the difference.

"Are you going to fall in love with my daddy like they do?"

That was going too far. "Holly—" Leslie rested both hands on the tabletop and gave the child a look that was a mixture of exasperation and amusement "—I only met your father once. I don't even know him. I've hardly even talked to him."

She thought about that for a minute. "After you get to know him, then are you going to fall in love with him?"

Leslie didn't make another attempt to answer the question. "Where do you get ideas like this?"

"They just come to me," Holly declared with a shrug and an innocently batting blink of her eyes. Bending over the table, she squirted glue from the bottle onto a band of red paper.

"It might work better if you used less paste," Leslie suggested as it went on the table. At least it was the kind that washed off with soap and water.

"Okay." There were already a dozen links to the paper chain. Holly stretched it out to see how it looked. "It's really going to be pretty on our tree, isn't it?"

"Um-hmm." It was an agreeing sound, which allowed Leslie to stop short of voicing an outright approval for the tree-trimming tradition that had lost its meaning over the years.

The double barrier of the storm windows muffled the voice calling outside the house. "Holly!"

"Whoops! That's my daddy." She scrambled off her perch on the chair and darted to the door.

"Your coat—" Leslie protested, thinking the little girl intended to run outside without it.

But she only opened the two doors and stuck her head outside. "I'm over here, Daddy!" Without waiting for a reply, Holly blithely shut the doors and skipped back to her chair.

Leslie stared, slightly taken aback by the child's lack of concern. While Holly seemed a little precocious, she hadn't acted spoiled or overindulged. If it wasn't the latter, she was certainly extremely confident of herself.

From the corner of her eye, Leslie caught the movement of someone passing the kitchen window. That was followed by a knock at the door. She didn't need three guesses as to who it might be.

"Come in." She called out the permission to enter, rather than hobble ungracefully to the door to admit Tagg Williams. Unconsciously she bit her lips to force color into them, aware she hadn't bothered to put on makeup.

The storm door opened, then the inner door, and her aunt's tall, dark neighbor walked in. His strong and sun-browned features were wearing a curious expression, his piercing blue eyes slightly narrowed. Without the dullness of fatigue and soreness, Leslie absorbed the full impact of him beyond the striking coloration of coal black hair and light blue eyes. Lines were grooved into his lean cheeks, indicating the frequence of his smiles. His mouth was thin and firm, clearly defined. There was a vitality about him, a virility that came from the combination of the whole rather than any single part of him. Leslie thought she glimpsed a sense of humor perpetually lurking in the blue of his eyes.

"So this is where you got off to." He eyed his daughter with a trace of reproval.

"I'm sorry. I thought you knew she was here." Leslie had presumed Holly had told him she was coming over. Even though it wasn't her fault, she felt a little guilty for not questioning the girl.

"I thought she was playing in the kitchen until I became suspicious over how quiet she was." His mouth lifted in a faint smile. "I guess parents develop a sixth sense about such things."

"I was going to tell you, Daddy, but you were busy," Holly explained in defense of her oversight. "I knew you wouldn't mind. And I knew I'd hear you call."

"You still should have asked." He walked to Holly's chair and lightly tugged at a strand of black hair, then rested his hands on her shoulders.

"I knew Leslie was here alone. I thought we could keep each other company. Look." She held up the paper chain. "See what we've been making for the tree."

"Let me guess—you did the pasting and made the chains while Leslie got the boring job of cutting the paper," Tagg Williams said dryly.

"She cuts straighter than me," Holly defended the system she'd arranged.

"I didn't mind," Leslie inserted. Actually, his little girl had livened up a dull afternoon for her.

"Thanks." When he looked at her, she felt warmed by his smile. If she wasn't convinced she had passed the blushing stage, she might have believed she had. But it was just an inner glow that heated her skin. Then he was patting his daughter's shoulder. "Get your things gathered up so we can go home. You've taken enough of Leslie's time."

"We haven't finished the chain." Holly looked at the paper still to be cut.

"You and I will finish it tonight. How's that?" He slanted her a grin with a downward tilt of his head.

"Okay." She began scooping her papers, scissors, and glue into the sack, leaving the incomplete paper chain to add last. "We're going out into the woods on Friday to cut our own Christmas tree. Why don't you come with us, Leslie?" she invited without checking with her father.

"Thank you, but—" She paused in time to check the impulse to inform Holly that she thought it was a crime to cut down a valuable tree just to hang some ornaments on it.

"—I don't think Leslie would have much fun hiking through the snow on crutches, Holly," Tagg inserted an excuse in the pause.

"She could ride on my sled and you could pull her," Holly suggested, finding a quick solution to the problem.

"Thanks, but as clumsy as I am, I'd probably fall off," Leslie refused.

Holly appeared to reluctantly accept her decision not to accompany them on their tree-cutting expedition. That idea was no sooner abandoned than another occurred to her. "Would you like us to cut you and Mrs. Evans a tree?" she asked, then turned to her father to verify it. "We could do that, couldn't we?"

"We could." He nodded.

"My aunt and I have talked it over and we aren't going to have a tree this year," Leslie stated to eliminate the offer.

"But you've got to have a tree!" Holly looked properly shocked. "Santa won't have any place to put your presents if you don't have a tree."

In her opinion, the myth of Santa Claus was a cruel hoax perpetuated by unthinking adults. She remembered her own traumatic discovery that he didn't exist when she was Holly's age. She had cried for two days.

Leslie worked to control her expression so her personal opinion of the subject wouldn't show. After all, it wasn't her place to correct the child's mistaken belief in something that didn't exist, but she really felt her father should. Some of that inner conviction must have shown in her eyes, because when she glanced at Tagg Williams, the measuring study of his gaze took on a mocking gleam.

She bristled ever so slightly before finally replying to Holly's remark. "My aunt and I have decided we don't want a tree," she stated again. "So I guess Santa Claus will just have to pass this house without leaving any gifts."

The large pair of china blue eyes viewed Leslie with solemn roundness. "Santa wouldn't do that unless you've been bad." She seemed worried that Leslie might have been bad.

"I don't believe Leslie has been a bad girl." Amusement was edging his mouth as Tagg affectionately squeezed his daughter's arm in reassurance. There was no mistaking the mocking light that danced so disturbingly in his eyes when he glanced at Leslie. "I think Leslie is saying that she doesn't believe in Santa Claus."

Holly's mouth opened in a round circle of discovery. Then a pitying expression stole over her innocently drawn features. "Don't you believe in Santa Claus, Leslie?"

"No." There was absolutely no reason to lie about it. Still, she felt defensive about admitting it to a child. She was irritated with Holly's father for putting her on the spot, so she challenged him. "Do you believe in Santa Claus?"

"Of course," he answered without hesitation as a smile broke across his face.

"Gee, I'm sorry you don't believe in Santa Claus anymore," Holly declared sadly. "Maybe Daddy and me can help you believe in him again."

She had the uncanny sensation she was being backed into a corner, assaulted from two sides. Leslie was determined to stand her ground and not be talked into an admission that was contrary to her beliefs. "I don't think you can, Holly." Her voice was cool and firm. It seemed wisest to bring this discussion to a close. "I enjoyed your company today. Maybe you can come visit me again. Only the next time, be sure and tell your father where you're going."

"I will." Holly's response seemed more off-hand than assuring. Picking up her snow jacket, she thrust a hand through an armhole. Tagg helped her find the second. "Since Leslie doesn't want to come with us when we get the tree, maybe she can come over to our house and help us decorate it. She did help me make the chain."

"We'll see." His glance at Leslie seemed to say that he knew she would refuse if the question was put to her now. She suspected he wanted to avoid letting his daughter suffer any more rejections of her invitations. Holly gathered up her paper sack and jumped off the chair to walk to the door. "Where are your boots?"

Holly peered up at him through her long lashes, so innocent and so beguiling. "I forgot to wear them," she admitted. "But I wiped my feet real good so I wouldn't track on Mrs. Evans's floor."

He didn't appear completely mollified by her reply. "Next time—" he began on a warning note.

"—I won't forget to wear them. I promise," Holly inserted quickly and turned the doorknob. As she pulled it open, she looked across her shoulder at Leslie, smiling and waving. "Bye, Leslie!"

"Bye," Leslie responded, but Holly was already pushing open the storm door.

Tagg paused by the door, his hand holding it open. A fine thread of tension seemed to run through the room, tying them together. Her heartbeat seemed louder, but it might have been just the sudden silence. She was fascinated by the polar blue color of his eyes, but their look was anything but cold. There was a latent sexuality about him that Leslie hadn't noticed before. It was no wonder that his daughter had observed that women fell in love with him. It would be so easy. Mentally she pulled back from the thought. It seemed to break the spell that had held them both silent.

"I hope Holly wasn't too much trouble," he said.

"She wasn't." The words, the subject matter seemed all wrong. It was an empty communication, a poor substitute for another that neither of them were prepared to make.

"She'll probably be back over another time to visit," Tagg inserted, almost as an amused warning. "If you're busy, just send her on home."

"Okay."

"Take care of that leg." It was said in parting, along with a quick, disturbing smile. Then the two doors were shutting behind him. Leslie had a glimpse of him through the window as he made a skimming descent of the back steps and cut across the driveway to catch up with his daughter.

The house seemed quieter and emptier. Leslie reached for the deck of cards and idly began shuffling them to play another game of solitaire.

After lunch on Friday, Leslie volunteered to do the dishes. When the last pan was rinsed and stacked in the dishdrainer to dry, she pulled the sink stopper and washed the suds down the drain. Hopping on one leg and using the crutches for balance, she tugged the terry towel from its wall rack and wiped the moisture from her hands. Her aunt was bending down to search through one of the bottom cupboards.

"What are you doing?" Leslie asked with a half-smile as her aunt nearly crawled inside the cupboard in her search.

"I'm trying to find my roaster pan." Her voice came hollowly from the inside of the cupboard. "I thought I'd fix a pot roast for dinner tonight. Ahh, here it is."

There was a noisy rattle of pans before she backed out of the cupboard with a mottled gray roaster pan and lid in hand. Patsy Evans pushed to her feet and set the pan on the countertop.

"At the rate I've been eating since I came here, I'll need to go on a diet before I leave." Usually Leslie was too busy at work to eat three full meals a day.

"We'll diet together when the time comes," her aunt declared with a twinkling look. "It's such a pleasure to cook for two people and not be faced with a refrigerator full of leftovers."

"There aren't many recipes to fix a dish for just one person," Leslie agreed. "Is there anything I can do to help?"

She barely got the question out when someone knocked at the side door. "Yes." Her aunt changed the negative response she had been about to make. "You can answer that."

After being on crutches for two weeks, Leslie was becoming adept at ambulating with them. She moved with relative swiftness to the door, balanced her weight on one crutch, and opened the door with her free hand. She was startled and a little unnerved to find

Tagg Williams standing at the threshold, holding the storm door open with his shoulder.

"Hi." His glittering gaze made its usual run down her length before coming back to hold her glance.

"Hello." Leslie was instantly conscious of the baggy pair of gray slacks she had borrowed from her aunt. None of hers would fit over the plaster cast. They were hardly flattering to her slim figure. The same was true of the sloppy-fitting maroon sweater. It almost made her look flat-chested.

"Taggart, come in." Her aunt had glanced across the room to identify her visitor. She didn't believe in shortening a person's given name, and never abbreviated his. "—Before you let all the cold air in," she added the admonishment.

Leslie shifted to one side so he had room to step in and close the door. He didn't bother to unbutton the charcoal gray wool parka he was wearing, which indicated he didn't intend to stay long. Leslie had always considered herself to be tall, at five foot six inches in her stockinged feet, but standing beside him, she was conscious of his superior height. The top of her head would just brush his chin, if she were closer. The latter thought sent a small quiver over her spine.

"I came by to see if Leslie wouldn't change her mind and come along with us on our search for a Christmas tree." Tagg stated the reason for his visit, not letting his gaze stray from her face. "I borrowed an old dogsled for you to ride in so you won't have to worry about falling off Holly's sled. I even have a couple of old fur blanket robes. They might smell a little musty but they'll keep you warm."

Leslie was slightly stunned at the trouble he'd taken to insure she'd be comfortable, but none of that altered one salient point. "I don't think you understand. I don't believe in chopping down trees just to use them for Christmas decorations."

"Are you an ecology nut?" he countered smoothly, a suggestion of a smile showing around the corners of his mouth. He gave no sign that he was deterred by her response.

"No. Not exactly." Leslie faltered at the unexpected question. She supported many of the ecology issues, but she wasn't an extremist or fanatic—or a "nut," as he put it. "It's just something I don't believe in."

"No." His mouth slanted in a crooked, and amused line. "I don't suppose you believe in the Easter Bunny or the Tooth Fairy, either."

"As a matter of fact, I don't." Her reply was unnecessarily sharp, but Tagg Williams didn't appear to notice.

"Holly and I would like you to come with us. When I get out the axe, you can look the other way," he suggested.

"Really, I don't—" Leslie started to repeat her refusal, but she was interrupted by her aunt.

"Forget all that tree business. It will do you good to be outside in the fresh air. It's just what you need after being cooped up so long," her aunt insisted in a mildly scolding tone. "Don't take any more arguments from her, Taggart. She'll go with you."

"Aunt Patsy." Leslie turned on her aunt, irritated that she had intervened.

"Now admit it, Leslie. You would enjoy being outside in the wood," she said in challenge.

That part of it did sound fun, Leslie had to admit it—if only to herself. She battled for a silent moment with her inner convictions and decided to take advantage of the opportunity to be outdoors. The dogsled was the ideal vehicle to accomplish it so she wouldn't have to rely on the dubious support of her crutches on ice and snow. Since she had already stated her views regarding so-called Christmas trees, she wasn't really compromising her position.

"I'll come," she agreed, then added, "—as long as you understand that I think what you're doing is wrong and a waste of a good tree. So don't ask me to help you pick one out."

"We won't." His smiling look gave Leslie the impression that he knew in advance she'd agree to come with them. "While you get your coat and scarf, I'll start the car and get it warmed up. We'll be ready to go in five minutes." He reached for the door to open it. "Don't change your mind." It was a warning against second thoughts.

"I won't." Leslie rarely backed off a decision once she'd made it. She wasn't the type to waver or regret impulsive decisions.

A rush of cold, December air swept into the kitchen when Tagg departed via the side door. Leslie shivered in a reflexive action to the sudden chill. In addition to her winter coat and scarf, she'd need a ski hat and her fur-lined gloves—and a couple of wool socks for her bare toes.

Chapter Three

Holly was in perpetual motion in the front seat of the station wagon, too excited to sit still. Leslie had the entire back seat to herself, sitting sideways with her legs stretched over the seat and leaning against the locked, rear passenger door. The used dogsled was stowed on its side in the back, surrounded by the blanket robes so it couldn't slide all over.

"How much farther now, Daddy?" Holly wanted to know.

They were traveling down one of the many unpaved backroads that laced the rural countryside of Vermont. A brief snowfall the night before had coated mountain, tree and valley with a pristine whiteness. It was a scene of picture-postcard perfection.

"It's the next farm just up the road," Tagg replied patiently to her oft-repeated question. He partially turned his head in Leslie's direction without taking his eyes off the road. "Abe Bellows gave us permission to take a tree from his woods."

"I wasn't going to accuse you of trespassing on someone else's property," she responded dryly.

"Come spring, he's going to brush-hog most of it so he can use it as a pasture for his dairy cattle," he informed her. "Most of the smaller trees will be cleared out of the valley area when that happens."

Leslie made no reply. She understood the reason Tagg was telling her this. He wanted her to know the tree they'd be cutting down for Christmas would be one that would be bulldozed out when the land was cleared the following spring. There was a degree of consolation in that knowledge, yet it didn't change the fact that she found this whole business of Christmas deplorably overdone.

Slowing the station wagon, he turned it into the farm lane already snow-packed from the comings and goings of other vehicles. There was a crunch of tires in the hard snow and the metallic rattle of chains with each rotation of the wheels.

A big collie came bounding out from a red barn to announce their arrival and escorted them past the buildings to a far gate. It continued to bark when Tagg stopped the car, but its flag of a tail waved the air in a manner that seemed more friendly than threatening. The minute Tagg opened the driver's door, the dog was pushing its cold nose inside to have its head scratched.

"Some watchdog," Leslie laughed.

"He told everybody we were here, didn't ya, fella." Tagg rubbed its ears, then gently pushed it out of the way to step outside. "You might as well stay in the car until I get things unloaded."

"I'll help." Holly shot out of her side, certain her father wasn't talking to her.

Unless someone opened the rear door by her feet, Leslie had very little choice but to stay in the car. It wouldn't do any good to open the door she was leaning against because she couldn't possibly swing her left leg with its rigid cast around—and going out backward didn't exactly appeal to her. There wasn't any way she could reach the other door handle without a lot of wriggling and twisting. So she resigned herself to sit and wait until they had unloaded the things from the back.

Tagg lowered the tailgate of the station wagon and pulled the sled out. Holly was so busy playing with the brown and white collie that she forgot she had volunteered to help. Righting the sled, Tagg set it on its runners and tossed the fur robes onto it. Only two items remained in the back, an axe with its blade encased in a leather pocket and a leather rifle case. When he started to remove both, Leslie frowned in confusion.

"Why are you taking the rifle?" she asked, then arched a dryly mocking eyebrow "Don't tell me you're going to shoot the tree before you chop it down."

"No," he chuckled, his warm breath turning into a vaporous cloud when it came in contact with the cold air. "I thought we might see some mistletoe while we're out."

"And you're going to shoot it?" That didn't make any more sense than her first question.

"Yes." His smile widened at the absolute confusion that took over her expression. "It's a parasitic plant that you usually see growing in the tops of other trees. There's only two ways to get it. You can either climb the tree or shoot the mistletoe out of it."

"You'd have to be a pretty good shot," Leslie declared.

"So I've heard," he replied with a deepening smile.

It was a crazy combination of arrogance and modesty. She laughed softly, in spite of herself. Tagg shut up the rear of the wagon and pushed the dogsled around the car to the fence gate. It was already standing open, so he took the sled on into the thickly wooded field.

Without the car's heater running, Leslie was beginning to feel the nipping cold of the winter afternoon. She lowered her chin so the wool scarf around her neck would cover more of her face and partly warm the air she breathed. Tagg was doing something to the sled, but she couldn't see too well since Holly and the frolicking dog had joined them. She glanced upward at the pearl gray sky overhead. It seemed to blend with the white snowscape that surrounded them.

When she heard footsteps approaching the station wagon, she pulled her gaze down. As Tagg walked back to the car, he pulled a ski cap out of his jacket pocket and covered his dark head with it. She reached down to pick up her crutches that were lying on the floor, then noticed Tagg was coming to the wrong side.

"Open the other door." She motioned to the one closest to her feet, but he gave no sign that he heard her. Half-turning, she rolled down the car window to repeat it. He reached through the opening and pulled the door lock. "Not this door," Leslie protested, but it was already swinging open behind her.

"You aren't going to need those crutches," Tagg advised her and hooked an arm around the front of her waist.

"What are you doing?" She almost panicked when he began dragging her backward out of the car, but she had already guessed his intentions before he slipped a supporting arm under her legs. "You can't carry me—not with this heavy cast."

Instinctively she wrapped an arm around his neck to hold on and gripped at the ridge of his shoulder with her other hand, afraid he might suddenly drop her. When he had her free of both the car seat and the door, he straightened and threw her a little higher in his arms to get a firmer hold. Her heart seemed to catapult into her throat. He turned his face to her, his blue eyes lazy with amusement.

"I tell you what. If it looks like I'm going to drop you, I'll make sure you land in a soft snowdrift. How's that?" he mocked.

She was so close to him that she caught the lingering scent of the tangy after-shave lotion on his smoothly shaven jaw. The cold temperature had already begun to stiffen his mouth, limiting the movement of his lips as they formed the words. It was difficult to keep her gaze from straying to his mouth, only disturbing inches away from hers. Leslie tried to concentrate on what he said and stop this purely sexual attraction from holding sway with her. But it wasn't easy with the warmth of his breath trailing over her skin.

"You'd better make sure it's a soft snowdrift. One broken leg is bad enough." Her voice was husky with the inner disturbance of his nearness.

"I promise." He started toward the sled, carrying her in his arms with her left leg sticking rigidly and awkwardly in the air.

Although Tagg carried her with seeming ease, Leslie noticed the muscles standing out in his neck, which proved it was requiring no little effort. When he reached the sled, he dropped down on one knee and carefully set her on the furry robe draped over the sled and its backrest. The second robe he took and covered her with it, tucking in the sides.

His breath was coming quicker after the exertion of carrying her, but Leslie didn't think he was actually puffing. "Just think." This time, she was the one who had a mocking gleam in her eye. "Now you get to pull me."

"You aren't exactly a lightweight, are you?" An eyebrow lifted in laughing, good humour.

"Can I ride in the sled, too, Daddy?" Holly requested eagerly.

He paused, resting an arm on his bent knee, looked at his daughter, and mildly shook his head in a gesture of defeat. "You can ride for a little while," he agreed.

"Oh, goodie!" She clapped her hands together in excitement and jumped up and down. The dog began barking, certain this was some new game.

Tagg picked her up. "You have to be careful of Leslie's leg," he warned as he set her toward the front of the sled. "And you have to sit still. No bouncing around or you might overturn the sled. We didn't ask Leslie to come with us just to get hurt. Agreed?"

"Yes, Daddy." She sat primly still, mischief darting out of her blue eyes.

"If she gives you any trouble—" Tagg glanced at Leslie "—just boot her into the snow."

"I will." Leslie snuggled deeper under the warm robe, burying her cold nose in the soft fur, and watched Tagg move to the front of the sled.

He'd rigged up some kind of a shoulder and chest harness to pull the sled. After he had shrugged into it, he adjusted the straps over the thickness of his wool coat. The collie sat forlornly beside the sled, whining at Holly and brushing at the snow with its tail.

"Can the dog ride in the sled, too, Daddy?" Holly couldn't resist the appeal of the dog's brown eyes.

"No. He's got four legs. He can run beside it." Tagg was definite in his refusal to haul another able-bodied passenger. As he leaned into the harness, the sled's runner glided cleanly through the few inches of new snow.

"Mush! Mush!" Holly ordered loudly and immediately began giggling. Leslie laughed, too, but she made sure hers was muffled by the robe.

"I'll 'mush' you," Tagg threatened, but there was a smile in his voice.

The ground fell away from the fence gate in a gentle, downward slope. It was relatively easy pulling the first forty yards until the land leveled out and became densely populated with trees. Then it became more of a trick maneuvering around them and finding a fairly straight path through them. The collie trotted along-side, sometimes dashing off to chase a squirrel or a rabbit, but always coming back.

The novelty of riding in the sled quickly wore off for Holly. The dog seemed to be having more fun than she was. "I wanta walk, Daddy. Stop the sled."

He halted so she could climb off, his breath run-ning out in large white puffs. "Watch her leg," he warned Holly again, but she scrambled off the right to avoid bumping Leslie's cast. His gaze lingered on Leslie, buried under the robe until only her eyes and part of her nose were showing. "Are you warm?"

"Yes." She nodded, in case he couldn't hear her muffled answer.

The briskness of the cold air sharpened all her senses while the rest of her managed to stay warm and cozy under the robes. When Tagg began trudging on-ward again, Leslie relaxed and enjoyed the relatively smooth ride.

A blue jay flitted from tree to tree, following them through the woods and calling raucously to warn the other creatures of the humans' presence. There was hardly any breeze, but every now and then, its faint breath would blow at the clumps of snow on the skel-etal branches of the maples and the birch and send crystalline flakes drifting downward.

Their trek was taking them down the length of a meandering and narrow valley, with mountains rising up on each side. There was a small stream running through, frozen over in places and running free in others. Sometimes they were close enough for Leslie to hear the musical tinkle of the water spilling over the rocks.

They were some distance from the fence gate when they finally reached an area where a stand of firs was growing at the base of the mountain. Tagg halted and shrugged out of the harness.

"We should be able to find a tree in that bunch," he said to Holly and walked to the sled for his axe. As he bent down, he winked at Leslie, "Be sure to look the other way when I start chopping."

She lowered the robe away from her mouth long enough to say, "Are you afraid I'll start shouting, 'Woodsman, spare that tree'?"

"I wouldn't be surprised." Tagg tried to smile, but the cold had stiffened his mouth. His eyes crinkled up at the corners instead.

As Leslie watched him walk away to the stand of pines, she wondered how she could joke about something she believed in so strongly. Maybe it was just that Tagg Williams made it difficult to be angry, and stay angry.

"Let's get this one, Daddy." Holly picked out a tree that was at least ten feet tall.

"It's too big. This one's more your size."

Their voices carried clearly across the snow. Leslie didn't have to strain to hear them. She couldn't see which tree Tagg had chosen, her view blocked by larger ones. It wasn't long before she heard the biting thud of the axe blade into a tree trunk. She looked away, not really to avoid the scene that was transpiring, but to assess the area. With fewer trees, more grass would grow in the valley to provide the farmer with pastureland for his dairy herd.

There was the splintering crack of wood giving way. Leslie tried to make it an abstract sound, not wanting anything unpleasant to intrude on this outing. She was enjoying herself and she was determined to continue enjoying herself.

The dog started barking. When she looked around, she saw Tagg dragging a small tree through the snow with the dog running alongside. The leather case was covering the axe blade he carried by its wooden handle. Holly broke away and ran toward the sled.

"Do you see our tree, Leslie? It's a pretty one, isn't it?" she declared excitedly.

Fortunately for Leslie, Holly didn't seem to expect a response, so she wasn't forced into a position of pretending or offending. Tagg noticed her silence, however, as he approached the sled.

"I'm afraid the tree is going to have to ride with you. I hope you don't mind too much," he said.

"It's all right."

He tied it onto the front part of the sled with a couple lengths of twine. It was a small, well-shaped tree, about four feet tall. The resinous smell of its needles scented the air Leslie breathed, making it pungently clean.

"Hold on," he advised her. "I'm going to turn the sled around."

Picking up the front runners, he held them just inches off the ground and used Leslie's weight at the back of the sled as an anchor point to make a slow pivot. With a few adjustments of the rear, he soon had the sled turned around and pointing in the direction they had come.

Before he strapped himself into the harness, he took the rifle out of its leather carrying case. "I saw some mistletoe along the way," he explained.

It was about a third of the way back along their trail. Before he took aim, Tagg pointed its location out to Leslie. It was growing on some of the highest limbs of the tree. Holly stood behind her father with her hands clamped over her ears and her eyes squeezed tightly shut.

Even though Leslie was prepared for it, she jumped involuntarily at the initial explosion of the first rifle shot. A squirrel scolded them in a loud, chattering voice from its perch in another tree. Its tirade nearly drowned out the sound of something falling through the tree limbs to the ground.

Holly and the dog went scampering through the snow to retrieve it, while Tagg waited until both were standing beside him before shooting again. After the third time, he removed the remaining bullets and started to slip the rifle into its case.

"But, Daddy, there's more," Holly protested when she and the dog came running through the snow with the last sprig of mistletoe.

"We have all we need," he replied. "Put the mistletoe in the sack with the rest. It's time we were headed back to the car."

Leslie caught something in his tone of voice. It was a full second before she realized the flakes of snow drifting in the air hadn't been blown from the trees.

The temperature had warmed up a little and it had started to snow.

"Daddy, it's snowing!" Holly made the same discovery, and turned up a hand, trying to catch a flake in her mitten. "What if we get lost? What if it snows so hard we can't see to find our way back? We should have left pieces of bread like Hansel and Gretel did."

"I think the sled made some very plain tracks. If we follow them, I bet we'll find our way to the car," he replied dryly.

"Let's pretend the tracks aren't there. It'd be more fun," Holly insisted, wanting to taste a little thrill of adventure.

"Okay, you pretend." He glanced over his shoulder at Leslie. "And I'll follow the tracks."

There was something enchanting and magical about the return trip with lazy flakes spiraling down through the trees. All was quiet and hushed, except for the crunch of footsteps and the slicing sound the sled's runners made through the snow. It seemed much shorter going back to the car.

This time Tagg pulled the sled through the gate and right up next to the rear car door. He was breathing hard when he shrugged off the harness and came back to help Leslie out of the sled. The last stretch had been a steady uphill pull.

"If I tried to carry you this time, I probably would drop you," he admitted with a cold-stiffened grin, and helped her to stand up on her good leg, supporting her with an arm around the waist while he opened the car door to the rear seat. "Can you make it, or should I get your crutches?"

"I can make it." She grabbed hold of the door frame and made short little hops. Then she slid into the car backward, dragging her casted leg onto the seat.

Once he was sure she was safely inside, Tagg shut the door. It took a few minutes more to load the dog-sled, the robes, and the tree into the back of the wagon. Holly hugged the collie goodbye for at least the fifth time and climbed into the front seat. Shuddering, Tagg slipped behind the wheel and pulled off his right glove to blow on his fingers.

"Now to get warm," he declared and started the motor with the ignition key.

By the time they drove out of the farmer's lane onto the backroad, warm air was blowing from the heat vents. The heat intensified the scent of pine needles in the air. It wasn't long before Holly became infected with the smell of the tree and broke into song, a loud if occasionally off-key rendition of "O Christmas Tree." Tagg joined in, and his voice was a rich baritone. Leslie sat silently in the back seat, feeling alone, unable to take part in this spontaneous joyfest of Christmas carols.

The singing ended when they turned into the driveway to the brick house next door to her aunt's. Tagg helped Leslie out of the car and passed her the crutches.

"Thanks for asking me to come along." She stood awkwardly on her crutches, aware that earlier she could have expressed herself with more genuine feeling behind the words. But the caroling had taken something away. "I did enjoy myself."

"You can't go home yet," he stated. "I wouldn't be much of a host if I sent you home without any refreshments. Come in and have some hot cocoa with us."

"I—" She was going to accept the invitation, but Holly seemed to think she wouldn't.

"Yes, do, Leslie." She grabbed at her hand to lend force to her plea. "Daddy makes the best cocoa you ever tasted, with lots of gooey marshmallows melting on top."

"All right, I'll come," she laughed. Her pleasure in the day had returned. Leslie couldn't sort through the reasons and come up with the right one, but it had something to do with being included, and sharing, of being a part of a whole. It didn't really matter as long as it felt good.

The living room was done in warm colors—cranberrys and golds with a smattering of orange. Richly grained maple woodwork was used throughout, including the staircase to the second floor. The house was comfortable and old and lived-in.

"Have a seat," Tagg invited, giving her the choice of the sofa or the matching chair with an ottoman.

Leslie chose the chair with the ottoman so she could rest her leg on it. When he started toward the dining room with the kitchen presumably beyond it, she asked quickly. "Would you like me to help you fix the cocoa?"

"Thanks, but I can manage," he refused with an easy smile.

"Look." Holly claimed her attention. "Over here is where we're going to put our tree. Right in front of the window. And when we turn on the lights at night, everyone who goes by can see it."

"That's true," Leslie agreed.

"Daddy and I finished the paper chain. Let me show you." She didn't wait to see if Leslie wanted to see it or not, and dashed off to another room.

Before Tagg brought the mugs of cocoa to the living room, Holly had an endless number of things to show Leslie. Some of them were Christmas oriented and some were not. Leslie looked at all of them and listened patiently to the little girl's prattle.

"Has she talked your leg off yet?" Tagg asked as he handed Leslie a mug of cocoa with frothy, melted marshmallows floating on top.

"Almost," she smiled in understanding.

Holly immediately took a sip of her own cocoa and stretched the tip of her tongue way out, trying to reach the sticking ring of marshmallow on her upper lip. "I got a white mustache just like Santa Claus," she laughed.

"You certainly do. You'd better go get a napkin," Tagg advised. "And bring some back for us."

"Okay." She set her mug carefully down on a coaster, then took off at a run for the kitchen.

"Believe it or not, she wears down about nine o'clock every night," he said to Leslie.

"She's certainly full of life and energy," Leslie agreed. "She was right about your cocoa, too. It's delicious. I've never had an instant mix that tasted this good."

"It isn't instant." He leaned forward, as if he was telling her a secret. "I made it from scratch. You are drinking the real McCoy, with milk, cocoa, sugar—the works."

She felt she'd really put her foot in it this time. "I...I'm sorry," she awkwardly laughed out the apology. "I just assumed—"

"I couldn't always cook. You should have tasted some of my first biscuits. They were harder than any bride could make." He smoothed over the situation by making light of it. "But like a bride, a father can learn to cook out of necessity, too."

"I guess so," she conceded and took another sip of her cocoa.

"Your aunt mentioned you work for a large advertising agency in New York." Tagg made the comment as Holly came racing back into the room and passed napkins around.

"I'm an assistant to the senior vice-president— which is a fancy way of saying I'm a glorified secretary," Leslie explained with a ruefully dry smile, and didn't mention that she earned a salary considerably higher than a secretary's. "I'm on a first name basis with the maître d's at the best restaurants in New York even though I've never eaten in one of them. And I know where you can get a suit cleaned in an hour— and the birthdays and anniversaries of my boss's children. But I don't make coffee."

"And you don't have to report for work until after the holidays?" The rising inflection of his voice turned the statement into a question.

"That's right," Leslie nodded and patted the hard cast under her pant's leg. "My cast will be off by then."

"Seems to me, your boss missed a good bet." A smile was tugging at the corners of his mouth.

"Why?" Curious, Leslie tipped her head to the side, not following his meaning.

"It's rather obvious." There was a wicked glint in his blue eyes, dancing and mischievous. "If a man took a notion to chase a girl with a broken leg around the desk, it's a sure thing that she couldn't run very far or very fast."

She had a sudden vision of that scene with Tagg as the pursuer. Her heart seemed to do a funny little somersault against her ribs. The breath she drew in became lodged in her throat, making it difficult to laugh off his little scenario.

"Why would he want to chase her?" Holly frowned in bewilderment.

"To catch her, of course." He reached out and rumpled the top of his daughter's head, then his gaze swung back to Leslie with veiled intensity. "That's why every man chases a woman—and vice versa.

There was a message in his remark, a statement of his interest in her. It quivered through her nerve endings, but it was accompanied by little fingerlings of personal doubt. She didn't want to rush into something, only to discover she was in over her head. In her experience, it had proved wiser to test the water by stages and not jump in.

"What happens when he catches her?" Holly's curiosity was thoroughly aroused.

"That, little lady, is something you'll discover for yourself when you're older," Tagg dodged the question. "That's part of the fun of growing up."

Holly turned to Leslie, a somewhat bored look on her face. "I'll bet he kisses her. Bobby Jenkins is always trying to kiss me."

There was a second of stunned silence as their glances met above Holly's dark head. Tagg couldn't keep a short laugh from escaping his throat. "When I was her age, I was putting spiders down Lucy Vining's dress. They grow up quick nowadays."

The conversation shifted to less provocative topics. A half an hour later, Leslie had finished her cocoa and made excuses to leave. Tagg accompanied her the short distance to her aunt's house. A fine film of snow had collected on the steps, just enough to make the footing slippery, but it had stopped snowing.

With a crutch propping the storm door open, Leslie rested her weight on her good leg and one crutch and turned to thank Tagg for seeing her safely home. He was standing on the next to the top step.

"Thanks to you, I made it without one slip," she said, smiling.

"We'll be putting the tree **up** Sunday afternoon. Why don't you come over and help us?" he suggested.

"No thanks," Leslie refused with a quick shake of her head.

"You don't believe in Santa Claus and you don't believe in decorating Christmas trees." He shook his head at her in mock dismay.

"I just don't like anything associated with Christmas period," she admitted without apology. "There's nothing 'merry' about it."

"You're too young to be such a cynic," Tagg declared and stepped down a step. "I'm going to have to have a talk with Santa Claus."

"Sure," she laughed without humour. "And his flying reindeer, too." She pushed the inner door open and hopped inside before the storm door banged shut on her.

"Leslie?! Is that you?" Her aunt called from the living room.

"Yes, it's me. I'm back!" She balanced on her crutches and began taking off the layers of outer garments she'd worn for warmth.

Footsteps approached the kitchen in advance of her aunt's arrival. "I thought I heard the car drive in some time ago. Are you just getting back?"

"No. That was probably us you heard," Leslie said and hopped over to a chair so she could take her snow boot off. "Tagg invited me in for cocoa."

An eyebrow was lifted at the ease with which she used his given name, but Patsy Evans made no comment on that. "Did you enjoy yourself?"

She thought about it a minute, then nodded. "Yes, I enjoyed myself." Oddly enough, it had been more fun than she had thought it would be.

"It isn't often that you meet someone who gets so much pleasure from their child," her aunt observed. "It's very heartwarming to see them together."

"I don't imagine it's easy for a man to be both father and mother," Leslie mused and tugged off her boot, tossing it onto the rug. A smile made a quick slant on her mouth. "Holly certainly isn't suffering any hardship having a bachelor father. Tagg is quite domestic. He made hot chocolate from scratch. That's something even I can't do."

Chapter Four

Sunday morning at Patsy Evans's house meant a late breakfast of pancakes with homemade Vermont maple syrup, sausages, and eggs. When the dishes were washed, Leslie took a cup of coffee into the living room and arranged herself in a chair with the Sunday newspaper spread around her to begin reading it section by section.

She was halfway through when she heard the floorboards creaking overhead. There was a brief moment of curiosity, certain her aunt had mentioned that she'd already made her bed. Then Leslie shrugged it aside and thought no more about it until she heard her aunt coming down the stairs. Her eyes widened in mild surprise at the red pantsuit her aunt was wearing.

"Are you going somewhere?" Leslie asked.

"The local nursing home is having its Christmas program this afternoon. I volunteered to help with the refreshments. Didn't I mention it?'' her aunt replied with an absent frown.

"No. Or, if you did, I'd forgotten."

"You're welcome to come with me," her aunt hurried to assure her of that.

"No, thanks, I'll stay here and read the paper." She turned down the invitation, which came as no surprise to her aunt.

"It will probably be close to six o'clock before I'm back." Her aunt slipped on her good coat with the dark mink collar and started for the kitchen. "Enjoy yourself."

"I will."

A few minutes after Leslie heard the side doors opening and closing, there was the muffled sound of an engine as a car reversed out of the driveway. The newspaper rattled companionably in the ensuing silence.

It didn't last long as a series of knocks loudly intruded. Leslie started to reach for her crutches, then guessed who it had to be. Since her aunt never locked the back door, she simply called out, "Come in!" Two sets of footsteps entered the kitchen, one light and one heavier. "I'm in the living room!" Leslie added.

Holly was the first to come dashing into the room, followed closely by Tagg Williams, his long strides making up for his slower pace. Holly leaned over the arm of Leslie's chair and claimed her attention.

"What are you doing?" she asked brightly.

"Reading the Sunday paper," Leslie stated the obvious, not needing to look at Tagg to be aware of the impact his presence made. He was standing a few feet away, his jacket unbuttoned to expose an ivory-colored sweater in a heavy ribbon-stitched knit.

"How are you with a needle and thread?" he asked.

The question momentarily threw her. "I can sew on a button. Why?"

"We need some help stringing popcorn and we thought we might be able to talk you into volunteering to give us a hand." There was a hint of a challenge in his look. "Have you got anything better to do on a Sunday afternoon?"

"I'm sure that's a matter of opinion," Leslie replied because she knew he wouldn't regard reading the paper as something better.

"Please, will you come over?" Holly added her plea. "Daddy's good at popping popcorn, but he's all thumbs with a needle."

"It's true," Tagg insisted with mock force and held out his left hand, wagging his fingers. "I stuck myself twice with the needle already. Holly thinks it ruins the popcorn to have dots of blood on it."

Two flesh-colored bandages marked the wounded areas on his middle and forefinger. A tiny smile edged her mouth as she tried to picture someone as decidedly masculine as Tagg Williams pricking himself with a sewing needle.

"I know you're not into tree-trimming, but I've got a fire crackling in the fireplace, cocoa warming on the stove, and lots of popcorn to eat...or string, if you're more adept with a needle than I am." He grinned crookedly, making it very difficult for Leslie to resist his appeal.

"I'll help you," Holly promised. "It will go faster with both of us doing it."

"I can't believe I'm letting myself get talked into this," she declared on a laughing breath because she knew she was going to agree.

"Then you will help!" Holly realized with delight and spun away from her chair. "You were right, Daddy. You said she'd come."

Her side glance at Tagg held a hint of accusation along with a touch of droll amusement. "Did someone let the cat out of the bag?"

"Let's just say, I knew you'd take pity on a couple of helpless souls." His darkly tanned features were gentled by the suggestion of a smile.

"I wouldn't be surprised if you poked yourself with the needle on purpose," Leslie accused, but without anger.

Tagg drew back in mock dismay. "Do I look like the kind of guy who would do something like that?"

"I don't think I'll answer that." The dryness in her voice was deliberate, indicating that he might be capable of such devious behavior.

"Here's your crutches." Holly gathered them up from where Leslie had them stored on the floor next to her chair. Now that Leslie had agreed to come, Holly was in a hurry for them to get under way.

Snowflakes were swirling out of a leaden sky as they crossed the driveway that separated the two houses. Woodsmoke was curling from the chimney of the Williams's house, its pungent odor being carried down by the heavy air. Holly was quick to point out the tree framed by the front window, but it was difficult to see beyond the reflection of the glass in the daylight.

Boxes of tree ornaments and tinsel garlands were strewn across the chair and matching ottoman in the living room. The sofa seemed to be the only piece of furniture that had escaped the litter of Christmas decorations. A huge bowl of popcorn was sitting at the coffee table in front of it, plus a six-inch-long strand of strung popcorn.

Balancing on first one crutch, then the other, Leslie took off her coat and passed it to Tagg to hang in the coat closet. She ran a hand through the length of her desert tan hair, trying to rid it of the static electricity that was making it cling to the green plaid sweater vest she was wearing.

"Daddy, can I plug in the tree lights so Leslie can see how nice it's going to look?" Holly was already beside the tree with the electric plug in hand.

"First you get a pillow for Leslie so she can prop her leg on the coffee table. Then you can plug in the lights," Tagg answered.

When she was comfortably settled on the sofa with her injured limb cushioned on a pillow, Holly plugged in the tree lights for Leslie to admire. After a few seconds, the white fairy lights began winking on and off in a haphazard pattern. Atop the tree, an aluminum star with a pale blue bulb shone down on the branches.

"It's very nice, Holly." Leslie had to make some comment for the child's sake, but Holly sensed her lack of enthusiasm.

"It will look lots better when we put the rest of the stuff on the tree," she insisted and wandered over to

the sofa to sit down beside Leslie. "This is the popcorn string I started." She picked up the one lying beside the popcorn bowl. "I threw Daddy's away. That's
his needle and string—what's left of it anyway."

"Shall we set the bowl between us and start in?"
Leslie suggested.

"If you want to." But Holly sounded preoccupied,
her mind on other things than stringing the popcorn.
Almost dutifully she nestled the bowl of popcorn on
the sofa between them and handed Leslie the unused
needle and string.

Out of the corner of her eye, Leslie was aware of
Tagg walking to the fireplace and bending down to
poke the glowing red coals. Another split log was
added. Flames sprang up to pop and snap over the
fresh fuel. Leslie began spearing popcorn on the needle and pushing the bunches down the string.

"How come you don't like Christmas, Leslie?"
Holly broke the short lull.

She flashed a quick glance at Tagg. He was watching her, but he gave no sign that he intended to jump
in and field the question for her. Leslie hesitated,
choosing her words carefully.

"It isn't that I don't like Christmas," she tried to
qualify her aversion to the season. "It's all the fuss
that goes along with it. It's the decorations and the
gift-giving and all the meaningless things that go along
with them. Too many people are making too much
money off a day that's supposed to be a religious holiday. I guess I believe the meaning of Christmas has
become lost under the fancy foil wrappings and bright
ribbons."

"That's why you don't believe in Santa Claus, too."
Holly seemed troubled by Leslie's failure to perpetu-
ate the myth.

"Do you know what Christmas is?" Leslie didn't
want to go into the business of Santa Claus. It wasn't
her place to puncture the child's belief in that myth.

"It's the day Jesus was born. And we give presents
to each other because the Three Wise Men brought
gifts to the baby Jesus," she answered without hesitation. "Our Sunday School is going to have a
Christmas program, telling the story of Baby Jesus
being born in the manger because there was no room
in the inn. I'm going to be one of the sheep that came
with the shepherds. Sally Tuttle says I'm going to be a
black sheep because of my hair. She gets to be the angel." Holly sighed at the unfairness of it.

"Black or white, you'll make a good sheep." Tagg
straightened from his crouched position beside the
hearth, joining the conversation.

"I don't mind being a sheep, 'cause I get to sit and
watch everyone else." Holly made it clear that she
wasn't bothered by the simpleness of her role in the
pageant. "When you were a little girl, what did you do
in your Christmas program?"

"I played the cow—and please—" she glanced
wryly at Tagg as he approached the sofa "—no comments from you."

"I was the inn-keeper who turned Mary and Jo-
seph away," he said to prove his childhood role had
been nothing to brag about. Reaching over, he
scooped up a handful of popcorn.

"You aren't supposed to eat that, Dad," Holly scolded him. "It's for the tree."

"Sorry." Tagg crunched away at a half dozen popped kernels.

"Did you like Christmas when you were a little girl?" Holly was back on her previous subject.

"Mostly I think I liked all the presents under the tree," Leslie admitted.

"Did Santa bring them?"

She held her breath a second, trying to find a way to avoid the question and not lie. "My parents gave me most of them."

"It must be sad not to believe in the goodness of Santa Claus," Holly declared.

The phrasing of her response shook Leslie a little. She glanced at the child, jet black hair falling forward across her cheeks as she bent her head to the task of stringing popcorn. She longed to question what Holly had meant by believing "in the goodness of Santa Claus," but she didn't.

"Which do you want me to put on the tree next, Holly?" Tagg had moved to the armchair with its assortment of decorations. "The red garland or the gold one?"

"The red one." Holly tossed her partially strung strand of popcorn onto the coffee table and pushed off the couch. "I'll show you where I want it to go."

Although Holly lent a hand now and then, Leslie ended up stringing most of the popcorn. She had to admit it looked very pretty draped around the green boughs of the tree like some lacy white ribbon.

After the garlands of tinsel and popcorn came the shiny Christmas balls in a variety of colors and sparkling patterns. Tiny strips of tinsel added the finishing touch. Holly took part in the last with gay abandon, throwing handfuls at the tree. Almost as much landed on the floor and Tagg as stayed on the limbs.

"You've still got some tinsel in your hair," Leslie advised Tagg when he lowered himself onto the adjacent sofa cushion.

He combed his fingers through the thickness of his ebony dark hair, raking out the short pieces of tinsel. There was a wry light in his blue glance, warm with humor.

"I have the feeling we're going to find tinsel in everything," he murmured.

"She did get rather carried away," Leslie agreed and half-turned to glance over the sofa's back at his daughter. She was sitting cross-legged on the floor in front of the lighted Christmas tree.

Her elbows were propped on her knees to support her chin on her hands while Holly gazed at the glittering sight before her. The solid overcase beyond the front window pane had brought a premature darkness to the late afternoon sky. The clear glass reflected the winking lights of the tree, creating a magical scene.

"I think it's just beautiful." Holly sighed with theatrical exaggeration.

"It's the most beautiful Christmas tree I've ever seen," Tagg agreed with tongue in cheek, then looked around the room. "The stockings are hung by the fireplace...with care. The nativity scene is on the mantel. The wax carolers are adorning the dining room table. All the decorations are out. All that's left is for a little girl named Holly to clean up the mess."

"Ahh, Daddy, not now," she protested in a wheedling voice.

"Yes, now." He remained firm under the coaxing appeal of her dark blue eyes. "Put all the boxes and packages in the closet. When you're done, we'll have some cocoa."

"All right," Holly gave in grudgingly and rolled to her feet with an agility that only the young seemed to possess.

"There's a bright spot to all this," Leslie said above the background noise Holly was making as she stacked the smaller boxes inside larger ones.

"What's that?" Tagg tipped his head back to rest it on the top edge of the sofa. He rolled it to one side to look at her.

"In three weeks, you can take it all down and put it away until next year," she teased.

"Don't remind me." He faked a groan and shut his eyes with seeming weariness. "I haven't recovered from chopping down the tree, so I can't say I'm looking forward to hauling it out."

"Your muscles are stiff, hmm?" Leslie guessed.

"I wonder why," Tagg murmured dryly. "It couldn't be because I pulled you on that sled for nearly two miles, plus chopped down the Christmas tree."

"You left out the part where you carried me from the car to the sled," she reminded him.

"That's right," he remembered, thick lashes sweeping up to let his blue eyes study her again. "A really good secretary would be an expert at shoulder and neck massages. I've had a hard week. Why don't you give me a good rubdown?"

"Sorry. I draw the line at coffee and a massage." Her refusal was brightly casual and offhand, but the hint of intimacy in his probing gaze made her feel anything but casual inside.

"I have the feeling that's not the only time you draw the line," Tagg said with a throaty chuckle.

"Hey, Dad! Look!" Holly cried excitedly from behind the couch, rattling a paper sack. "We don't have all the decorations up."

There was only so far Leslie could turn without moving her rigidly braced leg. Her head was turned as far to the side as it would go, but all she could see of Holly was her arm resting on the back of the sofa. The girl was evidently standing directly behind her. Something made Leslie glance at Tagg. His gaze was locked on a point a few inches above her head. She looked up and saw the sprig of mistletoe Holly was dangling above her.

"Now you've got to kiss her, Dad," Holly challenged with a giggling laugh.

"That's right, I do," he agreed.

Before Leslie could react, he was leaning toward her. Her pulse skipped a few beats when she found herself gazing into the black centers of his eyes. Her glance lowered to the strong, smooth line of his mouth, coming steadily closer. Her lashes came down a second before she felt the fanning warmth of his breath and the light pressure of his mouth so briefly touching hers.

It was over almost before it began. She blinked in vague surprise, feeling cheated. Which was silly since she'd always said that the business about kissing under the mistletoe was ridiculous.

There wasn't any time to assimilate her reaction or her response. Something was going on above and behind her. Tagg had grabbed his daughter's wrist and taken the sprig of mistletoe away from her. He was moving back to his own side of the sofa, dragging Holly with him. The little girl was convulsing with laughter and he was smiling broadly. He held the mistletoe over his own head.

"Now you have to kiss me," he informed his daughter.

Laughing, Holly leaned across the back of the sofa and gave him a loud smack on the lips. Only then, did he let go of her. She disappeared behind the sofa and popped back up with the sack of mistletoe in hand.

"Where are we going to hang this, Daddy?" She wanted to know.

"I have no idea." Tagg opened the sack to drop the sprig into it. "Just put it up for now. We'll find a place for it later."

"I'll put it on the coffee table so we won't forget it again," Holly decided.

"I'll get the cocoa." Tagg pushed off the sofa and headed toward the kitchen.

Just like that, the incident was over and forgotten—or so it seemed to Leslie. A kiss that hadn't been a kiss at all, leaving no lingering awkwardness or sense of unease. It was just as if it had been too unimportant to dwell on. At least that appeared to be Tagg's attitude. Leslie discovered she couldn't dismiss it so easily.

With Holly around, there wasn't any lack of conversation while they drank their cocoa. When Tagg turned on a lamp beside the sofa, Leslie realized how late it was.

"I'd better be getting back. It's almost six and I didn't leave any note telling Aunt Patsy I'm here." Leslie reached for the crutches propped against the side of the sofa.

"It's been snowing. I'll walk over with you in case the steps are slick," Tagg volunteered, and started for the coat closet.

"Thanks for coming over and helping us." Holly hovered close by while Tagg helped Leslie into her coat.

"It was fun—and you have a lovely tree." The last was added as an afterthought, but she meant it. This time it wasn't an empty compliment.

As they went out the door, Tagg paused long enough to tell his daughter, "I won't be gone long. If you get bored, you can wash the cocoa mugs." There was no response from Holly as he shut the door. "She's at the age where she thinks washing dishes is a treat. I'm sure she'll grow out of it."

"Everybody does," Leslie agreed with a quick smile. The snow had melted from the steps, but there were patches of ice and snow mixed in the driveway.

"Even though I'm prejudiced in her favor, I think Holly is turning into a little lady," he said with a degree of pride, then glanced at Leslie when she remained silent. "What? No comment?" he mocked.

"I was just thinking." She started not to tell him, then changed her mind. It was something she had observed and she was curious about it. "Holly never talks about her mother."

When Tagg came to an abrupt halt, Leslie stopped, too, wondering if she had unwittingly brought up a highly sensitive subject. A disturbing light had darkened his eyes; their gaze was centered on her as a profoundly pleased expression stole across his ruggedly handsome features.

"Well, well." It was a lowly voiced expression of satisfaction. "It's about time."

"I beg your pardon?" Her hazel eyes scanned his face in confusion, bathed in the light thrown from the windows of his house. The subdued light highlighted his angular features, emphasizing their planes and hollows.

"You've finally asked about Holly's mother." Again his voice was ringed with satisfaction. She noticed the faint deepening of the grooves etched into his tanned cheeks that indicated a suppressed, but dimpling smile.

"I don't understand." Leslie shook her head slightly in vague bewilderment. "Was I supposed to ask about her before or what?"

"Not necessarily." He spread his hand across her back to begin guiding her again toward her aunt's home. "It's just that when a woman asks about a man's past, it usually means she's interested in his future."

"I was asking because of Holly," she responded quickly, which was partially true—but only partially.

"Of course." His voice dryly mocked out an agreement. "It isn't too surprising that Holly doesn't talk about her. Cindy—my wife—died a month after Holly was born, so Holly has no memory of her."

"What happened?" Since he didn't appear to object to talking about his wife, Leslie went ahead and asked the question.

"There were complications in the delivery; infection set in; then pneumonia." It was a very clinical explanation with no insight into how his wife's death had affected him.

Leslie made a tactful attempt to probe into that area. "It must have been a difficult time for you—losing your wife and having a newborn baby to take care of and raise."

"Yes." It was a detached admission that lost even more of its credibility when he slanted a dry smile in her direction. "But Holly and I managed to survive it without any lasting damage. Although—" Tagg paused and briefly lifted his gaze skyward in a thoughtful attitude. "I guess a person never stops wondering what might have happened if things had turned out differently."

Which meant what? That he still longed for his wife? Did he think his life would be better or worse, if she had lived? It was impossible to come to a conclusion either way. His remark hadn't revealed enough. Leslie shied away from delving into something that was so personal.

As they reached the steps to the side door, Tagg moved in front of her to take the lead. "I'll turn the lights on for you."

By the time she mounted the steps, he had the doors opened and the kitchen light turned on. Tagg waited inside for her and helped remove her coat, an awkward task when one had to balance on crutches. For the time being Leslie draped her coat over the back of a kitchen chair, then turned back to him. He stood on the large rug, his hands thrust into the pockets of his open jacket.

The gesture of her hand as it brushed her silky, sand-colored hair away from the side of her face was almost a self-conscious one. His features were relaxed in a warm smile, but they didn't mask the inner probing of his gaze on her.

"I know a tree-trimming party is not your idea of fun, but I hope it didn't turn out to be too much of an ordeal," he said.

"It didn't." As a matter of fact, this was the second time she had enjoyed taking part in a Christmas-type activity. Perhaps she'd simply had too many bad memories associated with Christmas and not enough happy ones to off-set them.

"I meant to apologize for Holly's behavior. I hope she didn't embarrass you with that mistletoe incident." The curve of his mouth increased, taking on a rueful line in the rest of his expression. "I noticed you didn't look too pleased about it."

"I didn't?" Leslie hadn't thought it showed. "I've always regarded kissing under the mistletoe to be a silly tradition. It's forced on both parties whether either one wants it or not."

"It can be a useful ploy sometimes when a man wants to kiss a woman and he hasn't been given the opportunity. But, as you say—" he lifted a shoulder in a vague shrug "—it doesn't necessarily mean that the lady is willing. She could be just tolerating it. I suppose that's happened to you."

"More times than I care to count." It was one of the reasons she'd sworn off office Christmas parties.

"Was today one of them?" Tagg asked and immediately widened his smile. "That's a leading question, isn't it?"

"Very leading," she agreed with a self-conscious laugh. A warmth was beginning to spread through her veins and heat her skin until she felt slightly flushed.

"I guess you know where it's leading, too." He withdrew his hands from his pockets and took a step closer, reaching for her waist. Their touch just seemed to add to the warmth already coursing through her. His glance flicked upward, above her head, then down to hold her gaze. "There's no mistletoe—no obligation to kiss or be kissed."

"No," Leslie agreed, feeling oddly breathless in anticipation.

When he began bending his head toward her, he blocked out the overhead light. In an automatic response her chin lifted. His mouth settled onto hers with natural ease, its warmth melting away the little hesitancy that remained. Her lips moved against his, liking the stimulating feel of them.

His arm slid to the back of her waist, taking more of her weight so she had to rely less on the crutches for support. With his other hand, he took first one, then the other away from her and set them against the kitchen counter. Her hands found a way inside his jacket and circled his middle as he gathered her more fully into his arms.

A heady pleasure was building inside her as his mouth continued to roll over her lips, exploring their softness and inciting their response. That tangy fragrance clinging to his skin filled her senses with each deepening breath she took. His hands made a slow foray over her shoulders and back, traveling over the curve of her spine and shaping her to his length. Leslie was distantly conscious of his flatly muscled build, and the heat his body generated combining with hers.

When he ended the kiss, the moist heat of his breath continued to warm her lips. No attempt was made by either to pull back and increase the distance between their lips. Through the veiling screen of her lashes, Leslie studied the firm line of his chin and the attractive grooves that lined his mouth. She was conscious that his breathing was disturbed, not coming as evenly as it normally did. She knew her pulse was racing wildly, indicating the kiss had a similar, stimulating effect on her.

"I've been wanting to do that." His husky voice was pitched just above a whisper. It seemed to vibrate through her.

Lights flashed on the kitchen window as a car turned into the driveway. "That must be Aunt Patsy."

Leslie reluctantly loosened her circling arms to draw away from him. "You'd better hand me my crutches."

"Children and relatives; they don't have the best timing," Tagg declared dryly and kept a supporting arm around Leslie while he reached for her crutches. "Holly with her mistletoe this afternoon and your aunt arriving at this particular moment."

"She could have come home sooner." She slipped the crutches under her arms and shifted a small distance away from him.

"The cynic sounding like Pollyanna?" Tagg mocked that she had found something good in the intrusion.

"Even Scrooge had his moments," Leslie retorted, hearing the slam of a car door.

"Which reminds me," he said. "Holly goes to school in the mornings. One day this next week, I planned to drive into Montpelier. Would you like to ride with me and keep me company while Holly's in school?"

"Don't tell me. Let me guess," she said. "You're going Christmas shopping."

He laughed silently. "Clever girl. How did you figure that out?"

"It just seemed logical. So far I've gone along when you went hunting for your tree. You asked me over to help trim it. So the only thing missing is the presents to be put under the tree," Leslie concluded.

"Most of my Christmas shopping is done, but I do have a couple of items yet to buy. I promise I won't drag you through all the toy departments. We'll have brunch somewhere before we come home." He arched an inquiring eyebrow. "Will you come?"

"Yes." It didn't seem necessary to add more than that.

"I'll pick a day when the weather's nice and let you know," he said.

"All right," Leslie nodded.

When the storm door was opened from the outside, Tagg pivoted and opened the inner door for her aunt. Patsy Evans looked momentarily surprised to see him, then recovered with her usual aplomb.

"Hello, Taggart," she greeted him with a curious look. "Was there something you wanted?"

"No. I was just making sure Leslie got in safely. I have to be getting back. I left Holly at the house alone," he excused himself and moved to exit through the door Patsy Evans had just entered.

"I saw your Christmas tree when I drove in. It looks beautiful," she stated.

"I'll tell Holly you said so," Tagg smiled, then nodded to Leslie. "I'll see you."

When the door closed behind him, Leslie realized her aunt was watching her. She turned and Patsy busily began taking off her coat.

"I'm glad you didn't have to spend the afternoon alone," she commented.

"I helped string popcorn to hang on the tree," Leslie explained.

"I must say I like the way Taggart does things—going out and chopping down his own Christmas tree, encouraging his daughter to make things to hang on it." Her aunt elaborated on her initial comment.

"Yes." Leslie moved over to the sink. "Shall I heat some water for tea?"

"Sounds good. Please."

"By the way—" she held the teakettle under the faucet and began filling it with water "—he is a widower. His wife died of complications from childbirth a month after Holly was born."

"Really?" Her aunt appeared vaguely surprised by the news. "Somehow I had the feeling he was divorced. Not that it really matters." Her shrewd glance ran keenly over Leslie. "It was thoughtful of him to see you home."

"Yes." She hobbled over to the stove to put the kettle on to heat. "Some morning this next week, he asked me to ride into Montpelier with him."

"Are you going?"

Leslie turned, her eyes widening slightly at the question. "I thought I would, yes. Why?"

"No reason." Her aunt shrugged. "I guess I was just wondering whether this was the start of a holiday romance."

Her mouth opened to refute the idea, then closed without saying a word. It probably would turn out to be a short-lived relationship. It would be foolish to think that this time would be different from any of the others in the past.

Chapter Five

The gold dome of the granite Capitol Building glinted in the morning sunlight. A snow-covered, wooded hillside rose abruptly behind it to form an appropriately rural backdrop for the white statue of Ceres, the Roman Goddess of agriculture, standing atop the glittering gold dome.

There was little traffic on the street as Tagg drove by the State House. Leslie's gaze was drawn to the statue of Ethan Allen, standing proud and tall on the front portico of the Capitol Building, his arm upraised. This famed leader of Vermont's Green Mountain Men seemed to be standing guard over the independence they had battled to win from Britain, an independence Vermont had retained for fourteen years before finally joining the Union formed by the original thirteen.

"Small but impressive, isn't it?" Tagg noticed her interest in the Vermont State House and commented on it.

"Yes." Its size wasn't imposing, but there was a quiet majesty in its classic architecture and a solid strength about its granite walls.

"It always fascinated me when I was growing up. I often wondered whether my perspective as an adult would change that, but it hasn't," he stated.

"Are you from Vermont?" Leslie ran her glance over his profile. It was a piece of information she didn't recall her aunt mentioning.

"Yes, I grew up here." His attention remained on the street they were traveling, watching the intersections and glancing at the businesses. "Then I left for college, and came back only once or twice since." His gaze flicked briefly to her, absently amused. "Don't I look like a crusty native to you?"

"No." Although she conceded that Tagg had retained that air of reserve even if it was behind a smiling mask. "Did your work bring you back?" It was a probing question since he didn't appear to do any kind of work.

"No." The answer was accompanied by a brief, negative movement of his head, but he didn't seem to regard her question as prying into his personal affairs. "It was time for Holly to start attending school on a regular basis—and I guess I wanted her to grow up in the kind of background I did. How about yourself?" A traffic light turned red and he slowed the car to a stop, sliding a glance at her. "Are you from New York—or somewhere else?" And Leslie realized that she didn't know any more about what he did for a living than she had before.

"I was born and raised right in Manhattan," she answered his question while she tried to think of a tactful way to ask her own again.

"Then you're a city girl." The light changed to green and Tagg started the car smoothly forward.

The faintly mocking tone of his remark made Leslie add, "I've never thought of myself as a city girl. My parents had a house on Fire Island so we usually spent the summers there. In the winter, we'd go skiing—sometimes here to Vermont and visit Aunt Patsy. So I had a blend of citylife and countrylife, until the divorce changed things."

"Your parents moved away from New York after they split up?" he asked if that's what her remark meant.

"Eventually." She nodded and huddled into her coat, not from the cold since the car's heater kept the interior warm. Mainly Leslie was withdrawing from unpleasant memories. "Both of them remarried. Dad and his new family live on the West Coast; and Mom and her family live in Baltimore. 'And never the twain shall meet,' as the saying goes." The last was issued with a certain rawness.

"It was a bitter divorce," Tagg guessed by her tone.

"It was a bitter marriage." She shrugged, trying to make believe neither had mattered.

"Do you see them very often?"

"Not any more than I have to," Leslie admitted dryly. "I'm the spoils of their war, so they're both still fighting to claim me as theirs alone. And I don't like being the rope in a tug of war. That's why I came to stay with Aunt Patsy."

"I'm glad you did." Tagg smiled at her briefly, then noticed the store just ahead on the right. "There's where we're going—and there's an empty parking place out front. We're in luck."

There wasn't an opportunity for Leslie to turn the conversation back around and question Tagg about his occupation. So she had to bury her curiosity for the time being while he did his Christmas shopping.

Over an hour later, they returned to the car with his purchases made. Tagg stowed the brightly wrapped and ribboned packages in the back seat of the car, then held her crutches while Leslie maneuvered into the front passenger seat.

"And now to find someplace to eat," he declared as he slipped behind the wheel and took the car keys out of his pocket. "Hungry?"

"Just starting. I cheated and had toast and jam this morning," she confessed.

"So did I." Tagg chuckled softly, his glance moving over her. As he turned the car onto the street, he said, "I think I've figured out why you pretend not to like Christmas. It gives you a perfect excuse not to go through all this rigamarole of buying presents for people."

"Wrong." She laughed. "I just don't wait until the last minute to do all my shopping. My parents insist on giving me gifts—and a few of my friends. So I'm blackmailed into buying presents for them."

"A lot of people are too proud to accept a gift in the spirit that it's given," Tagg replied in understanding, then winked at her. "Of course, that's where Santa Claus steps in. How can a person say no to Santa Claus? He combines the joy of giving with the joy of receiving."

"I suppose that's true." Leslie leaned back in her seat to mull over that perspective of the Santa Claus myth.

The restaurant Tagg picked was relatively empty of customers. It was too early for lunch and the coffee break crowd had already left to return to work. So their service was quick and their food was hot. After the waitress had cleared away their dishes, she refilled their coffee cups.

Leslie noticed Tagg glance at his watch to check the time. "Is it getting late?"

"No. Holly won't be getting out of school for another hour. We'll be able to take our time driving back," he assured her.

There was a stirring of activity at the restaurant entrance, the relative quiet disturbed by the arrival of a small group of businessmen meeting for lunch. The distraction brought a lull to their conversation as the hostess led them to a table. One of the men, a white-haired gentleman still in the prime of health, spied Tagg and immediately broke away from the group.

"As I live and breathe, if it isn't Tagg Williams," he declared and grabbed Tagg's hand to shake it before Tagg could stand up. "I didn't know you were back in these parts. How are you, son?" The man didn't wait for a response as he turned a twinkling look at Leslie. "What pretty lady are you romancing this time?" He reached across the table to shake Leslie's hand and introduce himself. "The name's Kyle Clarehorn. I'm an old friend of Tagg's family. And who might you be? I have to ask because he'll never tell me your name. He's afraid I'll steal you away, that's why."

"Leslie Stiles." She was half-surprised that she was being given the chance to answer, but the man had to draw a breath sometime. His greeting had turned into a non-stop spiel. She was both amused and amazed at his energy, considering he was probably seventy if he was a day.

"Fine-looking woman, but you always did know how to pick them," he informed Tagg with an admiring shake of his head. Again, he split his attention to Leslie. "Better watch your step with this guy. Every time I see him, he's with a different lady. He draws them like flies to maple syrup."

"Holly has already warned me about him," Leslie assured him on a laughing note.

"Holly?" The name threw the white-haired gentleman for a moment.

"My daughter." Tagg pulled his keen glance from Leslie long enough to jog the man's memory.

"Your daughter, of course." He snapped his fingers in a gesture of self-impatience for forgetting. "How is that blue-eyed little charmer? It must be three years since you stopped by with her to visit. Cute as a button, she was. I'll bet she's got a long list made out for Santa Claus."

"Not a long one," Tagg replied. "But she's got a dog at the top of the list. Thankfully she's old enough to know that when she *asks* Santa for something, it doesn't necessarily mean she's going to get it."

"Every child should have a dog," the man insisted. "You tell Santa I said so. You couldn't pick a better Christmas present to teach a child the true meaning of love. Try spelling *dog* backward once. It's *god*. And if you think about it, a dog is always sad when you leave it and happy when you come back—never asking where you were in between—just as long as you come home. You make sure Santa brings that girl a dog," he ordered. "I wish I had time to stay and chat, but I have clients waiting." With a wink at Tagg and a hand gesture at Leslie, he said, "Better hang on to this one."

In the same flurry of energy that he had descended on them, the man was departing to rejoin his group. Leslie felt slightly out of breath, and the elderly man had been the one who did all the talking.

"He's quite a character," Tagg declared wryly.

"You can say that again," Leslie agreed.

"What did you mean when you said Holly had warned you about me?" His gaze narrowed on her with sharp curiosity.

"Oh that." Leslie tried to shrug it away, but realized he would persist until she explained. "She told me that all the girls fall in love with you and wondered if I would, too."

"I'm going to have to talk to that girl," Tagg declared in mild exasperation. "Between her and Kyle, they're making me sound like a regular ladykiller."

"Aren't you?" she chided to get his reaction.

"Why would anybody want to be labeled a ladykiller or a playboy?" he reasoned. "The first implies that you kill ladies and what man would want a dead woman on his hands? And a playboy might have spent a lot of time in the company of the female sex, but I doubt if he's ever known one woman well.''

"And you feel that's important?" Her voice was soft. Something inside her was waiting for his answer.

"You can't love an object, but you can love a person." Tagg reached for his coffee cup, breaking the intangible spell that had led them both into a topic with such underlying seriousness. "There's supposed to be a full moon Friday night, providing the sky is clear. How would you like to go on a sleigh ride with Holly for a chaperone?"

Leslie followed his lightning change of mood, arching a light brown eyebrow. "Jingle bells in a one-horse open sleigh?"

"You've got it," he said, grinning.

"I came here to escape all the Christmas hokum and I'm being deluged with it instead," she decried in mock protest.

"Bah humbug," Tagg mocked. "Even Scrooge was converted into a believer. And I don't think you're as tough as he was."

"Is that right?" Leslie didn't attempt to deny it. Her position was steadily being undermined.

"Are you game for the sleigh ride, weather permitting?" he asked.

"Why not?" Her shoulders were lifted in a helpless shrug of mock defeat.

Tagg finished his coffee and glanced at Leslie as he set his empty cup on the table. "Are you ready to start for home?"

The ride back began in a companionable silence with Leslie gazing out the window at the picturesque countryside. The mountain state was sparsely populated, consisting of mainly valley farms, quaint villages, and small cities. The winter snows had given the rolling and wooded hillsides a serenely peaceful look, slumbering restfully to prepare for spring's burst of green growth.

As the road curved past a farmhouse, Leslie noticed a man out back, chopping wood. The sight turned her thoughts to her curiosity about Tagg's occupation. Candor seemed her only hope in obtaining an answer.

"What kind of work do you do?" Her sudden question after such a long silence seemed to briefly startle him.

As his attention swung back to the road, the side of his mouth was lifted up by a smile. "At the moment, none," he replied dryly. "I have a law degree and I'll probably open an office here after the first of the year. My father was a District Court Judge for a number of years before he died. I'm finally getting around to following in his footsteps."

"But what did you do before now?"

"I was a professional skier. Unlike golf or tennis pros, professional skiers are a relatively unknown breed. Unless a skier has competed in the Olympics, which I didn't, the public generally never hears about him. So don't be embarrassed because you've never heard of me," Tagg said as if he knew Leslie was trying to remember if she had heard his name before.

"I admit I haven't," she said.

"Mostly I competed on the European circuit. That's how I met Cindy. She was the daughter of one of my sponsors," he explained with no expression showing on his face. "After we were married, she discovered the skiing circuit wasn't the glamorous life she thought it would be. Two years later, we separated. I didn't know she was pregnant until a mutual friend told me before a meet in Grenoble. I flew to Colorado to see if we couldn't work things out. That was in November, and Holly was born the day after Christmas that year. You know the rest of the story."

"Is that when you quit skiing?" Leslie quietly studied him, realizing now how his skin had become so darkly tanned from the constant exposure to the glare of sun and snow and why he was in such superb physical condition when many men in their thirties were developing paunches.

"Not right away. Initially I only entered competitions in the Rocky Mountain area so I could keep Holly with me most of the time. When you compete, you have to go all out every time. You can't worry about accidents or injuries. Suddenly I couldn't do that, because I had Holly. I never felt like that when I got married, but I suppose I knew Cindy was old enough to take care of herself. Holly needed me, especially with Cindy gone. My present to her on her third birthday was to hang up my racing skis, and buy a resort in the Colorado mountains."

"Then you sold it and came back here to Vermont," Leslie guessed.

"That's about the size of it," he agreed. "It was a good business, but it didn't give me enough time to spend with Holly." His shoulder lifted in an idle shrug. "Maybe I just got burnt out on skiing. I have no more desire to be on the slopes. Maybe that will change someday and I'll enjoy the sport of it again."

"In the meantime, you're going to practice law."

"I enjoyed studying law," Tagg told her. "I suppose the skiing interlude in my life was part of the wild oats I needed to sow. I don't regret it. It gave me Holly and sufficient funds to know that her future will be secure if anything happens to me." He flashed her a white smile. "And there you have my life story, my credentials, and even a glimpse at my bankbook."

"Was I being nosey?" She hadn't thought so. But most of the information, he had volunteered.

"No." He reached for her hand and threaded his fingers through hers. "I think you have the right to know something about the man who asked you out for a sleigh ride."

"That's true. I couldn't go sleigh riding with a total stranger," Leslie responded with the same bantering lightness he had used.

"I should hope not," Tagg mocked, then glanced at his wristwatch. "Everything is turning out perfectly this morning. I'll be able to take you to your aunt's, get the presents hidden in the house, and still have time to pick up Holly."

"That's good."

"I thought so, too." He squeezed her hand affectionately, a warm sensation spreading through her.

In the lull that settled, Leslie thought over the things Tagg had told her about himself, his life and his previous career in professional sports. It started her thinking about the comment Holly had made.

"When you were skiing, I imagine you had all sorts of beautiful women for company. I suppose that's where Holly got the idea that girls always fell in love with you." The minute she made the comment, she regretted it. "Now, I am being nosey. You don't have to answer that."

"I don't mind." He smiled at her briefly, letting his glance leave the road for a scanning second. "I didn't lack for female company, but I wouldn't go as far as to say there was an endless bevy of beauties. But it was the glamour of the ski slopes that attracted them—like Cindy. I doubt if it would have mattered to some of them if I was five feet tall with a receding hairline."

But he was six feet tall and unconventionally handsome. Leslie wasn't fooled. Those vital statistics had increased the attraction of the members of the opposite sex for him. She had no illusions about her own sex. Some were positively brazen in their pursuit of a man—single or not. She suspected the attentions of other women might have been one of the reasons for his marriage to go bad.

When they arrived at her aunt's house, Tagg parked the car in the driveway. "Do you need some help getting out?" he asked as she gathered up her unwieldy crutches.

"No, I can manage."

"I'm glad you came with me today." His hand lightly fitted itself to the curve of the back of her neck, holding it while he leaned across the seat and kissed her with lingering force.

Leslie was conscious of the trip-hammer beat of her heart when she finally opened the car door. Her lips could still feel the warm pressure of his mouth. It was a decidedly pleasant sensation.

He waited until she had reached the door and turned to wave to him. Then he reversed out of the drive to pick up his daughter from school.

Chapter Six

The bay mare tossed its head in a show of eagerness, jingling the bell strap on its harness, but the horse stood calmly while Tagg lifted Leslie into the shiny black sleigh with its red leather seats. The fur robes that had kept her warm on the dogsled ride were folded on the seat.

"Where on earth did you find this horse and sleigh?" she asked in amazement. "It's something out of a Currier and Ives print."

"The horse and sleigh belong to a local farmer. He usually rents them out for the winter through the ski resorts in the area," he explained and swung Holly into the sleigh, then climbed in himself to sit between them. The fur robes were spread out lengthwise to cover all three of them against the numbing chill of the night air.

"Are we going to go 'dashing through the snow,' Daddy?" Holly was bouncing on the seat, unable to sit still.

"Not unless the snow is on the road," Tagg informed her dryly, just in case she had visions of them racing across some meadow.

Picking up the reins, he lightly slapped the horse's rump with them and clicked his tongue to signal the mare forward. There was a slight jerk, then the sleigh was pulling smoothly onto the snow-packed dirt road.

A huge silver-dollar moon gleamed brightly on the white ground and highlighted the snow clinging on dark tree branches. It was a magical wonderland of sight and sound, muted bells jingling in rhythm to the horse's trotting hooves. The cold air was sharp and invigorating and rosied Leslie's cheeks as she sat shoulder to shoulder with Tagg, unconsciously snuggling closer to his body warmth. Her hands and arms were buried under the thick, furry robe that insulated them against most of the frigid air.

"Let's sing, Daddy," Holly suggested.

"Let's don't," he replied. "Mr. Grey told me the horse stops every time people start singing."

"Smart horse," Leslie murmured *sotto voce*.

Holly leaned forward to look her father square in the eye, skeptical and challenging. "Is that true?"

"No," Tagg admitted. "But let's spare the horse's ears anyway."

"Okay." She sat back in her seat and hugged the fur robe around her chin.

All was quiet and still around them as they traveled down the back road. It didn't seem to matter where

Leslie looked, some nostalgically familiar scene would leap out at her, painting a picture that she was certain she'd seen before. Whether it was the glitter of the moonlight on a meadow of snow or a farmhouse with lights shining from the window and smoke curling out of the chimney.

Tagg's hand found hers under the robe and curled around it. His head tipped slightly toward her. "Are you having fun—jingle bells and all?" A teasing light sparkled in his night-darkened eyes.

"Yes. Jingle bells and all," she smiled the admission, her gaze absently wandering over his features; the straight bridge of his nose, and the strong cut of his mouth.

"Look, Daddy. There's a covered bridge ahead!" Holly pulled her hand out from under the robe long enough to point out the houselike structure spanning a river.

"It certainly is."

"Are we going to go through it?" Holly wanted to know.

"I guess so," Tagg replied. "That's where the road goes—unless you want me to turn around and go back."

"No, I want to go across the bridge," she insisted.

As they drew closer, the white snow on the bridge's roof made its opening into the wooden tunnel appear even blacker. On the far side, the moonlight showed the way out.

"Why did they put covers on bridges?" Holly asked as she made a frowning study of the structure.

"These bridges were built a long time ago when most people traveled by horse and wagon. If it started raining or snowing, they could take shelter under the roofs of these bridges," Tagg explained, and slowed the mare to a walk as they entered the bridge tunnel.

Wind had whipped some snow and ice onto the reinforced woodplank floors. The horse's hooves echoed hollowly, disturbing an owl perched on a rafter. It hooted and swooped low to fly out into the night. Involuntarily, Leslie cringed and ducked, moving closer to Tagg before realizing it was just an owl. His hand tightened on hers, lifting her glance toward his shadowed face only inches away.

"I've also heard that during the old days when young men took their girl friends for courting rides in the buggy, these bridges made ideal lover's lanes," he murmured loud enough so Holly would think he was talking to her while he bent his head to claim Leslie's lips.

Initially his mouth felt cool against her lips, but it warmed up quickly, pressing on hers with a moist, demanding need. Her response was just as quick and just as hungry, trying to make up for the necessary shortness of the kiss.

There was the faintest sound as the contact was broken, seconds before they emerged from the covered bridge into the moonlight. His glance held hers for another second while his hand tucked hers more closely to him under the robe, their forearms resting together.

"Are we going to come back this way?" Holly asked.

"We could," Tagg admitted. "Why? Is that what you want to do?"

"No, but I thought it might be what you wanted to do." There was an impish little glint in her eyes when she looked at him.

"What makes you think that?" he asked with a trace of amusement in his voice.

"Oh, Daddy, I'm not a baby anymore," she chided him in exasperation. "I heard you kiss Leslie. Besides, I know what a lover's lane is."

"I have an idea," Tagg said. "Why don't we sing?" He slid a sideways glance at Leslie. "Sorry, but if you can't beat 'em, join 'em. And you know what they say about little pitchers having big ears."

"You sing along, too, Leslie," Holly urged.

The choice of songs was a foregone conclusion. Under the circumstances, it had to be "Jingle Bells." This time Leslie did sing with them, her mellow mood making her overlook her usual prejudices about caroling.

And the singing didn't stop until their long, circling route brought them back to the house. The farmer was waiting in Tagg's driveway with a pickup truck and horsecar. When they turned in, the back door to her aunt's house opened and Patsy Evans stepped outside.

"You're invited over for cider and gingerbread!" she called.

While Tagg stayed to help the farmer load the horse and sleigh, Holly and Leslie crossed the yard to her aunt's house. After being outside in the cold so long, the kitchen felt toasty warm, the air fragrant with the spicy smell of freshly baked gingerbread.

"We had so much fun, Mrs. Evans!" Holly chattered nonstop while she peeled off her snow jacket and pants. "We sang and sang. And there was this covered bridge—"

"I think I sang so much I lost my voice," Leslie interrupted her, not certain how much the little girl would reveal. "My throat feels hoarse."

"It probably is, from the sound of it," her aunt declared, standing at the stove and ladling mulled cider into mugs for each of them. "There's a fire burning in the fireplace. Take these and go in there and get warmed up."

Leslie curved both hands around the mug of hot cider, shivering in delayed reaction to the cold now that she was getting warm. "Can you carry mine, too, Holly?" she asked, certain she'd spill it if she tried to carry it and use only one crutch.

"Sure." Holly took it from her and headed for the living room where the crackling fire beckoned.

The furniture was grouped around the fireplace. Leslie settled into the chair with the footstool in front of it and propped her leg on it. Just the sight of the fire was warming. Holly gave her one of the mugs, then sat on the floor, facing the burning logs. The hot apple cider was sweet with brown sugar and laced with cloves and cinnamon. Its spicy sweetness seemed to activate her tastebuds again.

The feeling had returned to her toes when Tagg finally joined them, bearing his own mug of mulled cider from the kitchen. He set it on the mantel and held his hands out to the flames, rubbing them briskly together.

"Cold?" Leslie asked him teasingly.

"Yes." His gaze challenged her. "Do you want to come warm me up?"

"Put another log on the fire instead," she countered.

"The other way would be faster," he insisted, amusement glinting in his eyes.

"Too bad I'm comfortable." She turned her head when she heard footsteps. Her aunt entered the living room, carrying a tray with steaming gingerbread squares, dollops of whipped cream melting over them. After they were passed around, conversation was forgotten until every last crumb had been consumed. Tagg washed his last bite down with a swig of mulled cider.

"That was delicious, Mrs. Evans," he stated.

"It was good," Patsy Evans agreed with him. "I thought you'd enjoy it after your sleigh ride." She started to gather up the dishes.

"I'll do that for you," Tagg insisted. "Leslie can show me where to put things."

Her aunt didn't argue with him as he stacked the dishes onto the tray and waited for Leslie to lead the way into the kitchen. Once there, it was a simple matter to put the dirty dishes in the sink, cover the whipped cream with a plastic lid and set it in the refrigerator.

"Two shakes of a lamb's tail and we're done," Leslie announced turning on her crutches and finding Tagg blocking her way.

"It didn't take very long, did it?" He curved an arm around her and gathered her body to his length. His hand moved caressingly over her cheek, down her neck, and tunneled under her hair. "Do you think they'll miss us? It sounds like Holly has your aunt occupied."

"Yes, it does." Her pulse accelerated under his touch, heat running through her veins. The sound of it hammering in her ears was about all she could hear and his face was blocking everything else out of her vision.

Her head was tipped backward under the pressure of his moist kiss as his mouth rocked hungrily over her lips, eating at their softness. Then he was driving her lips apart and she was tasting the lingering spice on his tongue. Her breath was coming deep and fast, reacting to this intimate stimulation while a fiery inner glow seemed to melt her bones.

His attention gradually shifted to her cheekbone, the corner of her eye and the lobe of her ear. His nibbling and nuzzling sent off fresh waves of sensation, quivering over her nerve ends. She leaned more heavily against him, arching her spine to get closer to him still, yet her hands instinctively kept their grip on her crutches.

"Aunt Patsy is going to start wondering what's keeping us?" Leslie whispered against his skin.

"I'll bet she's already figured it out," he said thickly. His mouth searched out the corner of her lips, nuzzling it and letting their breath mingle. "Kiss me, Leslie."

She turned her lips into his mouth, a silent moan getting no farther than her throat. The shattering completeness of his kiss unleashed a greater need inside. Whirled away on this tide of intense longing, she forgot everything else and moved to put her arm around him.

Her crutches clattered to the floor with a resounding crash!

For a split second, it startled both of them, jarring them apart. Leslie realized instantly what she'd done and muttered impotently, "Damn this broken leg."

Running feet were already tearing toward the kitchen from the living room as Tagg bent down to retrieve the crutches. He was just handing them to her when Holly burst into the room.

"What happened?" she asked in wide-eyed alarm. "What was that racket?"

"Leslie dropped her crutches. It made a lot of noise, but that's all," Tagg assured her.

Her aunt appeared in the doorway behind Holly. "She didn't fall did she?"

"No," Leslie answered for herself. "The crutches just slipped out of my hands."

"Boy, it really scared me!" Holly declared, holding a hand to her throat. "I thought something terrible had happened."

"Nothing did," Tagg repeated. "You'd better get your things together. It's long past your bedtime."

"That's okay. I don't have school tomorrow. It's Saturday, remember?" she protested that the evening had to draw to a close so soon.

"Saturday or not, it's time you were in bed," he insisted, and crossed the kitchen to take his coat off the wall hook. "Thanks again for the cider and the gingerbread, Mrs. Evans."

"She said I could call her Aunt Patsy if I wanted," Holly informed him as she tried to get her arm into the other coat sleeve.

"Then tell her good-night and thanks." Tagg helped her find the opening.

"Good night, Aunt Patsy, and thanks for everything." Now that the decision was made to leave, she wasn't taking any time over it. "Good night, Leslie."

"Good night." To Tagg, she added, "Thanks for asking me along tonight."

"Jingle Bells, Holly, and all." His mouth twitched with a brief smile before his glance shifted down to her lips, then he was reaching for the door and pushing Holly toward it. "Good night, Mrs. Evans."

After they had gone, her aunt walked over to the sink. "I'll wash up those dishes, Aunt Patsy," Leslie volunteered.

"There isn't even a good sinkful here. We'll do them with the breakfast dishes in the morning. I thought that you might have gotten your hands wet because you'd put them to soak. But I guess your crutches fell for some other reason." Her aunt didn't elaborate on what she thought the reason might be.

"Yes, I guess so."

"There's enough cider here for two more mugs." Her aunt checked the contents of the pan. "Shall we finish it?"

"Sure." Leslie moved to get the mugs.

"I've been thinking," her aunt began. "Maybe we should ask Taggart and his daughter to come over Christmas Eve and have oyster stew with us."

"I think that would be a nice idea," Leslie agreed. "Maybe I could buy a little something for Holly—for a Christmas present."

"You could," her aunt nodded in an approving manner.

"I'll do it tomorrow," Leslie decided.

The next morning was as bright and clear as the previous night had been, and the temperature was almost as cold despite the golden sun shining down. Bundled up in her heavy jacket, gloves, and ski cap, Leslie was humming to herself as she did her three-legged walk down the driveway to the sidewalk.

"Where are you going, Leslie?" Holly came racing out of the house, her snow jacket unzipped and flopping open, and the hood barely staying on her head.

"I thought I'd walk into town. I need the exercise." She waited by the edge of the shoveled sidewalk while Holly came to a puffing stop beside her.

"Would you do me a favor?" Holly fumbled around, trying to get her hands into her pockets.

"What?" Leslie asked, discovering it was always wiser to ask first before agreeing.

"Will you mail this for me?" She finally found the crumpled envelope she had tucked in her pocket.

"Sure." Leslie took the envelope and slipped it into the coat pocket with her change purse.

"Thanks loads. Daddy doesn't know I'm outside, so I gotta go. Bye!" With a wave of her hand, Holly raced back for the house.

The village's small post office happened to be first along her route. Leslie paused by the drop box and reached in her pocket for the letter. When she checked to make sure it had a stamp, she noticed the address.

It read simply: "Santa Claus, North Pole."

"I can't believe I'm doing this," she muttered to herself and slipped the letter into the mail slot.

The village was small so naturally there were a few stores and the selection of gifts for an almost-seven-year-old girl was limited. Leslie did find a couple of books that had been her favorites when she was about Holly's age, so she bought them and a handmade bookmark. No doubt she'd get toys aplenty from Tagg—and Santa Claus.

With the wrapped parcel clamped between her arm and the crutch, she set off for her aunt's house again. A half a block away, she could hear Holly's giggling laughter. The bottom torso of a snowman was sitting in the middle of Tagg's front yard, but he was forgotten as Tagg and Holly hurled snowballs at each other.

Leslie watched them with a trace of sadness. Once she and her father had played like that—carefree and innocent. But that was long ago—before the arguments and bitter fights became so frequent. She hobbled forward, her head downcast.

A flying missile hit her shoulder with solid impact, splattering icy bits of snow onto her face. It knocked her off-balance. She heard Tagg shout as the tip of her crutch slid on a patch of ice. A startled cry came from her throat as she realized she was falling.

Out of instinct, she twisted her body to shield her broken limb and attempt to aim herself at the deep snow piled beside the walk. She landed hard, the packed snow making a crunching sound beneath. For the first few seconds, she was too shocked to move while her mind made a swift mental check to see if she was hurt. Nothing seemed to be damaged but her pride. She pushed a hand into the snow to lever herself upright.

Tagg came to a skidding stop beside her spraying snow in her face again. He dropped to one knee, bending over her. "Leslie, are you all right? I swear I didn't see you when I threw that snowball."

"I think I'm all right," she murmured shakily.

"Better let me help you up," he said and began to tunnel an arm under her side to lift her.

The shock of the fall had worn off, leaving a small, but vengeful anger in its place. Her gloved fingers dug into the snow, snatching up a handful which she tossed in his face as she turned as if to aid him in lifting her.

His head jerked backward as he sputtered and wiped at the snow that clung to his eyelashes and mouth. His look was first filled with surprise, then retaliatory amusement.

Off to the side, Holly laughed and jumped up and down. "She got you, Daddy!"

"You little witch," Tagg growled at Leslie, but his humor-riddled tone took any menace from his voice.

"You deserved that," she retorted and finished the turn so she could sit up and begin brushing the snow off her.

Out of the corner of her eye, Leslie saw Tagg reach down and scoop up a handful of snow. It triggered a warning of his intentions. With upraised arms, Leslie tried to shield herself from the expected snowball, but Tagg caught at her hand instead. He paid no attention to her laughter-laced outcry of protest as she struggled with him, warding off the hand with the snow. His strength and pressing weight was forcing her backward.

"Watch my leg!" she warned him with a squeal and tried to dodge the hand attempting to rub the snow in her face.

Breathless laughter was claiming both of them as they tumbled onto the snowbank, Tagg taking care to stay away from her legs. When he couldn't reach her face, he pushed the handful of snow down her neck. Leslie shrieked at the sudden cold against her skin and tried to do the same to him.

But he caught her wrist. A second later, her arms were pinned against the snow and the upper part of his body was lying across her to hold her down. Out of breath and laughing, Leslie stopped struggling and glanced at the male face above her. His mouth was parted in a panting smile of triumph.

"Give up?" Tagg asked, breathing hard from the short tussle in the cold, morning air.

"Yes." Her admission of defeat came out on a puffing breath.

His hold on her forearms relaxed, but it wasn't taken away. In the twinkling of an eye, the playful atmosphere changed and became charged with an elemental tension. Her breaths lengthened out under the darkening glitter of his gaze while her swiftly racing pulse took on a disturbed beat.

An awareness ran through both of them at the intimate positions of their prone bodies. The searching probe of his gaze moved over her face and became diverted by her parted lips. More of his weight began to settle onto her as Tagg began to slowly lower his head.

"Aren't you going to let her up, Daddy?" Holly's puzzled question short-circuited the volatile currents running between them.

Turning his head to the side, Tagg dragged in a deep breath and shifted his hold to clasp her arms. As he straightened backward, he pulled Leslie with him, sitting her up. The wryness in his blue eyes showed an amused regret when he met Leslie's sparkling glance.

"I swear, Holly—" his gaze slid to his daughter "—Cupid would never chose you for an accomplice."

Holly frowned at him. "What's an accomplice?"

"Get Leslie's crutches for her." Tagg ignored her question.

When his feet were solidly under him, he spanned her waist with his hands and lifted her up to stand precariously balanced on one foot, her fingers gripping the sleeve of his coat for support. Holly retrieved the crutches and dragged them over to Leslie. Tagg brushed at the snow sticking to her coat, slapping off the worst of it.

"Are you all right?" His warm and lazy glance moved over the subdued radiance in her eyes.

"Yes." She nodded briefly, a small smile showing.

There was a clump of snow on the collar of her coat. Tagg reached over and brushed it off, then let the gloved tips of his fingers touch her neck before lifting strands of golden tan hair outside her collar. Despite the coldness of his gloves, she was warmed by the light, tingling caress.

"I'd better walk you to the house so you don't get knocked off your feet again," he said.

Leslie took one step, then remembered. "I had a package." She looked around for it and spied the present sticking out of a snowdrift.

"I'll get it for you." Holly noticed it at the same instant.

At the sight of the Christmas-wrapped present, Tagg quirked an eyebrow at her. "What's this?" he murmured dryly. "I thought you didn't go in for last minute Christmas shopping."

"There's an exception to every rule," she retorted and started to take the package from Holly, relieved to notice the paper hadn't been torn.

"Better let me carry it." Tagg took it from his daughter, and gestured for Leslie to go ahead of him. "I'll catch you if you fall."

"Promises from the man who knocked me down," Leslie mocked.

"Ah, but I picked you back up again and brushed you off," Tagg reminded her with a twinkling glance as they started up the driveway toward the house.

Holly split away from them. "I'm going to work on our snowman."

"Don't be throwing any snowballs," Tagg warned with a faint smile and let his gaze follow his young daughter as she took off for their front yard where the partially constructed snowman waited.

"Do you have any plans for Christmas Eve?" Leslie asked, then explained the reason for the question. "Aunt Patsy and I would like you and Holly to come over and have oyster stew with us."

"We accept."

She remembered something else. "Oh, would you tell Holly that I mailed her letter to Santa Claus?"

A surprised frown flickered across his features. "When?"

"This morning. She saw me leaving and ran out to give it to me," Leslie explained. "Why?"

"We already mailed one letter to him last week." His glance strayed briefly to his daughter, a certain puzzled certainty in his expression; then Tagg shrugged it away. "I guess she decided to put in a second request for a dog."

"Is Santa going to bring her one?" A smile twitched at her mouth.

"Santa is still looking," he answered dryly.

Taking the lead up the steps, Tagg held the doors open for her and followed her into the kitchen with the gift-wrapped package. Her aunt was standing by the wall phone, the receiver to her ear. She half-turned when she heard them enter.

"My niece just walked in," she said to the party on the line. "I'll ask her and call you later to let you know. Goodbye."

"Ask me what?" Leslie inquired when her aunt hung up the phone.

"Hello, Taggart," she greeted him first before answering Leslie's question. "That was Maude Freer on the phone, a dear friend of mine who lost her husband this fall. She called to ask me to come have dinner with her Thursday night. When I explained you were visiting me, she asked you to come with me. Naturally you can stay here if you'd rather."

"Why don't you have dinner with Holly and me that night?" Tagg suggested.

"I'd like that," Leslie accepted his invitation, then glanced at her aunt. "You don't mind, do you?"

"Of course not. If I was your age, I certainly wouldn't want to spend an evening in the company of two widowed ladies when I could be with a good-looking man instead."

"Why, thank you, Mrs. Evans." Tagg inclined his head at the implied compliment, the corners of his mouth deepening with a suppressed smile.

"Then it's all settled. I'll call Maude back and let her know," Patsy Evans stated decisively.

Tagg set her package on the counter and reached for the doorknob to leave. "Thursday night, around six?"

"That's fine," Leslie nodded her agreement.

Chapter Seven

A hard crust had formed on the old snow. It crunched under her crutches like the breaking of ice, leaving clear-cut holes in the snow. New snowflakes swirled all around Leslie as she took a shortcut across the driveway and the Williams's front yard to the door. It was like being inside the glass dome of a winter scene after someone had shaken it.

The front porch light was on, throwing its light into the early evening darkness to show Leslie the way to the steps. The snow had begun falling as gentle flurries, but the flakes were coming down in earnest now. She clumped up the steps and across the wooden porch floor to the front door, punching the bell.

The muted echo of the doorbell had barely faded when Holly yanked the door open to admit her. Leslie swung across the threshold on her crutches and paused inside the door to lean her weight on them. The cold air had left her slightly out of breath. She smiled at Tagg when he came to greet her.

"I was hoping you'd come early," Holly declared. "We've almost got dinner ready, but I wanted to show you all the presents under the tree."

"Give Leslie a chance to take her coat off before you drag her off," Tagg said with an indulgent smile and moved forward to help her out of it.

"It's really coming down out there," Leslie loosened the wool scarf around her neck. White crystalline flakes were quickly melting to leave diamond drops sparkling in her tawny hair. "I hope it doesn't get too bad before Aunt Patsy leaves to come home."

"She's lived in Vermont most of her life. She knows how to drive in this kind of weather, so I wouldn't worry about her having any difficulty," Tagg replied, helping to slip her arm out of one coat sleeve, then the other.

When Tagg moved away to hang up her coat in the front closet, Leslie brushed at the melting snow on her clothes. Her calf-length skirt of camel tan concealed most of the plaster cast on her left leg. The rest of it was covered by a brown sock, the same shade as the tall, heeled boot she wore on her right foot. Adorning the plain white turtleneck sweater she was wearing, there was a large, gold medallion necklace in the design of an Aztec sun. She paused to adjust the clasp behind her neck.

Holly tugged at her arm, laughing up at her. "Leslie, Daddy's standing under the mistletoe."

When she lifted her head, she saw Tagg looking up at the ribboned sprig of mistletoe above him. "Sure enough. It's up there,'' he declared, bringing his glinting gaze down level with hers. "Now, I wonder how that happened.'' The faint curve of his mouth challenged her to carry out the tradition.

"I wonder, too,'' Leslie mocked, aware of Holly's silent urging.

It was only a few swinging strides to where he was standing. Leslie crossed the space and pushed on the crutches to raise herself on tiptoe while he tilted his head down. This mistletoe kiss wasn't as brief as the first one had been, their lips moving together in a warmly ardent greeting after being so long apart.

An involuntary sigh trembled through her when she drew away, the raw sweetness of the controlled exchange making her want to get rid of the bonds of propriety. Tagg held her gaze for a long moment, his nostrils distended as if drinking in the perfumed fragrance of her and memorizing it. Then his attention swung reluctantly to his daughter as if needing to remind himself of her presence.

"You can show Leslie all the presents now while I take the food to the table,'' he said.

"Come over here, Leslie.'' Holly waved her toward the lighted tree in the living room.

Leslie was slow to follow the little girl. Her gaze traveled after Tagg as he cut through the dining room toward the kitchen. Slim-fitting black slacks accented his narrow-hipped and long-legged build and the heavily ribbed smoke blue sweater hinted at the muscular strength of his chest and shoulders. As the other girls in the office would say, he was "some hunk of man" with his hair gleaming blue-black in the interior light.

"Do you see this one, Leslie?" Holly's voice demanded her attention, breaking into her thoughts. "It's so heavy I can't pick it up. And it's got my name on it, too."

"What do you suppose is in it?" Leslie asked the expected question.

"I don't know, and Daddy won't give me any clues," Holly grimaced in mild exasperation. "See this one."

After Leslie had dutifully looked at the packages under the tree, Holly led her into the dining room. "You sit here." She pulled out a chair for her as Tagg arrived with the platter of roast beef. All the rest of the food was already on the table.

"It smells delicious," Leslie declared, taking her seat.

"It should. We've been slaving in the kitchen all afternoon, haven't we, Holly?" Tagg asked his daughter for confirmation of his mocking remark.

"We've got pumpkin pie for dessert," she informed Leslie. "And I helped make it. I helped Daddy cook everything." After thinking about that, Holly qualified her expansive statement. "Well, almost everything."

Leslie wasn't sure whether it was the food or the company, but she couldn't remember the last time she had enjoyed a meal so much. Even clearing the table and washing the dirty dishes afterward was kinda fun with all three of them pitching in to do their share. Leslie washed, Tagg dried, and Holly put them away.

Then it was hot chocolate in the living room with the crackle of logs burning in the fireplace. It wasn't long until the hypnotic flames had weaved a silent spell on all of them. Leslie didn't notice the quiet until it was broken by the slap of Tagg's hand on Holly's leg. The two of them were seated on the couch while Leslie occupied the matching chair and ottoman.

"School tomorrow, little lady," Tagg stated lazily. "It's time for you to get to bed."

If Holly intended to protest, she thought better of it when she was overtaken by a sleepy yawn. "Okay." She pushed off the sofa and walked over to kiss him good-night. "Can Leslie come up and tuck me in?"

The request appeared to catch him off guard, then he threw a questing look at Leslie. "She might not want to climb the stairs." He offered her an excuse if she wanted to use it, but she was oddly touched by Holly's request.

"I think me and my trusty crutches can manage them," she assured Holly. "You call me when you're ready."

"Okay." She headed for the maplewood staircase at a running walk and went up the steps at the same pace.

"I hope you don't mind," Tagg said. "It's probably a novelty to have a woman tuck her into bed."

"It'll be a novelty for me, too," Leslie replied and listened to the muffled noises overhead.

"More cocoa?" he asked.

"No thanks." She shook her head.

"I'll just take these mugs out to the kitchen." He rolled to his feet and collected the empty cocoa cups.

Tagg was just returning to the living room when Holly called down, "I'm ready!"

"I'll be back," Leslie smiled at Tagg and headed for the stairs.

The steps were nice and wide, giving her plenty of room to maneuver her crutches. At the head of the stairs, a door was standing open to a lighted room. Holly was sitting cross-legged on the single bed with the covers turned back, waiting for Leslie. She came into the room, not too sure what was expected from her.

"You have a nice room, Holly."

Blue-flowered wallpaper covered the walls with matching light blue curtains and bedspread, as well as a skirted vanity table painted white like the rest of the woodwork. A few dolls and some of her toys were arranged neatly on white shelves. The bedside lamp had a frilly white shade.

"I'm glad you came up to tuck me in," Holly stated when Leslie lowered herself to sit on the edge of the bed.

"So am I." She lifted the covers so Holly could slide her legs under them.

"You like my daddy, don't you?" Holly folded her hands behind her head, watching Leslie with her round, innocent blue eyes. Long black hair spilled across the pillowcase.

"Yes, I do," Leslie admitted.

"He likes you, too. And I'm glad," she stated. "Because I like you a lot. I wish you lived here all the time instead of just staying here over the holidays."

"New York isn't that far away. I can come here to visit again," Leslie reminded her. "Because I like you a lot, too."

A happy smile split Holly's face. She pulled her arms down and snuggled under the covers. "Good night, Leslie."

"Good night, Holly." It suddenly seemed perfectly natural to bend over and kiss the girl's soft cheek. When she was standing, Leslie looked down at the child. "Shall I leave a light on?"

"No. I'm not afraid of the dark," Holly assured her.

She switched off the lamp and moved toward the lighted stairwell. The telephone rang as she started down the steps. She heard Tagg answer it, but her thoughts were on Holly so she didn't listen to his side of the conversation.

All the lights in the living room had been turned off except for the winking Christmas tree lights and the flickering glow from the fireplace. The room's dimness made for an intimate atmosphere. Leslie paused beside the ottoman, turning when she heard Tagg coming.

"That was your aunt on the phone," he informed her. "She decided the roads were too icy so she's going to stay the night with her friend rather than drive home."

"Is it getting worse outside?" Leslie glanced toward the steamed-over window but it was impossible to see out.

"It's coming down pretty thick," he admitted. "Your aunt said the weatherman on the radio is predicting six to ten inches by morning."

She lowered herself onto the ottoman so she could be closer to the fire. "As the song says, 'Let it snow.'"

"I agree." Tagg stretched out his length on the floor in front of her, propped on one elbow and looking into the leaping flames curling up from the charred white logs edged with red.

"What's with the lights?" Leslie asked with a faint smile, leaning forward to rest her arms on her knee. "Conserving energy?"

"I could have turned the lights down low, but I turned them off," he admitted, his mouth quirking on one side. He turned the upper half of his body toward her and held out his arm. "How else could I create the right mood to suggest you come down here with me?"

Accepting the invitation and his assistance, Leslie lay down on the warm carpet beside him with her head pillowed on his arm. He turned onto his side, facing her, and kissed at her lips, then drew back.

"Alone at last," he murmured.

"It's always possible Holly might decide she wants a drink of water," Leslie murmured to tease him.

"If she does, I'll drown her," Tagg growled the mock threat.

"No, you won't," she laughed softly.

"Don't be too sure," he warned. "I've been wanting to be alone with you for a long time."

When he lowered his mouth onto hers, its raw passion seemed to prove his patience had reached its limits. Her arms wound around him holding on while her senses were shaken by the answering rush of heat. With moist and mobile force, he kissed her lips apart and tasted the fullness of her response opening up to him. She was gathered close against him, her breasts feeling the solidness of his chest through the knitted material of her sweater.

For heated moments, the exchange continued while the blood pounded through her veins. Her breath was coming heavy and fast when Tagg grazed her cheek with kisses and pushed the hair away from her ear to take nibbling lovebites at the lobe. The high, rolled collar of her turtleneck sweater impeded his attempt to explore the sensitive cords in her throat and neck.

"Do you know what the trouble with winter is?" His warm breath spilled over her skin as his lips formed the words against her cheek.

"What?" she whispered, thinking it was a silly question at this particular time.

"People wear too many clothes, especially women," Tagg said quickly. Aware of his hand getting tangled in the knit folds of her loose sweater, Leslie laughed, but it was a breathless, barely audible sound. "You can never be sure what's under them until you take them off."

She felt his hand pushing up the hem of her sweater and the tightness in her throat began to spread upward, too. "A person could catch cold without them, so maybe it's wise."

"Wise men never fall in love." He began to sit up, bringing her with him.

For a second, she watched him take hold of the bottom of his smoke blue sweater to remove it. Then she pulled hers over her head, shaking her hair free and laying the sweater on the ottoman. When she turned back to Tagg, he was wearing a bemused look as he stared at her flesh-colored cotton camisole.

"What's this?" he asked, touching a shoulder strap with the end of his finger.

"A camisole."

"What happened to lacy brassieres with convenient hooks?" he complained as he searched for the camisole's hem and found it, lifting the loose undergarment over her head, and tossing it onto the ottoman.

Tagg gave her no time to become self-conscious with her partial nudity or his own. His arms were immediately around her and gently lowering her to the floor once again. The heat of his bare flesh was under her hands, the iron-solid muscles rippling with easy strength.

Their kisses became longer and hungrier while his roaming hands excited her with their touch. She was fast losing control over what she was doing. His teeth nibbled sensually at a white shoulder, sending quivers all through her nerve ends. Her fingers combed into the virile thickness of his hair as his mouth trailed up the slope of her breast to reach its hard peak. She felt herself slipping.

This was not turning out to be a simple necking and petting spree. It was becoming the preliminary to something infinitely more intimate. All the achings and longings of her flesh were seeking it but Leslie wasn't sure if she was ready.

Abruptly she pulled away from him and sat up, breathing in deeply in her fight for a sanity beyond lust. "You're going too fast for me," she stated unevenly and pushed at her hair.

His hand slid to the front of her waist. "You're going too slow for me," Tagg countered, and pressed his lips to the small of her back.

An exquisite shudder of raw pleasure ran through her, closing her eyes. "I can't think clearly." Especially now when his mouth was working its way up her spine. "And I don't like decisions forced on me if I'm not ready to make them. And I'm not ready to make this one." She felt him lifting the hair away from the nape of her neck and knew she had to stop his progress. Leslie half-turned and reached for her clothes. "It's time I went home."

His hand took the weight of her breast and pulled her back to him. Her sensitized skin felt the heat and solidness of his hair-roughened chest. She curled her fingers into her sweater and camisole, clutching them to her taut stomach.

"Honey, it's cold outside," Tagg murmured in a reasoning and persuasive tone. "Listen to that wind."

Above the thundering of her racing heart, Leslie could hear the muffled howl of the north wind and realized the storm had intensified. "It's just going to get worse out there. I might as well leave now." But her voice trailed off on a weakening note as he nuzzled at the erotic pleasure point at the base of her neck.

"Why go out in the storm when you can stay the night here?" Tagg asked. "With me."

"But that's just it," she protested and this time made a determined effort to escape both his touch and his kisses by twisting sideways and scooting backward out of his hold. "I don't know if it's what I want." That wasn't precisely true and Leslie shook her head in agitation. "It is what I want, but I'm not sure why."

"Do you have to analyze it?" he challenged mildly, but made no attempt to physically bring her back into his arms.

"Yes," she answered with a trace of impatience. "I don't know if I'm feeling this way because I'm lonely and I want to be held by someone—whether I've merely become sexually aroused—or if I feel obligated to let you make love to me because I've willingly gone this far already and you expect me to go the rest of the way. I just don't know."

She tugged the camisole over her head and followed it with the sweater, not even bothering to check front from back. As she adjusted the sweater around her waist, Leslie finally looked at him. Tagg sat there, braced on one arm, the firelight bathing his wide shoulders and the ruffed mat of hair on his naked chest, the corded muscles of his flat stomach standing out tautly. But the flickering light cast shadows on his tanned and angular features, making their expression unreadable.

His hand reached out to her and Leslie managed not to shy away from it. He lifted her sand-colored hair outside of the high collar of her turtleneck and let it lay about her shoulders.

"In all the reasons you mentioned, you left out an important one," Tagg said quietly and shifted his position to rest both hands on her shoulders near the base of her neck. "Maybe you love me. Maybe I want you to stay because I love you."

"It's a possibility," she whispered tightly, and felt pulled into the deep blue of his eyes.

"Leslie." His head moved slightly from side to side in faint negative movement. "It's more than a possibility that I love you."

A tremor vibrated through her at his low, charged statement. It was more than possible she loved him but there were too many purely physical sensations that were controlling her.

"Tagg, I'm not sure." It was imperative that there be no doubt in her mind. To her, love meant a lifetime commitment. It was too easy to be mistaken about emotions. How many people married someone they felt they loved only to discover their mistake in divorce courts? That wasn't going to happen to her.

Tagg let her go, reaching for his sweater. "Then I'll take you to your aunt's." His voice sounded gruff.

She guessed that she had inadvertently hurt him, but guilt was not sufficient reason to say something she wasn't absolutely sure about. She looked around for her crutches.

"Where are my crutches?" She didn't see them by the ottoman where she thought she had put them.

"I hid them," Tagg said dryly and reached under the coffee table to pull them out. "I said to myself, 'How far could a classy lady with a broken leg get without her crutches?' And I answered myself that she wouldn't get away from me if I didn't want to let her go.''

"That's terrible to take advantage like that," Leslie accused.

Anger flashed in his suddenly cold eyes. "I was only joking. I put them there so they'd be out of the way," he snapped.

"Oh." It was a small sound, tinged with guilt that she had been so quick to believe he might do that. "I'm sorry."

"You should be," he muttered and rolled to his feet, walking to the end table by the sofa to snap on the lamp.

There was a click, but no light came on. Leslie became instantly aware the only light in the room came from the fireplace.

"The tree lights are out," she told Tagg.

He moved toward the wall, his figure becoming partially obscured by the shadows. She heard the click of a switch, but the darkness remained.

"Stay there," he ordered. "I'm going to get a flashlight and check the fuse box."

Scooting along the carpet, dragging her leg with its cast, Leslie moved closer to the fire as the sound of his footsteps retreated toward the rear portion of the house. She stirred the glowing red embers with the brass poker. Flames shot up to throw more light into the room. Shadows eerily danced along the wall.

A long time seemed to pass before she saw a flashlight beam throwing a pool of moving light onto the floor and heard his footsteps behind it.

"The storm must have snapped a wire somewhere. There's no electricity and no lights showing anywhere outside," he stated grimly.

Switching off the flashlight to conserve the batteries, Tagg walked over and added another log to the fire. Sparks flew, lighting up his face. It took a minute for Leslie to realize he meant the power was out in her aunt's house as well.

"Like it or not—" his glance swung to her "—you're going to have to spend the night here. Without electricity, there isn't any heat, here or at your aunt's house."

"She uses oil to heat her house," Leslie corrected him.

"Yes, but it takes electricity to operate the blower motor and the thermostat controls," Tagg stated. "We'll have to rely on the fireplace."

"I'm going home." She levered herself up using the arm of the chair until she could get her crutches under her. "With no heat over there, her water pipes will freeze and break."

Tagg moved to block her way. "Leslie, I don't want you spending the night over there by yourself." He raked a hand through his hair in a gesture of agitated exasperation. "Listen, I don't want to come on like a heavy-handed male who is determined to have things his way. But—dammit! I'm not going to spend the night here, worrying about you over there with that broken leg—wondering whether you're warm enough—or if you've fallen. Whether you can take care of yourself or not, I'd worry."

"But the water pipes—" She was swayed by his genuine concern and the phrasing of his appeal—not claiming that he was stronger, but simply in a better position to cope.

"I'll go over there myself and turn the faucets on," he promised. "For my own peace of mind, will you please spend the night here? I can't leave Holly here by herself—and it would be foolish for all three of us to go traipsing over there."

"I'll stay," Leslie agreed.

His mouth curved in a faintly relieved smile. "Okay, first things, first. I'll go upstairs and bring Holly down. All three of us will have to sleep in front of the fireplace tonight."

"We should close off the living room, too, so we can keep all the warmth we can confined in here," Leslie suggested.

"Good idea." He looked at her with approval. "I can hang a blanket across the opening. We should have enough extra blankets to spare for that." He started for the stairs.

While he was gone, Leslie went over to the windows to draw the drapes and close out any drafts. She returned to the fireplace to wait.

Holly was certain it was an adventure as exciting as camping out when Tagg carried her down the stairs, wrapped up in her bed blankets. She wanted to get the candles from the kitchen so they could have lights, but Leslie convinced her there was more than enough light to see by from the fireplace and the candles should be saved for an emergency.

After Tagg brought down an armload of blankets, he nailed one of them across the living room archway. It immediately seemed warmer in the room. She and Holly spread the rest of the blankets on the floor in front of the fireplace to make one large bed.

"Are we going to have to cook breakfast in the fireplace, too?" Holly asked, all wide-eyed at the idea.

"Hopefully the electricity will be back on when we wake up in the morning," Leslie punctured that thought. "Climb under the blankets."

"I bet we won't have school tomorrow." Now that she was awake, Holly wasn't interested in going back to sleep and missing any more excitement. "It's snowing like everything outside, isn't it, Daddy?" She looked around, but he had disappeared behind the blanket curtain. "Where's Daddy? Do you suppose something happened to him?"

"No—"

The blanket lifted as Tagg stepped into the living room, all bundled up in his coat and ski hat. "I'm going over to your aunt's," he told Leslie. "Both of you get under those blankets. If you get chilled, it isn't going to be so easy to get warm again."

Following his advice, Leslie slipped under the blankets with Holly, letting the girl lie close to the fire. After Tagg had left, Holly chattered away, not expecting lengthy responses from Leslie. Eventually the dancing flames and the warmth of the blankets made the pauses between Holly's comments longer and longer.

In the quiet, Leslie listened to the creaking of the house and the wind prowling outside, occasionally rattling the windowpanes. With the reassuring crackle of the fire's warmth close by, she thought about Tagg, wondering whether he was still at her aunt's or making his way back through the snowstorm. It seemed he had been gone an awfully long time.

The front door opened, and the curtain-blanket billowed with the sudden sweep of cold air. Relief shivered through her when she heard the door being pushed shut and the stamp of his feet. Holly stirred sleepily beside her.

"What's that?" she murmured.

"Sssh. It's just your daddy," Leslie whispered.

Cold, cold air swirled into the room when the blanket was lifted aside and Tagg walked in, shuddering and rubbing his arms to get the circulation going. His glance ran first to Leslie, an attempt at a smile lifting his mouth, then to his sleeping daughter. Moving silently, he went to the fireplace and crouched in front of it.

"Is everything all right?" Leslie whispered.

He gave her an affirmative nod and stirred up the coals before adding another log to the fire. But he continued to shiver.

"You'd better get under the blankets," she advised.

When he slipped under the covers beside her, his clothes felt ice-cold. Leslie put her arms around him and cradled his head on her shoulder, absorbing the tremors shivering through him. His hair and skin were cold. As his body began stealing her heat, she felt the penetrating chill.

"I'm making you cold," Tagg realized.

"It doesn't matter. We'll both be warm soon," she murmured, and held him more tightly.

In time, her statement came true. By then, all three of them were sleeping in the glow of the fireplace.

Chapter Eight

The rumble of the snowplow wakened Leslie to the muted light behind the drapes drawn across the windows. She blinked sleepily in the semidarkness and tried to move, but she was sandwiched between two warm bodies.

Holly was curled tightly up against her, sleeping in the crook of her arm while Tagg's hugging length pressed itself to her other side. He was turned on his side, toward her with one leg lying across hers and a hand rested familiarly on her breast. His dark head was very close to hers on the pillow, his warm breath stirring the hair near her ear.

It was impossible to move without waking one or both of them, so Leslie subsided, resigning herself to the discomfort of the hard floor a little longer. She breathed in the air's chill and glanced sideways at the fireplace. The logs had burned down to chunks of white ash, the fire appearing to be out. But it was warm and cozy under the layers of blankets.

The hand on her breast moved, his fingers flexing and feeling in an intimately caressing manner. Leslie shifted slightly on the pillow trying to see if Tagg was awake. Her arm was pinned to her side by the pressing length of his body, so solid and warm. Thick and spiky male lashes lay together, leading Leslie to believe he still slept.

Then Tagg stirred, snuggling deeper into the pillow while his hand spread possessively over her breast. "What a wonderful way to wake up in the morning," he murmured without opening his eyes. "This is how it's supposed to be."

The lazy contentment in his voice sent a warm feeling of pleasure stealing through her. Leslie turned her head a little more in his direction, the corners of her mouth curving up. Through the screening veil of her lashes, she studied the easy strength in his masculine features, the shadowy growth of a night's beard on the teak brown skin stretched from cheekbone to jaw, and the attractive grooves that gentled his mouth. His eyes slowly opened, their dark centers ringed by a pale blue.

"I think the fire went out," Leslie whispered.

There was a lazy twitch of his mouth in amusement. "Do you want to bet on it?" Tagg murmured, putting another meaning into her words.

Her pulse gave a little leap of anticipation as he moved, without apparent effort, to lean slightly over her and lower his mouth onto her lips, moving over them in a mobile fashion.

It was a persuasive and pervasive kiss, warm with the fire of latent passion that started a curling heat spreading through Leslie. Even the faint scrape of the stubble on his chin seemed to be pleasantly rough, like the dry lick of a cat's tongue.

Tagg broke off the kiss with a degree of suddenness and turned his head to glance at his daughter nestled against Leslie's side. "You are supposed to be asleep," he accused with mock gruffness.

"I was pretending." Her voice bubbled with contained laughter. "I heard you and Leslie whispering and it woke me up."

His look was drolly resigned as his gaze slid to Leslie. "We should have shouted. She probably would have slept through that." Shifting his weight away from them, Tagg pushed aside the covers to get up. "I'll get the fire going again—the one in the fireplace," he added with a quirking smile.

"There won't be any school today, will there?" Holly asked, rolling onto her side and off Leslie's arm to watch her father poke at the slumbering embers before adding more firewood.

"We'll have to turn the radio on and find out." Tagg didn't hazard a guess.

When the logs started smoking, Tagg moved away from the hearth and crossed to the windows to pull the drapes. Sunlight burst into the room. Leslie flinched and turned her head away from the blinding brightness until her eyes adjusted to it.

"It looks like a beautiful day outside. Cold but beautiful," he stated, and rubbed his hands together to ward off the room's coolness. "I sure could go for some coffee."

"What are we going to have for breakfast? I'm hungry," Holly declared.

"I guess it will have to be cereal and milk," he shrugged.

"Can't we toast some bread over the fire?" His daughter was determined to do some kind of cooking over the open flames.

"You can toast some bread," Tagg consented. "The main road has been plowed, so it shouldn't be long before the power is restored. I'll let you two ladies use the bathroom first while I rustle together some breakfast."

"Brrr. I don't want to leave the blankets," Holly declared with an exaggerated shiver. "Do you, Leslie?"

"No, but we're going to have to sooner or later," she reasoned.

"Both of you, rise and shine." Tagg walked over and picked up the ends of the blankets. Holly squealed and grabbed to hold on to them, but he yanked them off, forcing them both to get up whether they wanted to or not.

Holly went scampering off to lead the way to the downstairs bathroom, shivering and carrying on with a child's theatrics, while Leslie followed at a necessarily slower pace. After sleeping in her clothes, her skirt especially was badly wrinkled. No amount of smoothing could rid the tan material of all its creases.

It was too cold for either Holly or Leslie to spend much time in the bathroom, making do with a quick, invigorating wash and a fast comb through their hair. When they returned to the partitioned-off living room, a cereal box and a pitcher of milk were sitting on the coffee table. Tagg entered the room shortly after they arrived, bringing a loaf of bread, a long-handled fork and a jar of strawberry preserves.

"You're in luck, Holly," he said. "I just heard on the radio there won't be any classes at school today."

"Yippee!" she shouted.

"Which means," Tagg continued, "you can help me shovel the sidewalks."

Holly groaned and ran to the window to see how much snow had accumulated in the night. But she was sidetracked by the discovery, "The treelights are on!"

With the power restored, it didn't take long for the central furnace to rid the house of its chill. Tagg made coffee, but Holly insisted they use the fire to toast their bread instead of the electric toaster. By the time they finished breakfast and a second cup of coffee, it was warm enough in the house for Tagg to take down the blanket across the living room opening.

"Let's get these blankets folded up, Holly," Leslie suggested and reached for the top one.

"We can do it later," Holly protested.

"I have to go home later," she reminded her, "and make sure everything is all right at Aunt Patsy's house."

"You'd better let me shovel a path over there first," Tagg said. "There's no sense trying to wade through all that snow on those crutches."

While he went outside to clear the walks, Leslie enlisted Holly's aid to pick up the front room and wash their breakfast dishes. When the housework was done, she checked his progress. There was a pathway through the snow nearly to her aunt's side door.

Anxious to make certain the blackout had not created any broken water pipes at her aunt's house, Leslie donned her heavy coat and wool scarf. Holly bundled up, too, to join her.

"Careful. It's slick!" Tagg called the warning to them when they emerged from the house.

As Leslie reached the edge of the driveway, she heard a car slowing down to turn in. It was her aunt returning home. She waited until the car was driven past her to the rear garage before she crossed to the side door. Tagg leaned on the snow shovel, his tanned complexion turned ruddy by the invigorating cold.

Holly went galloping through the snow to greet Patsy Evans as she waded toward the door. "We don't have any school today because of the snow," Holly informed her. "Did the electricity go out where you were? Ours was out all night."

"It was out at my friend's house, too," she replied.

"I came over last night and turned on the water in your sinks so the pipes wouldn't freeze," Tagg informed her. "Leslie spent the night at our place."

"That's a relief," her aunt stated. "I was concerned about her being in the house alone with no heat."

"We slept on the floor in front of the fireplace last night," Holly explained eagerly. "We had to huddle together under the blankets to keep warm. It was fun."

"I'm sure it was," Patsy agreed dryly.

"Did you have any trouble getting home this morning?" Leslie asked.

"It was a bit tricky getting out of Maude's driveway, but she lives on the main road so it had already been plowed. I had no trouble at all once I was on the road," she insisted. "But it certainly was nasty last night."

"Daddy—" Holly looked suddenly anxious "—will they cancel our Christmas program at church Sunday night because of this snow?"

"It won't be cancelled," Tagg assured her. "Not unless it snows again."

"Oh, good," Holly declared with very definite relief, and glanced up at the white-haired woman bundled up like an Eskimo in her fur-lined parka. "Are you coming to see our Christmas program?"

A pleased look brightened her expression, despite the chilling cold. "How nice of you to ask, Holly. I think Leslie and I would enjoy coming to watch your play." She glanced at her niece for confirmation.

"Aren't you coming?" Holly looked at her as if it had been a foregone conclusion that she would attend.

"Sure, we'll both come," Leslie promised, knowing how important it had been when she was a child to have people she knew in the audience at school or social functions.

"There's no need to take two cars," Tagg inserted. "All of us can go in our station wagon."

"That's very sensible," Patsy Evans agreed with his proposal. "What time shall we be ready?"

"The program starts at six-thirty, but Holly needs to be at the church early so why don't we leave at six?" Tagg suggested.

"We'll come over before six." She nodded her approval then glanced at Leslie with a no-nonsense briskness. "I don't know why we're standing out here in the cold when we can be inside. Thank you for looking after things, Taggart."

"It was nothing." He shrugged away her thanks and stepped to the side so they could get to the door. "Come on, Holly. Go get your shovel so we can get these walks cleared."

A check of the house showed a night of below-freezing temperatures had not resulted in any damage. Yet Leslie knew that events during the storm had resulted in changes within herself. As much as she was physically and emotionally attracted to Tagg, the feelings were also plagued by a vague apprehension. In the beginning it had been all right to take things as they came, but it was time she gave some serious thought about where their relationship was leading while there was still time to change its direction.

On Sunday evening, Leslie sat in the church pew between Tagg and her aunt, watching the Christmas story being acted out by the church's Sunday School class. Her view of Holly in a white and woolly sheep's costume was blocked by the people in front of her. When the angel appeared, Leslie remembered Holly mentioning the classmate who had gotten the part. It was obviously a case of typecasting since Sally Tuttle was an angelic-looking child with curly blond locks.

Tagg tilted his head slightly to murmur, "Holly could never look that innocent." It was an obvious reference to the girl playing the angel.

Leslie smiled briefly in acknowledgment, letting her hazel glance touch his profile. In a dark suit and tie, Tagg made a striking impression with his jet black hair, dark complexion and ice blue eyes. There was an air of maturity about him, travel and experience adding character to his handsomely chiseled features.

He had everything a girl could hope to find in a man—looks, personality, and sufficient wealth to be reasonably independent. Yet Leslie couldn't shake a sense of caution. She continued to hold back from any kind of commitment without being sure why she was. Some strong, protective instinct seemed to prevent it.

A choir of older members of the church class began singing Christmas hymns to bring the program to a close. The minister concluded with a brief prayer and an invitation for the parents and friends to partake of refreshments being served downstairs.

Still costumed, Holly met up with them in the church's small, outer lobby. "Can we stay?" she asked, wisps of black hair sticking out from her curly white hood with its floppy sheep ears. "They've got Christmas cookies and everything downstairs."

"Would you like to go down?" Tagg left the choice to Leslie and her aunt.

"Who can say no to Christmas cookies?" Patsy Evans asked and provided an affirmative answer with the question.

The refreshments were served in a small meeting room that quickly became crowded with children and adults. There was an empty space along the wall near the door where there was less chance of her crutches accidentally tripping someone. Leslie and her aunt waited there while Tagg and Holly brought them coffee and cookies.

As soon as Holly had eaten her cookies, she was lured away by some playmates. An acquaintance of Patsy Evans had drawn her off to one side to converse about a mutual friend, leaving Leslie and Tagg more or less standing alone.

The minister noticed them and came over. "Mr. Williams, I just wanted to tell you that I thought your daughter did a commendable job tonight. As a matter of fact, I don't have a 'baaaad' thing to say about it."

Leslie winced inwardly at the awful pun, but managed a smile.

"Thank you, Reverend August," Tagg pretended to smile, too. "I know Holly enjoyed it."

"Children are natural performers." The minister nodded and glanced curiously at Leslie. "Is this your wife? I don't believe I've had the pleasure of meeting her."

"Unfortunately she isn't my wife," Tagg corrected that impression. "This is Leslie Stiles."

"Of course." Her name produced instant recognition. "You are Mrs. Evans's niece, aren't you?"

"That's right." She nodded.

"I hope you'll forgive the mistake," the minister requested apologetically to both of them. "But when I saw the two of you standing together, it slipped my mind that you were a widower, Mr. Williams."

"No harm done," Tagg assured him.

Someone accidentally backed into her crutch, jostling Leslie's arm and sloshing drops of coffee onto her white silk blouse. "Darn." She breathed out the mild imprecation when she saw the stains. "Here." She handed her cup to Tagg. "Hold this, will you?"

"Did you spill it on yourself?" he asked.

"Just a few drops," she admitted. "I should be able to sponge them out with some cold water. Excuse me, Reverend."

"Of course."

After she'd worked her way out of the room, she went down the corridor to the ladies' room. She managed to get the coffee stains out, leaving only a damp spot on her blouse, which wasn't too noticeable.

As she emerged from the ladies' room, she heard Holly's voice. She was playing in the corridor with the Christmas angel, Sally Tuttle. Neither child noticed Leslie coming up behind them.

"Who's that lady with your dad, Holly?" asked the white-gowned girl with aluminum wings and halo.

"My mother," Holly replied with smooth nonchalance, and Leslie went white.

"You told me you didn't have a mother," Sally accused. "You said she died."

"She did, but that doesn't mean I can't have another one," Holly insisted.

"Then how come this is the first time I've ever seen her?" the girl challenged.

"Did you see her crutches? She has a broken leg and she's been in the hospital. That's why she hasn't been here before, so there!'' Holly stuck out her tongue at her doubting friend.

"Holly!'' Leslie spoke out sharply, realizing she should have stopped this before. She spun guiltily around and stared horror-struck at Leslie. "How can you say such a thing?'' Leslie asked.

Something crumbled in her face. With a lowering chin, she turned back to the blond-haired Sally. "I made that all up. She isn't really my mother,'' Holly confessed stiffly. "But she could be.'' The last was issued in a kind of desperation.

"I knew she wasn't,'' Sally declared with a degree of smugness and went flouncing down the corridor.

Holly turned her round blue eyes at Leslie. "Are you mad 'cause I said that?''

"No, but you shouldn't say things that aren't true,'' Leslie said firmly. "Your friend would have found out sooner or later.''

"I guess.'' She hung her head, scuffing the white toe of her shoe on the floor. "I'm sorry, Leslie.''

"We'll forget about it this time.'' She was troubled by Holly's pretence. "But please, don't do it again.''

"I won't,'' Holly promised with some reluctance.

"Let's go find your father and Aunt Patsy,'' Leslie suggested. "I think it's time we went home.''

During the drive home, Holly was more subdued than usual although she did talk to Patsy Evans about the Christmas program and some of her new friends. Leslie hardly said anything at all.

The incident had merely added to her own inner doubts. In the past, Holly had always seemed so happy and content with her father that Leslie hadn't suspected the girl yearned for a woman's presence in her life. So much of the time she had spent in Tagg's company had included Holly. Now, anything that happened between them affected the child.

Leslie knew all about innocent victims. She had stood helplessly by while her parents had argued themselves into a divorce court, caught in the middle of a conflict that she didn't understand. She didn't want that to happen to Holly. She didn't want to inadvertently hurt her if she decided to stop seeing Tagg. And it was obviously nearing the point where Holly was becoming too attached to her.

When Tagg braked the car to a stop in the driveway, he asked, "Would you like to come inside for some hot chocolate?"

"Not me, thanks," her aunt refused. "It's time I was getting my beauty sleep."

"Leslie?" Tagg arched a brow at her.

She paused in the act of opening the car door. "No, I'll pass, too. Thanks." Her aunt was already out of the car, but Leslie didn't wait for assistance from her or Tagg as she maneuvered out the side door on her own. She started down the sidewalk, following her aunt. Behind her, a car door was pushed shut as Tagg climbed out.

"Go into the house and get changed out of your costume," he told Holly, then called, "Leslie! Wait a minute."

She hesitated, then stopped to let him catch up with her, turning with a faint toss of her head. When he reached her side, his hands moved automatically onto her shoulders in a gesture that was possessive in its familiarity.

"Is something wrong?" He tipped his head to the side, his gaze probing.

"No. I've just got a headache." She took refuge in an old lie.

His gaze skimmed her, seeming to sense the falsehood, but he didn't press the issue. "Another time, then," he said.

"Yes." She accepted the ambiguous suggestion and smiled wanly. "Good night, Tagg."

She turned out of his arms and continued on her way to the house, conscious that he watched her for several long minutes before the sound of his footsteps carried him toward his own home. When she entered the kitchen, she pushed the door shut with her shoulder and leaned briefly against it, a troubled sigh sliding out with a long breath.

"Did you two have a lover's quarrel?" her aunt inquired bluntly, appearing without warning in the doorway.

"No." Her denial was cool and even. "And we aren't lovers."

"At a guess I'd say it isn't because Taggart isn't willing, so you must be the one holding back." Her aunt eyed her knowingly.

"I guess I'm not ready," Leslie shrugged.

"My dear girl, no one is ever ready to fall in love," her aunt informed her with a patient smile.

"I guess I'm not the exception," she declared with a wry and laughing shrug. "How about some tea?"

* * *

During the first three days of the week, Leslie only saw Tagg and Holly from the window of her aunt's house. She made no attempt to speak to them or make them aware of her presence. It wasn't easy, not as easy as she thought it would be. Tension wound around her until she thought she was going to snap.

After a restless night's sleep plagued by childhood nightmares, Leslie was late for breakfast. She swung into the kitchen on her crutches, an apology ready for oversleeping. It died on her lips when she saw Tagg sitting at the kitchen table drinking a cup of coffee.

"Good morning." His gaze was warm and bright with pleasure.

There was a curious singing in her ears, her spirits suddenly lifting despite her attempt to keep them on an even keel. "Good morning." She moved toward the table, glancing at her aunt. "Sorry I got up so late."

"I was going to come in and wake you when I heard you moving around. You have an appointment with my doctor this morning," Patsy reminded her.

"I'd forgotten." It had been made so long ago that it had completely slipped her mind, or been crowded out by too many other things. "What time am I supposed to be there?"

"Not until eleven. Don't worry. You have plenty of time," she assured, then cast a short glance at Taggart Williams. "As a matter of fact, Taggart said he'd be happy to take you to the doctor's office for your checkup. I think there's something he wants to show you, too."

"Something to show me?" Leslie repeated with a slight frown.

"That's why I came over this morning. I was going to take you by so you could see what you thought about it."

"You found a puppy for Holly," Leslie guessed.

"I found a puppy for Holly, but that isn't what I want you to see. Will you come?" Tagg asked. "It's right on the way to the doctor's."

"I—" She wanted to go with him, so why deny it? "I'll come."

There was only time for a light breakfast of coffee and toast. She changed quickly to a better outfit, then left to accompany Tagg in his car. Even though curiosity was getting the better of her, she refused to ask where he was taking her or what he wanted her to see.

Tagg was equally uncommunicative, not giving her any hints or clues about their destination. When he reversed out of the driveway, he made the turn toward town.

Chapter Nine

Tagg parked the car in front of an empty building located around the corner from the town's main street. She gave him a puzzled look.

"This is it?" she asked skeptically.

"Yup." He nodded his head toward the empty building. "What do you think of it?"

"It's a building. What am I supposed to think of it?"

His tongue clicked in mock reproval. "I should hope you would think something. You are looking at the future offices of Taggart J. Williams, Attorney-at-Law." His smile came quick and disturbing. "Come on. I want to show you inside."

Without giving her a chance to disagree, he climbed out of the car and walked around to help her over the snowdrift to the sidewalk. The lock stubbornly resisted his key and gave in after a few hard shakes of the doorknob.

A bare bulb hung from the ceiling of the small anteroom. There was no furniture or drapes to alleviate the bareness of the walls and windows. The building didn't give the appearance of having been used in a long time.

"It needs painting and some minor renovations," Tagg admitted as if reading her thoughts. "But I thought this could be used as the reception area. There's three more rooms back here."

Pausing to switch on the lights, he led the way through the inner door into a short hall with three doors branching off of it. He opened the one on his right and let Leslie enter another bare room.

"I thought this could be used for the secretary. There's room for her desk and some filing cabinets," he explained. "I'm going to have a carpenter cut an opening in the wall to connect this with the reception area so she can see whoever comes in."

One glance around the four bare walls took in all there was to see. Leslie had an impression of a comfortably sized office with adequate work space and floor space. Then Tagg was directing her into the hallway once more.

"This room is too small to be used for anything but storage of supplies and files," he said, opening the door to the room across the hall and letting her glimpse inside. "Down here will be my office."

It was the largest of the three rooms, but also the one in most need of repair. The ceiling was water-stained, indicating the roof had leaked at some point.

The paint was peeling off the walls, the plaster chipped in places.

"Most of this wall space can be used for shelves for all my law books—a kind of legal library," Tagg mocked. "The rest of the walls can be paneled. All I have to do is find a big oak desk and some maroon leather furniture and I'll be in the law business." He swung around to face her, his hands slid inside her coat onto the curves of her waist. "What do you think of it?"

"It seems ideal," she agreed. "Of course, it's going to take some work to fix it up."

"It won't take long once I get the carpenters and painters in here." His hands moved further around her waist to link together at the small of her back. Bending his head, he brushed his mouth over her cheekbone. The light caress trapped a breath in her throat. "I've got to start looking for a secretary." He rubbed his mouth over her lips, then straightened to look at her. "Have you ever given any thought to becoming a legal secretary?"

"No." It came out on that trapped breath.

"The salary probably wouldn't be as high as what you're being paid now, but you can't beat the fringe benefits that go along with the job," he insisted lazily. "What do you think?"

"I—" Leslie dragged her gaze down to the top button of his parka, staring at it and trying to make her heart return to its normal beat. "I already have a job."

She felt the stillness that went through him and the hard probe of his eyes, which she wouldn't meet. The silence ran for long seconds, growing heavier.

"Leslie—" Tagg began.

"Hellooo!" A voice called from the front of the building. "Anybody here!"

Tagg swore savagely under his breath and let go of Leslie, stepping away. "Yes! What is it?" His reply was short-tempered as he moved to the hall door where footsteps approached.

"Tagg Williams?" An older man in a business suit and topcoat appeared.

"Yes." He nodded, his eyes narrowed in sharp question for the man to state his business.

"You don't know me, but I was a great admirer of your father—the Judge." He reached out to shake Tagg's hand. "I was over to Bill Yates's store. He told me you had leased this building to open your law practice and said that was your car parked out front. My name's Davis Long."

"Mr. Long. I believe I remember my father mentioning your name." Tagg frowned as if trying to recall. "You're a banker."

"That's right." A smile widened his face, surprised and pleased. "Since I was here, I wanted to stop by and make myself known to you. Banks are always in need of legal advice. When you open your practice, I hope you'll come by and discuss the possibility of acting as counsel for us."

"It would be my pleasure," Tagg assured him.

"I won't keep you any longer," the man stated with a quick glance at Leslie. "I know you're busy. Welcome back to Vermont." He took a business card from his pocket and handed it to Tagg.

"Thank you. I'll be in touch," he promised.

For a long moment, there was only the retreating echo of the banker's footsteps as he retraced his route to the door. Tagg looked at the card and slipped it inside his pocket.

"My first prospective client." There was a sardonic note in his voice as he turned and glanced at Leslie.

"And you haven't officially opened your doors." Her attempt at a bright response came out stiff.

His glance ran over her, searching and testing before sliding away without finding what he wanted. "We'd better get started to the clinic or you'll be late for your appointment."

It was a short, but silent drive to the medical clinic. Tagg seemed preoccupied, an absent frown creasing his forehead.

Almost as soon as they arrived, Leslie was ushered into an examining room. It had been simpler to have all her medical records forwarded to her aunt's physician than to make the drive all the way back to New York to see her doctor. It was merely a routine checkup to make sure her leg was mending nicely.

The doctor was a young, bearded man named Hornsby. After he'd finished his examination, he picked up her chart. "How long has this cast been on? Five weeks?"

"Yes," Leslie nodded.

"How would you like an early Christmas present?" he asked.

"I beg your pardon?"

"From everything I've seen today, the bone has healed. There's no reason why your cast can't be taken off a week early," he explained.

"That's wonderful news." But she didn't feel as elated as she thought she would. Like Tagg and his first prospective client, she couldn't get excited about her cast being removed, either.

It was a strangely naked feeling when she limped into the waiting room without the cast and crutches, supported with the aid of a cane. Surprise pierced the aloofness of Tagg's expression when he noticed her freed leg.

"Congratulations," he said.

"I feel as if I've lost twenty pounds," she admitted.

Suddenly they both ran out of things to say. The silence was back, thickening until it seemed impenetrable.

"I guess we'd better go," Leslie suggested finally. "Holly will be getting out of school soon."

"Right." It was a grim sound, like his expression as Tagg escorted her outside to the car.

When they drove onto the highway, Leslie stared out the side window. She didn't see the mud-spattered snowbanks along the road. She didn't see anything. Tension knotted her stomach into a tight band.

His sudden braking startled her. She looked around, thinking they were about to hit something. But the road before them was free of traffic. Tagg shifted the car into reverse and backed up to turn into a lay-by.

"Why are we stopped?" She frowned at him.

Both hands rested on top of the wheel as the engine idled, keeping warm air blowing into the car's interior. Tagg breathed in deeply, then turned his head to study her hard.

"Because we need to talk," he stated. "What's the matter, Leslie? Have I been taking too much for granted?"

"I think so." She nodded, lowering her chin.

Shifting his position, he sat sideways in the seat, his arm lying along the back. Without any advance signal of his intention, Tagg leaned over and caught her chin between his fingers, lifting it so his mouth could cover her lips. His kiss was roughly demanding, licking through her like heat lightning.

Her fingers curled into the virile thickness of his hair in a response she was helpless to deny. There was a potency of feeling in his embrace that made her overlook other considerations. When she finally dragged her lips from the moistness of his, she lowered her head in a shaky reaction.

"Do you expect me to believe that when you kiss me like that, it means nothing?" Tagg demanded in a voice thickened by his disturbed state. "Why won't you admit it? Are you afraid?"

"I'm terrified," she whispered.

"Of what?" He pulled back, a darkening frown gathering on his features.

"Of you—of me. Of being wrong," Leslie admitted.

"So you aren't going to take the chance of finding out it's right?" he challenged angrily.

"You seem to be forgetting about your daughter," she retorted, her temper flaring from the sparks of his. "At church the other night, she was telling her friend that I was her mother. If I hadn't come along, who knows how many more of her friends she might have decided to tell."

"Holly did that?" he frowned skeptically.

"Yes."

"I've never known her to make up stories," he insisted.

"Well, she did. I was surprised, too, but I realized how easily she can be hurt. I know what it's like to want something so badly that it hurts inside. You pretend to yourself and others, hoping that if you pretend hard enough it will come true."

"Your parents," he guessed.

"Yes, my parents. The situation isn't the same. I know that. But I wanted so desperately for them to be happy together—for all of us to be happy—instead of constantly shouting and yelling." All the old hurt was back, twisting at her heart and squeezing her chest until it was difficult to breathe. "Even when they separated, which they did many times, I wanted them to get back together. I wanted it to all work out right— the way it did in the books." She stopped, lowering her head. "But it didn't. It still hasn't." There was a hint of moisture in her eyes when she looked at Tagg. "I don't want Holly to start hoping for something that might never be."

"Leslie." Involuntarily Tagg muttered her name and closed his eyes, a taut frustration hardening his features.

His hold tightened to gather her against his chest, his fingers burrowing into her hair to press her head to his shoulder, as he tried to comfort her and take away her fears. She trembled, haunted by the ghosts of things past, and shut her eyes to let the sensations of his solid warmth claim her. His head was bent to her, the side of his jaw, chin, and mouth rubbing against her forehead in an absent caress.

"It's perfectly normal for Holly to want a mother." His low voice was thick with tautly checked emotion. "I'd be more worried if she didn't. Instead of being upset that she picked you for the role, you should be flattered. It's quite a compliment when someone chooses you to be their parent, even if it's only pretend."

"I know," Leslie whispered, but that wasn't the point.

"God knows I approve of her choice," Tagg muttered as he turned his mouth against her face, trailing rough kisses over her eyebrows and temples.

His fingers tightened in her hair, gently tugging her head back so he could find her lips. They parted under his hungry pressure, the blood drumming in her ears. She strained toward him, wanting to be absorbed into him forever and escape these doubts.

Equally frustrated in his attempts to feel her against him, Tagg let go of her briefly and shifted his hold to pull her across his lap where there was no more awkwardness of position. Her arms went around his neck and shoulders as she came back to seek the heady stimulation of his drugging kiss.

With his arm supporting her shoulders and back, his hand pushed its way inside her coat, spreading across her waist and ribs to feel and caress with roaming interest. Desire fevered her flesh with raw and wild longings as she sought the excitement of his tongue, deepening the kiss with fierce pleasure.

There was a growing pressure in her loins, a need for assuagement. It swelled within her, expanding her breast under the cupping caress of his hand. He dragged his mouth from her lips to graze along the skin of her throat. She tipped her head back to allow him greater access, a moaning sigh coming from her lips.

There were too many clothes, too many layers of material to give either of them the closeness they desired. Their temperatures were rising. Between their combined body heat and the warm air blowing from the heater vents and their own passion, the windows were steamed over. Leslie could taste the perspiration on his skin.

When his hand invaded her sweater, it was prepared for the camisole she wore underneath and slipped under the loose garment to glide onto the naked skin of her breast. She shuddered under the sensual stimulation of his stroking thumb, circling the hard point.

His mouth returned to her lips to mutter against them, "I didn't intend for this to happen when we met, any more than you did. But it has. You can't change it." The moistness of his breath was in her mouth, filling every hidden corner.

"I know." The attraction was too strong. It wouldn't be ruled by caution, but it was its very strength that troubled her.

He dragged his hand away from her breast, faint tremors quaking through him as he made a shaky attempt to control his desires. Lifting his head, Tagg traced his fingers over her flushed and softened features. His expression was taut, a nerve twitching in his jaw while his searching gaze probed with a tearing earnestness.

"I've done everything but come right out and say it, Leslie," Tagg murmured. "Before a man tells a woman he loves her, he likes to have some indication that she feels the same. When you offer someone your heart, you don't want them to refuse it. You said I was rushing you, so I've waited. How much longer is it going to be?"

"I don't know." They were troubled words coming from a wary heart.

His mouth tightened. "All right, I'll say it then. I love you."

She looked at him with a sad skepticism that challenged. "How can you be sure?"

His breath came out in a short, humorless laugh, as if concealing his hurt at her doubt. "Well, I don't hear any bells ringing and I haven't noticed any fireworks displays, but I know what I feel. It's love."

"But you were wrong once before," Leslie reminded him in a quietly reluctant voice. "You separated from your first wife...and only reconciled after you found out about Holly. You must have known a child can't hold a marriage together once it's fallen apart."

"Yes, I knew there was only a remote chance that my marriage to Cindy could be salvaged," Tagg admitted with a hard glitter in his blue eyes, a hint of

impatient anger showing. "But I owed it to our un-
born child to find out, didn't I?"

"Yes," she conceded that point. "But you must
have thought you were in love with her, too, when you
married her. If you were mistaken then, you could be
mistaken now."

"I made a mistake—once." He stressed the last
word. "Does that mean I'm not entitled to another
chance?"

"It means you could be wrong again," Leslie murmured.

"I'm not," he stated. "There isn't any way I can
prove it. You'll just have to believe me. Part of loving
a person is trusting them."

"That isn't easy." Her protective instinct was too
strong; there were too many scars and too much potential for more pain for her to lightly accept his word.
Leslie shifted out of his arms and moved to her own
side of the car seat, straightening her coat. The silence grew, finally pulling her glance to Tagg.

"Love doesn't come easy—not the kind that lasts,"
he said quietly. "It requires work and effort from both
parties involved. It only *seems* to happen on its own.
I think you love me but you're afraid of it. You have
to be willing to take that last step. I can't take it for
you."

He didn't seem to expect a reply from her as he
shifted out of parking gear to drive onto the road. Instinctively Leslie knew that he was speaking the truth.
Yet it didn't ease any of her misgivings. Tagg believed
he loved her but did he? Until she was sure, how could
she risk taking that last step?

Turning into the driveway to her aunt's house, he stopped the car and let the engine idle. "I have to pick up Holly at school," Tagg said to explain why he was letting her out here.

"Of course," she reached for the door handle, but his hand on her arm stayed her.

When she looked back, he leaned across the intervening space and kissed her, tasting the soft curves of her lips and lingering on them for a moist second before drawing back. "I'll see you Christmas Eve."

His remark had the sound of a deadline, that she had to make up her mind by then or lose him. She silently railed at the unfairness of putting a time limit as she climbed out of the car, moving more freely without the cumbersome cast. A threading and weaving tension wound through her nerves when she watched him reverse out of the driveway.

"Merry Christmas! Merry Christmas!" Holly chimed the happy greeting to Leslie and her aunt in turn as she bounded into the kitchen, almost running Leslie down when she opened the door. "You should see all the stars in the sky. Santa Claus won't need to have Rudolph show him the way tonight," she declared.

After avoiding a collision with the red-bundled whirlwind of Christmas cheer, Leslie swung her attention to the man who followed, too conscious of the hinted deadline to listen to Holly's mythical observations. By then, Tagg was almost beside her.

"Merry Christmas." His swooping mouth kissed her startled lips with tormenting swiftness and moved away. An eyebrow danced above sparkling blue eyes. "Mmm, that was nice. Maybe I should try it again."

"Tagg." She was stunned, in a delightfully reluctant way, by his boldness in stealing a kiss not only in front of Holly but her aunt as well.

He chuckled at her halfhearted protest and came the rest of the way into the kitchen. "Merry Christmas, Mrs. Evans."

"Merry Christmas. What's this? Presents?" her aunt declared, drawing Leslie's glance to the gift-wrapped packages Tagg carried.

"Just a little something from Holly and me," he shrugged lightly and handed them to her while he took off his coat.

Holly had already scrambled out of hers. "Why don't you open them now?" she urged the woman. "One's for you and one's for Leslie."

"Why don't we all go into the living room by the fireplace?" her aunt suggested. "I believe I remember seeing a present in there with your name on it and we can open them together."

"With my name on it?" Holly asked with wide-eyed wonder. "Really?"

"Yes. Come. I'll show you," Patsy Evans curved a hand on the little girl's shoulder to guide her into the living room.

Which left Leslie to walk with Tagg. Although her leg was still weak, the exercises she'd been doing since the cast had been removed had strengthened it so it could bear her weight without relying on the cane. She still favored it, walking with a slight limp. Tagg's hand rested on her waist, for support if she needed it.

In the living room, Tagg guided her to the sofa and sat on the cushion next to her, casually resting his arm along the back. When Patsy Evans handed a rectangular-shaped gift to her, Leslie was reluctant to unwrap it, thinking it might in some way compromise her position. Instead she watched Holly eagerly tearing away the paper on her present.

When she lifted out the books, she held them up for Tagg to see. "Look, Daddy. Books." She was obviously pleased with the gift. "I haven't read either one of them before." Then she noticed Leslie hadn't opened her present. "Hurry up, Leslie, so you can see what book we bought you. Whoops!" She clamped a hand over her mouth. "I wasn't supposed to tell."

"I still don't know which book it is," Leslie assured her, sliding a finger under the tape to loosen it from the paper. Inwardly, she was relieved to have some idea of what the package contained.

In the meantime, her aunt had opened her gift. "A collection of poems by Robert Frost—and one I don't have. Thank you."

Underneath the Christmas paper and ribbon, there was a leather-bound edition of *A Christmas Carol* by Charles Dickens. A smile of amused disbelief wavered on Leslie's face.

"Daddy said you liked the hero of that book," Holly explained and waited for Leslie to confirm that it had been an appropriate choice.

"It's one of my favorites by Dickens," she said.

"I thought it would be good bedtime reading for Christmas Eve," Tagg murmured, a wicked light glittering in his eyes.

"Without a doubt," Leslie agreed, unable to keep the amusement out of her voice.

"I'm going to start reading my books now," Holly declared and opened up the first one to begin reading aloud.

All three of them became involved, helping her with the words she didn't know. When the story reached a point where it could be stopped, Patsy Evans suggested it would be a good time to put the book aside and have their supper. Everyone lent a hand in the kitchen to carry the crackers and bowls of steaming oyster stew into the dining room.

"I almost forgot to tell you." Holly was trailing after Patsy Evans with a bowl of little, round oyster crackers. "Do you know what I heard when we were coming over here to your house? I heard Santa's sleigh flying high in the sky."

Tagg leaned his head toward Leslie and murmured, for her ears alone, "It sounded very much like a puppy whining because it doesn't like being in the garage all alone."

"Of course, that's not what it was," she said dryly, guessing he had smuggled Holly's Christmas puppy into the garage.

"It had to be the whine of Santa's sleigh," he insisted with a wink.

After supper was finished, Tagg and Holly didn't stay long. As he explained, they opened their gifts on Christmas Eve so there would be room under the tree for the presents Santa brought.

"And I have to go to bed early tonight," Holly added. "'Cause Santa only comes when you're sleeping."

Leslie was about to conclude that Tagg was not going to raise the issue of their last conversation. But while her aunt was helping Holly into her coat, Tagg drew her to one side.

"Have you thought about what we discussed?" There was a watchful quality in his gaze.

"Yes." It was nearly all she'd thought about.

"And?" Tagg prompted.

"I'm still thinking," she said.

There was an uneasy quavering in her stomach as she watched him breathe in deeply. A smile of reluctant acceptance finally edged his mouth to show his continued patience with her. When Leslie smiled, it was out of relief that he hadn't been setting a deadline, giving her a now-or-never kind of ultimatum.

When he bent to kiss her, she ignored the fact there were spectators and kissed him back. For a second, it almost got out of hand, then her aunt cleared her throat and they drew apart, exchanging intimate and self-conscious looks.

"It's a shame Santa has such a busy night ahead of him," Tagg murmured.

"Yes, it is," she agreed.

"I'm ready to go, Dad," Holly hurried him along.

Chapter Ten

Early on Christmas morning, there was a loud pounding at the kitchen door. Leslie was still in her quilted robe, not having taken the time to dress before her first cup of coffee. She set the freshly poured cup on the counter and limped to the door in her furry brown slippers.

Holly was standing outside, both arms wrapped around a wiggling ball of white and brown fur. She was wearing the biggest smile Leslie had ever seen as she stepped into the kitchen to show off her new puppy.

"Look what Santa Claus brought me." She offered the puppy to Leslie so she could hold it. Its pink little tongue immediately began washing her face, a fluffy bundle of love. "His name is Chris. That's short for Christmas, 'cause that's when I got him."

"He's beautiful," Leslie laughed, managing to get the squirming pup away from her face so she could elude its licking kisses. When she glimpsed its long, thin nose, she guessed that it belonged to either the shepherd or the collie breed.

"When I came downstairs this morning, there was a big box under the tree," she explained. "I went over and looked inside—and there he was. There was a big red bow around his neck, but he chewed it off. I guess it tickled him. When he saw me, he got all excited—just like he knew he belonged to me."

"I'll bet that's because he knew you would love him." Leslie handed the puppy back to Holly and smiled at the way she hugged with such affection. It whined with excitement.

"I just had to come over so you could see Chris," Holly said, wanting to share the joy of this moment. She glanced beyond Leslie. "Aunt Patsy, look what Santa brought me."

The explanations started all over again as she showed the puppy to Leslie's aunt. She made all the suitable comments about what a fine-looking animal it was.

"Is this what you asked Santa to bring you?" her aunt inquired, rubbing the puppy's ears.

"Well, I did ask him for something else," Holly admitted with a thoughtful frown. "But I guess Santa can only bring certain kinds of things like toys and puppies. I'm glad I've got Christmas."

"So am I." Patsy smiled. "You'll have to take real good care of him."

"I will. Santa even brought dog food and dishes for his water and his puppy food." She turned suddenly to Leslie. "I almost forgot. Santa Claus left a present for you at our house."

"What?" A startled frown flickered across her face.

"I told you that you should have a tree," Holly reminded her with a knowing nod of her head. "Since you didn't have one, Santa had to leave your present under our tree. He knew we'd make sure you got it."

"I think there must be a mistake—" Leslie made a confused protest.

"No. Santa doesn't make a mistake," Holly insisted. "Daddy looked at the package and said it had your name on it. I'm supposed to tell you to come over and get it."

"I'll come over later—" she began.

"No, come over now," Holly coaxed. "I want to see what Santa brought you."

"But I'm not dressed." She glanced down at her quilted lounging robe in a chocolate brown trimmed with gold ribbing.

"Nonsense, you have more clothes on than you usually do," her aunt scoffed at that excuse. "You're covered from head to foot. Just throw a coat on and go over."

"Yes, Leslie. Please." Holly pleaded. "There isn't any snow on the walk and the sun is out."

"All right." She gave into their urgings, but she was conscious of her heart racing.

After donning her coat, she followed Holly outside. It was a bright Christmas morning with the sunlight glinting off the snow. Holly put the puppy on the ground and the pair of them ran ahead of the limping Leslie.

By the time she reached the front porch steps, Holly had the door open and was announcing her arrival. "Daddy! Leslie's here to get her present from Santa."

When she entered the house, she saw him standing in the living room, a coffee cup in his hand. He was dressed in a long-sleeved, flannel shirt in a gray and black plaid and gray corduroy slacks. There was a faint accusation in her glance when she met the knowing glitter of his gaze.

"Your present's under the tree." He used the cup to motion in the direction of the tree.

There was only one square package under the tree, so there could be no doubt which was hers. Her leg was tired and beginning to ache; her limp was more noticeable as she approached the tree.

"Maybe you'd better sit down," Tagg suggested and pushed the ottoman closer to the tree.

She sank gratefully onto it, conscious of him towering beside her. The puppy romped about her feet in uncoordinated play while Holly hovered anxiously behind Leslie as she picked up the lightweight box wrapped in silver foil.

"This isn't fair," she said stiffly to Tagg, sliding him an irritated glance. "I didn't buy you anything."

"Don't look at me." He drew back in mock innocence. "This present is from Santa Claus."

"Oh, hurry up and open it, Leslie," Holly urged impatiently. "I want to see."

When she removed the emerald green ribbon, the puppy grabbed it and began chewing and tearing it to shreds. He pounced on the silver foil, too, when it fell to the floor. Leslie slipped off the lid and began lifting aside the tissue that protected the contents. She just kept encountering more tissue.

"What's inside?" Holly was leaning over her shoulder, trying to see into the box.

"A lot of tissue." Then her fingers felt a second small box inside.

Her gaze darted to Tagg as she slowly lifted it out. He silently held her glance. She could hear the thudding of her heart as she stared at the ring box.

"Another box!" Holly exclaimed with delight. "Open it up, Leslie."

There was a tightness in her throat. Very slowly, she pushed back the hinged lid. Nestled on a bed of blue velvet sat a diamond ring, a solitaire in the center with smaller diamonds designed around it in the shape of a five-pronged star.

"Ooooh!" Holly was awed by the thousands of lights that sparkled from the diamond cuts. "It's beautiful."

Leslie didn't say a thing, her breath coming painfully shallow. There was the sting of tears in her eyes. Her fingers tightened their hold on the box, her knuckles turning white under the pressure.

"It looks just like the Christmas star, doesn't it, Daddy?" Holly declared in amazement. "It sparkles brighter than anything."

"Yes, it does." His voice was calmly quiet, but to Leslie, it seemed to come from some great distance. "Now that you've seen it, why don't you take your puppy outside?"

"Okay." Holly needed no second urging, unconcerned by Leslie's silence. "Come here, Christmas!" she called the bounding puppy to her side and scooped it into her arms. "We've got to go outside so you don't make any messes in the house. You've got to learn to be a good puppy."

All the while Leslie seemed to be frozen in position. It wasn't until the front door closed and there was silence in the room that she finally lifted her gaze by degrees to Tagg. There was a mute appeal in the shimmer of her hazel eyes. He ignored it and took a sip of his coffee.

"There's a card inside," he said. "Why don't you read it?"

This time her fingers were trembling when they searched through the tissue-filled box and came up with a small white card. There was a message written on it in a neatly lettered scroll.

"There is a man who loves you very much," it read. "I would appreciate your assistance and ask that you wear this ring so he may have the Christmas present he wants."

It was signed: *Santa Claus*.

Moisture collected in her eyes, blurring the words when she tried to read them a second time. She was shaking inside, deeply moved by his touching ploy. Yet she remained in the grip of her silence.

Tagg crouched down in front of her, the study of his gaze becoming intense. "Am I going to get my present?"

Her head made a slow move from side to side, but it wasn't a gesture of denial. It was an expression of helplessness. With all her heart, she wanted to give him the answer he sought but that fear of making a mistake held her motionless.

"I want you to marry me, Leslie," Tagg said huskily. "I want you to be my wife."

She looked again at the ring. A star of hope. A star of love. A Christmas star shining out at her from a heaven of blue velvet.

"I want to marry you," Leslie admitted in a wavering voice that was still not an acceptance.

"I haven't made it a habit of proposing to women. You're the first one I've asked since Cindy died. I don't mean to sound like I'm bragging, but I've been with a fair number of women in the interim—and there were willing takers among them if I'd asked. But I didn't ask because I didn't love them. I know the difference."

"I'm sorry." Her voice trembled, because she didn't mean for her doubt to be interpreted as a belief he treated the vows of marriage lightly.

"I understand why you are wary," Tagg said. "Your parents' divorce must have been a painful and traumatic experience for you. But I also went through it—as one of the parties directly involved, not just an innocent victim as you were. It isn't something I want to go through again, either."

The shaking stopped as she slowly lifted her gaze to him. She searched his face, suddenly realizing she had not considered what he had been through. Foolishly she had been thinking that she was the only one who knew the agony of a broken marriage.

"Christmas is all about God and love. It's something you can't see or touch, but you have to have faith. You have to believe in love," he stated.

It was all so simple when put in that context. Leslie could almost feel the peace stealing over her as she accepted what he said. With new calmness and confidence in what lay ahead, she removed the star ring from its box and gave it to Tagg.

"Would you put it on my finger?" she asked, finding it suddenly so easy to take that last step.

It was as if he had braced himself for something else. For a pounding moment, Tagg could only stare at her, not quite believing she meant it. But her left hand was extended to him, steady and sure.

His expression became filled with highly charged emotion, a bursting of wild joy and inexpressible pride. He gripped her hand and slid the ring on her finger. Both of them looked at it, sparkling there with a radiant light that seemed to shine with the fullness of their love.

When he swept her into his arms and crushed her mouth under his, happiness spilled through her like a raging torrent. All the doubts and fears were washed away by the flood of emotion. His mouth bruised her with his desire, but the pain was exquisitely sweet.

Dazed by the radiant joy that claimed her, Leslie was certain she heard bells ringing, muffled and far away, but it sounded very much like them. She wondered if she wasn't a little bit crazy when the kiss finally ended and Tagg held her tightly in his arms.

"I can't believe it," she murmured.

"Believe what?" he asked thickly, drawing his head back to look at her.

Her fingers stroked his strong features in a tactile exploration. "I actually thought I heard bells." She lazily studied his mouth, fascinated by its firm line and latent sexuality.

It quirked. "You did."

"What?" There was a lilt of absent curiosity in her voice, too, intrigued by little discoveries to pay close attention to words when actions were more satisfying.

"You did hear bells," Tagg repeated. "They were the church bells ringing out the message of Christmas."

She laughed and traced a finger under his jaw. "Just think—we can tell our children that I heard bells the day you proposed to me."

His eyes darkened with smoldering desire. "I want you, Leslie. I want you. I want your children. I want your love for the rest of my life and beyond."

The smile left her face as Leslie looked at him with sober intensity. "And I want you and your children—and your love for the rest of my life and beyond. Because I love you, Tagg." She finally said the words that no other man had heard, the ones she'd saved so they would have meaning and commitment behind them.

As his mouth moved onto hers, her fingers curled themselves into his hair, the star diamond ring winking its light in the blackness. The driving force of his kiss pressed her backward on the ottoman while his restless hand traveled over the point of her hip and the curve of her waist, caressing and stimulating.

The slam of the front door sent a draft of cold air blowing over the intertwining bodies. There was no time to sit up or disguise the passionate embrace before Holly dashed into the room with the awkwardly galloping puppy at her heels. It was all done after she was there.

Leslie's cheeks were flushed with an embarrassed heat, and Tagg noted the face with amusement. To avoid Holly's wide-eyed stare of curiosity, Leslie made a show of straightening her robe and brushing back the ends of her hair.

"What are you doing, Daddy?" Holly asked.

"I was kissing Leslie," he said candidly and reached out an arm to draw his daughter to his side.

"You kissed her the morning after we'd slept in front of the fireplace, but it wasn't like that," she said.

"That was a good morning kiss. There are different kinds of kisses," Tagg explained, more accustomed to fielding such questions than Leslie was.

"What kind of kiss was that?" Holly asked, meaning the one she had interrupted.

"That's the way a man kisses a woman when they are going to get married—and after they get married," he added the last as an advance warning of other kisses to come that "big eyes" might see.

"Are you going to marry Leslie?" She seemed to hold her breath.

"Yes." Tagg reached to clasp Leslie's hand, the one with the ring.

"And when you marry her, she'll be my mommy, won't she?" Holly asked, excitement beginning to bubble from her.

"Yes."

"I did get my present from Santa!" She began jumping up and down. "I did! I wanted Leslie to be my mother more than anything! I thought Santa couldn't bring me a present like that."

"I didn't know anything about this." Tagg frowned and looked at his daughter curiously. "How come you didn't tell me?"

"Because—I didn't want to tell anybody," Holly declared. "I was afraid Santa wouldn't do it. That's why I wrote him the letter all by myself."

"The letter I mailed to Santa Claus," Leslie realized.

"Yes, that's the one," she admitted with a quick nod of her head. "Now you're going to be with us all the time—every minute. And you won't be staying at Aunt Patsy's any more."

"Whoa! What a minute before you damage my future wife's reputation." Tagg called a halt to Holly's opinion of how it was going to be. "Before Leslie can stay with us all the time, there has to be a wedding."

"How would you like to be one of my bridesmaids, Holly?" Leslie asked.

"Can I?" she asked excitedly.

"I wouldn't want anyone else," she smiled.

"When can we have the wedding?" Holly wanted to know. "Can we have it tomorrow—on my birthday?"

"No, not tomorrow," Tagg chuckled. "Not that it wouldn't be nice, but it takes a little longer than that to arrange a wedding. But it will be soon."

"Boy, just wait until I tell Sally Tuttle that you're going to be my mother!" Holly exclaimed. "I can hardly wait until the vacation's over and school starts." A thought suddenly occurred to her. "If Leslie is going to be my mother, then Aunt Patsy is really going to be my aunt."

"That's right," Leslie nodded.

"Can I go tell her?" She was bursting to tell someone.

"Sure. Why not?" Leslie laughed softly.

In a flash, Holly was out the door and racing down the porch steps to run next door and break the news. With a hopeless shake of his head, Tagg turned back to Leslie and kissed the ring on her hand.

"It seems both Holly and me got our present from Santa Claus," he murmured and started to draw her back into his arms.

She snuggled into his arms, enfolded in their warmth and his love. "Why did you pretend my ring was a present from Santa Claus?" she asked. "Why didn't you simply propose to me?"

"How could anyone turn down Santa Claus?" Tagg countered, murmuring the question against her hair.

"That isn't an answer," she declared with amused reproach.

"Because I wanted you to believe in the goodness of Santa Claus and to know that he gives from the heart. He's love and he lives in the heart."

"Christmas is going to be my favorite time of the year from now on," Leslie sighed in contentment. "In the past, it has been such an unhappy season. Until this year when I came here and met you. Now it's the happiest."

"I still remember how you looked that day when you helped Holly make the paper chain for the tree." Amusement riddled his voice. "You were so indignant when I said I believed in Santa Claus. I expected any minute to be accused of corrupting my daughter with fairy-tale nonsense."

"If Holly hadn't been there, I probably would have," she admitted, remembering well how she had scorned any perpetuation of the Santa Claus myth.

"Indignant and so vulnerable," he murmured. "It was an intriguing combination. You tried to be so tough—and so cynical."

"You made me laugh at myself, and not take everything quite so seriously," Leslie realized.

"All of us have to believe in Santa Claus and Peter Pan. We need to keep a bit of a child's faith," Tagg said.

"I can see that now," she agreed.

"And you can see that I love you and want you to be my wife." The roughness of need was in his voice, making it husky. "How soon can we set the wedding date?"

"I've been thinking about that," Leslie admitted with a faintly troubled sigh. "Naturally my father is going to want to give me away. And if he comes, my mother won't."

"That's easily fixed," Tagg told her. "We'll elope—and not invite either of them."

"Tagg," she said in a reproving tone.

"I'm serious," he insisted. "There aren't going to be any undercurrents of unhappiness on our wedding day. After we're married we'll fly to Baltimore to see your mother, then honeymoon in Hawaii and see your father."

"It sounds wonderful," Leslie agreed and wrapped his arms a little tighter around her. "What about Holly? Are we going to take her along?"

"I love my daughter very much but I have no intention of taking her on my honeymoon," he stated without hesitation. "There will be plenty of opportunities in the future for us to vacation together as a family. This trip will be ours alone."

"Maybe Aunt Patsy will look after her," she suggested the possibility. "I think Holly would like that. And my aunt seems to have become quite fond of her."

"We'll ask, but either way, we'll make some kind of arrangements to have the time alone," Tagg answered her. "When we get back, that will be soon enough for you to assume the responsibility of being a mother."

"And a legal secretary?" she teased.

"I'll make sure your duties are light," he promised. "I know what a demanding husband you'll have at home."

"And how demanding is that?" It was a deliberately provocative challenge, fully aware that Tagg would show her, and he did.

* * * * *

EMILIE
RICHARDS

Sweet Sea Spirit

To the crazy McGees,
who have taught me everything I
need to know about big, loving,
Southern families.

Chapter One

A glossy-leafed magnolia tree towered over the front porch of the sprawling farmhouse, a sentinel guarding the house's inhabitants from the ravages of the Georgia sun. On one afternoon in May, however, the sun had disappeared behind a friendly cloud and the magnolia tree was just biding its time. Rustling softly in the spring breeze, it stood stoically as a teenage boy shimmied and clawed his way up to its highest branches, shaking them with enthusiasm to signal his arrival and subsequent departure.

"See if you can beat this!" the boy called, an adolescent quaver in his deepening voice.

"With my hands tied behind my back!" A young woman, two blond braids trailing down to her waist, stood with hands perched defiantly on her hips, feet planted wide apart. "I was climbing trees when you were still in diapers!"

Beside the young woman stood the twin brother of the tree-climbing teenager, who was now swinging from the bottom limb of the tree to land on the rubber-tipped toes of his dirty sneakers. "You did it, Randy," shouted the other boy. "You beat the record!"

"Of course." Randy modestly polished his fingernails on the front of his threadbare flannel shirt. "Care to show us what you're made of, Sandy?"

If there was one thing that Alexandra Kathryn MacDonald couldn't resist, it was a challenge. Growing up in a family of twelve children, life had always been one challenge after another, and she thrived on it. Now at age twenty-one she was still responding to her sixteen-year-old twin brothers with the same competitive spirit she had always shown. So much for the social graces, she thought as she watched her brother James reset the stopwatch.

"Do you want us to give you a handicap?" Randy asked with an audible sneer in his voice. "We could spot you a couple of seconds."

"You're going to have a handicap if you don't shut up," Sandy said calmly. "Just don't try to cheat me."

"We won't need to."

Sandy tucked her golden braids under the collar of a blue work shirt and pushed the shirttail into her faded jeans. She would take no chances of getting caught on any of the smaller branches. "Whenever you're ready."

"I left the penknife on the outside edge of the tree house at the top of the tree. You have to get it and bring it back in less than ninety-two seconds to beat my record," Randy instructed.

"A piece of cake," Sandy said, waving her hand gracefully in front of her as if she were shooing flies.

"You've grown soft, reading all those textbooks, typing all those reports." James was trying to apply a not so subtle form of psychological harassment.

Sandy ignored him. "Ready, boys?"

Simultaneously the boys yelled "Go," and like a monkey seeking coconuts, Sandy was scrambling up the tree. Her slender, lithe body twisted and stretched as she felt for toeholds and leaned into space to grab the sturdy branches. Every limb, every whorl and crevice was familiar. Climbing the magnolia tree was as natural as breathing or saying her bedtime prayers.

Every MacDonald child was intimate with the gnarled magnolia. The tree had figured prominently in the wild games that all of them had played on hot summer evenings as their parents sat in wooden rockers on the front porch, resting for a few minutes before the inevitable nighttime chores began. Raymond and Eldora MacDonald were protective parents, but they never protected their children from using their bodies or developing their skills, and not an eye was blinked as child after child swayed from the top branches of the proud, old tree.

Sandy couldn't count the times she had reached the midsection of the magnolia where a vital branch was missing. Readying her body for the most difficult part of the climb, she tensed, then sprang, wrapping her long fingers around the nub of the broken branch and swinging her feet to another foothold. Her years of expertise were being put to work, but the exhilaration of the climb left her feeling giddy with the sheer joy of being alive. She might be a recent college graduate about to embark on a new career, but she was still Sandy MacDonald, teenage tomboy, at heart.

"You'll never make it in time," came the chant from far below, and Sandy's laughter filtered down through the leaves as she continued her climb. *One more branch*, she thought, *half a circle, swing your left foot, grab with your right hand and push off hard*.

The tree house was right above her. Holding firmly to a branch, Sandy felt along the sturdy structure's edge, her fingers contacting and grabbing Randy's rusty penknife. Quickly she stuffed it into her pocket.

Turning to begin her descent, her eyes caught movement on the winding clay road that ran in front of the MacDonald farm. A cloud of red dust billowed behind what Sandy recognized as her father's faithful pickup truck. In its wake and following closely was a long sleek automobile that even from a distance shone with the muted glow of hand-rubbed pewter.

Forgetting momentarily about the race, Sandy parted branches to get a better look. Visitors were not rare, the MacDonald family had kin all over northern Georgia, but visitors usually came in pickup trucks or rusting station wagons. Fancy cars that showed no signs of having been driven on dusty roads were unheard of.

"Thirty-nine seconds left!" came the jubilant report from beneath the tree.

"Darn!" Woolgathering had cost her precious moments. Calculating the chances of making up her lost time, Sandy grabbed branches and swung and slid down the trunk of the tree, letting gravity do its job.

With nothing on her mind except beating Randy's record, she poured every ounce of physical skill and mental concentration into the task at hand.

It was the touch of daredevil in her that caused her defeat. Two-thirds of the way down, two branches grew side by side. From experience she knew that one was actually inches lower than the other. She also knew that landing on the bottom branch would put her in a better position to leap to the lowest branch of the tree and then to the ground. The problem was that her legs had never been quite long enough to reach. Instead, she always had to sacrifice seconds by hitting the top branch first, turning and stepping down to the lower one, and then, finally, to the lowest.

Today, with the smell of success in the spring breeze, Sandy jumped for the lower branch, hoping that her twenty-one-year-old legs were a scant inch longer than her teenage legs had been.

Unfortunately, they weren't. With a small cry, Sandy felt herself slipping out of the tree, falling, bottom first, to the lowest branch. In the split second before impact, she stiffened her legs, preparing them to wrap around the limb if she was lucky enough to land there before tumbling to the ground. Through the worn seat of her jeans, she felt the bark scrape as she bounced against it. Twisting with one fierce movement, she slid along the branch, wedging one shapely leg in a small crevice where the branch joined the tree trunk.

Gravity had been defeated, but so had Sandy. Hanging upside down by one leg, her long braids almost dragging the ground below, Sandy had to admit that Randy's record was safe. Even more embarrassing was the fact that in addition to James and Randy, who were lying under the magnolia bellowing with laughter, a very dignified man was standing ten feet away watching her attempts to swing upright and jump down from the tree.

Even upside down, the man looked important. He was dressed impeccably in a dark three-piece suit that fit his tall, wide-shouldered body to perfection. His hair was dark, too, with silver sprinkled at the temples, but the man's face was young with only the pleasant lines the aging process provides a male in his early thirties. With the blood rushing to her head, Sandy couldn't tell the color of his eyes, but she could tell that he was smiling at her with the paternalistic smile an adult saves for a rebellious child.

"Sandy! Get out of that tree!" Raymond Macdonald's voice rang clear in the spring air. Sandy watched as her father joined the stranger. His arms were crossed against his chest in what she knew was his most disapproving stance.

Acutely aware of the picture she was making, Sandy realized that her father was embarrassed. With chagrin she made one mighty effort, swung her dangling leg over the branch, and pulled herself upright. Waiting a moment for the blood in her head to drain back to its rightful arteries and veins, she finally slid out of the tree, leaping at the last moment to fall on top of James and Randy, who were still collapsed on the ground in hysterics. The moment was too good to resist, even though the look on Mr. MacDonald's face was warning enough that she should. Sandy threaded her fingers through each twin's hair and bumped their heads together before rolling off of them to rise to her feet.

"Are you trying to shame me, Alexandra?" Mr. MacDonald's soft Southern accent had completely disappeared to be replaced by arctic tones.

"Of course not, Daddy." Sandy brushed crumbled bark and dirt off the seat of her jeans, flashing her father a wide grin that changed her winsome features into the portrait of a tomboy madonna. Her eyes, the rich deep green of the ocean, were wide and innocent as she stared up at her father through long, sable lashes.

As always, Mr. MacDonald was incapable of staying angry. A stern man with a face burned brown by the Georgia sun and shoulders bent from almost fifty years of backbreaking farm work, Raymond MacDonald was putty in the hands of any of his five beautiful daughters. "Come here and meet Mr. Hamilton," he said gruffly, gesturing to the man beside him. He ignored his twin sons, flashing messages with his eyes that told them he would deal with their behavior later.

Sandy turned slightly and studied the stranger. Now that she was right side up, she could see that his eyes were blue. Piercing, soul-examining blue. She smiled hesitantly, moving closer to extend a grimy hand. "How do you do," she said politely.

"A pleasure to meet you." The Southern accent was soft and cultured; the voice was deep and musical. His words resonated with promises of Old Georgia wealth and social status, and Sandy decided that the man's voice exactly matched the elegant, completely masculine lines of his face and body. When he took her hand and shook it, his grasp was strong and his hand warm.

"Come on inside, Tyler." Mr. MacDonald climbed the porch steps, skirting the kitchen entrance to opt for the formality of the living room. Tyler Hamilton dropped Sandy's hand, nodding with a half smile and turned to follow.

Tyler Hamilton. Sandy watched the man climb the steps and disappear into the house. Tyler Hamilton. One of the most prominent lawyers north of Atlanta. The head of one of the law offices where Sandy had intended to apply for a job. "That was Tyler Hamilton," she muttered inanely to James and Randy, who were approaching to rub in their victory.

Even James and Randy had heard of Tyler Hamilton. "Wait till I tell Mom and Wendy what you were doing when Tyler Hamilton drove up," James bellowed. With a whoop, the twin terrors were off, and Sandy followed them at a slower, safer pace.

Mentally she reviewed what she knew about the elegant stranger. Tyler Hamilton lived in the medium-size town of Cameron, Georgia. He'd won several controversial cases in recent years, and since then his fame had spread throughout the state. But even before the controversy, he had been well-known. Because he'd been born into a wealthy family with roots sunk deep in Georgia clay, Tyler Hamilton's name had been bandied about for years as a potential candidate for any number of offices.

Never one to be impressed by status, Sandy was still well aware of the top quality of the Hamilton and Stone firm. In her four years on scholarship at a local girls' college, she had made it her business to find out about every important law office north of Atlanta. Sandy had been one of a rare breed of college students who knew exactly what she wanted to do with her life. Someday she would attend law school and become a public defender, but first she wanted practical experience to guide her studies. To further her goals, she had taken every available course to ready herself for a job as a paralegal. With utmost care, she had compiled information that might lead to a challenging job in one of the state's better law firms.

Unquestionably, there was one firm she could now strike off her list.

At the kitchen door, Sandy ran her fingers over the soft wisps of hair that had escaped from her braids to frame her face. With distaste she rubbed her hands on the seat of her jeans. Stepping into the kitchen she found her mother perched on a high stool, chopping tomatoes.

Eldora MacDonald was an older, well-seasoned version of her blond daughters. No stranger to hard work, she still believed in looking her best, and today she was wearing a clean housedress covered by a spotless apron.

"Salad with dinner?" Sandy asked.

Mrs. MacDonald looked up and smiled at her second daughter. Not as malleable as Mr. MacDonald, she was still outrageously proud of all her children. "When hasn't there been a salad with dinner?"

Sandy leaned over to kiss her mother on the cheek before washing her hands in the chipped enamel sink. "Did James and Randy tell you about our race?" she asked casually.

"They came through hooting and hollering about something they want to tell all of us over dinner."

"Such lovely, polite boys. A credit to the family," Sandy muttered. About to don an apron, she saw her mother's eyes flicker over the disreputable condition of her jeans. "All right," she said, holding up her hands and rolling her eyes in mock defeat. "I'll change before I help with dinner."

"Such a lovely, polite girl. A credit to the family," Mrs. MacDonald teased.

Picking up a tomato to eat on the way upstairs, Sandy tiptoed through the hallway toward the stairwell. Tomato juice dripped unnoticed down her chin as she plotted how to get past the living room without drawing attention to herself. The men's voices stopped her cold.

"Is Alexandra the daughter that you said was a paralegal, Raymond?" Sandy recognized Tyler Hamilton's deep voice.

"She's the one, though you sure couldn't tell today."

"She's a pretty girl, but she doesn't look old enough to be in high school."

"Doesn't act old enough, either," came her father's scathing reply. "We've let her run wild with the boys." His tone softened as he added, "Can't think we did too much harm, though. She just graduated with honors from college. Got offered a place in a couple of law schools, too, but she's determined to stay out and work for a year. Stubborn as a horse in a burning barn."

Resisting her impulse to stick her tongue out at both men, Sandy stood immobile in the hallway until the tide of the conversation began to turn. With her nose in the air, she darted past the living-room door, her braids flying out behind her.

"Alexandra?"

One foot on the stairs, she stopped, surprised by the sound of Tyler Hamilton's summons. "Yes?"

"Would you mind joining us for a moment?"

Yes, she would mind, but no, she wasn't rude enough to refuse a guest in her home. With a sigh, and a fruitless search of the hallway for a place to deposit her tomato, she muttered, "I'm coming."

Tomato in hand, she strolled into the living room, trying not to notice her father's disapproving assessment of her appearance.

"Your father tells me you've had some legal training. I thought you should know why I'm here." Tyler Hamilton was sitting comfortably on the sofa, his arm draped along the back, but he stood with old-fashioned courtesy when she entered. The only chair that was vacant was all the way across the room, threatening to make conversation awkward. Feeling on trial, Sandy dropped onto the sofa next to the well-known lawyer and wished that her jeans were cleaner, she wasn't wearing yesterday's work shirt and the half-eaten tomato clutched tightly in her hand would disappear.

"Mr. Hamilton's here because Chester Barkley up the road called him about a chemical dump bordering his property. Chester thinks the chemicals are leaking, and he wants Mr. Hamilton, here, to sue the Lanier Chemical Company."

Sandy leaned back against the soft cushions and flipped her braids in front of her shoulders. "Mr. Barkley's land borders ours, doesn't it?"

Mr. MacDonald nodded.

"Is he talking about that vacant stretch of ground on the northeast corner of the farm, over by the livestock pond?"

Mr. MacDonald nodded again.

Sandy frowned. "If the chemicals were really leaking, they could contaminate the groundwater and our pond, too, couldn't they?"

This time it was Tyler who nodded, twisting in his seat to face her. "Chester Barkley says that your family has more to lose than anyone, but there are several farms in danger. He also believes that there's another dump in the area with the same problems, too. A lot of land could be involved."

Sandy liked the thoughtful way Tyler spoke; the forceful quality was belied by a faint hesitancy that was Southern manners at its best. Up close she could see the blue-black shadow of his beard emerging against the lightly tanned skin of his cheeks and chin. His features were sweeping and aristocratic, his eyebrows bushy but well-suited accents to his penetrating eyes; his dark hair fell in perfect masculine layers to the top of his collar. Tyler Hamilton looked the part of a well-bred politician with charisma and power radiating from him in waves. Despite the fact that he thought she didn't look old enough to be in high school, Sandy was completely charmed.

Pulling herself reluctantly from her observations she turned to her father. "Daddy, have you noticed any problems with the cattle or with Jennifer's pony?" Turning back to Tyler, she explained, "They're the only animals we water at the pond."

"Nothing as far as I can see."

"I think we should check them carefully after supper, but if the chemicals have been leaking for some time, the effects are probably subtle and long-range. Don't you think, Mr. Hamilton?"

Tyler Hamilton was watching her, a half-smile twisting his mouth again. "Exactly. My guess is that you'd have noticed something by now. At this point, we know nothing about what kinds of chemicals were stored there, whether they're leaking, or whether they're even dangerous if they do leak. That will be my job to find out."

"That sounds like a lot of research," Sandy said, her delicate features screwed up into a thoughtful expression. "I should think you'd need substantial assistance on the investigation."

"You're right, of course."

"It sounds like fascinating work," she went on enthusiastically.

"Here the farm under your very feet is threatened, and you're getting excited about how much fun the investigation will be," Mr. MacDonald admonished.

"Daddy, I'll bet you dollars to doughnuts that the farm isn't threatened at all. In every case I've ever heard of where a dangerous chemical spill has occurred, someone or something develops symptoms. Has Chester Barkely complained of anything specific, Mr. Hamilton?''

"Call me Tyler. As a matter of fact, his only evidence is some concrete canisters the rain exposed a month or so ago. They've got Lanier Chemical emblazoned on them. Chester called the company and they refused to talk to him, so he hired me."

"There are plenty of good lawyers in Gainesville," Mr. MacDonald said. "How come he called someone from Cameron?"

Tyler was silent, obviously weighing the question. Finally he said, "Well, he heard about some other cases I've taken in the past that were similar, and he wanted someone with experience." Stretching his long legs in front of him, Tyler smiled a full smile, almost knocking Sandy over with its brilliance. "I guess I'm just that good," he drawled.

Raymond MacDonald laughed, slapping his knee in appreciation of Tyler's conceit. The small joke seemed to bridge the gap between the two men, and Sandy knew she was being treated to a sample of Tyler's courtroom style. No jury on earth could deny the charms of this man.

"I'd like to help," she found herself saying, after the room had quieted. "I mean, you're going to need researchers, and I've got a solid background for it. Until I start working full-time I've got time to spare."

She could feel Tyler's eyes as they politely examined her. Her fingers clenched convulsively on the dripping tomato. Sandy never thought of herself as especially pretty, although enough men had told her differently to make her wonder. Her green eyes were huge and striking with her golden hair, but she was sure her mouth was too generous, her nose too tilted.

By a fraction of an inch she missed having the all-American beauty of her oldest sister, Stacey, or the ethereal loveliness of her younger sister, Wendy. Instead she was a grown-up pixie with a face pleasing enough to look at but not to grow rapturous about. As Tyler swept his eyes over her body, she found herself wishing that her slender figure, an asset even she couldn't find fault with, was better displayed.

"I'd like to have your help," Tyler said finally. "Why don't you drive over to Cameron next Monday and see my office. We can talk then." Leaning forward, he drew out a kidskin wallet and found a business card.

"I'll be there," she told him.

Tyler rose, extending his hand to Mr. MacDonald. "Thank you for talking with me, Raymond. I'll be sure to keep in touch with you." Sandy watched as her father walked Tyler to the door. "Good bye, Alexandra. I'll look forward to seeing you next week."

Without thinking she raised the hand holding the tomato in a casual wave. In a moment, Tyler Hamilton was gone.

When Mr. MacDonald turned to face his daughter, his eyes shone with suppressed laughter, but his voice was stern. "Come here, girl."

Sandy joined him in the doorway and stood quietly as he pulled a big handkerchief out of his pocket and wiped drying tomato juice off her chin. "Are you planning to grow up soon?'' he asked when he was finished.

"I'm working on it," she said with a sigh. "Don't give up on me yet, Daddy."

A quick squeeze was answer enough. Mr. Mac-Donald kept his arm around Sandy's shoulder as they walked into the hallway.

"Just why do you suppose that a man like Tyler Hamilton would want to get involved in a lawsuit against a powerful corporation?" she wondered out loud.

"I don't know, but I'm going to keep both eyes open," Mr. MacDonald observed quietly.

"I liked him, Daddy. He has style and quiet conviction. I'll bet he's doing it because he believes in it."

Mr. MacDonald stepped away from his daughter wondering, as he had countless times before, why God had blessed him with five beautiful young females to protect. He was never going to get a good night's sleep until he married the last one off, and at that moment there were still four to go. "Whoa, girl," he warned. "Tyler Hamilton is trouble where you're concerned."

Used to her father's worrying, Sandy gave him a big grin as she stood on tiptoe to peck his cheek. "You think everyone male is trouble where I'm concerned."

Mr. MacDonald shook his head. "Some are worse than others."

"And Tyler Hamilton is one of those?"

Sandy watched as her father straightened his shoulders. "There are Georgia folks and Georgia folks, honey. Folks like us have nothing to be ashamed of because we're the ones that have made Georgia grow and prosper. But it's folks like Tyler Hamilton who have done the prospering. Those folks stick together, Sandy. Don't ever forget it.'' Shaking his head again, Mr. MacDonald disappeared into the kitchen.

Sandy finished her tomato, replaying her father's words. Had he meant his comments in a general sense, referring to the possible lawsuit? Or was he warning his daughter not to become personally involved? Shutting her eyes for a minute she pictured Tyler Hamilton as he had looked sitting next to her on the sofa. The man was masculine grace, charisma and elegant charm wrapped up in a six-foot-two package, with the most arresting blue eyes she had ever seen. Tyler Hamilton was a force to be reckoned with.

Somehow, without understanding exactly why, Sandy was absolutely sure that her father's warning was already too late.

Chapter Two

"Then she swung her leg over the branch and hung upside down like a chimpanzee at the Atlanta Zoo." Randy was scooping up his black-eyed peas with cornbread and waving it over the table to make his point. "You should have seen Tyler Hamilton's face!"

"That's enough, Randy. You've managed to thoroughly embarrass your sister. Finish your dinner," Mrs. MacDonald instructed.

"Did it really happen like that?" Wendy MacDonald asked in her lilting voice. "Tell me you didn't behave like a thirteen-year-old hooligan in front of northern Georgia's prime bachelor."

"You make him sound like a cut of beef," Sandy said dryly, narrowing her eyes at her sister in warning. Discussing Tyler's bachelor status at the dinner table did not seem like a good idea, considering the feelings her father had already expressed on the subject. But Wendy's brown eyes were half-closed, and she completely missed her sister's signals.

"The things I've heard about Tyler Hamilton!" Wendy continued, running her fingers through her short white-gold curls as if she was unconsciously primping. "How could you have missed your chance with the most eligible man in this part of the state?"

"If I spent my life expecting to be introduced momentarily to an eligible man, I'd never get anything done. I'd have to spend all my time polishing my nails and simpering," Sandy replied sensibly. "Pass the chicken, please."

"Don't take the wing, I want the wing!" shrieked twelve-year-old Jennifer.

"It's my turn for a drumstick," James inserted.

"Save the other breast for your father, dear," Mrs. MacDonald said, raising her hand in the air to command silence.

Having changed the direction of the conversation, Sandy sat back and smiled. "Actually, I'm not really hungry, forget it."

But Wendy had been a MacDonald almost as long as Sandy, and she knew large-family survival tactics as well as her sister. She recognized the attempt to change the subject and she ignored it. "That's not true, you know. You don't have to simper to get male attention, you just have to be available."

"Wendy doesn't simper," seventeen-year-old Sarah pointed out calmly. "And half the men in Hall County are after her."

"Jealous, jealous!" chanted the four boys in unison.

This time Mrs. MacDonald banged her fist on the planks of the ten-foot redwood picnic table that was their sole dining-room furniture. "A little less noise, please. Boys, apologize to Sarah."

"We're sorry, Sarah," they chorused. Mrs. Mac-Donald rolled her eyes and resumed eating.

"I may get a lot of male attention," Wendy said, trying to smooth over the discussion, "but I've always thought it was because Sandy wouldn't give any of the local men the time of day." She smiled at her sister. "You always seem to be too busy."

Sandy smiled back in gratitude. Because she and Wendy were only nine months apart in age, Sandy had always felt especially close to her younger sister, who in many ways was more mature than she was. Although they were very different, there was a common bond of shared experiences and an unwavering loyalty between them.

"Are you sure Tyler Hamilton is a bachelor?" Mrs. MacDonald asked Wendy. "I just caught a glimpse of him, but he seems kind of old not to be married."

"His wife died several years ago. His name comes up in the Atlanta *Constitution* social column with regularity now."

"How do you remember all those details about strangers you don't even know?" Sandy asked with a sigh. "Can't we drop the subject of Tyler Hamilton, please?"

"Is that the same Hamilton that was about to run for the state legislature a couple of years ago?" Mrs. MacDonald went on, ignoring Sandy's request.

"They say he dropped out of the race when his wife got sick." Wendy raised her eyebrow at her sister. It was another signal of warning. If you protest too much, Wendy was telling Sandy, everyone's going to wonder why. Sandy bit her lip and kept silent.

"The Hamiltons own half of Georgia." Sarah was the quietly studious MacDonald. At age seventeen, she knew more about the way the universe worked and why than all the rest of the MacDonalds put together. Nothing ever got past Sarah. "They made their money in peanuts, lumber, real estate and tobacco. The town of Cameron revolves around them, and Tyler Hamilton could probably buy himself any political office he wanted anywhere in the state."

Sandy put her hands over her ears. "The FBI needs your talents, Sarah. By the way, has anybody heard anything from Stacey and Ryan lately?" This time her ploy worked. Talking about Stacey MacDonald Cunningham, her architect husband of two years, Ryan, and their four children, was everybody's favorite pastime. The Cunningham kids, who were really Ryan's orphaned nieces and nephews, were the only grandchildren that Raymond and Eldora had, and spoiling them was the MacDonald family's greatest pleasure.

Sandy listened as the conversation ping-ponged back and forth across the table. She was glad to be off the family hot seat. For some reason, chatting casually about Tyler Hamilton unnerved her. But looking up from her empty plate, she caught Wendy's eye.

"You might fool everyone else, but you don't fool me," Wendy said in a voice only Sandy could hear. "You don't fool me at all."

* * *

The town of Cameron was almost a two-hour drive
to the southeast of Sandy's home. On Monday morning she pulled her six-year-old Mustang into a parking spot on Main Street, directly in front of the law
firm of Hamilton and Stone. Before finding Tyler's
office, she had driven slowly through the picturesque
town, admiring the spacious, white-pillared houses in
what was obviously the original Cameron.

The newer sections were packed with brick ranch
houses separated by moderate-size yards, and Sandy
had discovered one housing development, Cameron
Estates, that gave new meaning to the phrase *nou-
veau riche*. On the outskirts of town she had passed
the inevitable ramshackle shanties complete with
patched tin roofs and chassis of rusting cars in the
front yard. Cameron was a town no different from
many others just like it throughout the South.

Stepping out of the car, Sandy paused to straighten
the gold cotton sweater and matching skirt that she
had carefully chosen for her meeting with Tyler. She
had braided her hair with extra care and had wrapped
the thick braids around her head and pinned them se-
curely. The reflection that stared back at her from the
rolled-up car window was disgustingly wholesome.
"Get me a dirndl and a couple of goats, and I could
pass for Heidi," she muttered.

Tyler's office was in a rose-colored brick building
that had once been a private residence. Carefully
tended shrubbery and flower beds softened the effect
of the wooden sign with neat black letters that adver-
tised the firm of Hamilton and Stone. Pausing on the

porch, Sandy took a deep breath before opening the door to step into the reception area.

"May I help you?"

Sandy admired the dark skin and shoulder-length curly hair of the young black woman at the receptionist's desk. "My name is Sandy MacDonald. I'm here to see Mr. Hamilton."

The woman reached for her appointment book. "Alexandra Macdonald?"

"That's right."

"Mr. Hamilton said to make you comfortable when you got here. Unfortunately, he's got someone with him right now. My name is Dorothy Carlin." Dorothy smiled in welcome.

"I'm happy to meet you."

"I'll be glad to show you around if you'd like."

Ten minutes later, the two women were chatting like old friends. Sandy had seen the law library, the conference room, the kitchen and all the offices except Tyler's. Matthew Stone, Tyler's partner, was out of town, but Sandy had been introduced to Mrs. Howell, a sixtyish woman with spectacles who examined Sandy minutely as they talked. Mrs. Howell ran the office, Dorothy informed Sandy as they walked back to the reception area. Somehow the crack legal secretary managed to take care of more typing and secretarial chores than any other three people could have managed.

After four years of classes, being in a real office with people who were doing meaningful work almost seemed like a vacation. "What an interesting place,"

Sandy told Dorothy. "I'll bet there's always something going..."

They were passing Tyler's office door, which was now ajar. Without meaning to draw attention to herself, Sandy lifted her eyes and found the elegant Georgian staring at her. There was a half smile twisting his aristocratic features, and he seemed to have stopped in the middle of a sentence too, because the man with him was asking, "What was that you said?"

For a moment, neither Tyler nor Sandy moved. As Sandy stood in the hallway, staring at him through the open door, her heart gave an uncharacteristic lurch. She smiled shyly and Tyler gave her a nodding salute before he turned back to his client. Passing on, she wondered why she felt so light-headed.

Minutes later she looked up from a copy of *The New Republic* to find Tyler standing patiently in front of her.

"How long have you been there?" she asked with chagrin.

"Long enough to wonder if you were the same young woman who hung by one leg out of a magnolia tree last week."

Sandy stood, smoothing her skirt over her stockinged legs. "I'm sorry, Mr. Hamilton, but you must have me confused with someone else. I just glide with ladylike grace over the veranda and drink tea with my pinkie crooked."

His smile was magnificent as he honored her words with flashing white teeth. For pure physical appeal, Tyler Hamilton was unbeatable.

"I think I'll miss the tree climber," he said, taking Sandy's arm to guide her into his office. "But veranda gliders have their place."

"How about law researchers?" she suggested.

"Have a seat, Alexandra." Tyler removed his hand, and with it, the friendly intimacy that had developed so quickly between them. Suddenly he was all business.

"The only person who ever calls me Alexandra is my father and then only when he's angry. Please call me Sandy," she said, watching him take his seat across the desk from her. She had expected something more casual, and suddenly she felt as though she was at a job interview.

"Is your father angry with you often, Sandy?"

"My father's my biggest fan," she answered candidly. "You know the story about the man who wanted a son and had a daughter so he makes her the son he never had?" She paused for a breath, and Tyler looked as though he was having trouble keeping a straight face. "Well I was the daughter of a father who already had a son, three in fact, and he was glad to have another daughter, but I decided sons had more fun, and so I . . ."

"Became his fourth son?"

"Definitely not!" she said, raising her eyebrows. "But with a little wheedling, I discovered that my father would let me help him with the chores instead of making me do the dishes with my sisters. We became very close milking all those cows, catching all those chickens."

"Catching chickens?"

"We have a broiler house. On a certain day in the chickens' life cycle you have to send them to market. They don't willingly fly into their coops, so you have to catch them by the neck. A professional chicken catcher can grab eleven in each hand."

"And your record is?"

"Ten. Five in each hand." Lowering her eyes to an imaginary speck of lint on her skirt, she continued. "You'd be a terrific chicken catcher. With those long fingers, you could beat my record easily."

"I'll file that away in case my law practice folds."

Sandy looked up again and treated Tyler to a wide grin. "But I didn't come here to educate you on the care and feeding of chickens. I came to offer my services for a while."

"Why?"

Tyler was leaning back in his desk chair, tapping a gold fountain pen on his leg, and he was examining her minutely. Sandy was surprised to find that she was enjoying the examination. She thought about his question awhile before answering. "I've always wanted to be a lawyer. I could have gone right on to law school, but the more I thought about it, the more I felt that I needed some practical experience."

"Why was that?"

"It seemed to me that a good lawyer is someone who knows her way around a little bit. If I had some experience, I could take advantage of my course work. I'd know what to study and the reasons why."

"Anything else?"

Sandy nodded her head, watching with mesmerized fascination as Tyler continued to bounce the pen on his thigh. The perfectly tailored gray suit pants were pulled tightly around his long legs, and she was torn between admiring the masculine attractions of his body and desiring to appear intelligent and professional. With effort she shifted her glance to his face, trying to remember what he had asked her.

"Anything else?" he repeated with his characteristic half smile.

"Well, to be honest, I also needed a break from school. I was on complete scholarship all four years, and I had to maintain a high grade average to continue getting it. Law school didn't sound like much of a rest."

"What was your average?"

One of the few things Sandy wasn't comfortable with was bragging about herself. She could feel her creamy skin tinting to a light apricot. "I graduated with a 3.9," she answered, picking the imaginary lint off her skirt.

Tyler whistled softly. "Very good."

"I was happy with it," she said, meeting his eyes again.

"Did all that work leave you with any time for a social life?"

Although the question seemed impertinent, Sandy realized that it was really quite relevant. "No," she admitted. "I lived at home while I went to school, so I helped out as much as I could on the farm. Between that and studying, I probably set a record as the most reclusive college student in history."

"Is that another reason for delaying law school?"

Sandy nodded, surprised at his perception. "When I come home from work, I'll be free to see people and have a life of my own. If I were in school, I'd come home and study."

"Is there a special man in your life to spend those extra hours with?"

This time, Sandy couldn't think of a reason for the personal question. She was thrown off balance, and she shrugged helplessly. "Would it matter? If there were, it wouldn't interfere with my research for you."

"Humor me."

"No. There's no one. I went to a women's college, and I'm not interested in any of the boys I grew up with."

"Tell me about school. What you liked and why."

Wondering why Tyler was taking so much time to interview a volunteer, Sandy gave him the information he was looking for. At least when she began her real job interviews, she would have had some practice.

"Dr. Hendrickson is a friend of mine," Tyler said, referring to the professor whom Sandy had just said she admired most. "Would you mind if I called her for a recommendation?"

"No, of course not," she answered. "But Mr. Hamilton..."

"Tyler."

Sandy smiled. "Tyler, are you always this conscientious when someone volunteers to do something for you? I can't even promise to help for very long. I'll need a job by summer."

"I'm offering you a job as my paralegal. If your references check out, that is."

Stunned, Sandy searched his face for the joke's punch line. But an assessment of Tyler's features indicated that he was not kidding. "Why on earth would you want to hire me?"

Tyler threw back his head and bellowed at her question. Not ever having expected to see the dignified Tyler Hamilton convulsed with laughter, Sandy was delighted that she had caused the remarkable transformation. "Well, that answers my question," she said when he sobered a little. "You need a comedienne in the office."

"I need an intelligent paralegal to take over some of Mrs. Howell's chores, and I think you're right for the job."

"If I ask why again, will I send you into hysterics?"

Tyler's piercing blue eyes were unguarded, and Sandy gulped a little at the devastating warmth of his smile. "Anyone who can climb up and down a sixty-foot magnolia tree in ninety-five seconds is the kind of person who can get things done," he answered finally.

"Thank you." Basking in the radiance of Tyler's smile, Sandy allowed herself the pleasure of imagining how nice it was going to be to work with him. Not until that moment had she admitted that she felt regret over her adolescent behavior at their first meeting. But despite her hoydenish antics, Tyler Hamilton still thought she had potential. She was going to be working with a first-class attorney and a terribly attractive one to boot.

Through the discussion of salary (generous) and job responsibilities (mammoth), Sandy felt the warm glow inside her igniting into outrageous excitement. She could hardly believe her good fortune. "Since the references are just a formality, let's brainstorm about possible living arrangements for you," Tyler said after they had finished with the details.

"I hadn't even thought of that."

"There's a new apartment building for singles that opened several months ago. There may still be a vacancy."

Sandy shook her head, trying to hide a smile, but Tyler, who like any good lawyer was sensitive to everything around him, caught the humor in her eyes. "Why was that funny?"

"Can you truly imagine my father allowing me to even set foot inside one of those apartments?"

"You're twenty-one. Legally you've been emancipated."

"That's one emancipation proclamation that my parents would fight to the death to abolish." The look on Tyler's face was proof that he still didn't understand, so Sandy went on. "Tyler, if I'm not married at age fifty, my parents will insist that they have a say in how I conduct my life. They're staunchly old-fashioned."

"And you agree?"

"We're very close. They only want the best for me."

Tyler made a steeple with his fingertips and rested his chin on them. "What do they want for you, Sandy?"

"A happy marriage, kids, a career if I want one." She began to be uncomfortable with his direct gaze but she continued to meet it. "My folks have very traditional values."

"I gather you've inherited them."

"I guess I have. My life certainly smacks of it."

"You should wear a warning sign then. You're going to frustrate an awful lot of young men."

Sandy guessed that she had just been complimented, but she wasn't sure she liked it. Before she could come up with a reply, Tyler was standing, and she stood too, assuming the interview was at a close.

"Would you like a walking tour of downtown Cameron?"

Sandy had intended to take one on her own, but having Tyler as a tour guide was definitely an improvement on her plan. "I'd like that."

For the next hour they strolled through the streets, with Tyler pointing out places of interest and Sandy filing away the information she heard. She learned where to shop and where to mail her letters, where to do her laundry and where to have an ice cream soda. Tyler waited while she flirted with the puppies in the pet shop window, and Sandy waited while countless people stopped to pass the time of day with him.

There was a certain quality of deference in the way that Tyler was treated by the town's inhabitants. Although no one actually fawned over him, there was respect in their soft Southern voices. It was a universal reaction, true of rich and poor, young and old, male and female. With the females, however, there was something more.

"Tyler," Sandy said casually, as they turned down a side street lined with classic Southern colonial houses that had survived the passage of a century. "I've never seen so much Scarlett O'Hara charm displayed in my whole life."

"I gather you're not talking about these houses."

"Well, honey," she mimicked in perfect imitation of the last fading belle they had encountered. "How fortunate for you that Tyler, *heah*, would be the one to *hiah* you. You'll be the envy of *hey-af* the women in Cameron."

"Cameron is a small town, and I'm a bachelor. The combination can be lethal."

"Well, if you're not serious," she said, tongue in cheek, "then you should wear a warning sign or you'll frustrate an awful lot of young women."

Tyler's laughter rumbled through the empty street and for just a second, he put his hand on Sandy's shoulder in appreciation. "I deserved that."

At the last house on the end of the short block, Tyler stopped, turning to face Sandy for a moment. "How would you like to live here?"

She examined the stately old home. It was huge and white, like most of the houses on the street, with square pillars at regular intervals around the wraparound porch and leaded glass panes in every window. The house was in better condition than some they had passed, with a neat yard planted with azaleas and camellias. The one thing that made the house unique was the row of rabbit hutches on the front portion of the porch. "What do you mean?"

"My Aunt Charlotte lives here by herself. She's quite a character, but somehow I think you'll like her."

Tyler seemed to be filled with strange compliments. Sandy waited for the rest of the explanation.

"Aunt Charlotte is still going strong, but I think she'd like to have your company and perhaps some help with her animals."

"Animals?"

"Let's see. At last count she had four cats, the rabbits—" he swept his hand in front of him to indicate the hutches "—a blind cocker spaniel, six parakeets and a boa constrictor, Julius Squeezer."

"And mice to feed Julius."

"Of course."

Sandy knew immediately that she had found a home. "Does she know about me?"

"I mentioned you this weekend. She seemed pleased with the idea."

"I'd love to meet her."

"There are no trees suitable to climb," Tyler pointed out, his light blue eyes sparkling with humor.

"I'll swing sedately from the chandeliers."

Aunt Charlotte was a silver-haired eccentric with Tyler's blue eyes and a cane that she swung back and forth to accent every syllable she spoke. Since Tyler had last visited, a trio of guinea pigs had been added to her menagerie and Tyler and Sandy were called on to visit every animal and exclaim over its virtues.

Although the house was filled with pets, it was immaculately clean, and after the animal visitation rights had been performed, Aunt Charlotte gave Sandy a tour. Originally built for a large family with live-in servants, the house was big enough to get lost in. By the time they progressed to the second floor, Aunt Charlotte had offered Sandy a room, and Sandy had happily accepted.

"Will this one do?" Aunt Charlotte flung open the door of a room that was almost as big as the entire upstairs of the Macdonald farmhouse. Blue-and-white flowered wallpaper covered the walls and the high ceilings were painted blue to match. There were floor to ceiling windows leading out onto a small balcony, and the resulting view of Cameron was charming.

"I love it."

"It's yours."

Tea and sandwiches provided by Aunt Charlotte's elderly maid finished off the visit. Sandy expected Tyler to hurry away, but visiting with his aunt seemed to be as important to him as his law practice. He listened to the old woman's comments with apparent fondness.

"She liked you," Tyler told Sandy as they were walking back to his office.

"She's wonderful. I hope I'll be that charming when I'm seventy."

"Eighty. Aunt Charlotte is my father's half-sister and the bane of his existence."

"Why?"

"He wants her to move into a retirement home and sell the house. It's their old family home and Aunt Charlotte refuses."

"Good for her!"

"I can see you two will get along."

Too soon they were standing on Main Street in front of Sandy's Mustang. "Thank you for everything, Tyler. The job, the place to live, the time you've spent with me."

"You're not difficult to spend time with."

"Well, thank you," she said, lifting her head to smile at his words. She was surprised when he moved closer to stand within touching distance.

"You look very different with your hair up." His hand brushed a wispy curl from her face before he lightly touched her coronet of braids.

"Do I look old enough to be in high school?" she asked, remembering the comment she had overheard at their first meeting. Her body was reacting to his casual touch with a series of delicious little tremors, and she was trying to be grown-up about it.

"So you heard that."

She nodded, smiling to show she wasn't upset.

"Yes, you look old enough to be in high school. But no older."

"Just think what a raving beauty I'll be at Aunt Charlotte's age then."

"You don't have to wait that long. You're a lovely girl."

Tyler Hamilton definitely had a way with words. But as nice as the compliment was, Sandy felt the need to change one word. "Woman. I'm a woman, not a girl."

"Define your terms." Tyler leaned casually against the door of her car, and Sandy knew immediately that correcting an excellent lawyer had not been a good idea.

"I'm twenty-one, old enough to drink and vote. That makes me a woman."

As his blue eyes swept her body, Sandy knew that she had just lost her first case. "If you think that's what makes you a woman, Sandy," he drawled, "then you're more of an innocent than I thought."

"I have a feeling that being 'more of an innocent than you thought' is impossible."

Tyler laughed, obviously enjoying the apricot blush that was tinting her cheeks again. "I shouldn't tease you."

"Actually," she admitted, "I like to see you laugh. Your whole face lights up."

The moment was surprisingly intimate as a number of moments throughout the long morning had been. For just a second, Sandy forgot that Tyler Hamilton was her new boss and, therefore, completely off limits for her. They stood close together, a man and a woman very aware of each other.

Finally she pulled herself away from his gaze. "I'd better go," she murmured.

"I'll call you on Wednesday about your references."

"I'll look forward to hearing from you."

Tyler waited until she was in her car before he waved and walked away. Sandy watched him disappear through the door of the law office as she backed up to pull out of her parking space. She had come to Cameron as a volunteer researcher, and she was leaving with a paid position in Tyler's law firm. But along with that startling realization came another.

Sandy knew that working with Tyler Hamilton was not going to be easy. There was an attraction between them that she couldn't deny or ignore. Although Tyler was much too well-bred to chase her around his desk, Sandy knew that unless the faint sparks that were kindling between them were stamped out, her plans would be in jeopardy. Tyler Hamilton was a man she could lose her heart to, and with it, her new job.

Resolving not to let that happen, Sandy pulled out into the light traffic. She had a two-hour drive ahead of her, and she was sure she'd need every second of it to talk herself into believing that Tyler Hamilton was not the most attractive man she had ever met.

Chapter Three

"Do you really think you'll need five pairs of blue jeans in Cameron?" Wendy lifted a particularly disreputable patched piece of denim in the air and waved it under Sandy's nose.

"What else will I fill my suitcases with?" Sandy answered sensibly. The phone call from Tyler Hamilton had come. He had checked her references, approved them and asked her to start work immediately. Sandy had spent the previous day selecting books to fill her room in Aunt Charlotte's house, and now she was finishing up her packing by stuffing what clothing she had into two worn suitcases.

"Take some of my clothes. I have more than enough for both of us." Wendy went to the closet and began to pull perfectly coordinated skirts and blouses out of the closet. "Here, these will look better on you, anyway."

"Don't be silly. I'm not taking your things."

Wendy ignored her sister, carefully folding three outfits and neatly packing them in the second half-filled suitcase. "All those hours I was learning to sew, you were out hoeing corn with the boys. Think of this as your reward."

Sandy watched as Wendy discarded three of the blue jeans, refolded another dress that had already been packed, and began to list the necessities that Sandy would have to buy before Monday when her job began. "What am I going to do without you?" Sandy asked.

"You'll only be two hours away. And we're expecting you to come home on weekends. Whatever happened to the brown leather purse I gave you for Christmas last year?"

Sandy dug through the back of her closet, pulling out the purse, a forgotten sweater and two unmatched slippers. "I kept saving it for a special occasion," she said as an apology to her sister as she flopped down on her bed. "Are you going to miss me?"

"You know I am."

"I'm a college graduate, and the only time I've been away from home was in high school for our senior trip to Atlanta."

Wendy sat on the twin bed, too, and tucked an errant strand of hair back into Sandy's braid. "It's time then, don't you think?"

"You'd like to take my place, wouldn't you?"

Sandy watched Wendy's curly head nod a scant inch. "But it's not time for me yet. I've still got three years before I graduate. Then I'll be gone so fast everyone will wonder what that gust of wind passing by was." There was no self-pity in Wendy's soft voice, only determination.

"Is home such a bad place to be?"

"Being with people you love is never bad. It's just that I want something different from this." Her hand swept the room, but Sandy knew that the encompassing motion referred to the house, the farm, rural Georgia and the provincial life they led. Wendy was an exquisite butterfly who was not happy being asked to live the life of a honeybee.

"One by one, we all move on. First the older boys, then Stacey." Sandy played with the ends of her braids thoughtfully. "So far I'm the only one who's had to be dragged kicking and screaming into maturity. For two cents, I'd climb to the top of the magnolia and stage a sit-down strike."

"You've never liked change." Wendy pulled Sandy's braid out of her hand and tugged on it. "A prime example."

"Think I should chop them off?"

Wendy gasped and shook her head. "One change at a time, please. Just be sure you remember to wrap them around your head on weekday mornings."

There was a noisy toot followed by another and another in the yard below. Sandy jumped off the bed and loped to the window, throwing it open to stick her entire head out. "Stacey!" she shouted. She motioned for Wendy to join her. "Stacey, Ryan!"

Doors to the blue van below flew open and four small bodies flung themselves into the yard. "Aunt Sandy! Aunt Wendy!"

"Did you know they were coming?" Sandy asked Wendy as she closed the window in preparation for a hurried flight down the stairs to join the gathering family in the front yard.

"Ma told me last night. They're on their way to their cabin in North Carolina for the weekend, and they wanted to surprise you since you're going to be moving Saturday."

In the yard below, hugs were being exchanged and excited children were leaping up and down, indiscriminately grabbing the person nearest them. Sandy squatted at the edge of the crowd talking to four-year-old Christy, Stacey's and Ryan's youngest child. The little girl was a petite picture of health, and Sandy was admiring her newly expanded vocabulary.

"I could eat you up, Christy," she said, giving the tiny child yet another hug.

"How about one of those for her father?"

Sandy stood to give Ryan a bear hug, ending by rumpling his dark brown curls. "You're all looking terrific," she proclaimed with a big grin.

"And you have turned into another blooming Georgia beauty," he said, holding Sandy away for a moment to examine her carefully. "Any man wanting to marry into this family has quite a choice, doesn't he?"

"Don't let your wife hear you say that," came a musical voice from behind them, and Sandy turned to throw herself into Stacey's arms.

"Stacey!" The two young women hugged, oblivious of the noise and confusion around them. Finally Sandy pulled away to give her sister the once-over. "You're even more beautiful," she marveled. "How do you do it?"

"I'll tell you my secret later," Stacey promised.

Later came after everyone had been properly greeted. Sandy and Wendy helped their mother serve endless glasses of iced tea and pieces of Mrs. MacDonald's special pecan pie. In the melee, Sandy kept her eye on her oldest sister, watching the looks she exchanged with Ryan and the excuses they found to touch each other.

Stacey and Ryan had married after a whirlwind courtship. There had been times at the beginning of their marriage when Sandy had wondered if the wedding had been a mistake, but now there was no question about that. The love they felt for each other was so obvious that, watching them together, Sandy almost felt like an intruder. When Ryan bent to brush a quick kiss on the top of Stacey's honey-blond hair, Sandy felt with a deep certainty that if the man she fell in love with ever looked at her the way Ryan looked at Stacey, she would be the happiest woman alive.

"Sandy?" Stacey asked, catching Sandy's eye.

Sandy smiled at her sister and held out her hand. "I'm going upstairs to finish packing," she told her. "Can you come up for a few minutes?"

Although Sandy and Stacey were only three years apart, separated by a brother, Jerry, who was now in the Coast Guard in New England, their relationship had always held overtones of mother to child. As the oldest girl, Stacey had been second mother to all the younger children, enjoying her nurturing role in a family where everyone pitched in to help when they could. Now Stacey had four children of her own to nurture, but she still managed to be available to Sandy for advice.

"Coming home is so strange," Stacey mused as she sat on the bed and watched Sandy drop odds and ends of clothing on top of the neat piles Wendy had made. "Nothing has changed, and yet of course everything really has. I feel like I'm in a time warp."

"Please, I'm having enough problems with leaving," Sandy pleaded. "Tell me it's going to be okay."

"More than okay. It's going to be spectacular. And home will always be here for you. We'll all be here for you."

"Did you feel this way when you left?"

Stacey shook her head, her hazel eyes lighting up with private memories. "Not when I left home, when I got married. I was scared to death."

"Well, I'm sure glad you went through with it. I've never seen you look so happy." Sandy sat on the bed next to Stacey and patted her on the knee. "Tell me your secret."

"I'm pregnant."

Sandy was stunned, staring at Stacey as though she had announced that she had just grown a new head.

"No one in the family knows but you," Stacey said with a glorious smile. "I'm going to tell Ma and Daddy tonight. Think they'll be pleased?"

"Ecstatic. But how did it happen?"

Stacey laughed and patted her sister's hand. "Sandy, if you don't know how it happened, I'd better have a long talk with you before you move away."

"I'm so happy for you," Sandy said, sniffing as a tear trickled down her cheek. "I've never been happier in my life."

"Then you knew," Stacey said quietly. "You knew that the doctors told me I probably wouldn't ever be able to have children."

Sandy nodded, turning her hand palm up to grasp Stacey's fingers and thread her own through them. "Ma told Wendy and me. She didn't want us blurting out anything stupid at your wedding. But the doctors were wrong, Stacey. They were wrong!"

"Not wrong exactly. They just told me that my chances were very small. When I married Ryan, he didn't care if I was infertile. We have our children and neither of us cared that they hadn't come from our bodies. So I just ignored the whole issue until last month."

"What happened?"

"Ryan made an appointment with a fertility specialist in Miami. He decided that we ought to know exactly what the chances were and whether microsurgery would be helpful. He's very satisfied with the four kids, but he didn't want me to miss out on being pregnant if it was a possibility."

"And the doctor operated?"

"He didn't need to. I was already six weeks pregnant."

The two sisters hugged, Sandy's tears dampening Stacey's cotton blouse. "Do the kids know?"

"Not yet, we're going to tell them tonight along with everybody else."

"Do you know how lucky you are?" Sandy asked, pushing away to search Stacey's face.

"Yes." They smiled into each other's eyes for a long moment. "Sandy," Stacey added finally, "someday you're going to meet and marry the right man, too."

Sandy flipped her braids over her shoulder, wondering why Tyler Hamilton's picture filled her mind at Stacey's words. "I want a career," she said, staunchly attempting to ignore her subconscious.

"You can have both," Stacey pointed out, reading Sandy's face like the open book it always was. "Who's the man, Sandy?"

Sandy shook her head, but she couldn't miss the opportunity to ask for advice. "Stacey, do you ever worry about the age difference between yourself and Ryan?"

"Never." Stacey waited patiently, finally sighing and patting her sister's knee. "Who's the man, Sandy?"

"My new boss," Sandy answered, meekly giving up the fight. She was used to the fact that there were never any secrets in the MacDonald family. "He's very attractive and I just wondered about the difference in our ages, but there's really no reason to wonder because..."

Stacey's smile stopped Sandy cold. "Tyler Hamilton is a terribly attractive man and you're a beautiful woman. You're right to wonder. But I'd say the age difference is the least of your problems, honey."

"What should I be worrying about then? I'd hate to think I was wasting my time worrying about the wrong things when there are better things to worry about."

"The differences in your experience and life-style are going to be more important than your ages. Tyler's only in his early thirties, after all."

Sandy realized that Stacey was speaking as if she knew Tyler Hamilton. "Tell me how you know all this."

Stacey leaned back against the pillows and curled up with her hand behind her head. "When I was Miss Gainesville, I had to go to countless parties to represent the community. Mrs. Hamilton, Tyler's mother, was at a lot of them because she was active in the Cameron beauty pageant. She introduced me to Tyler and his wife, Kay, at one of the parties. They were such a striking couple that I've never forgotten."

Sandy digested Stacey's words, wondering if she could safely ask anything more without appearing to be too interested. As if she sensed Sandy's concern, Stacey went on.

"At the time, I didn't know that Kay was dying. She was tall and blond, very poised. I remember that Tyler hovered over her and, of course, later I understood why. At the time, the most interesting thing was that they both seemed to be cut from the same bolt of cloth. Old Georgia warp and woof. Dignified, refined, with flawless manners and just the right amount of warmth."

"You're warning me, aren't you?" Sandy asked quietly.

"No. I'm telling you what I know."

The two women were silent for a moment, thinking about Tyler Hamilton. "Wouldn't I make a fabulous politician's wife?" Sandy asked, making an effort to treat Stacey's information lightly. "I could climb trees at all the political barbecues, wear my blue jeans to afternoon teas..."

"You're probably just what Tyler Hamilton needs," Stacey said. "But be careful, honey. You're going to be so easy for some man to hurt."

"Not me. I'm going to be a hard-as-nails attorney with a facade no one can crack with an icepick."

Stacey examined the gamine face and sparkling green eyes so close to her own, and her heart twisted at the innocence she saw. "Ah, but it's not the ice-picks I'm worried about, honey," she answered with wistful sadness. "It's the kisses that are going to get to you. It's always going to be the kisses."

Sandy thought about her sister's words after Stacey had been dragged off to spend time with other family members. If the small chance existed that Stacey was right and Sandy was vulnerable to a man like Tyler Hamilton, she was sure she was still as safe as a baby in a cradle. There would be no kisses exchanged, no careless seductions to resist. Tyler Hamilton was her boss. That was all the protection she needed.

"So calm down, heart, and do as you're told," she whispered to herself as she sat on a full suitcase and snapped the lock shut. "When it's safe for you to beat faster, I'll let you know. Until then, it's business as usual."

* * *

On Saturday afternoon, with her Mustang packed to the limit, Sandy pulled up in front of the Southern colonial house that was to become her home. "Hello, Aunt Charlotte," Sandy said when the old woman opened her door to find her new boarder with a cardboard crate of books in her capable hands. "I hope Tyler told you that I was coming this afternoon."

Swinging her cane, Aunt Charlotte followed Sandy through the house. "Yes, he certainly did. Said he'd be here to help you unload if he could get away. He's got some sort of 'to-do' over at City Hall this afternoon. Anniversary of somebody or something."

The two women chatted, Aunt Charlotte keeping up with Sandy's fast pace as though she was a big city jogger. Pushing her door open, Sandy admired the room again, noticing the addition of several comfortable pieces of furniture and a tall wire cage. She stopped in front of the cage, setting the book crate at her feet. "Aunt Charlotte, you shouldn't have."

"He liked you. I could tell."

Julius Squeezer stared out at the two women, his three-foot scaly body drooped comfortably over a long branch. "Do you really think so?" Sandy wondered out loud. "I couldn't tell."

"I'm sure of it."

Spontaneously, Sandy hugged her new landlady, and the two women stood together watching Julius wave his head back and forth. "I think you're right," Sandy agreed finally. "I think he's trying to let me know he likes being in here."

"Next there'll be rabbits and cats, then before you know it, Aunt Charlotte will have installed a horse in your closet." The deep male voice came from the doorway, and with pleasure Sandy turned to see Tyler leaning against the door frame, arms folded as he watched the two women.

"You're as bad as your father," Aunt Charlotte said airily, swinging her cane in Tyler's direction.

"Not a chance." Pushing away from the door frame, Tyler walked toward the cage and stood nonchalantly by Sandy's side. "Welcome to Cameron, Sandy."

Glad that she was wearing her best blue jeans and a kelly-green shirt that made her eyes seem as though they were the same color, Sandy smiled shyly. "Thank you, Tyler."

"Every time I see you, this is different," he said, lifting an impossibly long strand of hair that Sandy had caught into a simple pony tail before leaving her parents' house. As Tyler bent to kiss his aunt on the cheek, Sandy watched the old woman's face light up. It was obvious that Aunt Charlotte adored her nephew, and Sandy was having no trouble understanding why.

Tyler was wearing a dark blue suit with a conservative cranberry-colored tie and a crisp white shirt. At the farm Sandy had tried to tell herself that Tyler wasn't as good looking as she had thought, but now, seeing him again, she had to admit that he really was. In fact he was even better looking than she remembered. The blue suit emphasized his eyes and the silver strands just beginning to streak his thick dark hair.

"I noticed that your car still has a few books in it," Tyler told Sandy, smiling lazily as he caught her investigating eyes.

"Did I hear that you were here to help?" she murmured, wishing that Tyler had some fatal flaw she could single out and dwell on.

"Just tell me all those boxes aren't full of books."

"All of them aren't. Some of them are filled with my priceless rock collection."

"Rock and roll?"

"Rock and stone."

"Thank heavens!" Aunt Charlotte said gratefully, vacating the room as Tyler groaned.

"Don't feel you have to carry anything," Sandy addressed Tyler sweetly. "Of course if I'm not in first thing on Monday you can check the local hospital to find out where to send flowers."

Three boxes of books later, Sandy was exhausted, and she sat on the floor unpacking as Tyler continued to bring in box after box. Six boxes later, Tyler took off his coat and tie, unbuttoned the top two buttons of his shirt and rolled up his shirt sleeves. Sandy watched in fascination as his almost-black hair swung over his forehead, which was faintly beaded with perspiration. Rumpled, he was gorgeous.

"Too informal?" he asked, watching Sandy's fleeting expression of awe.

"Come off it, Tyler," she said, determined to make a joke of her transparent admiration. "You must know there are women who would kill for a man who looks like you."

His answer was a heart-melting grin that threatened to wipe the teasing smile right off her face. It seemed that no matter what she said or did, Tyler Hamilton came out on top.

"Do you know what my only reservation about hiring you was?" he asked, dropping to the pile of books at Sandy's feet and stretching out comfortably beside her.

"You were afraid I was too dainty to stomach legal work."

"I was afraid that working beside you every day was going to test my self-control to the limits."

"I'll try not to make mistakes or embarrass you," she said meekly.

"Are you trying to misunderstand me?"

After falling prey to his grin, Sandy had managed to avoid meeting Tyler's eyes, but his remark forced a visual confrontation. The teasing was over, and this was certainly not a scolding. The air between them vibrated with unformed energy. "Please be direct," she said softly.

"All right. I find you very attractive. Maintaining a strictly professional relationship is not going to be easy. But I decided that it was the very worst kind of sexism not to hire you just because you're young and beautiful and so full of life I can almost touch it."

"Why are you telling me this?" Sandy asked in a small voice.

"Because I think you're attracted to me, too, and I wanted us to clear the air." Tyler put two fingers under her chin and tipped her head back so that she was forced to look at him again. "I'm not going to take advantage of your feelings or act on my own. You have nothing to worry about."

She wanted to protest that deep down inside she was worried he wouldn't take advantage of her, but wisely, she kept silent and nodded her head.

As if the conversation had never occurred, Tyler picked up one of the books at his feet and began to leaf through it. "Isn't this rather heavy reading material for a girl who wants to relax a little?"

The book was a text entitled *A History of United States Law in the Decade 1910—1920*. Sandy had an entire series beginning with the nineteenth century that she had gotten at an estate sale. "You should know if it's heavy. You carried it in."

Tyler peered in the unopened box at his feet and groaned. "When I moved my own law library, I hired men to do it for me."

"I'm sorry," Sandy apologized. "While I'm working for you, I intend to study in some of my spare time. Then when I get to law school, it won't be so difficult."

"You're quite a determined young lady, aren't you?"

"I'm not a bit afraid of going after what I want." She thought about her words and realized that they only extended to her professional goals. At least one of the other things she wanted was entirely too frightening to pursue.

"Tell me, when most of your contemporaries are floundering around trying to decide what to be when they grow up, how did you get to be so single-minded?"

"I grew up on hard work. A lot of my contemporaries didn't." She turned a little to watch Tyler as she talked. If they were never to be more than boss and employee, at least she could still enjoy looking at him. "In our family the Protestant work ethic made sense. If we all pitched in, we survived and prospered. All the kids, at least so far, have made something out of themselves as adults, and I think it's because of the way we were raised."

"Tell me about your brothers and sisters."

"Do you have a few hours?"

Tyler laughed and patted her knee casually. "A quick sketch will do."

"Greg's twenty-seven and the oldest. He's married to a local woman, Sue, who was his high-school sweetheart. They have a small farm near ours, but they both work in town. Next year they hope to be self-sufficient and start a family."

"Are you next?"

Sandy shook her head. "There's Thomas next. He's out in Washington state managing an apple orchard. He married recently and his wife is half-Indian. We can't wait to meet her. Then comes Stacey, who's the oldest girl." She stopped, wondering if Tyler would remember meeting Stacey. "Actually, you've met her. She was Miss Gainesville about five years ago."

Tyler wrinkled his brow in concentration. "Describe her."

"Stacey's beautiful," Sandy said with pride. "Honey-colored hair and hazel eyes with a real Georgia peaches-and-cream complexion."

"She came close to winning the Miss Georgia title, didn't she?"

Sandy nodded. "First runner-up."

"I remember." With a hand on either side of Sandy's face, he turned her head as if examining her for similarities to her sister. "Your hair is lighter, and your eyes are definitely green, not hazel. But I'll bet the skin tones are the same."

Embarrassed by the close scrutiny, Sandy looked away. "All the MacDonald girls resemble each other. But each of us is unique."

"You are definitely unique," Tyler agreed, caressing her cheek with his thumb before he dropped his hands.

In a daze Sandy went on to tell him about the rest of her siblings, finishing up with Jennifer. "At age twelve she still hasn't outgrown her ambition to be a bareback rider in the circus."

"She sounds the most like you."

"She was always my pet. I used to pretend that Jennifer was my baby."

"You like kids then?"

"You can't grow up in our family without liking kids. Even Wendy, who swears she doesn't want any of her own, likes kids."

"I think I envy all of you. What a wonderful, unfettered childhood you had."

"It's interesting that you would see it that way. Most people think we were terribly fettered. No privacy, no long vacations or luxuries that others take for granted. Just plenty of good food, hard work and love."

"I grew up with all the privacy and luxuries one person could stand. I'm not sure it's the best way to raise children."

"Were you an only child?"

Tyler laughed at Sandy's tone. "You know, if you had asked me if I was an escaped convict, you would have done it just that way."

"I'm sorry," she said, blushing a little. "My prejudices always show."

"You'll have to work on that before you hit a courtroom."

"I know."

"Yes, I was an only child, an unexpected one at that. My parents had given up hope of having children, so when I came along, they lavished every possible luxury on me."

"You don't seem spoiled. Are you?"

"I almost always get what I want. But I have such excellent manners, it doesn't show."

Sandy shivered a little. Death had cheated this man out of at least one thing that he had wanted. She wondered what effect his wife's death had on his life now. "You're certainly successful enough," she agreed carefully.

"And if that's how you measure life's quality, then I guess I have what everyone wants."

Sandy watched an expression of such utter bleakness cross Tyler's aristocratic features that she wanted to throw herself into his arms and comfort him. Instead, she put her hand on his shoulder for a moment, in silent recognition of what he had just unconsciously shared. He looked at her with surprise as if he couldn't believe that she had understood his feelings.

"Thank you for helping me today, Tyler," she said, casually removing her hand. "I think I'm going to like it here."

"And we're going to like having you here," he answered. The words were absolutely correct, but Sandy understood that behind them was a mixture of confusing feelings. She watched as Tyler stood and brushed off his pants.

"I'll get the suitcases, myself," she said, following him to the door. "You've done enough."

"They're at the bottom of the stairs. I think the car is all cleared out."

He stood aside as Sandy preceded him down the staircase. Stopping at the bottom, she lifted both suitcases easily and stood beside him. "Thanks again," she said with a smile.

Tyler bent and brushed a kiss across her cheek. It was done with such lazy Southern gallantry that Sandy could not find any reason for the rush of excitement that culminated in a blush on her cheeks where his lips had been. "Have a good weekend," he drawled. "I'll see you first thing Monday morning."

She watched as he walked into the living room where she could hear Aunt Charlotte talking to one of her cats. Promising herself to have another instructive session with her speeding heart, Sandy turned and trudged slowly up the stairs.

Chapter Four

Sandy found that late June in Cameron seemed to be cooler than June on her parents' farm had been. Perhaps, she decided, it was because she sat in air-conditioning all day instead of sweltering outside in the overheated air. Whatever it was, she found herself walking back and forth to work every day just to experience summer's delights and tortures.

In the month that she had been at Hamilton and Stone, Sandy had devised a routine before work that had become as much of a ritual as anything in her life. She rose every morning, fed the rabbits and guinea pigs, cleaned their cages and then progressed to the mice. She always lavished special attention on the tiny white creatures, since they eventually came to such an infamous end. Aunt Charlotte took care of feeding Julius Squeezer, even though he was housed in Sandy's room, and Sandy resolutely ignored the fact that on some mornings, the mice cage was conspicuously less crowded and Julius was conspicuously fatter.

After showering and changing for work, Sandy would sit on the balcony, untangling her long hair as she watched the town of Cameron wake up. Across the street lived a family blessed with three teenage boys, and Sandy always waved as they came through the door, pushing and shoving to see who could be the first one down the steps. The oldest boy, a likely-looking young man of sixteen who reminded her of James and Randy, always shouted something funny, and Sandy was beginning to suspect that he had a crush on her. It made her feel very old.

When her hair was neatly braided and coiled around her head, Sandy went to find Aunt Charlotte to spend a few minutes with her before she began the walk to work. Sandy had developed a special place in her heart for Tyler's aunt. Instinctively she felt a kinship with her, hoping that when she was eighty years old, she too would be full of life and eccentric to boot.

On the way to work Sandy invariably made three stops. The first was the newspaper stand, because Aunt Charlotte refused to have the paper delivered. Rabbit hutches on the porch were all right, but newspapers on the porch were low-class. After exchanging gossip with the proprietor of the stand, Sandy always took the paper to the drugstore where she had coffee and toast and read the front page and funnies.

There was a regular group of people who were always at the drugstore when she arrived, and Sandy had become involved in their lives, teasing, laughing at their antics and offering advice when it was warranted. When she finished there, she followed the sidewalk to the pet shop where the owner was, without fail, washing the front window or sweeping the sidewalk under the gaily striped awning. They always chatted, and the old man reported on the new additions to his stock so that Sandy could carry the news to Aunt Charlotte that night.

By the time she reached the door of Hamilton and Stone, Sandy had made contact with almost a dozen people. Cameron felt like home.

Inside the office her feeling of acceptance changed to one of cautious withdrawal. Sandy had made firm friends with the receptionist, Dorothy Carlin, and even the stern-faced Mrs. Howell had warmed up nicely. It was Tyler Hamilton and Matthew Stone who presented the problems.

True to his word, Tyler treated Sandy in the most professional manner possible. He was businesslike, remote, and usually shut tight in his office. In the four weeks she had worked for him, there had never once been a return of the intimacy that had touched their first meetings. At work, Tyler was all dignified attorney. And after work, Sandy never saw him at all unless it was from a distance. When she did catch sight of him, he was invariably escorting a beautiful woman. There had been no occasion for Sandy to lecture her speeding heart again.

Matthew Stone was an entirely different problem. Older than Tyler, Matthew was a big man with curling hair and large square hands that continually found a reason to rest casually on Sandy's shoulders. He was an excellent lawyer but an even better flirt, and he was also quite married. Had he been ten years younger and a bachelor, Sandy would not have been interested. As it was, Matthew's advances were anathema. No matter how promising her walks to work were, if she opened the door and realized that Matthew was going to be in the office that day, her heart always sank.

On this day, after her morning ritual had been completed, Sandy opened the office door and found Matthew waiting for her. "Well," he drawled in his gravelly voice, "it's little Miss Summertime."

"Hello, Mr. Stone," she said evenly.

"When are you going to call me Matthew, honey?"

"When you stop calling me honey, Mr. Stone." Sandy looked past the lawyer's bulky body to catch Dorothy's wink. "Will you excuse me?" She tried to move quickly around him, but his hand on her arm stopped her.

"You need to friendly up a little, honey."

"You need to friendly down a little, Mr. Stone." Sandy could feel the tension building up inside her. Certain that Stacey or Wendy would know just what to say to send this maddening man on his way, Sandy felt very inept. She was beginning to have dreams where she found graphic ways to punish Matthew for giving her trouble. Her favorite centered around a whip and a chair.

"Quick on the draw, aren't you?" He let go of Sandy's arm and patted her on the shoulder. "Be a good girl and get me some coffee."

Since getting Matthew coffee was the least of her problems with him, Sandy gracefully complied, adding just enough extra sugar to make it undrinkable.

She was setting it on his desk when Tyler entered the room. "Matthew, have you..."

"Hello, Tyler. Last time I saw Mr. Stone he was heading down the hall to the library."

"Hello, Sandy." Tyler stopped and examined her. She was wearing an outfit Wendy had given her that was cool and comfortable and just a little bit unprofessional. The raspberry dress with tiny straps was covered with a pink linen jacket, but the neckline was still more revealing than it should have been. If she had thought about Matthew Stone when she had put it on that morning, it would have remained in her closet. Tyler didn't seem to mind, however. "Don't you look lovely." he said.

It was the first personal comment Tyler had made in a month, and Sandy was stunned. "Thank you."

"Sandy, I'd like you to go to lunch with me today. Will you be able to?"

She nodded, wondering if one skimpy dress had wrought this miracle. Before she could come to any conclusions, Matthew came strolling into the room. "Ty, old man. Admiring our girl, here?" Matthew affectionately clapped Tyler on the back. "She's a beauty, isn't she?"

Sandy promptly relegated the miracle dress to the back of her closet and silently vowed to come to work in high collars and long sleeves. "What time, Tyler?"

"Around one o'clock." Tyler turned to Matthew. "Can you come to lunch with us then? I want to talk about the Lanier Chemical case, and I don't have any other time available."

Sandy's heart sank as Matthew gave an obscene grin and nod. "Only if I get to sit next to Little Miss Summertime."

"Since there are only three of us," Sandy pointed out coldly, "I hardly think there's a chance you won't." Head high, she walked out of the office to the sound of Matthew's booming laughter.

The rest of the morning passed without incident since both lawyers were continuously involved with clients. Sandy caught sight of a young divorcée who seemed to spend an inordinate amount of time seeking Tyler's counsel, and an old black man who shuffled into Tyler's office with the help of a walking stick and Tyler's strong arm.

Sandy was busy with her own work. Tyler had assigned much of the mundane research for the Lanier Chemical case to her, and she had tenaciously gone after facts, often giving him more information than he needed. She thoroughly enjoyed her job, only asking for help when she absolutely had to. She preferred to find answers on her own. Even Mrs. Howell had told her what a good job she was doing.

At one o'clock, Sandy turned off the copy machine and straightened the piles of documents she had been copying. After splashing cold water on her face and repinning her braids, she emerged from the bathroom to find Tyler and Matthew. A knot in her stomach pointed out how much she was dreading this luncheon. In her month with the firm, she had never been in the position of having Tyler present while she defended herself from Matthew's advances. *Maybe*

Matthew will behave, she thought hopefully. *Maybe Tyler will tell him to leave me alone if he doesn't.*

They walked to a nearby Italian restaurant, and by the time they arrived, Sandy knew that her optimism was unwarranted. Matthew had managed to put his arm around her twice, stroke her hair once and bang his hip against hers more times than she could count. When the waitress arrived, Sandy had absolutely no appetite left, and she ordered a small salad for lack of anything less substantial on the menu.

They were sitting in a booth, a possibility that had not occurred to Sandy, and Matthew had guided her in, seating himself next to her to effectively pin her against the wall. Tyler sat across from Matthew, ignoring her discomfort.

"Matthew, I don't know how closely you've been following the Lanier case, but we're about at the stage where we can confront them with some pretty hard evidence. Sandy has done a very thorough job of researching the sites of all their dumps and exactly what they contain."

"Summertime, you're incredible," Matthew said, draping his arm around her. "How did such a pretty little thing get such a good head on her shoulders?"

Sandy shut her eyes for a minute, willing Matthew's arm to disappear. When it didn't, she opened them again to find Tyler staring at her, a half smile on his face. "Mr. Stone, it's a little crowded. Would you please remove your arm?"

Matthew did, with a laugh. "She plays hard to get," he confided to Tyler, "but I know she eats it up."

A whip, a chair and a cage, Sandy decided. A cage full of hungry lions! "What are you going to do next, Tyler?" she asked, struggling for composure.

"She calls you Tyler, but she calls me Mr. Stone. Now why do you suppose that is?"

"Respect for the aged, Mr. Stone," Sandy said with all the sarcasm she could muster.

Tyler threw back his head and his laughter filled the little booth. "Matthew, you've met your match."

"She loves me," Matthew bragged. "Don't you, Summertime?"

Sandy took a sip of her ice water, refusing to reply.

Surprisingly, Matthew backed off until halfway through their meal. Satiated by manicotti and two glasses of wine, the big man leaned back and looked Sandy square in the eye. "If you don't loosen up a little, honey, you're going to end up as an old maid. And what a waste that would be." The words were blatant enough, but they didn't begin to compare with the big hand he firmly planted on Sandy's thigh.

With a squeal she whipped around and gave the surprised lawyer a hard shove. "Get you hands off me, you overgrown Casanova!" Balling up her napkin, Sandy threw it on top of his plate and tried to push past him. When Matthew didn't budge, she grabbed her ice water and dumped it in his lap. This time Matthew squealed and slid out of the booth like a greased pig on the Fourth of July. Sandy slid out right behind him.

"I am not up for grabs," she said fiercely. "Most especially not to a married man. This one-sided flirtation has gone entirely too far." With both men staring at her, Sandy stomped across the room, threw a five-dollar bill in front of the startled cashier and slammed the restaurant door behind her.

Out on the street she debated where to go. Home was terribly appealing. Not home to Aunt Charlotte's but home to the farm. Even in her anger, Sandy knew that she owed too many people an explanation to do that so precipitously. Without having any desire to face either of her employers, she still turned her steps back to the office.

Managing to get past Dorothy's concerned questions and Mrs. Howell's motherly frown, Sandy closed her office door and began to sort through her belongings. She had neatly gathered everything she owned into piles to put into shopping bags when the door opened. Without turning around she knew that Tyler was standing there.

"What are you doing?"

Sandy was sure that she was about to be subjected to one of Tyler's famous interrogations, and she pushed her shoulders back and tilted her chin before turning around. "I am packing," she said, clearly enunciating every word.

"And why are you packing?"

"Because I am certain that you are going to fire me."

Tyler was frowning at her, but he didn't look nearly as angry as she had expected. Sandy's chin descended a notch.

"You're behaving foolishly."

"There is nothing foolish about telling an octopus to keep his hands to himself. I will not be manhandled and smile sweetly about it."

"Nor should you."

"Then why am I behaving foolishly?" She concentrated on keeping her face blank with lawyerlike detachment.

"You're acting like a child, not a professional woman. Don't run away. Stay and face your problems."

"I've been facing my problem every day since I started working here. Believe me, Matthew Stone doesn't go away."

"Matthew's a notorious flirt, but he's harmless if he's not encouraged."

Sandy knew that her face was no longer a polite mask. "How dare you! I have never encouraged him. Never!"

Tyler walked behind her desk to stand inches from her enraged body. "Calm down. I didn't mean to intimate that you had. I'm sorry."

An apology from Tyler Hamilton was what she had least expected, and Sandy wilted like a tired daisy. "I'm sorry I raised my voice," she muttered, wiping her hand across her eyes in a gesture of defeat.

"Don't be. No one has ever yelled at me before."

She raised her head and tried to smile. "Not even irate clients?"

"No one I like," he amended. "And I like you. Don't leave."

"I can't live with Matthew's groping. I wasn't raised to accept careless intimacies," she said, her anger completely dissolved. Tyler's words were paving a warm path to Sandy's heart, and she was beginning to bask in the glow of his concern.

"Tell me what's been going on," Tyler demanded softly.

Sandy told him as succinctly as she could, but somehow, in the telling, her qualms about Matthew began to sound petty. When she was finished, Tyler nodded as if he had suspected the exact level of the flirtation. "You're not used to men like Matthew, Sandy, but there are a lot of them around. You'll need to deal with them from time to time."

"Actually," she admitted with a spark of humor, "I thought the ice water in his lap was a touch of genius."

"You know, don't you, that you're very lovely and your independent spirit is going to be a magnet to men. Perhaps you should carry a thermos."

There was a knock at the door, and a very chastened Matthew Stone stuck his head in the office. "Summertime," he drawled, "I went too far, and I apologize. The ice water sobered me up."

Sandy blinked and then giggled. Matthew's face was immediately wreathed in a big grin. "You're just too tempting," he said, "but I'll try to behave."

"You will behave," Tyler said quietly as he pulled Sandy to stand in the crook of his arm. "I don't want her bothered anymore, Matthew."

Matthew nodded sheepishly and the door closed behind him. Expecting to be released, Sandy was surprised when Tyler kept his arm around her, turning her to rest against his long, hard body. "Don't wear that dress to work again," Tyler warned as his arm tightened momentarily, "or Matthew won't be the only one after you."

When he finally removed his arm and strode out of her office, Sandy knew that Tyler was not teasing. The attraction between them, so recently set to simmer on the back burner, was now boiling rapidly once again.

Two weeks later, Sandy walked through the door of Hamilton and Stone, humming a song that she had just heard on a teenager's box radio. It was possible, now, to walk through the door and retain her good mood. Matthew was friendly, still teasing her from time to time, but keeping a discreet distance. And Tyler, well, Tyler wasn't keeping his distance at all.

The all-business manner her favorite boss had treated her with had been replaced by an open warmth that Sandy found simultaneously confusing and intriguing. Never out of line, Tyler still found ways to communicate his interest, and Sandy sometimes found it difficult to concentrate on her work. Try as she might, forgetting that Tyler Hamilton was sitting in the next office was impossible.

Sandy no longer tried to talk sense to her heart. She was completely infatuated with Tyler and she knew it. She tried to tell herself that she was due for this, that the life she had led previously had delayed this passionate reaction to a man, and that it would soon pass. When it didn't, she told herself that she had chosen Tyler for her object of affection because he was perfectly safe. But when she caught him looking at her with unabashed desire in his eyes one morning, she knew that another theory had been destroyed.

How had this totally irrational turn of events come about? In her six weeks in Cameron, Sandy had met several eligible young men through her work and through her attendance at the local Baptist church. She had dated one of them and found him charming and fun to be with, but when he asked her out again, she had no desire to go. When the other young man asked her to attend a church social, Sandy had turned him down flat. She was so caught up in her attraction to Tyler Hamilton that dating other men seemed ridiculous.

Finally, after some serious soul-searching on her own, Sandy had confessed her predicament to Wendy, who was visiting Cameron for the weekend.

"Are you willing to sleep with him?" Wendy asked.

Sandy shook her head emphatically. She wanted Tyler, but she wasn't willing to lower her standards to have him.

"Then you're playing with fire. Tyler Hamilton isn't going to be led around by an innocent who has no intention of giving him what he's after."

Wendy had been born understanding men, and Sandy sat dejectedly beside her sister wondering why her own genes were so deficient. "Why are you so sophisticated and I'm so dumb?"

"You're not dumb. Just inexperienced."

So Sandy had come no closer to a solution to her problem than before. And in her innocence, she continued to try to deny that there was any problem to worry about.

On this morning, with the popular love song resounding through her head, Sandy ran up against her problem immediately.

"Sandy, will you come into my office, please?"

With a smile for Dorothy and Mrs. Howell, Sandy trotted down the hall after Tyler. Once inside his office she watched as he closed the door and came to sit beside her instead of at his desk. "I'm going to Atlanta this weekend," he told her after some pleasant small talk. "I want you to come with me."

There it was. The summons she had simultaneously dreaded and longed for. Sandy gulped convulsively. "I don't think that would be a good idea," she said.

Tyler laughed, as though he had expected her refusal. "Whoa, Miss MacDonald. I'm not making any illicit offers. Mrs. Howell will be coming, too. I finally got an appointment with the president of Lanier Chemical for Friday afternoon. I want you to come with me and see how these things are done. You've done most of the work. You deserve to be there for the kill."

Sandy lifted her eyes, trying to wipe all expression off her face. Tyler had approached her this way on purpose, and she refused to let him see how unhinged she felt. "Since there will be a chaperon," she said formally, "of course I'll come."

Tyler leaned back, his long legs thrust out in front of him. He was wearing blue again, and Sandy wished he would try not to look so devastating. "You realize, don't you, how things have changed around here?"

She denied it to the last, pretending to misunderstand. "Thanks to you, Matthew treats me decently now."

"And how do I treat you, now?"

He was toying with her with the instincts of the hunter who knows his prey is trapped. Sandy stopped pretending. "Tyler," she said, her voice barely above a whisper, "I don't know how to handle this."

"You're going to have to learn," he said steadily.

"Is this another one of those lessons I need before I become an attorney myself?"

"You'll have to decide that yourself."

Tyler didn't touch her, he didn't even move closer, but the sensuous web he wove around her as she sat there, searching his blue eyes, was as powerful as any approach he could have used. When she finally got up and left the room, Sandy knew that her dreams were over and reality had set in with a vengeance.

Atlanta was bustling with chaotic energy. Sitting in the back seat of Tyler's luxurious Lincoln, Sandy peered out of the window at the crowded streets and wondered why anyone wanted to live in a city. Farm girl, small-town girl, she accused herself with no malice. Quite simply, she knew beyond the shadow of a doubt that this kind of life, as invigorating and exciting as it was, was not right for her.

They had traveled for most of the morning with minimal conversation. Mrs. Howell rarely talked anyway, and somehow Sandy knew that she and Tyler had little that was casual enough to talk about in front of a third party. When he pulled up to a sky-scraping luxury hotel near the center of the city, she was grateful to finally get out and stretch her legs.

Their rooms adjoined, Mrs. Howell and Sandy in one, Tyler in the other. Knowing that Tyler was asleep in the room next to hers was not going to be easy, but Sandy was glad that she could keep track of his comings and goings. Atlanta was a second home to Tyler, and Sandy had no doubt that he had an active social life here. Perhaps if she was submerged in the reality of his involvement with other women, she would be able to get on with her life and accept the futility of romantic daydreams.

For their meeting at Lanier Chemical, Sandy changed into the only conservative suit she owned and rebraided her hair into one long braid, twisting it into a knot on top of her head. When she was ready to go, she knocked at Tyler's door.

He let her in, buttoning a clean shirt with one hand as he held the door for her. Sandy glimpsed more of Tyler's hard, sleek body than she felt old enough to see, and when she averted her eyes to his face, she saw that he was grinning at her reaction. "I gather you're not used to half-naked men in hotel rooms."

"I grew up with half-naked men," she quipped. "Nothing is sacred in a big family."

"But we aren't related," he reminded her, "and that makes it different."

It was different, all right, and as she looked for a place to sit, Sandy wondered how Wendy would handle this situation. One chair had Tyler's suitcase on it, the other his briefcase. The only alternative was his bed. "Maybe I'd better wait downstairs while you finish dressing," she suggested with a nervous smile.

Tyler inclined his head toward the bed. "Sit."

She did as she was told, perching on the edge like a sparrow ready to take flight. Tyler had turned to the mirror to knot a navy blue tie, and Sandy watched with fascination as his long fingers casually flipped the silk back and forth, under and out.

"I'm beginning to understand why your father is so protective of you." Tyler was still turned toward the mirror, and Sandy watched his mouth move in the silvered glass.

"I told you, my family's old-fashioned."

"I'll bet it's more than that." Tyler finished the tie and turned to lean against the dresser with his arms folded and a half smile on his face. "I imagine that your father realizes that as innocent as you are, you're a sitting duck."

"There was a time in history when innocence was valued," Sandy said primly.

"A tomboy in Victorian wrappings."

"Don't make fun of me."

"I'm sorry, but you look like you'd spring off that bed if I even moved in your direction."

Sandy blushed, leaning back on her elbows to appear more comfortable. "Better?"

Tyler just smiled.

"I could take off my jacket, unpin my hair and smile seductively," she added, "but it would take so long, we'd be late for our appointment."

"If you did any of those things, we wouldn't even make the appointment."

Sandy sat up straight, perched for flight again. "We'd better go."

"We'd better," Tyler agreed.

After weeks of hard work the appointment with Lanier Chemical's president, Melvin Howard, was a huge letdown. They were ushered into the balding man's fourteenth-floor office, which had a view of Atlanta that Sandy thought was breathtaking. Tyler ignored it completely, coming to the point of his visit with unerring accuracy.

Everyone had done their homework. Tyler presented Mr. Howard with the facts they had obtained; Mr. Howard presented Tyler with a complete report of what was in the two dumps near Sandy's parents' farm and what Lanier Chemical intended to do about cleaning them up.

The two men argued civilly about who should oversee the cleanup and who should test for possible pollution. Mr. Howard explained that the company had been running studies all month, a fact that Sandy knew to be true. They would be glad, however, to pay an independent lab to duplicate their research.

Sandy was relieved to hear that Lanier Chemical had found no indication that there had been any damage to the environment at all. Mr. Howard's willingness to have more tests run convinced her that he was telling the truth. In return for the company's compliance with his requests, Tyler promised to keep publicity about the cleanup to a minimum and to portray Lanier Chemical in an advantageous light.

The entire meeting took twenty-four minutes. With handshakes all around, Sandy and Tyler were on their way down the elevator and walking toward the street before she was sure what had happened. Outside the building, she allowed Tyler to guide her to his car and help her inside.

"It was so easy," she said, her head still spinning from the brief encounter. "It was all so easy."

"It could just as well have been another Love Canal," Tyler said. "Frankly, I expected it to be."

"That's why you took the case?"

"I took the case because I wanted to see justice done."

Sandy wriggled around to face Tyler and touch his suit sleeve. "For all of us then, let me say 'thank you.'"

"Let's celebrate tonight. Let me take you to dinner."

"Mrs. Howell too?"

"Mrs. Howell too," he said with a harsh sigh.

"Afterward," she said tentatively, "would you show me a little of the city?"

"Mrs. Howell too?"

"Not necessarily," Sandy murmured.

Tyler brushed his hand over her hair, tucking a stray wisp behind her ear. "It's a date," he said, his voice husky.

Sandy snuggled back into the seat cushions and shut her eyes.

Chapter Five

Mrs. Howell refused to go anywhere. Tyler had planned several appointments for early the next morning, and his secretary planned to go to bed at eight o'clock sharp in order to be ready to go with him. After trying politely to persuade Mrs. Howell otherwise, Sandy slipped out of the room to let Tyler know they would be dining alone that night. But Tyler was gone.

Torn between walking through the city to explore and taking her time getting ready, Sandy allowed her feminine instincts full rein. She washed her hair, combing out the tangles as it dried, and wrapped in her old flannel bathrobe she filed her nails as she watched reruns of *My Favorite Martian*.

The only dress she had brought to Atlanta was a conservative shirtwaist that covered her adequately but had no other virtues. Wishing that she had brought the

raspberry sundress instead, Sandy was just getting
ready to step into the shirtwaist when Mrs. Howell,
who had gone for a walk, unlocked the door.

"You are not wearing that," she told Sandy after
she took one good look at the limp fabric in Sandy's
arms. "What else did you bring?"

"Blue jeans?"

With an exasperated shake of her graying head,
Mrs. Howell ordered Sandy to get dressed and follow
her downstairs. Still faintly terrified of Tyler's dragon-
lady secretary, Sandy obeyed immediately.

On the ground floor of the hotel there was a variety
of shops. Hotel patrons could shop for Oriental art,
exotic souvenirs, floral arrangements or luxurious
clothing. The boutique that Mrs. Howell steered
Sandy into was the kind of place where normally
Sandy didn't even window-shop. But with Mrs. Howell barring the doorway, she meekly looked at the collection of frivolous dresses, wondering how she could
possibly make a selection.

Sensing her predicament and a sale besides, the
store's proprietor came over to help, and Sandy found
herself in the dressing room with rapidly failing courage and three outrageously priced dresses. In the end,
the choice was simple to make. All the dresses looked
good, but one, a sea-green crepe with a tightly fitting
bodice and a flaring skirt that emphasized her slender
waist and long legs, was stunning.

Mrs. Howell added two jeweled barrettes to the bill,
and Sandy came out of the boutique determined never
to shop again. She had forgotten about shoes and a
purse, however. Mrs. Howell hadn't. The older

woman marched Sandy to the next store like a teacher
taking a recalcitrant pupil to see the principal. When
they were finally back in their room, Sandy was so
overwhelmed by the amount of money she had just
spent on herself, that her shaking fingers couldn't
braid her hair.

Her clumsiness turned out for the best, anyway.
Mrs. Howell insisted Sandy wear her hair down,
caught up on the sides with the two barrettes. It cas-
caded down to her hips like a waterfall in the sunlight, and Sandy, sitting on the bed to wait for Tyler,
suddenly felt very exposed.

"Don't you think the neckline of this dress is too
low?" she asked Mrs. Howell.

"No."

"Maybe I should take a sweater."

"No."

Sandy shut her eyes in defeat, completely missing
the maternal smile on the dragon lady's face.

Tyler was right on time, dressed elegantly in dark
blue slacks and a dinner jacket that accented his tall,
broad-shouldered body. He stood in the doorway and
stared at Sandy while murmuring polite regrets that
Mrs. Howell wouldn't be joining them.

Sandy smiled tentatively to see if the muscles in her
face had frozen solid in fear. They hadn't, and as she
stood she managed a lopsided smirk. The answering
grin that lit up Tyler's face almost knocked her back
down to the bed.

The walk to the hotel parking garage had a calming
effect. By the time Sandy was settled comfortably next

to Tyler in the front seat of the Lincoln, she was beginning to feel almost normal.

"Where are we going?"

"We're having dinner at a nearby hotel." Tyler put his arm on the back of the seat as he turned to pull out of the parking space, and his fingers brushed Sandy's hair. With his foot on the brake, he let his fingertips tunnel through the golden mass to find her neck and caress it lightly. The sensation was like a thousand butterflies dancing down her spine, and Sandy shivered in appreciation. "I wish I'd known that Mrs. Howell wasn't coming," Tyler said, moving his fingers back to the seat. "I would have chosen someplace more intimate.'

"Is it too late?"

"My parents are in town, and I invited them to eat dinner with us at their hotel. I had no idea that you and I had a chance to be alone. I'm sorry."

"Don't be, Tyler. It will be fun."

But it wasn't. Mr. and Mrs. Hamilton obviously doted on their only son and only slightly less obviously disapproved of his choice of a dinner companion. Tyler's mother seemed especially concerned. By the end of the meeting, the silver-haired matriarch had made two comments about Sandy's youth and one condescending remark about her rural background. She had also raised her perfectly arched eyebrows so many times that Sandy was beginning to think that Mrs. Hamilton resembled Groucho Marx.

Mr. Hamilton warmed up considerably as the meal progressed, caught helplessly in the snare of Sandy's innocent charm. Since Sandy's major experience in

dealing with men came from dealing with her own father, she treated Mr. Hamilton to the same mixture of
deference and sauciness that worked with Mr. Mac-
Donald. By the end of the evening, she was rewarded
with a smile.

Even though she was under examination herself,
Sandy was also sensitive to the other undercurrents
swirling through the conversation. Georgia politics
were discussed with fervor, especially by the elder
Hamiltons. Sandy watched as Tyler's face became
more difficult to read, his comments terser, his body
rigid. Even though she was a stranger in the midst of
a closely-knit family group, Sandy could see the battle lines being drawn. The senior Hamiltons, especially Tyler's mother, wanted their son to run for the
legislature in the next election. Tyler did not want to
discuss it.

By the time the meal ended, Sandy was exhausted
from the emotional battle that had been waged behind careful smiles and polite conversation. Without
meaning to, she found herself comparing this occasion with the family dinners she had grown up with.
The hotel dining room was magnificent, the food excellent. There was fine china, fresh flowers and candles on the table. But Sandy was sure that she wouldn't
trade any of it for the indoor picnic table in the
MacDonald house and her mother's black-eyed peas
and cornbread. There was love in both places, but
Sandy knew she preferred the unquestioning kind that
flowed with abundance in the overcrowded farmhouse in northern Georgia.

"I'm sorry I had to put you through that." Tyler and Sandy had said restrained goodbyes to his parents and were seated once again in the Lincoln.

"Is it always like that?" she asked, deciding not to pretend that she wasn't aware of the tension.

"It's not usually that bad. They're getting older, though, and they're desperate to see me settled in the life that they think is right for me." Tyler looked as tired as Sandy felt, and she put her hand on his arm in comfort.

"You look beat. Why don't we skip the sightseeing?"

Instead of the nod she had expected, Tyler put his arm around Sandy's shoulders and pulled her to sit close to him. "I want to be with you tonight."

Sandy knew that if she turned her face up to his, Tyler would kiss her. Shaken with apprehension, the girl who had hung upside down from a magnolia limb without a single thought for her safety couldn't make her head move.

"Tip your head back," Tyler said quietly, forcing Sandy's compliance with two fingers under her chin. The kiss, when it came, was gentle and reassuring. Tyler moved his lips over hers with an aching sweetness that threatened to dissolve every bone in her body. With her eyes tightly shut, she let the kiss take her where it would, her body responding to his increasing pressure with an increasing pressure of its own.

Tyler's hands tangled in her hair and his tongue began to caress her lips. Just at the point where Sandy moaned and opened her mouth to receive him, he drew back, pushing her head to his shoulder while his hands played with her hair. "In all my fantasies," he said softly, "I never imagined that kissing you would be that sweet."

The kiss had been wonderful. Hearing that Tyler had fantasies about her was wonderful, too. "Thank you," she murmured, pressing her body softly against his to feel his warm, hard strength against her. Tentatively she lifted a hand and placed it against his chest. Through the fabric she could feel his heart pounding.

"I know a place we can go and you can see as much of Atlanta as you want without even leaving the room," Tyler said, reaching up to cover Sandy's hand with his.

For a moment, she thought he meant his hotel room, and she went rigid with shock at the idea. "Tyler, Mrs. Howell would be right next door," she whispered, shaken to the core.

Tyler's laughter filled the luxurious car. "You're way ahead of me, Sandy. Let's take this one step at a time."

The place Tyler had in mind was a private club at the very top of an office building near Lanier Chemical. Obviously accustomed to seeing Tyler there, the guard at the lobby door just nodded as they walked through to take the elevator to the top. They were greeted by a hostess in a slinky lamé gown who showed them to a table at the edge of the room. The glass walls surrounding them did nothing to impede the view of the Atlanta skyline.

There was a broad terrace that wrapped around the building on three sides, and with a nod, Sandy stood to let Tyler lead her outside.

"Tyler!"

His features in rigid control, Tyler turned as they neared the door to the terrace to see three men bearing down on them.

"I'm sorry, Sandy," he apologized, waiting for his acquaintances.

The three men were Atlanta attorneys visiting the club with their wives, and the scent of Georgia politics wafted through the air. "Come on over and sit with us," one of the men, a commanding presence in a brown suit, ordered them. "We've been trying to get hold of you for weeks now."

"No, not tonight," Tyler told them, after he had introduced Sandy.

"Just for a while," another man, whose name Sandy had recognized from the newspapers, insisted.

"Gentlemen," Tyler explained with lazy charm, "if you were here with Miss MacDonald, would you let yourselves be persuaded to join anyone else?"

Good-natured backslapping followed and a sly wink at Sandy's blushing face. In a moment the gentlemen were gone, and Tyler was steering her onto the terrace as rapidly as he could manage.

They leaned over the chest-high railing, and Sandy let the breeze ruffle her hair. Tyler pointed out some of Atlanta's landmarks, stopping only when he noticed that Sandy was watching him instead. "Come with me," he said quietly.

Holding hands they followed the terrace to the one side of the building that was not glass. This section had been designed for privacy, with tall shrubbery in clay pots screening visitors from view. With amazement, Sandy realized that they were absolutely alone.

"Dance with me," Tyler demanded, putting his arms around her to pull her close. They stood together, swaying to the music of the small orchestra inside. Sandy was so intrigued by the feel of Tyler's body against her own that she was hardly aware when he stopped dancing and pulled her behind two potted hibiscus.

Without wanting to, she stepped back just far enough to read his expression. "Everything has changed, hasn't it?" she asked.

"Yes."

"I have to know. You're not a notorious flirt like Matthew, are you, Tyler? Because I couldn't stand it if you were just passing time with me."

The look in his eyes was answer enough. When his mouth found hers, she was ready. Her hesitation was gone, her body was so flooded with rippling desire that she couldn't get close enough, couldn't share enough. This kiss wasn't sweet. It was undiluted passion. Tyler's hands explored the slender lines of her sides and back, his tongue explored the inner sanctum of her mouth. The kiss became another and then another until Sandy stopped counting, unable to do anything except whimper softly and kiss him back.

In her inexperience, she didn't realize that rubbing her soft breasts against his shirt and rotating her hips against his was a signal. She only knew that she wanted to feel every part of him, to be devoured by the shaking passion that was filling her innocent body. When her tongue answered his, beginning its own exploration, Tyler groaned in response. Accepting her honeyed warmth, he cupped her bottom in his hands to move her slowly up and down against his hardening body.

Still innocent of signals, Sandy tangled her fingers in Tyler's hair and allowed him to deepen their intimacy. "Tyler," she whispered against his mouth, her own slanting over his once more to claim it in a kiss that kept nothing from him.

But when her tongue sought his this time, he pulled back, holding her away from his body with his long fingers locked on her shoulders. "Lord, Sandy, don't do that," he said, pushing her even farther away.

She was dazed, a rosebud commanded to stop unfolding. "What did I do?" she asked, tears filling her eyes at the reproachful expression on Tyler's face.

"It's what you won't do...what I won't let you do," he amended cryptically. Tyler dropped his hands to his sides, and Sandy turned to stumble blindly to the terrace wall, resting her head on folded arms as she looked out over the city.

Tyler joined her a few moments later, and his hand pushed beneath her hair to rest on her back in an unspoken apology. Still confused by his reaction, she continued to count the city lights until he finally put his arm around her and turned her to face him. "I didn't mean for it to go that far," he said. "I should have known how generous you would be, how much you would give."

I was warned about this, Sandy thought. *Stacey tried to tell me.* But she had no words for Tyler. She couldn't meet his eyes.

"There you are." The three attorneys, trailed by their attractive wives, appeared from around the corner of the terrace, and Tyler straightened, pulling Sandy to stand beside him.

"I'll get us out of here," Tyler promised quietly, and after a minimum of polite conversation, he did just that, escorting Sandy quickly through the club, down the elevator and into the parking garage to retrieve his car.

Inside their hotel, Sandy headed quickly to the elevator, but Tyler stopped her with a strong hand on her arm. "We have to talk."

Too confused to protest, she let him steer her to a quiet table in the hotel bar. The corner he chose was dark and perfect for a romantic tête-à-tête, but Sandy understood that Tyler had chosen it to give them anonymity.

The waitress took their order, and Tyler waited until their drinks arrived before he began. "I'm not sorry I kissed you," he said, taking Sandy's hands in his. "I've wanted to from the first time I saw you upside down, braids hanging all the way to the ground."

"What's the problem then, Tyler?" she asked softly, her thumbs covering the backs of his hands with unconscious caresses. "When you finally worked up your nerve, I'm sure you could tell that I liked it."

She had intended to destroy the tension between them, and for a moment she did. Tyler was smiling when he said, "You liked it entirely too much."

"I see. I wasn't supposed to enjoy it. I'm sorry, I didn't realize. Is that another lesson I'm supposed to learn?"

"That kiss was the beginning of something that can't be allowed to happen between us."

Sandy might be innocent, but she wasn't ignorant. She understood clearly what Tyler was referring to. She lifted her eyes to his, but before she could speak, he continued. "I could never insult your father by taking advantage of your youth and your sweetness, Sandy. If you had an affair with me Raymond would never forgive either of us."

Shock waves crashed through Sandy's body at his words. She was furious at his masculine arrogance, and she narrowed her huge green eyes in preparation for battle. "Are you so used to women clamoring to jump into your bed that you think that's what I'm trying to do?"

"The thought entered my mind."

"You conceited chauvinist." She watched Tyler's eyes narrow, too, but she was too angry to be careful. "I'm going to share a name with the man I love before I share his bed. And right now I'm still Alexandra Kathryn MacDonald."

"Let me give you some advice, then. Don't kiss a man like you kissed me if you're not extending an invitation." Tyler held her hands tightly, forcing her to remain in front of him.

Fury destroying every sensible cell of her body, Sandy tried to pull free, but Tyler wouldn't let her go. "Men don't like to be teased," he added, making his point with a cruel exclamation mark. "Someone else might have taken you up on your offer. Remember it."

"Have you been so hurt by the tragedy in your life that you can't recognize honest emotion anymore?" she asked, her voice low and charged with feeling.

"Just what does that mean?"

Tyler's fingers were biting into the back of her hands, forcing Sandy to stay seated even as she tried once again to pull away. They were a satire on lovers, she thought. Sitting in the darkened bar, holding hands and looking into each other's eyes. Only they knew the complete absurdity of the analogy. They would never be lovers, after tonight they would never even be friends. The pain in her hands was nothing compared to the pain that thought gave her.

I'm in love with Tyler Hamilton, she realized as he continued to hold her prisoner. I'm twenty-one with my whole life ahead of me, and I've fallen hopelessly, terribly in love. I am the worst kind of fool.

There seemed to be no way to salvage the remnants of a relationship. Tyler was waiting for an answer, and Sandy had none to give him. "Please let go of me," she pleaded softly, her eyes focused on the hands that had captured hers.

"Look at me."

She shook her head, but her eyes lifted anyway. Dreading what she would see in Tyler's face, she tried to erase the expression from her own. She was not successful.

"You think you're in love with me," Tyler said, his voice tinged with amazement.

"Please, let go of me."

He did, but his hands still lay on hers, and she didn't have enough strength or pride to leave him yet. "Sandy," he said with quiet intensity. "Don't fall in love with me. I can't love you back. I don't want to marry again."

For just a moment all the agony of unfulfilled dreams and the devastation of loss was written across Tyler's face in bitter lines. His need for comfort seemed so immediate that Sandy could only give it, even in her own misery. "I'm sorry you've been hurt, Tyler. I can understand that you'd never want to face that much pain again," she said, turning her palms up to grasp his hands.

Her understanding seemed to be the last thing he wanted. He removed his hands from hers, folding them in front of his chest to form an impenetrable shield. "You'll be over this in no time," he said in an emotionless voice. "You're very young."

It was a slap in the face, but it gave Sandy the courage to leave him. "Just like I got over my seventh grade English teacher, you mean." She stood and moved gracefully to circle the table. Honesty stopped her; they were not finished. "Even at my tender age, Tyler, I know what love is. I'm not going to embarrass you with my feelings. I'll just need a reference so that I can look for another job." She waited for him to say something, anything, that would allow them to pick up the pieces of their shattered relationship and begin again. But Tyler was silent.

She continued out the door to the elevator and up to her room. Mrs. Howell was asleep and Sandy packed quietly, leaving a hastily scribbled note explaining her decision to take a bus home.

She arrived in Gainesville in the early hours of the morning, exhausted and resigned to her misery. No one had made her fall in love. Sandy couldn't blame Tyler at all.

It was entirely her own fault she was such a fool.

The sun was just beginning to rise when she slipped into the pay phone at the bus terminal to call her parents' home. After a brief conversation with Wendy she stood, back rigid against the outside wall of the bus station, and waited for a ride back to the farm.

Chapter Six

Sandy rocked monotonously back and forth, her golden braids slapping the side of the pot into which she was dumping shelled crowder peas. A fat fly buzzed around her head and she wearily lifted her arm to swat at it, not even coming close to her target. In the distance she could hear the shouting of the twins, who were teasing Jennifer as she practiced tricks on her pony.

"I thought you'd be down helping Jennifer." Wendy took the rocker next to her sister and stared over the porch railing in the direction of the raucous laughter that probably signaled one of their little sister's many failures.

"Not today."

"Did you go for the job interview in Gainesville this morning?"

"Yes. I can probably have the job if I want it. Tyler gave me an outstanding recommendation."

Wendy took note of the bitter tone of the last sentence, but she restrained herself from commenting on it.

"Are you going to take the job then?"

"I suppose. They want me to start in September."

Wendy stood and walked to the porch railing where she turned and faced her sister. She watched Sandy meticulously shell the peas as if doing the tedious job correctly could somehow keep her misery at bay. "It's been two weeks. Are you going to tell me what happened?"

Sandy shrugged her shoulders. "I made a fool of myself. What more needs to be said?"

"I can't believe it."

"Believe it." Sandy closed her eyes and rested her head on the back of the rocking chair. The punishing July heat shimmered over her rigid body and she could feel perspiration forming under her shirt to run down her sides. It seemed a miracle that she could feel anything at all.

"Falling in love isn't something to be ashamed of, Sandy. Making a mistake isn't something to be embarrassed about."

"How would you know?" The voice that emerged was a snarl.

"I've made some, too."

Sandy opened her eyes to stare at the beloved sister she wanted desperately to pick a fight with. She restrained herself with difficulty. "Never like this you haven't. I do everything big and on impulse. You're careful, you think everything through."

"Once I didn't." Wendy watched Sandy's expression change to disbelief. "I fell in love once too, with the wrong man, though he wasn't a man then."

"This wasn't a high-school romance."

"Pain is pain."

Sandy was jolted out of her self-pity by the understanding on Wendy's face. She fought against the wave of love sweeping over her for this friend who knew her so well. She didn't want to feel anything except anger, but Wendy's liquid brown eyes were piercing her defenses. She could feel the tears welling inside her. "I'm going to cry," she said with a sniff.

"It's about time."

Scalding tears washed over the crowder peas, and Sandy set the pan down to wipe her eyes with the hem of her skirt. "It's going to hurt worse now," she accused her sister between sobs.

"It's going to hurt better." Wendy waited until the storm had passed before kneeling beside Sandy to stroke the golden head and long braids.

"When I grow up and leave home again, will you come, too, and take care of me?" Sandy asked finally, and Wendy knew that her sister was telling her "thank you."

"You are grown up."

"If so, I think I hate it."

Although Sandy had called Aunt Charlotte to let her know that she would be moving her things out of the house, she had persistently put off the trip to Cameron. The day after her talk with Wendy, she knew that she couldn't wait any longer. Wendy agreed to go with her to help pack and move.

By the time the two sisters had reached Cameron, Sandy had poured out the entire story, and Wendy had listened in accepting silence. Parking in front of Aunt Charlotte's house, they walked up to the front door and waited for the old woman to answer their knock.

"You're as peaked looking as one of Julius's mice," Aunt Charlotte greeted Sandy.

"And you're still as frisky as a kitten," Sandy observed with saddened affection. Inside the house, she waited as Wendy and Aunt Charlotte made small talk. "I want you to know I loved being here," Sandy told the old woman when she and Wendy had finished. "I'm sorry if my leaving has caused you any problems."

"I'm not the member of the Hamilton family with the problems," Aunt Charlotte said with a snort. "That nephew of mine's the one who's upset."

Sandy tried to picture the elegant Tyler Hamilton upset. The image was incredulous. "I'm sure he hates to lose a good worker."

"I'm disappointed in both of you."

Sandy was taken aback by the blunt tone of Aunt Charlotte's voice. "Why?"

"I was counting on you to pull that boy out of his shell and take notice. I didn't expect either of you to behave this way."

Sandy's face was suffused with color. "I don't..."

"You do, too. I never saw two people who needed each other more, but both of you are as hardheaded as rhinoceroses.'' The old woman walked spryly through the house shaking her head.

"I think I'd better pack and get out of here fast," Sandy told Wendy.

"Yes. If you don't move fast, you might actually have to think about what she said," Wendy agreed, with the innocent smile of an angel.

Halfway through the fourth box of books, there was a knock on Sandy's door. "That will be Aunt Charlotte to apologize," Sandy said. "Will you get it?" She heard the door swing open and footsteps. A prickling sensation at the back of her neck warned her that her visitor wasn't Aunt Charlotte and that Wendy had discreetly left the room. Refusing to look, Sandy continued to sit and pack books, her back to the door.

"I don't suppose I could persuade you to stay."

It wasn't fair, she thought with a surge of panic. It had been two weeks since she had heard Tyler's voice, and still, one sentence could turn her inside out. Without moving, she sat stiffly, contemplating his words. Finally she shook her head, and picked up another book.

She felt rather than heard him come up behind her but she still jumped when he knelt and put his hands on her shoulders. "I never meant to hurt you," he said softly.

"I know." It took all her energy to raise a hand and cover one of his in order to assuage his guilt.

It wasn't enough for Tyler, however. His hands gripped her shoulders and forced her to turn to him. Kneeling face to face, Sandy raised her eyes to his, and she was stung by the sorrow in the blue depths. She wanted to reach out and caress the sadness from his face, but she could not risk touching him again. She waited.

"I don't want you to go. We could pretend that nothing ever happened."

"I can't lie to myself, Tyler. I never learned how."

They searched each other's faces for clues, for ways to return to the first, casual days of their relationship. But there were no roads back. "It would be awkward for us both if I stayed," Sandy said finally.

"I would try very hard not to make it awkward."

"And when I saw you with other women and knew..." Her voice wavered and she stopped to swallow. "I'm not sophisticated enough to handle that."

"Sandy, there is no special woman in my life. There hasn't been anyone special since Kay died."

She shut her eyes briefly at the revelation, but the surging hope inside her was all the warning she needed. "Tyler, if there was no one to stand in my way, and you continued to look at me like that, I think I'd end up in your bed. And that would destroy me."

Tyler was silent, his hands still resting on her shoulders. When she opened her eyes, she found that he was examining her face with the eye of an artist trying to memorize features for a portrait. Wide-eyed she watched as he bent slowly to take her mouth.

The kiss was clearly a goodbye, a tender farewell to emotions that neither of them could have controlled or predicted. But the kiss was unpredictable, too. Abandoning herself, knowing this was her last chance to be close to him, Sandy leaned forward and put her slender fingers on the back of his neck. Her caress, as gentle and undemanding as it was, seemed to send desire sweeping through Tyler's body.

He arched against her, his arms wrapping around her back to pull her as close as she could come. She could feel her breasts flatten against his hard chest and she knew the exact moment when the insidious heat of his body crept inside her to light tiny, dancing bonfires. Tyler broke away, but only for an instant before he reclaimed her lips and the velvety inside of her mouth with his tongue.

Sandy knew she was moaning. Her fingers burrowed into his hair and she let the silky feel of it tantalize her fingertips as his body and mouth tantalized the rest of her. The kiss went on and on and she was dizzied by it, but when Tyler finally broke away, the absence of his mouth was even more dizzying. "Tyler?"

"Damn!"

She sat back in confusion and covered her face with her hands when she saw the savage anger in his eyes. The slam of the bedroom door announced the new beginning of her loneliness.

"Sandy has more dates than Wendy does these days," James noted gleefully. Trying to make the MacDonald females angry at each other was one of the twins' favorite games.

Mrs. MacDonald looked disapprovingly across the supper table at her son, silencing his maneuvers immediately. "I don't believe that Wendy and Sandy are competing, are you, girls?"

Sandy finished the last bite of sweet potatoes on her plate and shook her head. Next to her Wendy was doing the same. "In fact, we're double-dating tonight."

To combat the heat of the August evening, both young women were dressed enticingly in simple cotton sundresses, and Mr. MacDonald sighed heavily. "Do I know the young men?"

Wendy obligingly filled her father in on the names of their dates, where they were going, when they would be back and whether they intended to kiss them good-night.

"I raised a smart aleck," Mr. MacDonald grunted.

"Just being a dutiful daughter."

Sandy watched the byplay, a bright smile pasted on her face. Since the disastrous trip to Cameron, she had thrown herself into family life and the local social scene with an energy that, even for Sandy, was unusual. Her fervor had garnered her more dates than she could count. But it hadn't even begun to touch the empty place inside her. Tonight was another attempt to kill time. She had given up hoping that she would ever feel better.

"Sandy, I have some news for you."

Sandy looked at her father and read the concern written on his face. Her smile began to fade.

"Tyler Hamilton called me today. He's driving down tomorrow to meet with all the local farmers. He has the final laboratory reports for us."

"Good news, I hope?" she asked, her voice carefully polite.

"It seems so. He asked that you be present since you did so much of the work."

"That was considerate."

"The meeting's at ten o'clock at Chester Barkley's house."

"I won't be there."

For once, the MacDonald supper table was quiet. Although Sandy had only shared her story with Wendy, preferring to tell the rest of the family that the job just hadn't worked out, she knew that her parents suspected the truth.

"Ma, Randy ate all the peaches." Jennifer's wail broke the long silence. As if Sandy had never spoken, the family rallied around, quickly returning to normal.

Sandy pasted a pleasant smile back on her face and wondered how she was going to survive the next twenty-four hours knowing Tyler would be so close and still so very far away.

Even though she ran her date ragged with a supply of nervous energy ample enough to light the city of Atlanta, Sandy was not able to sleep after she and Wendy said their good-nights. At dawn, she rose with the roosters, pulling on blue jeans and a frayed T-shirt to help her father with the early-morning chores.

At nine, after a shower and a change into shorts and a blouse to prepare for the onslaught of the day's raging temperatures, she wandered aimlessly through the house, trying to decide what new job to take on. Mrs. MacDonald took pity on her and gave her two loads of laundry to hang outside to dry.

At ten of ten, Sandy watched her father's truck pull out of the drive. At ten-thirty, heartsick and too tired

to pretend anymore, she sought the comfort of the
magnolia tree. This time there was no race to worry
about. She climbed carefully, taking as long as she
needed to find a secure hold on the branches. At the
top she swung herself into the scrap-wood tree house
and settled to wait for the sight of Mr. MacDonald's
truck. She knew that when Tyler Hamilton completed his business here, he would be gone from her
life for good.

There would be no more tentative ties. No more
waiting for phone calls that never came. Tyler would
be gone, and Sandy could get on with the business of
living.

The local farmers must have had a lot of questions,
she thought as the burgeoning morning sun and her
sleepless night acted in tandem to shut her eyes. Although it was now past eleven, there was no sign of
Mr. MacDonald's truck. Her neighbors had obviously wanted to know all the facts. Sandy sighed, giving up the struggle to stay awake. The tree house was
safe and womblike around her as she fell asleep.

She awakened a little later to the rustling of tree
branches. That, in itself, was peculiar since the still
August day had no hint of a breeze. Slowly opening
her eyes, Sandy heard the unmistakable sound of
someone climbing up the tree. It was too labored a
climb to be Randy or James, too steady and determined to be the younger boys or Jennifer.

Lying quietly, she waited for the intruder to reach
the branches surrounding the tree house. If she was
lucky, the mystery tree climber would leave without
seeing her, and she would not be forced to make con-

versation. But the tree shook with the effort that was being made, rocking Sandy gently in its leafy arms.

Amazement gripped her body, as realization dawned in her brain. This was no child making the tree sway and jerk beneath him. There was an adult coming to join her. An adult with a marvelous sense of balance and purpose.

Shutting her eyes, Sandy labored to wipe all expression off her face. When Tyler swung himself into the tree house she greeted him with a polite, "How nice to see you."

Tyler was dressed in what had once been an immaculate white shirt with short sleeves, a concession to the blazing temperature. His beige pants probably matched a jacket on the ground below, and there was no tie around the collar, which had been unbuttoned along with the top three buttons of his shirt. His carefully cut hair was rumpled and his face was gleaming with sweat. Sandy knew immediately that the month she had tried to exorcise him from her mind had been a complete waste of time.

"I've missed you," he said with no preliminaries, stretching out to lie beside her, their bodies only a scant inch apart.

"Have you?" she asked, giving up the pretense of politeness. Her eyes were wide, vulnerable and fully awake. Please don't hurt me again, they pleaded. Leave me something. Some integrity. Some pride. Leave me something to continue living with when you go.

Pushing her onto her back, Tyler covered her mouth with his. Remembering the agonies her response had

caused during past kisses, Sandy lay rigid beneath
him. She tried to remember how he had rejected her
when she had responded with generous warmth to his
lovemaking. She held herself back from him, letting
him do what he would but not letting him know how
he affected her.

"Don't punish me," he pleaded against her mouth.
"Sandy, don't do this to punish me."

She would not bend; she would not melt. Shutting
her eyes against the pain in his, she lay still, telling
herself that she must. But Tyler would not be denied.
His arms circled her inert body, cradling her in his
arms as he pulled her still form even farther beneath
him. The feel of his hard body so fully against hers
made her tremble with fear and with the desire for him
that had never abated.

"Don't do this to me, Tyler. It isn't fair. It isn't
fair." The voice she heard was a sad surprise. There
was no strength in it, no conviction. She knew that she
had lost everything.

Moving to Sandy's side, Tyler started unfastening
the buttons at the top of her cotton shirt. He watched
her eyes blink open as shock and desire left their mark
on her expressive features. She raised her hand to stop
him, but the gesture was useless. She was a kitten with
unsheathed claws fighting a sleek and deadly leopard.

"Tyler, I can't," she whispered in a broken voice.
"Don't ask this of me. You know I can't."

He continued with the fourth button as if she hadn't
spoken.

"I can't!"

"Yes, you can." With her blouse open to his gaze he drank in the sight of her, her torso naked to his devouring eyes. She wasn't passive now, she was writhing beneath him, trying to escape, trying to cover herself. With his fingertips barely brushing the bared skin, Tyler felt every inch of her as she moaned in frustration. Wrapping her long braids around his hand, he held her head down as his mouth descended to one breast. Her startled gasp inflamed him and he pulled the sweet rosy nub into his mouth, stroking her with his tongue.

"Sweet heaven," she cried. "Don't do this, Tyler."

"This and more," he murmured roughly, abandoning one breast to taste the other. "Much, much more."

A voice from below drifted lazily through the leafy branches. "Did you find her, Tyler?"

Sandy groaned softly at her father's question and at the incredible things Tyler was doing to her. Her resolve had collapsed completely. There were no more protests in her repertoire.

Tyler straightened, a half smile on his face as he watched Sandy's expression. He continued to hold her down as he called to Mr. MacDonald, "I certainly did."

"Then I'll expect to see you both down here in five minutes."

"Good idea," Tyler agreed.

Even sixty feet above, Sandy could hear her father chuckling as he walked away. "He means it, Tyler," she warned, trying to sit up, but Tyler was on top of her again, pinning her more effectively than before.

She shuddered as he unbuttoned his shirt all the way to rub his pelted chest against her soft breasts. His mouth covered hers, cutting off any further lectures.

Resistance gone, Sandy arched to meet him, her tongue finding his tongue, her body melting into his body. With her arms wrapped tightly around his back, she held him against her, sure that he would disappear again if she didn't.

She was not as inexperienced this time. When Tyler groaned and moved away from her, she understood why. That was one lesson he had taught her, and she released him, waiting grimly for his anger. Instead, when she finally found the courage to search his eyes she found humor there, and something else that took her breath away.

"What on earth did you tell my father?" she asked as she sat up slowly, pulling her blouse closed with one hand as she straightened her braids with the other. "Did you tell him what you were planning to do to me up here? Is that why he only gave you five minutes?"

Tyler shot her a stunning grin that effectively destroyed her attempt to gain the upper hand. "I told him that I was going to ask you to marry me."

"Marry you?"

"Yes. As in long white dress, gold band... honeymoon."

Sandy was sure that she looked as confused as she felt. "Honeymoon?"

"And no matter what you think, I wasn't planning to have the honeymoon in a dilapidated tree house before the wedding. That's what your father is trying to prevent, by the way."

"But why?"

"Why? I don't know. I guess he wants you to get married in white in a church by a . . ."

Sandy shoved his wandering hand away from the cleavage of her unbuttoned blouse, her cheeks the color of a ripe peach. "You know what I mean. Why do you want to marry me?"

Tyler was silent, his fingers tracing beneath the vulnerable green eyes that still were filled with distrust. He sighed finally and pulled her close, carefully tugging the fabric of her blouse from beneath her twisting fingers. Slowly, he began to button it. "I need you."

Need she could understand. It was a close relative of desire, and other men had desired her. But need was a little more comprehensive. It indicated that she was different from other women, more special, more important. She was glad he needed her. But it wasn't enough.

"I see."

"No, you don't. And I don't know if I can make you understand." He finished buttoning the blouse and pulled her to sit on his lap like a small child. "You make me feel alive like no one else ever has, Sandy. You bring me joy."

"I thought I brought you anger."

"How can I even ask for your forgiveness? I didn't want to feel again. I was fighting what you had to offer me."

She shook her head, her long braids swishing softly against his hair-roughened chest. Tentatively she followed their path with her fingers, twirling a matted black curl around a trembling fingertip. "I never thought this far ahead. I wasn't trying to trap you, to tease. Marriage never entered my mind."

"Never?"

She turned her face to his chest. "I knew that it was an impossible fantasy."

"I don't understand how it happened, how you snuck past all my defenses, but here we are."

"I think I'm too young for this," Sandy said tentatively, gathering speed as all the objections she could muster spewed out in helpless anxiety. "I have law school ahead of me. What kind of a wife will I be for a man like you? I don't want to go off on the campaign trail. I've never even been to a country club. Your mother doesn't like me."

"I like you, and I'm the one you'll be marrying," he said, beginning at the end of her list to work back to the start. "A country club is a building with people in it and if you don't enjoy it, I'll drop my membership. I don't want to go off on the campaign trail, either. You will make a fabulous wife for a man like me, and you can commute to law school at the University of Georgia when you're ready. But, yes, you are too young. And there doesn't seem to be a thing either of us can do about that."

"The age difference worries you, too," she said sadly.

"Not the age difference. I worry that I may be taking away your youth."

A youth without Tyler didn't seem to be worth worrying about. "How about sharing it with me, instead?'' she murmured, her tongue beginning to explore where her fingers had lately been.

''With the greatest of pleasure.''

Sandy knew that she couldn't say no. Tyler could not tell her he loved her, but still, he had said she brought him joy. And she loved him. There were good marriages that were built on much less. She trembled as his hand began to stray beneath her blouse again.

''There are one thousand and one things I want to do to you,'' he said, his voice husky in her ear, ''and not a one of them can be done in two minutes and forty-five seconds. Marry me right away so that I can spend my life making up for the time we don't have today.''

She was lost again, her body betraying the cautious words trying to form in her brain. With a sigh, she surrendered to his kisses, to his hands and to his promises.

With thirty seconds left to them, Sandy agreed to become Tyler's wife.

Chapter Seven

St. David's Church filled up quickly. Cameron's finest citizens sat on the side of the sanctuary reserved for friends and relatives of the groom. Sandy's guests sat on the other side, the center aisle a wide gulf between them.

The little Baptist church in Gainesville where Sandy had always worshiped, had proved to be too small for the MacDonald family and all the guests whom Tyler's mother insisted on inviting. Generously, Sandy had suggested having the ceremony in Tyler's own church in Cameron. Since she had agreed to attend St. David's after they were married, it seemed fitting to begin their life together at St. David's altar.

As if he were afraid that he might scare her away with a repeat of his request to be married as soon as possible, Tyler had patiently retreated while Sandy allowed his mother to plan a wedding that was larger than Sandy or he had ever wanted. Mrs. Hamilton had deferred graciously to every suggestion Sandy made, but Tyler's mother had been the driving force behind the formal wedding that was finally taking place that day. Sandy had been too dazed to protest.

Now, dressed in the same wedding gown that Stacey had worn only a year before, Sandy began the long walk down the aisle on her father's arm. Against Mrs. Hamilton's advice, she had chosen to forego a veil, wearing her golden hair loose and garlanded with tiny white rosebuds and ropes of pearls. All her sisters were already at the altar, dressed in matching long dresses of forest green and gold. Tyler was there, too, and Sandy nervously sought his eyes.

He was watching her, his face composed, his eyes blazing with warmth. As she reached his side, the smile he gave her infused her with courage. When her father removed his steadying arm, she was ready to place her hand on Tyler's.

The unfamiliar words from the Book of Common Prayer fell around her. She knelt when she knew she must, stood when she was supposed to, murmured vows, exchanged rings and turned her face up to Tyler's for his kiss.

The sanctuary was quiet except for one ripple of laughter that occurred when she and Tyler knelt. Then the huge room swelled with organ music and the happy voices of the wedding guests. On Tyler's arm, Sandy made the trip back up the aisle to begin her new life.

The country-club reception was as elaborate as their wedding had been. Although Sandy's parents had taken care of the wedding expenses, the Hamiltons had insisted on doing the reception. It only made sense for the well-to-do Hamiltons to help, but Sandy was sure that the casual party her parents had planned to throw would have been much more fun. Stoically she stood in the endless receiving line, wilting under the introductions that seemed to go on forever.

The fact that she was being examined for her fitness in her new role was blatantly apparent. Matrons clucked over her, obviously comparing her to Kay, Tyler's first wife; unmarried women gave her the once-over, wishing they were standing in her satin shoes; unfamiliar men swept their eyes over her modestly clad body as if they were imagining the wedding night. She was kissed, hugged, pummeled and wept over. By the time she could gracefully leave the line, she was exhausted.

The Hamiltons had hired a small orchestra to play, and after Sandy and Tyler cut the largest wedding cake she had ever seen, he led her to the dance floor for the first dance. It was the only time all day that they had been able to talk.

"I should have put a stop to this," Tyler said grimly as he pulled her close. "What a nightmare."

Sandy was stunned, and she hugged him close against her. "I thought this was what you wanted."

"Would any sane person want this?"

Warmth replaced the formal chill that had settled around her heart. "Do you suppose you could have told me before this got out of hand?" she asked with a teasing grin.

"I thought you wanted it. I didn't realize until today how intimidating all this must be for you."

She turned her face to his and his lips covered hers in a not-formal-at-all kiss. "I think I'm going to make it," she reassured him. "Will you try to stay by my side until we can get out of here?"

"I'll even help you change into your going-away clothes."

"That's perfectly moral now, isn't it?" she said, wishing she could take him up on his offer. "But I'm afraid your mother would have a heart attack. Your marrying me was enough of a shock to her system."

"I'm tired of waiting to be alone with you."

After their tree house tryst, Sandy and Tyler had seen little of each other in the six weeks that it had taken to put together the elaborate wedding. Sandy had remained at her parents' house, coming to Cameron for weekends chaperoned by Aunt Charlotte or Tyler's parents. There had been parties to attend, wedding plans to finalize. The kisses and caresses they had been able to sneak had been few and far between. And there had been even less chance to talk seriously.

They had dined together at restaurants, discussing the thousand and one details of beginning their life together. They had driven back home to Aunt Charlotte's, discussing the impersonal decisions that needed to be made. When a few moments of blissful solitude were possible, they didn't discuss anything at all, preferring to show their feelings rather than talk about them. Now they were husband and wife.

It seemed impossible.

"I don't know how people survive long engagements," Sandy whispered in Tyler's ear as the song ended and everyone applauded.

"Not all brides-to-be are as steadfastly chaperoned as you were. Some prospective husbands are not mindless idiots by the time their wedding night rolls around."

Sandy blushed, and Tyler laughed as he handed her to her father for the next dance. She danced with two of her older brothers and her father-in-law, with Matthew Stone who behaved himself admirably and then with Ryan, who had accompanied Stacey and their children to the wedding and reception.

"I've only seen one other bride as lovely as you are," Ryan told her gallantly.

"Stacey looks beautiful today, too," Sandy pointed out. The slight thickening of Stacey's waistline and the mother-to-be flush on her cheeks made Sandy's sister more beautiful than ever. Just looking at Stacey made Sandy hopeful that someday she, too, would carry that look of absolute joy on her face.

"She was a lovely matron of honor," Ryan agreed.

"I've been meaning to ask someone," Sandy said when the dance was almost over. "Why did everyone laugh when Tyler and I knelt at the beginning of the service?" She could feel the vibrations of Ryan's laughter through his dark suit coat.

"I was sure someone would tell you right away. When Tyler knelt and the bottom of his shoes became visible, we all saw that someone had painted HE on one and LP on the other in fluorescent orange paint."

"HE...LP. Help?" Sandy stamped her foot, but her face was wreathed in an irrepressible grin. "Who on earth would do that?"

"James and Randy," they answered together.

"Don't worry, your father took them out behind the church to discuss it with them afterward," Ryan added.

Sandy was giggling uncontrollably when Tyler cut in. "You two are having entirely too much fun," he complained.

Ryan kept his arm around Sandy and looked his new brother-in-law straight in the eye before relinquishing her. "This one is very special," he said quietly. "Be sure you're good to her."

"Do you know how many warnings that makes?" Tyler asked Sandy when they were dancing again.

"Too many to count. You're lucky my brother Thomas wasn't able to come. He's always been outrageously overprotective."

"A MacDonald trait, obviously."

When Stacey came over a few minutes later to see if Sandy was ready to change into her going-away clothes, Sandy kissed Tyler quickly and followed her sister to the private room where she was to change.

"Sit down," Stacey instructed. "You look so tired."

Sandy sat still while Stacey unfastened the pearl and flower headdress and laid it on a chair. Stacey took a brush and began to pull it through Sandy's hair, and Sandy shut her eyes in blissful relaxation for the first time that day.

"It was a lovely wedding."

"I guess," Sandy said, eyes still tightly shut. "I'd have liked it better if it had been someone else's."

"Someone else marrying Tyler?"

Sandy laughed and shook her head. "Can you believe I'm actually married?"

"No."

Sandy's eyes flew open. "Me neither."

"You'll believe it soon enough." Stacey stopped, realizing how the remark had sounded. "I mean, eventually you start to feel married."

"I think I'm going to feel married tonight."

Stacey sat down next to Sandy and took her hand. "Is there anything you want to know? You're a little old for me to have to explain the facts of life, but can I answer any questions?"

Sandy shook her head, but Stacey saw the shadow of fear cross her eyes. "What are you afraid of?"

Sandy leaned her head back and watched her older sister for a few moments before she asked, "When you married Ryan, did you ever worry about pleasing him?" She rushed on. "Tyler's been married. Happily married. I know what's going to happen tonight, but I'm very inexperienced . . ." Her voice trailed off.

"It's very special to have your first experience with the man you love, the man you've chosen for the rest of your life. Don't be ashamed of your virginity."

"I'm not ashamed, just concerned."

"Can I give you some advice?"

"Please!"

"Love him. Just love him and be sure he knows it. Everything else will take care of itself."

"Loving him will be easy no matter what else is hard," Sandy said softly.

"Then you have nothing to be frightened of."

A series of knocks on the door announced the arrival of the other MacDonald women. Stacey stood to let them in. "Tonight's going to be beautiful," she promised her sister, before she opened the door. "Tyler Hamilton is a very lucky man."

Although Tyler had tried to consult Sandy about their honeymoon plans, she had preferred to be surprised. After she had thrown the bouquet, dodged countless pink net bundles of rice and said goodbye to the immediate families, she found herself in the Lincoln, next to her new husband, speeding down the highway with no idea at all where they were going.

"Are we really alone?"

Tyler checked his rearview mirror. "It would seem so."

"Hallelujah!"

"Come here, woman." Tyler put his arm around Sandy's shoulder and pulled her to sit against him.

"Are you going to tell me where we're headed?"

Tyler's long fingers were stroking the silk sleeve of her turquoise going-away dress, and Sandy shivered in response. Wherever they were going, they couldn't get there fast enough to suit her.

"I'm taking you to my beach house in South Carolina."

Sandy let the words sink in. As hard as she had tried to push Tyler's first marriage out of her mind, today had made it difficult not to remember. She had wondered all day if Tyler was comparing this occasion with his first wedding. She had been aware that others had been comparing her, unfavorably she was sure, with the socially correct, statuesque woman Tyler had been married to. Now they were going to spend their honeymoon in a place where Tyler and Kay had spent time together. She checked out her suspicion. "How long have you had the beach house?"

"Seven or eight years. Why?"

"I just wondered."

Tyler's fingers crept up her sleeve to her neck where he caressed the soft skin he contacted there. "I'm waiting."

"I'm being foolish," she said, her lower lip caught between her teeth. Tyler was silent. "It's just that...well, I'm not really jealous of your first wife...." She felt Tyler stiffen beside her. "It's just that...when you make love to me tonight, I want to be sure you know who's in your bed."

"What an extraordinary thing to say," Tyler answered after a charged moment of silence. With an easy movement he pulled the big Lincoln onto the shoulder of the road. "How could you think that I'd ever be confused?"

"I know you loved her. I can live with that. But making love tonight in the same bed where you made love to Kay? I don't think I can handle that."

"Kay was never at the beach house. She hated isolated places. It's always been my retreat, and no one's ever been there with me until now."

Contrite and humiliated, Sandy rested her head on his shoulder. "I'm sorry," she said, quick tears forming in her green eyes.

"Sandy, you won't be sharing your marriage bed with another woman. Not in any way."

Tyler tipped her head back, taking her soft mouth with his hard one, and his kiss convinced her that he was telling the truth.

The beach house was gray, weathered wood built off the ground on tall posts. It sat, surrounded by dunes, just off the ocean shore. Although the October weather was warm, the water was chilly, and tourists had abandoned the area for more favorable temperatures. Tyler's house sat on enough land to be private under the worst of circumstances. In October it was absolutely deserted.

"I love it. I love it!" Sandy scurried over the dunes, carefully avoiding the sea oats, as Tyler climbed the steps to unlock the back door. "I love it. I love it!"

The sun had recently set, and pastel streaks of light hovered on the horizon. White-tipped waves ran along the shore, beckoning Sandy's exploration, and she abandoned her new husband to the task of carrying suitcases as she ran along the water's edge.

"You look just right here," Tyler said from the shadows, and she turned to hold out her arms to him. "This is home."

"Have you ever seen the ocean before?"

She shook her head, not at all ashamed of her inexperience. "Never. But I think that now you may have to drag me away."

"Not for two whole weeks," he reminded her, catching her by the waist and twirling her effortlessly in his arms.

Sandy slid down his long body as he cupped her buttocks, moving her against him. "Two whole weeks.

What will we do all that time?'' she asked, fluttering her eyelashes.

"We'll think of something."

"Well, I don't see any movie theaters or restaurants nearby. The water's probably too cold to swim."

"I packed a deck of cards."

"We're saved then."

Tyler set her down gently, and with his arm around her waist, he firmly propelled her toward the house. "Are you hungry?"

They had stopped to eat on the way and Sandy had been too excited to do more than pick at her food. What she was hungry for now was something different. "No."

At the top of the steps, Tyler swung her off her feet again, carrying her over the threshold. She was thrilled by his newly-married chivalry and slightly saddened when he finally set her down. Fantasizing that perhaps he would carry her right into the bedroom and simultaneously relieve her desires and fears, she was immersed in disappointment. For a man who seemed to have been chafing at the bit all day, he was remarkably calm.

Inside, the house was irresistible. The wood was the same gray as the exterior, but the entire front of the house facing the ocean was glass. "Some retreat," Sandy said with pleasure. "I was expecting a cozy little shack."

"Would I bring you to a shack for our honeymoon?"

"You could have brought me to a mosquito-ridden hut and I would have been delighted," she said with a grin.

Tyler came to stand behind her, his arms around her waist. "I hired a woman to come in and open it up for us and to stock the refrigerator. If you like, she can come back and cook every day, too. Otherwise, she'll just be back every three days to clean."

"Over my dead body."

Tyler tightened his arms. "You're not supposed to work on your honeymoon."

"Taking care of you comes under the heading of pleasure."

"Oh, I think you'll be taking care of me quite nicely, Alexandra Kathryn MacDonald Hamilton. I'm counting on it."

It was a promising statement, but before it could lead to anything, Tyler broke away to show her through the rest of the house, explaining where to find anything she might need. There were three bedrooms. At the last, they stopped and Sandy self-consciously went to sit on the big double bed. "Is this our room?"

Tyler was watching her with a half smile twisting his features. "Bingo."

The room had floor-to-ceiling glass windows looking over a deck that led down to the beach. Sandy knew that with the lights off she would be able to see the ocean pounding the shore below. "I'm going to love it."

"I hope so. We'll be spending some significant blocks of time in here."

An attack of shyness made her examine her shoe. Sensing her discomfort, Tyler walked to the door. "I'm going to make a fire to take the chill off the air. Change if you'd like to or come as you are."

What did she change into? The almost-invisible nightgown that Wendy, Sarah and Jennifer had given her was not designed for anything except instant removal. The nightgown her mother had given her was as enticing as a flour sack. Sandy settled on a floor-length green nightgown and robe that exactly matched her eyes. Stacey had given them to her, and as always, Stacey knew best. After a quick shower Sandy put them on, and the filmy material slithered seductively around her hips and thighs as she went to join Tyler.

"You're as beautiful as you were in your wedding dress." Tyler made room for her on the sofa beside him, and she slipped down and snuggled against him as his arm encircled her.

Together they watched the flames dance. "I'm so glad to be here," Sandy told him, turning her face up to his. Tyler's eyes were shut, and there was a curious tautness about him that didn't seem to fit with the sensually charged atmosphere. "Tyler?"

He turned his head so that she could no longer see his face. "Sandy, I know you must be completely exhausted. I'll understand if you would just like to go to bed now."

She wasn't sure what he meant. "Whatever you say. But you have to get ready, don't you?"

"I'm not going just yet."

"Then neither am I." She settled back beside him, but his words had left her ill at ease.

They were on their honeymoon, this was the long-awaited wedding night, and suddenly, Tyler didn't seem to want her anymore. She pushed the thought aside. It was ridiculous. No matter what other areas of their marriage still needed clarification, their physical desire for each other had always been crystal clear.

"Aren't you going to kiss me?" she asked finally. "I think it's all right now, don't you? We've been married over six hours."

Something like a groan came from Tyler's side of the sofa. He complied with his mouth moving carefully against hers as if he were afraid that she would recoil at any pressure.

Now Sandy was genuinely puzzled. Deciding to take matters into her own hands, she put them on the back of his neck and pulled his mouth against hers again. Her tongue traced his lips, she pressed her soft breasts against his shirt while the material of her gown rustled sensuously around him.

Tyler's hand began to wander over the curves of her body, bunching the silky fabric and letting it fall against her. Sandy moaned with pleasure. But her response seemed to disturb him, and he pulled back a little, his eyes shuttered to her.

"Perhaps it's time for bed after all," he said.

He stood and disappeared down the hall, leaving Sandy to trail gracefully behind him. When he disappeared into the bathroom she pulled down the sheets and slipped off her robe. Her gown was held up by thin silvery straps and incorporated yards and yards of filmy green fabric. On an impulse, she twirled around like a small child in a ballet recital, letting the material float around her whirling body.

When she stopped spinning, Tyler was standing in the doorway wearing dark blue pajamas. Sandy's smile died at the expression on his face. It was a mixture of desire and torment and it sent her heart thudding down to her shoes. "Tyler," she whispered, "what have I done?"

He shook his head, reaching up to click off the overhead light. The room was suddenly dark, but he crossed it easily to open the curtains all the way and let the meager glow from the cloudy sky illuminate them.

Sandy watched as he approached her. She wanted to soothe away whatever troubled him; she wanted desperately to make whatever was wrong between them right. But when she reached for him, he held her gently away. "It's cold in here. Get under the covers."

She did as she was told, bewildered by his distance. When he slid under the blanket too, she turned on her side to face him. "Shouldn't I undress?"

"It's too chilly."

Sandy couldn't believe that a honeymoon in Antarctica would be too chilly to lie naked beside the man she loved, but she was in no mood to argue. "I'll bet if we snuggle together we'll warm up faster."

She was relieved when Tyler's answer was to pull her into the crook of his arm. She could feel the heat from his body against her breasts and the long muscled length of his leg through the thin fabric of her gown. The shiver that went through her had nothing to do with the nebulous chill in the air. "Are you comfortable?" he asked.

"Comfortable is not quite the right word."

Tyler began to stroke her hair as if to soothe her fears. She realized that she had given him the wrong impression. She was not frightened, not of him. She was only afraid that she might not please him. Snuggling closer, she reached across his chest to caress his cheek, running her fingertips over the perfect outline of his mouth. "It seems that all my life, I've wanted to be here like this with you," she whispered.

He didn't stiffen, not exactly, anyhow. But the peculiar tautness she had noticed before was still present, and at her words he seemed to pull even farther into himself. "Under those tomboy ways exists a true romantic," he said, kissing the fingertips that lingered on his lips.

Her limited bag of tricks was fast becoming empty. Slowly she began to unbutton the top of his pajamas, an act that seemed daring under the circumstances. When she had finished she felt a reassuring shudder pass through his long frame. Her inexperienced fingers began to play with the inky curls she had uncovered until his fingers circling her wrist stopped her. "Sandy, if you do too much of that, tonight is going to be a disaster."

Humiliation drained through her body. In her innocence she had thought that touching him would bring him pleasure. Instead he seemed angry. She moved away a little, waiting for the explanation that never came. "I'm sorry," she said finally. "You'll have to tell me what to do then."

"Let me take care of it," he said, his voice softening.

"Tyler, if you're too tired tonight, I'll certainly understand."

His laugh was humorless. "I'd have to be dead to be too tired to make love to you."

But though he said he wanted her, Sandy could find no real evidence of it in the controlled, almost calculated way he began to caress her. Her own response died time after time from lack of encouragement. It was as if Tyler had set out to make their union as passionless as possible.

His hands were steady and gentle, but they held no magic. His kisses were carefully tender, but they held no fire. He whispered words of affection, but no words of love or arousal. He did not undress her; he did not move against her with abandon.

Finally, with careful precision he made them one. And Sandy, who would have been the willing vessel of genuine passion no matter what the initial pain, lay back against the pillows and cried bitter, helpless tears.

Chapter Eight

Sandy woke up the next morning with humiliation as the nucleus of every cell in her body. After Tyler had sealed their wedding vows the night before, he had taken her in his arms and whispered soothing endearments as she tried to choke back her sobs. He had promised her that it would be all right, that the first time a man makes love to a woman is never the best. She had listened, trying hard to believe the carefully chosen words, but when he fell asleep she moved to her own side of the bed, finding solace away from the warmth of his body.

She had been a complete failure. The small doubts she had experienced had not even begun to prepare her for the depth of her inadequacy. She had not expected miracles. She had known that she might experience pain. But she had never believed that she would experience the complete rejection she had felt in Tyler's arms. He had not wanted her. Making love to her had been a duty.

Why did he marry me? she asked herself, her eyes still tightly shut, her body curled into a knot. If he didn't want me, why did he give me his name?

She listened for the sound of Tyler's breathing. The opposite side of the bed was quiet, and finally she turned slowly, as if in sleep, to peek through her eyelashes. Tyler was gone. A muffled crash from the kitchen pinpointed his location.

She stretched with no joy, and swung her feet on to the floor. Her body felt sore but not nearly as sore as it should have. She was a woman now, but she still felt like an untried girl.

Grabbing clothes at random from her suitcase, she went into the bathroom to prepare for the new day.

Later when she could delay no longer, Sandy walked through the house to find her husband. Tyler was sitting at the small round table placed near the glass walls that revealed the ocean. When he raised his eyes and saw her standing there, his expression was as carefully veiled as her own. *We've been married less than twenty-four hours, and already we have secrets to hide,* she thought sadly.

"Good morning. I made coffee if you'd like some."

"Thank you." She disappeared into the kitchen to compose herself and search for the coffee. "Have you eaten anything?" she called to him.

"I was waiting for you."

It was a good sign. At least he knew that she was there. He remembered he had married her. Now if she could just figure out why.

"Would you like eggs and bacon for breakfast?" she called. Strong arms around her waist stopped her.

"No. I'd like a good-morning kiss." He turned her slowly to face him. "Look at me."

She shook her head slightly, keeping her eyes on her bare toes.

"I'll have to kiss the top of your head then, and as lovely as your hair is, I don't want it in my mouth."

She was shocked that he could tease after the debacle of the previous night. Tentatively she tilted her head to read his expression. Instead she was subjected to a friendly kiss. "Good morning, wife," he said, kissing her again with the same detached affection.

"Good morning, husband," she answered softly. "How do you like your eggs?"

There was little conversation over the breakfast table. Tyler complimented her on her cooking; she told him how much she liked the house. They commiserated over the drizzling rain that was going to make it impossible to enjoy the beach. They managed to get through the meal.

Tyler insisted on doing the dishes, and Sandy let him. She wandered restlessly through the rooms looking for answers that weren't there. They had fourteen more days to be alone together. The next two weeks promised to stretch into eternity.

Although the air wasn't chilled, Tyler made another fire, and they sat together watching it as they had the night before. Sandy asked Tyler to tell her about some of his cases and surprisingly, the informal conversation relaxed them both. By noon, they were smiling and laughing with good-natured humor.

Tyler was careful not to touch her in more than a casual fashion, and Sandy was careful not to seem as if it mattered.

After a lunch they fixed together, Tyler pulled out a book and Sandy went to take a nap. Even though she and Tyler had finally been able to relax a little in each other's presence, the strain of the morning had given her a headache. With the curtains pulled tightly shut, she lay on their marriage bed and let the few tears that hadn't been cried the night before slip down her cheeks.

She fell asleep feeling sad, but she woke up angry. Somehow the nap destroyed her headache, leaving in its place a slow-burning fury at the way she had been treated. She was not Tyler's sister; she was not his best friend. Perhaps they had never been lovers before their wedding night, but there had been promises of great passion in his responses to her. For some reason she couldn't fathom, she had been cheated out of the one thing she had been sure would be good in their marriage.

She was no longer humiliated. She no longer felt inadequate. She was simply ready to claw his eyes out.

"You're awake."

"Yes."

Tyler was standing at the door watching her. He came to the bed but stood a foot away when he teased, "I thought you might sleep the whole day away."

"You can see I didn't."

If he was surprised by the venom in her tone, he didn't show it. "The drizzle stopped and the sun is coming out. I thought I'd take advantage of the last hours of daylight and walk on the beach."

"Be my guest."

"Sandy, I'm asking you to come with me."

There was amusement in his voice, and she swung her legs over the bed, standing directly in front of him. "Then why didn't you say so?"

"I just did."

"Communicating with you is like talking to an out-of-order robot, Tyler. You rarely say what you mean. Someone's switched your microchips around."

He threw back his head and laughed, his long arms pulling her close as he did. "Do you always wake up from a nap like this?"

His body against hers stirred the banked fires of the night before, and she pulled away sharply. "Always. You're going to hate being married to me."

"Impossible."

There was such affection in his voice that her tongue stumbled over her next angry retort. Before she could recover he covered her mouth with his, burying his hands in her hair. This kiss was not friendly, it burned through to her very core. She stood in stunned surprise as finally he washed her face with tiny kisses. When he pulled away she could only stare.

"You're adorable when you're angry," he said as if he needed to explain.

"Then perhaps I should have worked up a temper tantrum last night," she said, turning to rummage through her suitcase for shoes to wear.

"What do you mean?"

"Forget it, Tyler. Let's take that walk."

The cold front that the rain had signaled had not yet arrived. The air was pleasantly warm as they walked along the shore. Sandy stuffed her hands in her pockets to avoid holding Tyler's, and they were both quiet, immersed in their own thoughts. They walked for miles, turning to start back to the beach house when the sun was no longer visible.

Filled with enough pent-up tension and unexplored anger to make some psychiatrist a wealthy man, Sandy finally exploded as they neared the house. She was faced with the choice of picking a fight with her new husband or doing something drastic to shock her body into submission. The choice seemed obvious, and she sat on the sand and began to pull off her shoes.

"What are you doing?"

"I'm going to wade."

"It's too cold. I don't want you wading in that water."

She shook her head in disbelief. "Fine, I won't wade. I'll go for a swim."

"No, you won't."

Sandy stared at him openmouthed. "You are my husband, not my keeper." She continued to take off her shoes.

"You'll catch pneumonia. The water's cold this time of year anyway, but the rain's made it even colder."

"I'm healthy. I'll survive."

The sky was darkening. The beach was totally deserted. Hidden by the dunes, Sandy began to pull off her blue jeans.

"Do I have to carry you up to the house and talk sense into you?"

"Don't you touch me!" She pulled off her T-shirt, standing in front of him clothed only in a silky violet teddy. She didn't notice Tyler's indrawn breath as his eyes fastened on her exposed body. She had turned to run into the waves when he called her to come back.

The water wasn't just cold. It was ice against the warmth of her skin, and she gasped as she dived into a wave, letting it cover her for a moment before she came up for a breath. She spit out the salt water and coughed, diving back in again and again, punishing her body for its betrayal of the night before.

Finally she was shivering so hard that she could not stay in a second longer. She was farther out than she had intended, and the dubious warmth of the shore seemed far away. As she brushed long strands of hair from her eyes, she saw that between her and the beach was her husband, wading angrily through the ocean to retrieve her. She lurched through the small waves to collapse in Tyler's arms. Scooping her up as though she was weightless, he pulled her against his chest, shielding her from the slight wind as he carried her to dry land.

"You little fool," he ground out. Setting her on her feet, he stripped the soaked teddy off, exposing the slender curves of her body to his gaze for the first time. "Get dressed," he said, his voice a strangle.

As cold and miserable as she was, Sandy did not miss the expression on Tyler's face or the sound of his words. Shivering, she watched his eyes hungrily de-

vour her. The naked passion there sent fire blazing
through her to shut out the cold.

"No. I won't."

"You'll freeze!"

"Restore my warmth." With every bit of wanton
behavior she was capable of, she pressed her body to
his, moving against him with all the concentrated desire she had ever known.

He was a drowning man. He clutched her, his hands
running feverishly down her sides, to her breasts, to
her buttocks to bring her closer. She unbuttoned his
shirt with shaking fingers and let her mouth discover
him. When he scooped her up this time it was to carry
her to the shadow of the dunes. In a moment he was
undressed, too, and they were in each other's arms,
crying out for satisfaction.

There were sea gulls cawing in the distance. There
was the sound of the waves crashing on the sands below. There was the feel of Tyler's body against hers as
he united them, creating a vast ocean of longing within
her. There were waves inside her too, and finally a tidal
wave of pleasure that threatened to drown her in its
sucking, spinning, triumphant cascade of feeling.

Sandy clung to Tyler, her legs wrapped tightly
around him. They were on shifting sands, safe only in
each other's arms. And finally, incredibly, there was
peace.

When he tried to roll off of her a few moments later,
she wouldn't let him. Surprisingly, she could still talk.
"Don't go," she whispered.

"We have to. You're going to get sick if I don't get
you inside."

"I'm not cold."

"Humor me, damn it. Just this once."

Wishing that they could stay there forever, she acquiesced, taking the clothes he handed her and pulling them over her sand-encrusted, satiated body. When she was done, she looked up to see Tyler watching her, his face wary, his body covered now, too. He turned and she followed him to the house, skipping to keep up with his long stride.

He went straight to the bathroom, turning on the shower until the small room was steamy with warmth. Sandy, passing in the hallway, was snatched, undressed and set under the hot water before she could protest. When she emerged after washing her hair and enjoying the luxury of body heat again, Tyler was gone.

Wrapping a towel around her rosy flesh she went in search of her husband. "Tyler?"

There was no answer. Curiosity piqued, she dressed quickly in a coral velour warm-up suit, and then went to finish searching the house. Tyler was definitely gone. She discovered his discarded clothing in the tiny laundry room, her wet sneakers set carefully on the deck. But there were no clues to his whereabouts.

Shrugging her shoulders at the mystery, she returned to their bedroom to comb the myriad tangles from her hair and attempt to braid it neatly. She sat on the bed with the lights off, staring out at the ocean, remembering the feel of Tyler's arms around her while his lips traced fevered paths over her body. Their lovemaking had been everything she had ever dreamed about and more.

Sometime later she heard the door slam. A little hurt that he had left her so soon after their passionate encounter, she sat quietly on the bed waiting for him to find her. When he stood at the bedroom door, she didn't turn.

He came to the bed without speaking and sat beside her. "Are you warm enough?" he asked finally.

"Not without you here," she said, relenting. There was no point in throwing up new walls between them.

"How can you still say that?" he asked, self-blame heavy in his tone.

Sandy frowned, turning to read his face, but the room was too dark for success. "Once again I have no idea what you mean."

"I mean that after my behavior on the beach, how can you pretend to be glad to see me?" Each syllable was clearly enunciated.

"Pretend?"

"It's a seven-letter word meaning 'to playact.' "

Suddenly very tired of all the unexplained nuances of the past day and a half, Sandy got up from the foot of the bed, pulled back the covers and slipped under them. "Look, Tyler, if you want to have a conversation with me, you're going to have to do it in bed." She patted the place next to her. "All this tension is exhausting me."

He came around beside her, took off his shoes but none of his clothes and lay down, his hands folded beneath his head. "I never intended to treat you that way," he said without looking at her. "What happened on the beach wasn't planned."

"Of course it wasn't. That's what made it so spectacular."

"Spectacular?" He snorted. "Did your mother train you to make your husband feel good, no matter what he does to you?"

"What are you talking about?"

He propped himself on one elbow and faced her. "I know I frightened you, but I lost control. I've been so dizzy with need for you that I was just pushed over the edge. I've been trying to be so careful, so gentle...."

"You've been trying..."

"Not to hurt you." He ran his fingers through his hair in an uncharacteristic display of feeling. "Sandy, you're young and very new at this. I haven't wanted to scare you, and now..."

"Tyler!" She understood. Finally it was clear. It wasn't that he didn't want her; it wasn't that he wasn't attracted to her anymore. She rolled to her side and began to cover his face with kisses. "Poor Tyler," she murmured, wrapping her arms around him. "Who ever told you that a woman, even one with no experience, wants to be treated like spun glass?"

He was silent, but he returned her caresses. Already she could feel the heat from his body merging with her own. Soon there would be no more time to talk. "Tyler, why did you think I'd be afraid of you?"

He pulled away slightly, but only to settle her more comfortably beside him. As if she were a sponge, Sandy could almost absorb the tension draining slowly from his body. He ignored her question. "You weren't hurt?"

"Today was wonderful. *Last* night hurt because I thought you didn't want me." The wobble in her voice was a fitting punctuation to her statement.

"Didn't want you? Dear Lord, I wanted you so much I thought I'd die from it. And I was so afraid I'd spoil things for you. When you cried I felt like the worst failure in the world."

"I felt like the failure. No matter what I did, you didn't like it."

"I liked it too much. I was afraid I'd lose control. You do that to me."

"I thought I was supposed to do that."

"Not on our wedding night." Tyler was silent, and then, as if he had decided she deserved an explanation, he continued. "I didn't want anything that happened last night to have repercussions for our future together. I knew that it could."

His explanation spoke volumes. Sandy understood instinctively that Tyler was referring to his past. As personally revealing as his last comment had been, she couldn't let it pass unnoticed. Although openly discussing this was not something she had been raised to do, she pressed painfully onward.

"Tyler, do you remember when we were driving here and you told me that I wouldn't be sharing my marriage bed with another woman?"

She felt him stiffen beside her and his answer was a grunt. "I don't think you were telling the truth," she said.

His profile was chiseled perfection against the silver moonlight illuminating their room. Sandy knew that he was remembering another time, another wedding night, another marriage. "Tyler, I want all of you, not just the part your experience tells you is good for me."

"Sandy," he groaned as he pulled her to lie on top of him. "You make me go crazy."

"I'm so glad." She buried her face in his shoulder. "You need to go crazy once in a while."

"I have a feeling it may be more than once in a while," he said, beginning to unbraid her hair.

"That will be even better." She felt his hands stroking the now-loosened strands. "Why are you doing that?"

"Because as cute as you are with your hair in braids, when I make love to you in a minute, it's the woman in you that I want in my arms."

Later they dressed again and dug through the refrigerator, making huge double-decker sandwiches to eat out on the deck. Huddled together out of the path of the wind they watched the waves change the shoreline.

"This was the right place to bring you," Tyler said after they had finished the impromptu dinner. "You're like the ocean. Wild and constantly changing, generous and nurturing. Calm at times and furious at others. A sea spirit."

"What a nice way to describe a very ordinary person."

"You're not ordinary at all. I've never met anyone like you."

"Some people would say that made you a lucky man."

"Some people can't appreciate the finer things in life."

Sandy leaned over the table and gave Tyler a kiss that was all the thank-you he needed. "You also catch on to things very quickly," he added.

"I've had a good teacher."

When the cold chased them back inside, they lounged in front of the fire, talking about their childhoods. Sandy regaled Tyler with hair-raising tales of her escapades, and he sketched out a well-ordered, perfectly balanced youth that had left little time for just enjoying life.

"You've been cheated out of so much," she observed when he was finished. "Your childhood... then your wife."

"Kay and I had some good years together. I've regretted her death but never our marriage."

"Can you tell me about her? Does it still hurt to talk about it?" Sandy was curled up on the floor at Tyler's feet like a well-fed kitten, and she rubbed her head against his leg in comfort.

"No. The pain is gone now, too. What do you want to know?"

"How you met."

"We were in diapers at the time. Our families were close friends. We grew up together, almost as brother and sister. We dated in high school, got pinned in college, engaged when I was in law school and married when I graduated. I knew everything about her; in most areas our tastes were similar."

"What was Kay like?"

"Self-assured, poised, able to meet every challenge, even death, with finesse. She was a perfect candidate for a politician's wife."

"When she died you must have felt like you lost part of yourself."

"When she died, I felt relief. She was ill for a long time. Her death was a merciful blessing."

Alive and sitting at the feet of the man she loved with all her heart, there was no room inside Sandy for envy. "She had you, Tyler. She died too early, much too early, but she had years with you. In that way she was very lucky."

"I'm not sure that she always thought so."

Sandy was startled by his honesty. "May I ask why?"

"There were parts of our marriage that were less than perfect." He did not elaborate. He did not need to.

"No marriage is perfect."

Tyler slid off the sofa to join her on the floor. "I think if we'd had children, things might have evened out a little. It was one of the few things we openly disagreed about."

"I've wondered why you didn't have any. Was it Kay's illness?"

"No, actually Kay just didn't like kids. They tend to be noisy and dirty and rude. Being a mother had no appeal for her."

"We've never really talked about kids, Tyler."

"There's a lot we haven't talked about, sea spirit."

"Would you still like to have children? My children?" she asked softly.

"Just as soon as you're ready."

A warm glow spread through Sandy at the thought of giving Tyler the children he had wanted for so long. Now was not the time, but later, when their marriage was solid, she would proudly bear him sons and daughters.

"I'll give you children, as many as you want. But Tyler, I don't know what kind of a politician's wife I'm going to be."

"Have you ever heard me express an interest in running for any office?"

She thought about his words. "No," she admitted. "But your mother has talked to me at great length about it."

"My mother should run for president."

She wondered if, like a good husband, he was just trying to soothe her fears. One thing she was sure of, she would never stand in his way, no matter what it cost her to play the political game. She would never make Tyler sorry that he had chosen her to share his life with.

She wasn't jealous of Kay or the time that Tyler had spent with her. But Tyler's description of his former wife had pointed out clearly the differences between Kay and Sandy. And though Sandy knew that she could never compete with Kay's memory, she also knew that the time had come to make the supreme effort to grow up. She would take her place in Tyler's world, and she would make him proud. That much she could do.

In the meantime, two glorious, carefree weeks stretched in front of them. "Tyler?"

"Mmm..."

Sandy was beginning to understand her new husband's body, and unbuttoning his shirt, she sought out the most sensitive places on his chest. "Growing up on a farm has taught me the value of hard work."

"Mmm..."

"And wasting time is considered a sin in my family."

"Mmm..."

"You're not going to let me wallow in guilt, are you? I mean, I really feel that right now I should be doing something productive."

"Sea spirit, you're going to make an old man out of me."

"I think not doing this could make an old man out of you."

With his hands wandering the curves of her body, Tyler whispered against her searching mouth, "I think you're probably right."

"And I am absolutely sure I am," she answered, just before speech deserted her. "Absolutely sure."

Chapter Nine

The first thing Sandy noticed about Tyler's house in Cameron was that it had no trees. But that was not unusual. The developers who had designed Cameron Estates had begun their work with a legion of bulldozers, knocking down and setting fire to the magnificent oaks, poplars and magnolias that had grown there for decades. Now there was nothing to block the view of ostentatious Southern architecture at its worst.

Tyler's house, like half the houses on his street, was a Greek-revival-style mansion. Sandy had to bite her tongue to keep from asking where the slave quarters were; she had no desire to hurt Tyler's feelings. Perhaps he hadn't chosen the house at all. Perhaps the house had been Kay's idea.

"Well, it . . . it certainly is big," she stammered, for lack of anything kind to say about it.

Tyler misinterpreted her statement. "I...we," he amended, "have help. You don't need to worry about taking care of the house yourself."

"That's a relief." But it wasn't. The idea of living with strangers did not appeal to her. She wanted to take care of Tyler with no help from anyone. She wondered when they had children if a nurse would be hired automatically, making Sandy completely obsolete.

"My housekeeper, Mrs. Lamont, has been with me for years. There's a part-time gardener and a maid who does all the heavy cleaning. Mrs. Lamont has been doing the cooking since long before Kay died. We should probably hire someone else now."

"No!" She tried to soften her exclamation. "I mean, no thank you. Whatever Mrs. Lamont can't do, I will."

Tyler parked the car in the driveway, coming around to Sandy's door to help her out. "I'm sorry I never brought you by before this. It must feel very strange to be coming here to live without seeing it first."

"We were so busy. When we were alone there seemed to be better things to do." She smiled in memory of the stolen kisses that would never have to be stolen again.

"Still, there's no excuse. But you have met Mrs. Lamont. She was at the wedding and reception."

Sandy shook her head. There had been well over a hundred strangers who had come through the receiving line. She wasn't sure that she would recognize any of them again. "It's been two weeks."

"Two incredible weeks." Tyler's arm around her shoulders stopped her slow progress up the front walk. "Two of the best weeks of my life," he murmured, turning her face to his for a leisurely kiss.

It was like Tyler to reassure her. She was entering his world, and soon she would be attempting to find a place in it for herself. On the trip back from South Carolina Sandy had felt herself grow quieter, more subdued. Now she was almost speechless with insecurity.

"Come on, sea spirit, it's not that bad."

"I love you, Tyler."

He squeezed her shoulder in answer, pulling her along beside him. Just for a moment she let herself wonder if he would ever say those words to her. As happy as he seemed to be, he had never told her he loved her. Love was something different, deeper, than what he felt for her. She only hoped that when he saw how she could fit herself into his life, his affection for her would strengthen and grow.

The front door opened before they were halfway across the porch. A woman in her fifties, wearing a crisp white uniform, stood there to greet them. Sandy examined Mrs. Lamont with curiosity as the introductions were made. There were deep, harsh grooves around the housekeeper's unsmiling mouth, and she held herself as rigid as a Prussian soldier. She had small, almost beady eyes that seemed to take in absolutely everything. Sandy was properly intimidated.

"The staff welcomes you, Mrs. . . . . Hamilton."

The words had been hard for the woman to say, and Sandy hadn't missed the slight hesitation. She felt like a little girl dressing up in someone else's clothing. "Thank you," she said simply.

Tyler's hand on her back was insistent, and just for a moment, Sandy almost gave up the fight to remain in her place. Innate romanticism stopped her. "I'm not going anywhere, Tyler," she said firmly.

Obviously puzzled, he waited for an explanation, but Sandy wouldn't even look at him. Finally, a slow smile began to form on his face. "I already did this once," he reminded her.

"That was our honeymoon. This is our life."

Without another word, he scooped her off the ground, strode across the threshold and deposited her at the housekeeper's feet. "It's a good thing you're so light," he said in mock complaint.

"It's a good thing you're so chivalrous." She stood on tiptoe to kiss his cheek.

"Mrs. Lamont, please show Mrs. Hamilton the downstairs while I bring our luggage inside." Tyler gave Sandy a little push to start her trotting along behind the housekeeper.

The house was huge, and although it had an ample number of windows, it was gloomy. There was room after room of ornate furniture covered in elegant brocades and velvets. Even the so-called family room was uncomfortably formal with a fireplace that seemed never to have known a fire and a walnut pool table that seemed never to have known a pool cue.

The kitchen was cold and sterile, but at least the curtains were not drawn. Sunlight from the small window over the sink tried unsuccessfully to warm the room. An accomplished country cook, Sandy still could not imagine what half the small appliances on the counter were. The microwave looked as though it could fix dinner by itself, the food processor looked as though it could do everything except split logs. Suddenly even the most ordinary things seemed terribly complicated.

Following Mrs. Lamont back into the hall, Sandy asked, "I've noticed that most of the curtains are drawn. Why is that?"

"The first Mrs. Hamilton always specified that I was to close the curtains against the sunlight. So I open and close them as the sun changes angles. That way the furniture and carpeting will never fade."

Sandy winced at the thought of so much time spent on such a foolish endeavor. Furniture was to sit on; rugs were to walk on; sunlight was to appreciate. Furniture that looked as if it had never been used wasn't doing its job. "I see," she said, although she really didn't.

Tyler was on his way upstairs with the final suitcase when Sandy followed Mrs. Lamont back to the front of the house. He motioned for her to follow him. The second floor of the house was more of the same, but at least this time her tour guide held her hand. Even the MacDonald farmhouse didn't have as many bedrooms as Tyler's house. And what boring bedrooms they were. All of them were large, well designed and totally lacking in any interesting detail.

Mrs. Lamont had followed behind them, and when Tyler was finished, the housekeeper asked politely, "Which room shall I get ready for you, Mrs. Hamilton?"

Sandy was shocked. Her suitcases were still in the hallway, and she realized that Tyler also had been waiting for her decision. She threw back her shoulders and straightened her spine. "That's easy," she said. "I'll be staying in my husband's room."

If Sandy had announced her decision to climb up to the roof and tap dance, Mrs. Lamont would not have looked any more disapproving. "I see." With military precision she marched down the hall to see about Sandy's strange request.

"Well-to-do Georgia lawyers don't sleep with their wives?" Sandy asked in a whisper.

"Let's set a new trend." Tyler put his arm around her and pulled her close. "Forgive me, sea spirit, but it may take a while for all of us to get used to your enthusiasm."

They were still kissing when Mrs. Lamont passed silently on her way back downstairs.

Although Sandy had been given a small bridal shower at her mother-in-law's home, she had never been there with Tyler. One week after they returned from the honeymoon, Tyler and Sandy were invited to dine with his parents, and Sandy was nervously rehearsing the proper etiquette of a daughter-in-law.

The Hamilton residence was in an older, more gracious section of Cameron, and Sandy enjoyed the change from the arid, treeless environment of Cameron Estates. The house itself was traditional but attractively presented on a lot sporting several pecan trees among its wealth of foliage. Since Tyler had been back to work for most of the week, Sandy had found herself with almost nothing to do. Even socializing with Tyler's parents was a welcome change.

Polite hugs were exchanged, and Sandy followed her new in-laws into the living room with Tyler right behind her. She had dressed carefully for the occasion, using some of her free time to shop for a suitable outfit, and she had pulled her hair on top of her head in a braided knot. But the right clothes and an appropriate hairstyle did not take the edge off her nervousness. Facing Tyler's parents when she had thought they would remain strangers had been different from facing them as in-laws. Even the time Sandy had spent planning the wedding with Mrs. Hamilton seemed casual in comparison.

"Both of you are looking well. The beach agreed with you," Mr. Hamilton observed.

Sandy decided that she liked Tyler's father. As she watched him chatting with his son, she could see the occasional sparkle in his eyes and the deep affection he held for his only child. Instinctively she knew that if she made Tyler happy, Mr. Hamilton would accept her no matter what mistakes she made.

Mrs. Hamilton was a different story. Although her attitude toward Sandy was properly polite, she constantly seemed to be taking her new daughter-in-law's measure. Sandy was sure that she was never going to be as acceptable to her mother-in-law as Tyler's first wife had been. It was not Sandy's fault, it could not be changed, but it left her feeling faintly forlorn.

Dinner was delicious. The Hamiltons' cook had been with them since Tyler's infancy, and Sandy tried to imagine her husband, who insisted he loved his new

wife's fried chicken, growing up here dining on vi-
chyssoise and trout meunière. She ate with relish, not
only because the meal was so excellent, but because for
the past week she had eaten little.

Since they had come back to Cameron, Mrs. Lamont had insisted on cooking every meal, and Mrs.
Lamont was not an accomplished cook. She prepared
food as she did everything else, with self-righteous
discipline. The food was plain, and there was just
enough to stave off starvation. When questioned
about her menus, she succinctly revealed her philoso-
phy: food was meant to nourish you and keep you
healthy. Period. The first Mrs. Tyler Hamilton had
agreed with her ideas. Unfortunately the second Mrs.
Tyler Hamilton was pining for baked ham coated with
brown sugar, mashed sweet potatoes and lemon meringue pie.

After two helpings of apricot soufflé, Sandy obligingly followed her in-laws to the living room and settled back in an antique wing chair. "Well, Sandy,"
Mrs. Hamilton began. "Do you feel as though you've
settled in yet, dear?"

"I'm beginning to," Sandy answered cautiously.

"There are dozens of people just dying to get to
know you better. Just say the word when you're ready
to start socializing, and I'll pass along the message."

"The word" in Sandy's opinion, was "no." She did
not want to become part of the Cameron social scene;
she did not want to spend her free time, as plentiful as
it was, playing bridge and drinking tea or cocktails.
Tyler had never said that it was expected of her. He
was nonchalant about her role as his wife, apparently

convinced that everything would work itself out if she
gave it half a chance. He seemed to be content just
finding her in his bed every night and waking up with
her every morning.

But Sandy wanted to fit in. She wanted Tyler to be
proud of her, to think that she was a good wife. She
wanted Tyler to love her.

"I'd be glad to start meeting people," she answered quietly.

"That's good, dear. I'll be sure to let everyone
know."

Two weeks later the word was definitely out. No
longer did Sandy and Tyler have long, quiet evenings
after he arrived home from work. There were parties
to attend, dinners to sit through, charitable events to
patronize. Tyler gave Sandy free rein to accept or not
accept any invitation, and in her complete ignorance
as to what was appropriate, she accepted everything.
She was terrified of making a social blunder.

Mrs. Hamilton was her advisor. She made certain
that her new daughter-in-law met everyone important
and made a good impression on them. With eyebrow-
raised tactfulness she advised Sandy on the correct
clothing for each event, taking her shopping at Cameron's most exclusive shops if nothing Sandy already had was appropriate. In addition, she drilled the
family histories of the town's elite into her brain, until Sandy could recite entire genealogies by heart.

Two weeks before Thanksgiving, Sandy sat in front
of the mirror in the bedroom she shared with Tyler,
and tried valiantly to twist her hair into a sophisti-

cated knot for the party they were attending that evening.

"I think your mother's right," she said, jabbing hair pins into the heavy loop of hair. "I ought to get my hair cut."

"Another of mother's changes," Tyler said, his back turned to her as he searched for a clean shirt.

Sandy swiveled in her seat to watch him dress. Without a shirt the hard muscles rippling under his tanned skin were clearly visible, causing a familiar longing inside her. They had been so busy, and she had been so tired when they came home, that it had been almost a week since he had held her in his arms and made love to her.

"She thinks I would look more sophisticated and older, too."

"What do you think?" He turned to face her, and for a moment, she couldn't concentrate on his question. As he buttoned each button, covering himself from her gaze, her concentration returned.

"I've always been happy with it long."

"That should tell you something."

"But then, what do I know?"

"More than you've given yourself credit for lately."

Sandy heard the sharp edge in Tyler's voice, and she wondered what was behind it. "Are you angry at me?"

He shook his head, a weary shadow passing over his face. "No. But I will be if you cut your hair."

"All you had to do was tell me you like it long," she said, hurt by his tone.

"Look, Sandy, it's not what I like that's the point."

She tried to puzzle out his words, but the doorbell intruded. The couple who were taking them out to dinner had obviously arrived. Sandy turned back to the mirror and watched as Tyler came to stand behind her. Slowly he began to dig through the golden loop of hair, discarding hair pins as he came to them. "Wear it down," he told her. When he finished and her hair was once again hanging freely past her waist, he turned and left the room. Sandy sat and stared in the mirror at the place he had been and wondered what she had done wrong.

They dined at Cameron's finest restaurant, and from Sandy's viewpoint the evening went well. Their host was another local lawyer, and inevitably the talk turned to politics. Sandy listened as Tyler showed a grudging interest in the subject, warming up to a heated discussion that left the two men on opposite sides of the issue but energized by the argument.

Sandy stayed in the background, refusing to express the opinions that were constantly on the tip of her tongue. Although no one had ever told her so, she was certain that her interference in this aspect of Tyler's life would not be welcome. Instead she chatted comfortably with their hostess about local events, clothing and interior decorating.

They arrived home late again. Tyler had been very quiet in the car, ignoring her few attempts to draw him out. When they were in their bedroom, he changed into pajamas and pulled on a robe. "I'm going downstairs to my study. Don't wait up for me," he told her with a perfunctory good-night kiss.

Although she tried to sleep, she was still awake when, hours later, he slipped into bed beside her. "Tyler," she whispered, "are you all right?"

"I'm fine. Go back to sleep."

Instead, she pressed her body against his, caressing him with all of her softness. "I've missed you," she whispered in his ear, her hands beginning to unbutton his pajama top.

"Have you?"

She couldn't miss the faint sarcasm in his tone, and she removed her hands and rolled away from him. "I don't know what you think I've done wrong," she said, "but I don't deserve your scorn."

He was still lying rigid next to her and for a long time she thought that he would refuse to answer. "I'm sorry," he apologized finally. "I'm just tired. Go to sleep."

It was hours before she could. Long after Tyler's breathing deepened and evened out, she lay awake trying to understand how she had disappointed him. And finally when the sky began to lighten with a new morning, she knew.

All her effort to become the kind of wife Tyler needed was not enough. She could never compete with Kay; she would never be the perfect hostess or even the perfect guest. Tonight Tyler had shown an interest in politics again. But he was saddled with a young woman who had told him repeatedly that she didn't think she could be a good politician's wife. Tyler was torn between his dawning political aspirations and his duty to Sandy.

Sandy was not a MacDonald for nothing. She had been raised to go after what she wanted, raised to be self-reliant and strong. There was nothing stopping her from becoming the wife Tyler needed, except ignorance. She had made a good start toward fitting into the town's social structure, but she must do more, she must try harder. She must learn everything that she would need to know. She must make Tyler love her.

Finally she fell asleep, convinced that she could make her marriage work. And if the job of becoming the perfect wife was much less than appealing, that was too bad. She would not give up without a fight. Even if the fight was with herself.

Sandy arranged to spend Thanksgiving with Tyler's parents. The senior Mr. and Mrs. Hamilton had planned a large, formal dinner, and Sandy accepted the invitation without consulting Tyler. Actually, consulting Tyler was virtually impossible. He left for work early and stayed right up until it was time to come home and change for whatever event was scheduled that night. On the rare evenings that they had nothing to do, he shut himself away in his study, pleading a heavy trial schedule coming up after Christmas.

Sandy was distraught. She was certain that her plan would work if Tyler just noticed how hard she was trying. But he wasn't around enough to notice. Although they still made love occasionally, more often than not he turned over and fell instantly asleep as soon as his head hit the pillow. Sandy, who now had the unasked for luxury of sleeping as late as she wanted in the morning, would lie awake for hours and dream about their honeymoon.

On the Tuesday morning before Thanksgiving, after another rejection in Tyler's arms, Sandy sat at the dining room table, too defeated to pretend anymore. With her head in her hands, and her hair falling like spun gold down her back, she wondered where she would find the energy to get through the day. She was so lost in thought that she didn't hear Tyler come into the room.

"Sandy?"

Startled, she wiped away a lone tear with her fingertip and shook back her hair. "I thought you'd gone to work."

"I did, but I forgot something that I needed. Are you all right?"

"No, I'm not."

He crouched beside her chair and twisted a lock of hair around his finger. "If you're feeling bad about last night, I'm sorry. I was just very tired."

"Of me."

"Pardon me?"

"Tired of me," she repeated, enunciating every syllable.

"You're very wrong."

"Come off it Tyler," she said. "I'm not sure which of us was the bigger fool. Me for thinking I could make this work or you for giving in to your desires and marrying me to get what you wanted."

Tyler untwisted the hair curling around his finger and stood up. "You don't seem to be in a very reasonable frame of mind. We'll discuss this later."

"Oh, certainly. We'll do it at your convenience!"

"That's right."

"Fine, then you schedule it. We have a party tonight, a Thanksgiving dance to benefit the hospital tomorrow and Thursday is Thanksgiving day."

"We can talk on the way to your parents' house."

She was shocked out of her anger. "My parents' house?"

"I was going to surprise you. We're driving over early Thursday morning to celebrate Thanksgiving there. I thought you'd want to go. I've made arrangements to take the rest of the week off. We can come back Sunday."

"I told your parents we'd eat with them."

"Then I'll leave it to you to call my mother and get us out of it. But we're going to the farm. That's final." He bent and placed a casual kiss on her head. "I'll be back in time for the party."

In a moment he was gone.

Home. The thought of going back home was too sweet to ignore. No matter how Tyler felt about her, one hundred miles away was the family who loved her regardless of what she did or tried to do. The thought of basking in the warmth of that love for even just a little while gave her the courage to call Mrs. Hamilton.

Surprisingly, Tyler's mother understood. "We've had you to ourselves," she said pleasantly, "I can see why your parents want their turn now."

When Sandy hung up the phone, she spun on tiptoe through the living room, almost crashing into the disapproving Mrs. Lamont. "Take Thanksgiving and the weekend off,'' she told the housekeeper. ''We're going away.''

''I'll have to check with Mr. Hamilton about that,'' Mrs. Lamont said with a sniff.

But even Mrs. Lamont couldn't spoil Sandy's excitement. Tyler had thought enough of her to surprise her with this. Perhaps it was a start.

Chapter Ten

Determined to trust Tyler and the solidity of their marriage, Sandy did not bring up her concerns on the trip to her parents' house. And, too, she was afraid that they would fight again and spoil what promised to be a beautiful day. The weather was cold but the sun shone brightly. She dressed in a plaid kilt with a heavy kelly-green sweater, her hair in braids. She knew she looked as if she were ten years old, but she didn't care. With each mile, her resolve to become the sophisticated wife Tyler needed slowly disappeared. She had worked very hard. For the weekend she just wanted to be Sandy.

Tyler was quiet at first, concentrating on his driving and his thoughts. But as Sandy's irrepressible good mood spilled over and she began to tease him about his serious face, he relented, laughing and talking with some of the same warmth he had shown on their honeymoon. Sandy was enthralled.

He had been working too hard; she was sure of it. Getting Tyler away from the office was the answer to their problems. It wasn't that he was upset with her; it was just that his life was too difficult. Sandy made him a silent promise that she would become the kind of wife he needed to take some of the pressure off his shoulders.

But not this weekend. This weekend was for fun.

With the exception of the two brothers who lived out of town, the whole MacDonald clan had gathered for the holiday. Since the last time any of them had seen Sandy was on her wedding day, everyone tried simultaneously to hug her and her new husband. The chaos seemed wonderful to Sandy who, now more than ever, gloried in the unquestioning love and goodwill of her family.

Mrs. MacDonald had decided that four pecan pies were not enough, never mind the fact that there were also four pumpkin pies and two mincemeat to go with them. She set all her daughters on the sunny front porch with a bushel basket of pecans and five nutcrackers, and they chatted and teased each other as the pecan pile grew.

Stacey was now gloriously pregnant, and she sat like a queen bee in the most comfortable rocking chair, nodding and smiling at the activity around her. Ryan found excuses to stop and check on her from time to time as the lazy morning progressed.

As far as Sandy knew, Tyler had disappeared from the face of the earth. At first she was too busy to notice his absence, but when Ryan stopped to chat for the third time, she casually asked him if he had seen her husband.

"I think he went for a walk in the woods," Ryan said, exchanging a look with Stacey that Sandy tried not to see. It was apparent that they wondered why Tyler would leave his wife without a word.

"Good," Sandy said, trying to keep her voice steady. "He's been working too hard. He needs some time to himself."

They cracked enough pecans for a dozen pecan pies, and when they looked for another job to do, were soundly shooed out of the kitchen by Mrs. Mac-Donald who had the huge meal under control. The two younger girls scampered off.

"Let's go for a walk," Wendy suggested.

"I'm going to take a nap before dinner," Stacey stated sublimely. "You two have fun."

Since Tyler was reputedly in the woods, Sandy suggested walking to the pond on the northeast corner of the farm instead. She and Wendy set off at a fast pace, teasing each other about the need to make room for the fabulous dinner to come.

At the edge of the pond, they sat on an old bench and looked out over the water sparkling in the autumn sunshine. "I want to hear what it's like to be married," Wendy told Sandy. "Are you happy?"

Was it the reflection off the water that was bringing tears to Sandy's eyes? Or was it the fact that somebody loved her enough to ask how she felt? She took a shaky deep breath and waited until she was under control. "I made a mistake, Wendy," she finally said.

"I thought I could make Tyler love me. Instead he seems to grow farther away each day."

"He married you."

"To get me into his bed." She lapsed into silence, hating the pity that Wendy must feel but needing to share her pain with someone who loved her.

"Are you that passionate, that desirable, that a man like Tyler Hamilton would marry you, share his wealth and his life with you, just for a legal roll in the hay?"

Sandy couldn't believe what she had heard. She gasped and turned, her fingers itching to slap the superior look off of Wendy's face. But the two sisters hadn't touched each other in anger since they were six and seven, and when Sandy looked into Wendy's eyes there was only concern there. "How can you ask me such a question?" she managed to say.

"Because somebody needs to."

"And you were elected?"

"By a vote of one. But don't be surprised if Stacey tries to get you to one side to find out what's going on, too. You're as obvious to us as you've always been. When you heard that Tyler was off walking in the woods you looked as if you thought the world had ended."

"It's been a hard six weeks."

"Stacey had a hard time at first, too. Remember how we worried?"

Sandy nodded, wondering if there were any similarities to the adjustment problems of the two couples. She doubted it. "You're the one with the right idea," she told Wendy. "Don't bother getting married. Build your life without a man."

"Have you ever watched Ryan with Stacey?"

Sandy sighed in defeat. "I know. Somehow it seems that they've made it, and it was worth whatever pain and disappointment they survived."

"When I see them together, then I wonder about my life plans."

"When I see them together, I wonder where I've gone wrong."

The two young women stood and turned to start back to the house. "Sandy, I have no business giving you advice," Wendy said as they walked, "but I'm going to, anyway. Just hang on. Let Tyler know that you love him."

It was remarkably similar to Stacey's advice on Sandy's wedding day. Sandy firmed up her resolve to show her love for her husband by becoming the kind of wife he needed. "Oh, I'll hang on," she told Wendy. "I plan to be the best wife that anyone in Cameron has ever seen."

Wendy frowned. "Don't go overboard, Sandy." But Sandy was halfway through the front door and missed her sister's parting comment completely.

Tyler returned from his solitary walk in time for dinner. After the huge Thanksgiving meal that satisfied all the secret food cravings that Sandy had experienced in the past six weeks, the family fanned out, some on the porch, some in the living room, some to clean up the kitchen. Sandy took Tyler's hand and held tightly to it, afraid that he might leave again. They found a quiet corner and sat on a rag rug. Sandy settled herself between his long legs, and played teasing, tickling games on his thighs. Tyler retaliated by lifting her braids and licking the back of her neck.

They hadn't made love in such a long time that the intimate contact slowly began to drive Sandy wild. She twisted in Tyler's arms, turning her face up to his for a kiss and then straightened when she remembered where she was. There were other people in the room, and she didn't want to embarrass them.

"I took a long walk in the woods this morning," Tyler whispered in a husky voice as his tongue teased her ear. "Would you like to come with me and see where I went?"

"You'll miss dessert," her mother observed when Tyler and Sandy tried to disappear through the door.

"I don't think so," Sandy said, her arm around her husband's waist.

"Newlyweds!"

They made love with almost all their clothes still on as protection against the cold air. Despite the extra layers, there were no real barriers between them. For one glorious hour they pleasured each other mindlessly, letting the healing contact soothe the unspoken problems between them.

Finally, they prepared to rejoin the family. "Everyone will know what we were doing," Sandy said, her cheeks pink with the cold and embarrassment.

"There's a better chance we can keep it a secret if you'll let me pull the dead leaves out of your hair." Tyler stopped and held her by a long braid as he carefully picked the forest floor from the golden strands.

"I love you, Tyler." She had told him again and again as he made love to her, but now, slightly saner and more rational, she wanted him to know that it was still true.

"Ah, sea spirit," he said, pulling her close for one last kiss. "If everything could always be this perfect."

"It will be," she promised him. "I know it will be."

And for the rest of the weekend, it was. They visited with the family, played games with all the children, helped with the farm chores and found time for more walks in the forest.

Tyler made friends with Ryan and the two men were often seen in long, serious conversation. Sandy talked to Stacey and received the assurance that the first months of a marriage can be the worst. When Sandy and Tyler finally said goodbye and drove out of the MacDonalds' driveway, she was more at peace than she had been since their honeymoon. She knew that everything would be all right.

But back in Cameron there was Mrs. Lamont. There was the huge ostentatious house, and there was furniture that was too good to sit on. There were endless phone calls from people who issued invitations, and there was Tyler's job.

They slipped back into the same routine. Tyler worked; Sandy tried to mold herself into the wife she knew he needed. They both became quieter and quieter. Their lovemaking dwindled to nothing. And finally, Tyler began sleeping in another bedroom.

"I didn't want to wake you," he told Sandy when she woke up one morning to find that she had slept the whole night alone. She had run through the house searching for him, only to find him in the bedroom next to theirs. "I came to bed so late that I was afraid I'd disturb your sleep."

"Please, disturb me next time," she said, trying to remain calm. "I see little enough of you as it is. At least sleep with me."

But he didn't. More and more often he found excuses to sleep in another room. Sadly Sandy began to wonder when the moment would arrive that he would stop sleeping at home at all. There were plenty of other bedrooms in Cameron that were available to the handsome Tyler Hamilton. She had been told often enough what a lucky woman she was to tie down the town's most eligible bachelor.

She considered leaving him, but no MacDonald had ever given up on his or her marriage. And she still loved him. Being married to Tyler, even if it was in name only, was better than not having him in her life at all. She stopped trying to talk to him; she stopped asking him what was wrong. She became afraid that she might find out what the real problem was and thereby lose him completely. With self-control she hadn't even known she had, she just went on with her life as though everything was fine.

"Tyler," she asked him one night when they were dressing to go out, "were you aware that your parents' fortieth wedding anniversary is in three weeks?"

He nodded, pushing ebony links through the cuffs of his dress shirt. "I know."

"We ought to do something special for them. Don't you think it's about time we gave a party and paid back all these invitations?"

"It's awfully close to Christmas, don't you think? Is that how you want to spend our first Christmas together?"

"At least it will give me something to do while you go off to work," she snapped. "And at least I'll be guaranteed one chance to have you at home for the whole evening."

"Do what you want," Tyler said with a shrug. "But don't expect me to help."

"I wouldn't dream of so much togetherness," she said bitterly.

He came to stand behind her, and she stiffened as his arms went around her waist. "Don't!"

She heard the sharp intake of breath and he withdrew his arms immediately. There was a hideous silence, and finally he drawled, "I'm sorry, for a minute there I thought you were my wife."

Without another word, he turned and left her standing in the middle of the floor crying as though her heart were breaking.

Sandy moved her things into one of the guest bedrooms. Neither she nor Tyler mentioned her actions; it was hardly significant enough to matter. Although they still appeared together at social events, danced at the inevitable round of charity Christmas balls and lived in the same house, they were for all practical purposes, no longer married.

Sometimes Sandy would stare with longing at the dark-haired stranger who had given her his name and a few brief weeks of happiness. She remembered how it felt to be held in his arms, the pleasure he knew how to give her willing body, the love she had poured out to him.

Sometimes Sandy would find him staring at her, some undecipherable emotion written on his face. She would smile tentatively and he would smile back, but the smiles never progressed into closeness. They were careful not to touch, careful not to be rude.

Sandy threw herself into the anniversary party as if it might be the one thing that would salvage her marriage. Perhaps if Tyler could see how genuine her desire to fit into his life was, he might relent and forgive her for her unknown sins. She researched proper party etiquette as if she were a lawyer and the party a trial. She read volumes on being a hostess, what to wear, what to serve, whom to invite.

She went over the house with a fine-tooth comb dragging the unwilling Mrs. Lamont from room to room to help her check on details. She called some of the young women she had socialized with and asked for their advice, getting information about caterers, bartenders and Cameron protocol. When she was finished with her list, she knew that she had planned the social event of the holiday season.

The senior Hamiltons were delighted. "This will be very good for Tyler's career," his mother said, congratulating Sandy on the plans she had made. "You've become a wife to be proud of."

Even Mrs. Lamont gave Sandy a compliment. "The first Mrs. Hamilton gave a lot of parties here. This one looks as if it won't be too bad."

Sandy, who was beginning to feel she should genuflect at the phrase "the first Mrs. Hamilton," only smiled and started another list of things to do.

Although the party plans were going well, they had taken all the time that Sandy would have liked to use getting ready for her first Christmas in Cameron. There was no time to shop, to bake the traditional MacDonald family Christmas cookies and fruitcake, to decorate the house or buy a Christmas tree. Sandy promised herself that on Christmas Eve, which was the day after the party, she would raid the Cameron stores, buying everything that was left in them for the people on her list.

But there was one present she couldn't ignore. She had to get something special for Tyler. It could not be a last-minute gift. She rejected every idea she had. Some were too personal, some not personal enough. Some, like a beautifully bound volume of love poems, seemed to send too many hidden messages. Others didn't send enough.

She was walking by Cameron's only art gallery on the way to pick up the new punch bowl she had bought for the party when she discovered the perfect gift. An Atlanta artist was having a special showing of his work, and hidden among the scenes of snow-covered forests meant to entice the Christmas shopping crowd, was a large painting of the ocean.

Sandy could almost smell the salt spray. She was filled with such nostalgia that she had to blink back tears. In the painting the waves crashed against an uneven shoreline and the sun hovered over the horizon. There was a wildness and an uncultivated loneliness about the picture that tore Sandy's heart to pieces. Without looking at the price tag she handed the gallery owner her charge card and asked him to deliver the painting on Christmas Eve.

She had no illusions about her future with Tyler. She had tried as hard as she could to be the perfect wife, and he had repeatedly rejected her. She knew that she was going to be the first MacDonald to end her marriage. When she did, she wanted Tyler to look at the painting and to remember, if only for a moment, the passion and affection that once they had shared.

"Merry Christmas, Tyler," she whispered softly as she watched the gallery owner place the painting in his storage room. "Merry Christmas and goodbye."

Chapter Eleven

Sandy put off decorating the house for Christmas until the day of the party. Daily reminders of the season of love and peace seemed too painful. Because Mrs. Lamont had assured her that packed away in the attic were enough decorations to fill the house with good cheer, Sandy hadn't even bothered to investigate. Whatever was there would do.

That morning after breakfast, Sandy and the gardener went up to begin bringing down the decorations. A few minutes later she was searching for Mrs. Lamont. "I thought you said there was a tree," she accused the housekeeper. "There's no tree up there."

Mrs. Lamont took off her apron and marched up the stairs with an irritated Sandy right behind. Immediately zeroing in on the correct box, Mrs. Lamont opened the cardboard flaps and pointed. "There."

"I thought that Christmas trees were green and at least *looked* as if they dropped their needles on New Year's Day."

Mrs. Lamont sniffed and left the room.

Although Sandy had no Christmas spirit anyway, seeing the white, artificial tree was the final damper on her goodwill-to-all. She carried the box to the bottom of the stairs and dumped out its contents. Maybe once it's decorated it won't be so bad, she thought. And next year I'll get Tyler a real one.

But then, there probably wouldn't be a next year for them. They were doomed to celebrate their only Christmas together under the spiky, plastic bristles of a giant bottle brush.

Hours later when she had garlanded the house with silver net streamers and plastic mistletoe and decorated the tree with the fifty identical red ornaments she had found, Sandy stood back and surveyed her handiwork. At home there would be a real pine tree, cut from the MacDonalds' own land. It would be covered with handmade decorations, some of which Sandy had done herself as a child. The house would smell of cinnamon and love. Here in Cameron, the house smelled of fancy hors d'oeuvres and distrust. She was so homesick she wanted to die.

It was indicative of the worsening relationship between husband and wife that they hadn't even talked about where to spend Christmas. At that moment, gazing around the house that had never been a home for her, Sandy knew that she would spend Christmas day with her parents. By herself. And she doubted that she would come back to Cameron again.

* * *

Sandy's gown for the party was a marvel of good taste, elegant style and subtle, muted colors. She hated it.

She had allowed Mrs. Hamilton to talk her into buying the designer original on a day when she was feeling so depressed that she would have bought a gunny sack if she had been told she should. The dress had a high collar that choked her, a low waist that did nothing for her slender figure and an ankle length skirt that made her look like a teenager who was growing too fast.

The crowning blow came after they left the store when Mrs. Hamilton told her that the dress reminded her of one that Kay used to wear.

There was no way Sandy could rip the dress to shreds, not when her mother-in-law was the guest of honor at the party. Resolutely she waited until the last minute to put it on, hoping for a miracle. She hoped that moths would attack it, but there was no chance of moths in the efficient Mrs. Lamont's jurisdiction. She hoped that the bedroom closet would be struck by lightning or the dress would self-destruct on the hanger. But when none of these things came to pass, she slipped the dress over her head like a little girl who is made to go trick-or-treating as a witch when she really wants to be a princess.

She had been to a hair stylist that afternoon and had her hair arranged in a low, dignified chignon. The exhausted stylist had pleaded with her to let him cut several feet off the unruly locks, but stubbornly she had hung on to every inch. Not that Tyler would notice, anyway. He hadn't looked at her in such a long time that Sandy was sure if he ever had to issue a missing person's report on his new wife, he'd get every detail wrong.

"Sandy, have you seen my . . ." Tyler stopped in the doorway of the room Sandy now occupied, and stared at her. "Where did you get that dress?"

"At MacKent's downtown." She didn't have to ask him what he thought. Distaste was engraved on his features. "I'm afraid I let your mother pick it out. I don't like it, either, but I don't want to hurt her feelings."

"Mother would like the dress. It makes you look older, more sophisticated. The hairstyle helps too."

She was surprised by the compliment. "Well, that's the impression I was trying to make."

"Congratulations." He turned on his heel and disappeared down the hall as her smile died.

Things went quickly from bad to worse. The caterers forgot two trays of sandwiches and four trays of hors d'ouevres; next they discovered that they had locked themselves out of their shop. While one of the caterers went back to wait for the locksmith, the head caterer got tipsy on the party punch and had to be helped to walk around the block until he was no longer dizzy.

The classical guitarist who was to play soft Christmas carols in the background cut his finger and proceeded to improvise four-fingered. The hated artificial tree leaned precariously to one side because Sandy had not wanted to ask Tyler for any assistance.

Still, Sandy refused to be daunted. Privately muttering that she hoped every guest at the party contracted botulism from her clam dip, she put on a big smile and pretended to be the perfect hostess as people began to arrive.

True to his word, Tyler had been absolutely no help with the party. But when guests came streaming through the door, he was at Sandy's side, playing the host and loving husband as if the role had been written for him. Sandy had organized the party so well that, later, there was nothing for either of them to do except talk to their guests and make sure that they were having a good time.

As the party progressed, Mr. and Mrs. Hamilton glowed from the attention they were receiving. At some moment in the past tension-packed weeks, Sandy had begun to feel better about her in-laws. Mrs. Hamilton was demanding, and she was adamant about Tyler's career in politics, but she was also intelligent, well-read and interesting for Sandy to talk to. The two women had discovered that they shared a common interest in the law, and Mrs. Hamilton had confessed that if she had been born in a different era, she would have been a politician herself.

Mr. Hamilton never said much, but when he did it was always insightful and to the point. In addition he seemed to like his new daughter-in-law. It was Mr. Hamilton who asked her how she was feeling, Mr. Hamilton who seemed to notice that all was not well in Tyler and Sandy's marriage. It was Mr. Hamilton who had pulled her to one side at a crowded charity bazaar and given her a quick hug because she wasn't smiling.

The party had cemented the rift between Tyler and Sandy, but she was not sorry that she had decided to have it. In this the season of love and goodwill, she was glad that at least she had done something nice for Tyler's parents.

By ten o'clock, the party was in full swing. Someone put the top up on the Steinway baby grand in the parlor and played Christmas carols. A group gathered to sing along, and their wobbly voices sounded almost angelic. Another group had gathered around one of the guests who was an amateur magician, and were exclaiming over the most basic of card tricks. Clusters of people moved around the first floor, sampling food, greeting old friends. The party was relaxed and mellow. Sandy was suddenly very, very tired.

"You look absolutely beat."

Sandy looked up to see Matthew Stone standing in front of her with a glass in each hand. "For you," he said. "I noticed you haven't had a thing to drink all evening."

She was surprised that anyone would pay that much attention to her, and she accepted the glass with gratitude. "Thank you."

"Just don't pour it on my lap."

She giggled, remembering the scene at the restaurant, and when she looked at Matthew, he was smiling, too. "Where's Gloria?" she asked.

Gloria was Matthew's sainted wife. She was a lovely woman who adored her husband and ignored his philandering. Once at a party when Gloria had imbibed more than she should have, she had confessed to Sandy that Matthew was absolutely trustworthy no matter what his reputation. It was Gloria's money that placed them among Cameron's elite. If Matthew wanted to remain rich, he had to behave himself. Afterward, watching the two of them together, Sandy had suspected that there was more to the relationship than greed. Matthew Stone, consummate flirt, was in love with his wife.

"Gloria's singing her heart out. Why don't you sit down for a while, honey," Matthew answered.

Gratefully, Sandy did as he suggested, finding a quiet corner in the living room where she could rest for a few minutes. Matthew followed her, sitting a polite distance away. "This was a good idea," she said, stretching wearily.

"Your husband should be the one taking care of you. Where is Tyler?"

"I have no idea."

Matthew lifted an eyebrow. "So I'm not imagining it. There is something wrong between you."

Sandy refused to acknowledge his statement. "How are things at work?"

"Work has slacked off. I've been able to take quite a bit of time off for the holidays."

"Tyler must be doing all your work then. He's been busy night and day."

"He doesn't have to be."

Sandy looked at Matthew in wide-eyed disbelief. "What do you mean?"

"December is always a quiet time. Things will start up again after the New Year, but there is no reason to prepare for the onslaught until then."

"I see."

"I think you're beginning to," Matthew answered carefully. "Face it, Sandy."

"What do I have to face?" she asked softly. Knowing that Matthew could be trying to prepare her for almost any piece of bad news, she clasped her hands tightly in her lap.

"You and Tyler are both desperately unhappy. If things get any worse, there's not going to be any way out of your unhappiness."

"Is Tyler... Does Tyler have another..." She couldn't go on.

"No. He's much too decent to take a mistress when he's married to the woman he loves."

She allowed a shudder of relief to pass through her body at Matthew's assurance of Tyler's fidelity. Then the rest of his words began to sink in. "The woman he loves?"

"Yes. Hasn't he ever told you?"

She shook her head, surprised that she could admit something so personal to Matthew Stone. It was an indication of how overpowering her loneliness had become.

For once there was no humor in Matthew's face. "I think I can understand why. The last woman he said it to died in his arms. Tyler may be Georgia's most rational lawyer, but he's as superstitious about his personal life as the next guy."

"Thank you, Matthew, but I can't believe it." She tried to smile. "It's done me some good to talk about this, though."

"Then I'm going to give you one piece of parting advice." Matthew slid to the edge of his seat and touched her knee. "Give the man what he really wants, not what you think he needs." In a minute he had crossed the room and disappeared into the crowd clustered around the punch bowl.

With her head spinning, Sandy went to see about her guests.

"Mr. Hamilton, Mrs. Hamilton." Sandy bent to kiss her in-laws on their respective cheeks. "I know Tyler will be upset when he finds out that you've left. I'm just not sure where he went off to." She tried to sound like an indulgent wife, but she knew she missed the mark by a mile.

"That's all right, dear. Tell him thank-you for us." Mrs. Hamilton stopped in the doorway and examined her daughter-in-law. The examination no longer had the accusing quality that it had months before. Mrs. Hamilton looked genuinely concerned. "Sandy, promise me you'll take the rest of the holidays off to relax and recover. Tyler and your health are more important than the Cameron social set." She patted Sandy's cheek before going out the door.

"She's right," Mr. Hamilton said before he turned to follow his wife. "The sparkle is missing in your eyes. You tell that son of mine that he'd better be treating you right or I'll be having a talk with him."

The Hamiltons were among the last guests to leave.
Tyler had disappeared halfway through the party,
never to resurface. Sandy was left to perform the inevitable end-of-a-party tasks by herself. When she was
finished, she was so upset with her husband that she
was trembling with rage. Turning off the downstairs
lights, she marched up the stairs in an imitation of
Mrs. Lamont and went to see if Tyler was there.

She wasn't sure what she would find. A part of her
wondered if Tyler had taken one of the single women
at the party and gone somewhere else for the night.
Even Matthew's reassurances did not relieve her suspicion. Tyler was an attractive, virile man. He certainly had not been sleeping with her. It was not
outside the realm of possibility that he had found
someone else to meet his needs.

The door of Tyler's bedroom was shut. Sandy put
her ear to it and listened for noises. When she didn't
hear any, she took a deep breath and carefully turned
the knob. The door wasn't locked and it swung open
easily.

It took a few seconds for her eyes to adjust to the
darkness. When they did she saw Tyler, facedown on
the king-size bed that once they had shared, sound
asleep. By himself.

She was so relieved that he was there, sleeping alone
in his own bed, that she forgot to be angry. The subtle
light of the moon slanted across the exposed side of his
face, revealing weary lines that even sleep had not
erased. A lock of dark hair brushed his forehead giving him a sad little-boy quality that touched her heart.
He was hugging a pillow, his long frame spread over

most of the bed, and he had not bothered to undress. His tie and coat were gone, but he had fallen asleep in slacks and a now-wrinkled dress shirt.

On an impulse she sat gently on the bed and stroked the hair from his forehead. He appeared to be having a bad dream, and her hand seemed to soothe him. He sighed, and turned to his side. His eyes flickered open and then shut again as he tossed restlessly. He mumbled something, and Sandy lowered her head next to his. "Tyler?"

"Kay." He mumbled something else and turned away from her.

"What, Tyler?" she said louder, not caring now if she woke him or not. But he had finally fallen into a deep sleep and her words had no effect on it.

Carefully she rose from the bed and pulled a blanket out of the top of the closet to cover him before she left the room. In the hallway she leaned against the wall, eyes shut in defeat. She had worried about losing her husband to a living woman, but the reality was much sadder. Tyler was still in love with his first wife. Sandy could never compete with her memory.

Tomorrow I'll pack, she thought. Tomorrow I'll leave.

Rousing herself, she went to her room and closed the door. At her dressing table she sat to begin taking the carefully placed hair pins from the sophisticated chignon. Her hairbrush was not where she usually kept it, and she threw open the top drawer and peered inside. As she removed the brush, her eyes caught an unfamiliar object in the back of the drawer. She reached in and drew out a leather picture case. Snapping it open she stared at the face of her rival.

Tyler had other pictures of Kay. Her death had not erased the life they had shared, and Sandy had never been jealous that Tyler wanted to preserve his memories. Seeing the studio portrait tonight was different, however. Tonight Sandy was facing the woman she no longer wanted to compete with.

She stared at the photograph. Kay had been lovely, with a polished beauty that radiated poise and good breeding. In this portrait her hair was in a chignon low on her neck, and her smile was polite. But missing from the photograph were signs of the inner woman. Sandy knew instinctively that Kay, like Tyler, had been trained to cover up her feelings.

"I wonder what they talked about," she whispered. "I wonder if they ever really knew how the other felt."

She shut the case, placed it carefully back in the drawer and raised her hand once again to her hair. The face that stared at her from the mirror was familiar, but it was not her own. She watched as her cheeks drained of color. The resemblance was uncanny. Sandy Hamilton and Kay Hamilton could be sisters.

Their features were not the same, their hair was not the same blond, but the look of complete self-control, of wealth and careful sophistication were identical. Sandy had succeeded beyond her wildest dreams. Trying to become a good wife to Tyler, she had taken on the identity of the woman he had once loved. Sandy had become Kay.

The irony was that it hadn't worked. With each new bit of her hard-won poise, her husband had slipped farther away from her. Why? Wasn't that what he had wanted?

As she sat staring at herself in the mirror, she fought her rising suspicion. But it overwhelmed her, flooding her slender body with painful insight. The answer was obvious.

Tyler had married Sandy MacDonald, not the ghost of his ex-wife. If he had wanted sophistication, country-club manners or a woman to host gala social events, he would have chosen someone else. But Tyler had wanted her. As she was. He had not married her because of her soft body and intriguing face; there were many women more beautiful he could have chosen. He had married her for the indefinable essence that was Alexandra Kathryn MacDonald. And she had set out immediately to destroy that part of herself. No longer was she his sea spirit. She was an empty shell.

With her head in her hands she thought of all the social occasions she had insisted they attend, all the people she had insisted on meeting. She thought of the new sophisticated clothes she had bought to make herself look older, and the hairstyles and cosmetics she had experimented with.

She should have been home making love to the man she married. Instead she had socialized with people she hardly knew. She should have been home creating a happy environment for their love to grow in. Instead she had danced until dawn. She had done it all for Tyler, and in the process she had lost him. She had lost herself.

Matthew Stone's words were finally clear. "Give Tyler what he wants, not what you think he needs," he had said.

Tyler had told her that he didn't want to go into politics. She hadn't believed him, and so she had given him what she thought he needed. She had become a wife any candidate could be proud of. But the man she married had been looking for something else. He had wanted the spontaneous, unqualified love that she had so freely given at first. And she had denied him.

In the months of their marriage, they had only been happy twice. The first time was on their honeymoon, the second was at her parents' house for the Thanksgiving holiday. Both times she had stopped trying to be someone else, and Tyler had responded to her with the deep warmth and affection of which he was capable.

Why had she tried to give him a carbon copy of his first marriage? Not a man to discuss past intimacies, Tyler had still made it clear that although he had loved Kay, there had been differences between them. When he had chosen Sandy, he had chosen her with the hope that she could give him what he really wanted in a relationship.

Sandy had the sense of a tremendous burden being lifted off her shoulders. She had not been inadequate. Just confused. She had allowed her fears to push her into a role she did not want. No longer would she have to pretend to love the social whirl. She could be herself, and perhaps she could make Tyler happy too.

If it wasn't too late.

Quickly she pulled the pins from her hair and let it fall down her back. She brushed it with long strokes, dividing it in half to braid it. When she stood and removed her dress she neatly dropped it in the trash can beside her bed. She was torn between going to Tyler to throw herself in his arms and taking a walk to clarify her thoughts. As much as she wanted to confront her husband, she decided to wait until the next day.

Tyler had not been an innocent victim. He had never expressed his feelings to her. Instead he had become more and more unhappy without telling her why. Sandy knew with certainty that if they had talked about the problem when it first began that they could have solved it immediately. Tyler was at fault, too. Until she sorted everything out, Sandy did not want to be with him.

She grabbed a pair of faded jeans from her dresser and pulled a sweater over her head. Sneakers and a down jacket completed her outfit. Putting her house key in her pocket, she tiptoed down the stairs and let herself out the front door.

It was cold outside. There were optimistic Cameron residents who were predicting a light snowfall for Christmas. Sandy hoped that they were right, but the clear winter night with the moon shining brightly was lovely without it. The faint smell of woodsmoke was in the air and the ground crunched softly under her feet.

She walked for hours. The night was still with only the occasional barking of a dog, the occasional sound of a car's engine. With no conscious plan Sandy found herself in town, standing in front of Aunt Charlotte's house.

She hadn't seen Aunt Charlotte in weeks. It was difficult for the old woman to get around, and Sandy had been too busy planning the party to visit. A wave of shame swept over her. She had neglected a friend.

Her feet took her along the route she had always walked in the morning on her way to work. She stopped and peered in the window of the newsstand, the pet store, the drugstore where she had eaten breakfast. In front of Tyler's office, she stopped again. She had seen little of Dorothy or Mrs. Howell since she and Tyler had gotten back from their honeymoon. She had purposely stayed away from the office, believing that a good wife doesn't bother her husband at work.

Now she wondered why she had never asked Tyler if she could have her old job back. No one had been hired to take her place. Working with the man she loved would have been a pleasure. And it would have prepared her for law school.

Law school. She had put the idea firmly behind her when she had decided to become the wife she thought Tyler needed. Now she wondered how she could have abandoned the dream of a lifetime without a second thought.

The walk back to Cameron Estates gave her time to put the pieces of the puzzle that was her life back together. She walked slowly, examining everything as if she were a blind woman whose sight had just been restored. It had been a long time since she had taken the opportunity just to observe her surroundings.

Entering the exclusive housing development she paused with distaste and looked at the houses of her neighbors. They were unattractive fortresses, blemishes on the face of the planet. There was nothing original or tasteful about them. And there was not one house on her own street that looked as if anyone lived in it.

There were no tricycles, no swing sets. With the exception of one house that had a life-size plastic manger scene that blinked on and off, there were no Christmas decorations. No, she was wrong. There was another house that was decorated, too. It was a house with a white Christmas tree in the window and a plastic holly wreath on the door.

Tyler's house.

The night had grown colder, and even huddled in the down jacket, Sandy was beginning to feel chilled. But the chill was coming from inside of her, too. As she stood and stared at the house that had never been a home, she realized that their Christmas tree was a symbol of what she had let her life become. Decorative, sophisticated, and very, very artificial.

Chapter Twelve

The next morning Sandy lay in bed and pretended to be asleep until she heard Tyler's car pull out of the driveway. The pretense had been harder than she had imagined because Tyler had come into her room, walked to the bedside and stood watching her for long minutes. She resisted throwing herself into his arms. She was not ready to face another rejection. She had laid careful plans the night before, and she wanted to be sure that she had a chance to follow through with them before she and Tyler had their confrontation.

But, oh, how she ached for his arms around her, his body covering hers. When he was finally gone she allowed herself the luxury of a few tears for the months they had lost.

There was a no-nonsense knock at her door, and Mrs. Lamont entered with a breakfast tray. Since the housekeeper had never attempted to pamper her new mistress before, Sandy was immediately suspicious. "It was Mr. Hamilton's idea," Mrs. Lamont told her quickly, as if she were afraid that Sandy would think she had done it on her own.

"I'm glad you're here," Sandy told her. "You and I are going to have a little chat."

"I'm in the middle of polishing the..."

"Stay," Sandy commanded as if she were talking to a collie in a dog-obediance class. She looked the beady-eyed woman over carefully. "You seem tired, Mrs. Lamont," she said finally. "I think you need a long vacation."

Mrs. Lamont just sniffed.

"A lon-n-n-n-g vacation. Starting this afternoon you will be relieved of your duties until the middle of January."

"I take my orders from..."

"Me. Starting today. And if you think that Mr. Hamilton will support any rebellion, you had better think again. He will back me up one hundred percent!" Although Sandy wasn't sure the last statement was true, something about the way she said it convinced the housekeeper.

"Yes, Mrs. Hamilton."

"And when you come back, you will stay out of the kitchen unless I specifically ask for your help. Understood?"

"I've always cooked for..."

"Not anymore."

"Yes, Mrs. Hamilton."

"This morning," Sandy said, delivering her parting shot, "this morning you will spend your time taking down all the Christmas decorations we put up yesterday and disposing of them. And you will open all the curtains. All of them. And they will stay open."

"The furniture will..."

"Look like furniture," Sandy finished for her. "And this house will look like a home."

"Anything else?" Mrs. Lamont asked with a trace of reluctant admiration.

"That will be all," Sandy said as politely as she could. "Thank you."

Sandy wolfed down the butterless toast and the room-temperature eggs, eager to begin putting her plans into action. She dressed carefully, searching for her best faded jeans and her favorite green sweater. Unbraiding her hair, she brushed it, clipping it back from her face with two tortoiseshell barrettes. A pair of leather boots with one scuffed toe completed the picture. "Welcome back," she said proudly to the wholesome young woman in her mirror. "It's so nice to see you again."

There was not time for the luxury of another walk into Cameron. In her old Mustang she made the trip in a few minutes, parking near Tyler's office to begin her Christmas shopping. The stores were frantic, but she didn't mind. She bought extravagant or silly gifts for everyone on her list: a hand-crafted weather vane for her father, a food processor for her mother, angora sweaters for her sisters, Walkman radios for her brothers. For Stacey's children she bought a video game machine and cartridges to go with it. The shopping went on and on.

By lunchtime she was almost finished. She had been able to complete her buying spree quickly because she refused to be daunted by the speed at which the stores were being cleaned out. She just bought whatever was left that caught her eye, and when she finally finished with a piece of Depression glass that she knew Mrs. Hamilton would like, she delivered the last bundle to her car and drove to Tyler's office.

As she had predicted, Tyler had already gone to lunch. Everyone else was there, however, and she chatted, laughing at the looks on Mrs. Howell's and Dorothy's faces when they unwrapped the sexy nighties that Sandy had bought for them. Matthew was delighted with a first-edition Perry Mason novel.

There was one more gift Sandy had wanted to buy. A call to the pet store had confirmed her purchase. At Aunt Charlotte's house she parked and then gathered the biggest present of all from the back seat of her car. The covered cage was heavy, and she had just set it down on the front porch to ring the doorbell when the old woman flung open the door.

"It's about time you came to see me," Aunt Charlotte said sternly.

"Merry Christmas, Aunt Charlotte. Will you forgive me?"

"Of course. I was just wrapping your Christmas present."

They solemnly traded cages. Aunt Charlotte was delighted with Sandy's brilliantly plumed parrot, and Sandy was delighted to be presented with Julius Squeezer, a huge red bow laced through the bars of his cage.

"Believe me, he's exactly what our house needs," Sandy said sincerely.

"That's what I thought, too."

"Can you see the look on Mr. and Mrs. Hamilton's faces when they see him?" Sandy giggled at the thought.

"It'll do them both good," Aunt Charlotte said with authority. "That nephew of mine was never allowed to keep a pet when he was a child. He used to come over here and play with mine. That's how I got started on my collection."

There was a lot that Tyler had missed in life, Sandy thought sadly. And she knew she had the power to make up for some of it if he would only give her another chance.

Aunt Charlotte invited Sandy to lunch. Over sandwiches and tea the old woman promised to come to visit Sandy when it was necessary to feed Julius, and Sandy promised to visit Aunt Charlotte regularly to help out with the other animals. By the time Sandy left she was filled with the spirit of Christmas.

There were two more stops to make before she went back home. At a Christmas tree lot she bought the biggest blue spruce that was left, bribing the man to deliver it for her that afternoon and help her set it up. At the grocery store she bought the makings of a gala Christmas Eve dinner. With a car full of presents, groceries and pine boughs that the man at the tree lot had given her, Sandy turned her car toward Cameron Estates.

* * *

It was twilight before Tyler came home. They had accepted an invitation to a party that night, and as always Tyler arrived just in time to eat and dress. At just the hour she had predicted, Sandy heard him open the front door. She remained in the kitchen, humming "Jingle Bells" under her breath as she waited for him to find her.

It took about as long as she thought it would. With mounting excitement she could picture him moving from room to room downstairs, examining the changes that she had made inside. But first, she knew he would have noticed the big sprays of pine tied with red bows that decorated the hand rail leading up the steps to the front porch. He would have noticed that the plastic wreath was gone, and he would have seen the huge blue spruce in the front window, decorated with colorful plaid taffeta bows and twinkling white lights.

Inside he would find three fat red candles sitting at each window, surrounded by more pine boughs. Perhaps he would even notice that for the first time all the drapes were open, too. The fire burning brightly in the living-room fireplace, and the newly-purchased hand-carved crèche under the tree would be unfamiliar. The sound of soft Christmas carols from the elaborate stereo system would be unfamiliar, too.

Sandy bustled around the kitchen, spooning pan drippings over the glazed ham in the top oven, poking her fork into the sweet potatoes to see if they were done. The activity kept her mind off Tyler. She was simultaneously excited and terrified. She wanted desperately to believe that he would understand what the changes meant, but a part of her was afraid that he would be offended instead. The more anxious she became, the louder she hummed to block out the frantic beating of her heart.

The kitchen timer went off, and she bent over the lower oven to pull out the lemon meringue pie. When she straightened and turned to set it on the counter to cool, she saw Tyler standing in the doorway. She stopped, frozen in time, and tried to read the expression on his face.

"How long have you been standing there?" she asked, when she finally realized that she wasn't going to be able to tell what he was thinking.

"Long enough to think that a miracle may have occurred," he said quietly.

Her eyes had fallen to his chest. She knew that when she lifted them, there would be no more barriers between husband and wife. For better or for worse, she would know in an instant if there was any reason to hope. "I'm back," she said, meeting his gaze.

"And how I've missed you," Tyler answered, opening his arms.

She dropped the pie on the counter, whipped off the flour-covered apron and flew across the kitchen to throw herself at him. He swung her around and around until they were both breathless, and then he let her slide slowly down his long muscular body to stand close against him as he kissed her repeatedly.

She couldn't get enough of him. He tasted of the crisp winter air and Christmas. She rediscovered the pleasures of his tongue, the moist interior of his mouth, the even line of his teeth. She fell in love all over again with the feel of his skin against hers, the faint rasp of whiskers against her face.

Tyler explored her with the same wonder, running his hands down the curves of her body, lifting her with his hands cupped under her bottom to let her fall fully against him. She pressed her breasts against his chest, feeling the peaking excitement. "Love me," she said with a moan. "Tyler, please, please love me."

In a moment he scooped her up in his arms, and strode through the house. She had expected him to take her up to bed, but instead he stopped in the living room beside the Christmas tree and set her gently on her feet.

She could feel his hands begin to tremble as he undressed her. The moment was too sweet, and she could only whimper softly each time his hand brushed against her flesh. Her knees were weakening, and she leaned against him as he knelt to pull off her jeans. He placed warm, lush kisses along her bare thighs and just when she was sure she would collapse, he stood and faced her.

She wrapped her naked body around his still-clothed one, demanding immediate satisfaction, but Tyler pushed her gently away, sweeping his eyes over her inch by inch. When he lifted his eyes to hers and gave her a heartbreaking grin, she moved seductively forward, still caught in his gaze, and began to unbutton his shirt.

With demented control she took her time, slowly brushing her fingers across each portion of his body that she uncovered. She whispered hints of what she would do to him when he was fully undressed and promised him with her eyes and the slow, sweeping motions of her body that she meant what she said. When they were finally together, with nothing between them, she stood back and waited.

"It's been so long," he said, his voice a hoarse groan. "And I've wanted you so much."

"I'm yours," she answered, waiting for him to come to her. "Only yours."

In one step he was directly in front of her, his arms clasped tightly around her softness, and they were falling to the rug below. They came together with shattering force. There was not enough patience for gentle caresses and kisses. She was drowned in shock waves of sensation, her body greedy for what only Tyler could give her. She made him hers, and she knew the exact second when he took what she had to offer and gave himself to her.

They were irrevocably one.

Sandy stirred to life sometime later, still clasped in Tyler's arms. "I have to turn off the sweet potatoes."

"Stay here, I'll do it." She watched as, gloriously naked, he walked from the room and into the kitchen. She was curled on her side, her face pillowed on her hands when he returned. Her eyes followed his every movement, and she opened her arms to him when he came back down to the rug.

"Tyler, we have to talk."

He nodded, his hair slipping over his forehead with the same boyishness she had seen when he was asleep the night before. She sat up, brushing the dark strands away and tracing the faint lines of weariness around his eyes. "Tyler, no matter what else we say tonight, I want to start with the most important thing. I love you."

He didn't answer, pulling her to rest against his chest instead. For a moment, the contact was so reassuring that she sat quietly soaking it in. Then she began. "I love you, but I can't change who I am for you, Tyler. You'll have to take me as I am or not take me at all."

"What a choice," he said, the low rumble of laughter in his voice.

"And in exchange," she went on, "I'll stop trying to change you."

This time he was serious. "I've seen the changes in you, sea spirit, but I wasn't aware that you were trying to change me, too."

She was thrilled at the nickname. It had been such a long time since she had heard it. "I've been trying to make you love me, Tyler. It's been putting an awful burden on us both."

It was the hardest thing she had ever had to say. But she said it without expecting reassurances. It was a statement of fact; one that Tyler was entitled to hear. He had to understand what her motivation had been if they were to continue their marriage.

There was a long silence, but Sandy was no longer anxious. She had said what she had to say, and his arms were still around her. Relaxed against the strength of his body, she waited, suspended, for his reply. When it came, it took her breath away.

"I've been watching you struggle to find your place here, and it's love that's kept me from stopping you. I thought you needed to belong for your own sake, Sandy. I've missed you and needed you, but I've let you do all this because I love you.''

Having convinced herself that she never had to hear those words to be happy, Sandy could not comprehend their meaning. "You love me?" she asked in a small voice. "You love me?"

"I have for a long time."

"But you never told me!"

"I told you in a thousand ways. I married you, I asked you to have my children, I put up with all your damn parties."

"That's true," she said, tears beginning to run down her cheeks. She wasn't sure if they were tears of joy or sadness for all the misunderstanding that had kept them apart. "Tyler, all those 'damn parties' were for you. I thought that if I could be more like Kay, you'd begin to care for me."

Tyler turned her in his arms so that they were facing each other with Sandy kneeling in front of him. "Sea spirit, you're the other half of me. You round out my life and bring it meaning. I loved Kay, but she was so much like me, we had little to give each other."

"I didn't know!"

"I can't believe you didn't realize how I felt."

A good wife might have taken that statement at face value and accepted the fact that she had made a mistake. But Sandy had stopped being a good wife. "Listen to me, Tyler Hamilton," she said firmly. "If you're going to live with me, you're going to have to tell me what you think, what you feel. I'm not going to spend any more time trying to guess what's behind that elegant Georgia exterior!"

He bellowed with laughter, falling back on the rug to take her with him. "I can see that things have changed," he said.

"Yes, they definitely have changed."

"What happened to the Christmas tree?"

"Mrs. Lamont took it home with her."

"What happened to Mrs. Lamont?"

"She's on vacation."

"What happened to the house?"

"I decided to make a home out of it."

They were on their sides, curled up and smiling at each other. "Don't work too hard on the latter," he warned her with a lazy grin. "It won't be worth it."

Sandy traced a line down Tyler's nose. "Why not?"

"Because we aren't going to live here after August."

"August?"

"The house officially goes on the market in June and I've already had two offers. There are some people who would do anything to live in Cameron Estates."

"And some people who would do anything to get out!"

"I thought maybe you felt that way. Now, why didn't you tell me that?"

Sandy's smile was sheepish. Tyler was right; he was not the only one who had failed to communicate. "I didn't want to hurt your feelings. I thought maybe you liked living here."

"This house was never my idea. But our new one will be. Ryan is drawing up plans and I've bought seven acres right outside of town with the biggest old oak and magnolia trees you've ever seen." He lifted his head and kissed her. "Merry Christmas from me to you."

Sandy was stunned. "Twenty-four hours ago, I thought our marriage was over. And all this time you were planning to give me a new house."

"How could you think I'd let you get away, let you end our marriage? Last night was the final straw. I was going to confront you after the party and put my foot down. No more partying until we got our marriage back together. Half the reason I wanted a new house was to get you far enough out of town to make the social whirl a little less appealing."

"It's impossible for it to be any less appealing than it already is," she said, screwing up her face with distaste. "But last night, you fell asleep. Fell asleep at your own parents' anniversary party, I might add!"

"I've been working so hard to put you out of my mind and give you the room I thought you needed, that I was completely exhausted."

"It was a good party," she said.

"You can give one party a year. Your other evenings will be tied up with me."

She shivered, and he put his arms around her. "We've wasted so much time," she said mournfully. "Wasted time when we both wanted the same thing."

"It's over now. We have the rest of our lives."

They dressed, then dished up platters of food and took them back into the living room to eat beside the

Christmas tree. They talked about politics and law school, about having children and what they wanted their new house to look like.

Sandy gave Tyler his Christmas present and gloried in his pleasure over it. She watched as he took down a still life from over the living-room fireplace and replaced it with the painting of the ocean. "We'll go back," he promised her. "Soon, in fact. I've worked so hard these past weeks that I'm ahead of myself. We can go for New Year's if you'd like."

"Just you and me," she said dreamily, "and Julius."

He turned from the fireplace, and she saw he was grinning. "Aunt Charlotte's Julius?"

"Our Julius now."

"Let me guess where you put him."

Sandy smiled benignly.

"Our bedroom, right?"

"Yes, our bedroom. I figured that you'd demand that I sleep with you again, just to protect you from Julius."

"What a good idea." He crossed the room and pulled her to stand in front of him.

"Do you know what I'm thinking right now?" he asked her.

She knew, but she refused to admit it. "You'll have to tell me," she insisted. "From now on you have to tell me everything."

"I love you," he said, kissing her on the tip of her nose as he hugged her against him. His mouth dipped down to her ear, and Sandy stood silently, listening to the words he whispered.

"Communication received, understood and about to be acted on," she said, dragging him toward the stairway. "And the sooner, the better!"

Arm in arm they climbed the stairs, turning for just a second to take one last look at the Christmas tree. It stood, a symbol of what their marriage would be from that day forward. Sturdy, beautiful, and very, very real.

*   *   *   *   *